PRAISE FOR *LITTLE VOICES*

"An unsettling mystery with an unreliable narrator who will keep you guessing the whole way through. *Little Voices* is as haunting as it is gripping."

—Liv Constantine, bestselling author of *The Last Mrs. Parrish*

"Intricate, unpredictable, and deliciously addictive."

—Minka Kent, bestselling author of *The Memory Watcher* and *The Thinnest Air*

"*Little Voices* grabs you from the first chapter and doesn't let go until one shocking final twist. Vanessa Lillie is an author to watch, taking us deep into the world—and mind—of former prosecutor turned struggling new mom Devon Burges as she battles old politics, new money, big fish, and, worst of all, that little voice in her head to help solve the murder of her close friend. Psychological suspense at its best."

—Kellye Garrett, Anthony, Agatha, and Lefty award–winning author of *Hollywood Homicide*

"From the opening chapter to the last line of the book, Vanessa Lillie takes you on a ride you won't be prepared for, but at the same time, won't want to end. Twists, turns, suspects, and small-town motives are around every corner with an ending that will blow you away. One of the best books I've read this year."

—Matthew Farrell, bestselling author of *What Have You Done*

"Vanessa Lillie's *Little Voices* is my favorite kind of mystery: densely plotted, character rich, and full of sharp and perceptive writing. This is a stunning debut with a gut punch of a twist. You'll be reading all night long."

—Jennifer Hillier, author of *Jar of Hearts*

"*Little Voices* is an utterly original debut novel with a twist so unexpected I jumped from the last page right back to the first to start reading again."

—Victoria Helen Stone, bestselling author of *Jane Doe*

LITTLE VOICES

LITTLE VOICES

A THRILLER

VANESSA LILLIE

This is a work of fiction. Names, characters, organizations, places, events, and incidents are either products of the author's imagination or are used fictitiously. Any resemblance to actual persons, living or dead, or actual events is purely coincidental.

Published by Thomas & Mercer, Seattle

www.apub.com

ISBN-13: 9781542092265
ISBN-10: 1542092264

Quote from "Portrait of the Artist as a Young Mom" by Kim Brooks, *New York Magazine*, reprinted by permission.

Cover design by Shasti O'Leary Soudant

Printed in the United States of America

First edition

For my beautiful son, August, whose sleeplessness led me to this story, and for Zach, who supported us both along the way

There are moments when I feel like I'm dying a little more every day. I feel like a fish that's been caught and then abandoned on a dock, lying there, flopping and gasping, each gasp weaker than the last.

—Kim Brooks, "Portrait of the Artist as a Young Mom," *New York Magazine*

Chapter 1

September 30

My contractions have begun, but everything is wrong: the wrong day, wrong month, wrong person clutching my hand.

The pain in my lower abdomen eases to a dull shredding. I open my eyes and flinch at the yellow leaves flashing across the ambulance's back glass in the fading evening light. Those citrine hues are the first colors to appear in the New England fall and the last thing I should see on the day I go into labor.

The driver speeds down Blackstone Boulevard, where I collapsed after a rush of blood coated my thighs. Blinking back tears, I concentrate on the thin blur of telephone wires cutting through the trees along the road. Each tree is trimmed into a deep V to keep the power lines safe. No longer full and round, they've grown into broken hearts. I count four split hearts before I'm seized by another contraction.

A minute, maybe more, passes before the cramp disappears like a twig snapping, and I fully exhale. The pain is so much worse than the Braxton-Hicks practice contractions I've had the past few weeks. I grasp for some guidance from the books and classes and articles, but my mind cannot get beyond the terrible truth of what being on this gurney means.

More wetness spreads beneath my thighs, dampening the backs of my knees. The EMT loses all color in his face as he lets go of my hand.

His jittery stare creeps along my navy-and-white nautical dress until it reaches below my pregnant stomach. The stripes are now maroon to the point of shiny black. Our terrified gazes lock, and then he yells to the driver. The wail of sirens begins.

We're in trouble, baby girl.

Both my hands grab the metal handles, squeezing until I regain control of my breath. Finally, my mind shifts, but it's not an act. There is fight and there is flight, and I've done them both plenty. But there's a third choice for those of us who have experienced enough terror: focus.

The pain is on the left side of my abdomen. If the blood loss is from there, I have to do something. With a moan, I pull myself over, applying as much pressure as I can stand.

Panic returns, and my nostrils burn as tears descend my cheeks, pooling along the tight oxygen mask. This child, small and beautiful and mine, is almost in my arms. I picture her from last week's ultrasound and cry harder.

The EMT's chin wobbles as another contraction begins. He grabs my hand again.

"I'm okay." I repeat the words until I'm coughing, which doesn't make them believable.

This cramp pulls me to a primitive place. The EMT's murmured assurances barely register. My senses narrow onto the sharp pain. My muscles tighten as if in revolt, desperate to escape my body.

I feel the road change from the bumpy potholes and uneven city streets to smooth highway. I take a long, exhausted exhale in relief. Almost there, almost there, almost there. Women & Infants Hospital of Rhode Island, baby girl. We're almost there.

We stop at last, but it's seventy-eight breaths before the driver with a gut who loaded me into this ambulance can be bothered to help the panicked EMT get me out. They finally lower the gurney onto the ground as another contraction begins. I let out a deep guttural holler, then take short breaths from fear as much as pain. The gurney wheels squeak, and my noises continue as I see stars starting to appear above me in the evening sky.

They hurry me through the ER's sliding doors. In my own area, I'm surrounded by beige curtains and beige cabinets and blinking beige machines. A man in blue scrubs enters, though his face is beige, and he's got a scruffy dark beard.

"Devony Burges, I'm Dr. Keller. You have to slow your breathing."

No one outside southeastern Kansas calls me anything other than Devon. I hate the name my mother gave me, but correcting him isn't possible.

"Can you hear me, Devony?"

I slow my gasping to a shuddering trot under the oxygen mask. A burst of light passes across my left eye, then right, then left again.

"Are you with me?" he asks, pulling the penlight back for my response.

I grab his hand and gather up all I've got. "I'm twenty-eight weeks and a day. I don't . . . have any allergies. I'm O negative." I grit my teeth through another contraction, but it's gone soon. "I've been walking all day . . . the contractions got worse . . . I thought my water broke, but all I saw was blood." I pause as my voice catches. "There's terrible pain . . . my lower back."

He nods tightly once and joins the activity around me. The nurses cut away my dress and underwear, slipping my arms into a thin gown. The blood bag cart clinks against the gurney, and the pinch of the IV is a tickle compared to the pain within my body.

The nurse drops my purse in a plastic bag. The edge of a yellow day planner slides out as she ties it shut. I start to say the planner isn't mine, but there's another contraction, and all I can focus on is the overhead light behind the doctor's head.

"Can you tell me what happened?" he asks.

He's asking the wrong question. I count down from one hundred, and finally the contraction's grip dulls, and I have a few glorious moments of only burning back pain. I relax my closed eyes and think.

When I was in my first trimester, I made a list of probable complications that could occur during labor. Seventeen of them seemed worth categorizing and diagramming and obsessing over. They're tucked away in a tidy spreadsheet on my computer. In the ambulance, I was too scared to mentally cull through the symptoms to determine what's happening. That's the problem with logic. It doesn't stand a chance against terror.

I must be brave for my daughter. I visualize my spreadsheet, and every line item spins around like a slot machine. The variables of my day align with different columns until number seven stops: detached placenta. The system my body grew in my uterus to feed my baby and give her oxygen has stopped working.

"All day my back hurt," I begin. "I was . . . walking and then bleeding. It's my placenta."

Dr. Keller sticks out his stubble-covered jaw as he presses on my stomach. "Have you noticed increased urination prior to today?"

I shake my head no because I pee all the time lately. "First trimester, I bled some. Not . . . for a while."

He pauses his hands along my stomach. "Have you felt the baby move?"

Everyone stills. Even my breath goes somewhere else.

"No," I manage to gasp as another contraction begins. I groan and press my trembling hands along my stomach. I picture the cord, amniotic fluid, and my baby fighting to stay with me, mere centimeters below my touch.

The ultrasound machine appears, and familiar goo is plopped onto my bare stomach. The seconds are minutes.

"Please, please, please," I moan to no one and everyone.

The liquid silence of my womb continues. My head rears back, mouth falls open with a silent scream lodged deep in my chest. This is the real pain.

There's a murmur, distant like a record scratch in another room over and over and over.

Her heart is beating.

My body shakes as I cry hard. This is the only sound in the world that matters. That will ever matter.

Dr. Keller prints the ultrasound images. "You're correct. The placenta has pulled away. We have to stop the bleeding and deliver your baby. The heartbeat is weaker than I'd like, so a C-section is our only option."

I try to temper my sobbing, holding my breath to make childlike gasps.

"This blood loss will not slow down until we operate," he says to a nurse before getting closer to me. "Devony, we must operate immediately. We have to put you under."

I can nod while I sob, so I do while picturing my birth plan lying in a color-coded folder on my desk at home. There is no "completely alone, put under with anesthesia as I'm bleeding out" tab.

The sturdy nurse who's swabbing the blood off my thighs grips my knee. "We'll contact your husband," she says.

"He's in Boston." Even though it's after rush hour, there will be traffic. It will be an hour at best. My breathing speeds up, and I pull at the oxygen mask. "He'll never make it."

"You can do this," she says. "You've got to fight."

If it's just me, I can handle it. But my baby is an unknown variable. Does she have my tenacity that borders on myopia or Jack's quick compliance with circumstances? "I'm going to throw up," I say before heaving into a metal bowl she quickly provides.

After wiping my mouth, the nurse takes my hand. "You will be fine. We have the best doctors and nurses ready to help your baby. When you wake up, it will all be over."

I flinch at the implication. She leans back, inhaling sharply as if trying to take back the words.

She doubles down, pressing my hand tighter. "I'll pray for you both."

"I don't believe in God."

"I do," she says. "That's why I'm doing the asking."

I let her have the last word because I'm one of those lazy atheists who wishes there was a God, precisely for times like these.

The operating room is cold and sterile, the lights even brighter than those I left in the emergency room. They tie my hands down, Jesus style, and I'm crying, quietly but hysterically.

Most of my tears are angry ones at this point. Anger at Jack for not being here. Anger at myself for insisting he stay overnight an hour away with the rest of his team for his stupid retreat. Anger at delivering this way, so I don't have a moment of labor that isn't sheer terror or a complete blank.

This is my fault. The gray-and-pink nursery and soft knitted coming-home outfit were taunts to the God my nurse prays to. I should have remembered the voice I thought was God who spoke to me as a girl: *Turn your back on your family. Turn your back on me.*

The surgeon enters and begins moving nurses around before addressing me. "We don't have time for candles, but you can listen to music as we intubate you."

He's referencing a "gentle C-section," how natural birth plans that go off the rails can still have some nonsurgical significance. Sure, you don't get your home birth in a pool with your loved ones around you, but here are a few two-for-one Glade candles and Sade.

One of the surgical nurses, who has mostly been observing, heads over to a CD player. She smacks the top, and it's not relaxing music but talk radio. I read horror stories online about surgeons cranking up Metallica as a terrified mother is put under, so maybe I shouldn't care. Instead, I listen to the murmuring voice and will time to move faster, unconsciousness welcome at this point. Any reality but this one.

As the anesthesiologist does her magic, I feel as if I'm levitating. I tell myself the bright lights I'm heading toward are surgical, not spiritual.

"The bleeding has started again. I need to make an incision *now*." The surgeon yelling in his green mask blurs. I close my eyes, the tube starting down my throat.

The talk newsy voice on the radio grows louder. The medicine gives me something I haven't had in hours: calm. I can focus on the voice, the shock of the message numbed by the drugs.

"Murder rocks the East Side of Providence tonight. A woman, identified by exclusive sources as twenty-seven-year-old Belina Cabrala, has been found at Swan Point Cemetery off Blackstone Boulevard."

The announcer said my friend's name. I saw her today. She isn't dead.

With my eyes closed, the memory arrives. Six months ago, I was wandering through the gravestones at Swan Point when the dogwood trees were in bloom. I came upon a stroller and diaper bag I recognized, my friend's son dozing inside under a gauzy blanket. Not far away, there was a stunning woman I'd never seen before, thick black hair down her back and olive skin that glowed in the sun. I lifted a hand to introduce myself, but her focus remained on a nearby dogwood tree, as wide as it was tall. She lifted onto her toes to smell a branch heavy with blooms. She guided the branch with her hand until the face of the lowest flower caressed her forehead, then the length of her nose. Once it reached her lips, she opened her mouth and sank her teeth into the white petals.

She saw me staring, still standing near the stroller, and made her way over. I was unable to move. Embarrassed, intrigued, I wasn't sure. Just a few feet away, she paused to lick one corner of her red lips.

"Medicine from the old country," she said, staring me dead in the eyes. "Purifies the blood."

That was the first time I met Belina Cabrala. And now, is it possible we'll never meet again?

I hear a faint beep, a flatline. Please be me, not my baby.

Or maybe you'll be seeing Belina real soon, girlie.

Loud voices, a double beep, flatline again.

You'll finally get what you deserve.

Chapter 2

Monday, December 5

The new baby cry is gravelly and desperate, like the sound you make when breaking through water after believing you'd drown. The explosive wail is paralyzing at first. I read about it extensively, listened to hours of audio recordings of what different newborn cries could mean (hungry, wet diaper, overtired). Now that we're home, I realize preparation didn't help. Ester's scream is so piercing I can barely put her down for fear of that sound.

I focus on my movements to keep Ester calm. Up and down on the exercise ball, my thighs burn, but still I softly bounce her in my arms. I try not to get frustrated; it's her instinct to stay awake and survive.

At first I blamed all her crying on my inability to nurse. I pumped in the hospital, insisting Ester get my milk and not preemie formula. The difficult recovery meant I couldn't nurse, both of us hooked to machines in different rooms. Pumping was the only action that signified my new-mother status. I was told she was born two pounds, two ounces, by a nurse, or maybe Jack, but Ester steadily put on weight. I took her home eight weeks after we both almost died.

Despite the milk I pump every three to five hours and the new Deepfreeze in the garage that's filling with the small plastic bags, Ester still cries.

And she ain't stopping anytime soon with a mother like you.

I hate the voice in my head that began again when Ester was born, whispering, *Maybe you'll be seeing Belina real soon.*

I almost did. Death circled us both that day.

Them chickens can still come home to roost, girlie.

I flinch at the sound and shut my eyes as I bounce. To hear a voice that's not there is shocking and unsettling but not unfamiliar. It's older, wiser than I remember. There are new, vicious judgments about my motherhood failings. The worst part is, sometimes, the voice is right.

I haven't told anyone, but I can silently defend myself when I've got the mental fight. The less I sleep, the less it's possible to do anything but cry with my baby.

You fixated on having this baby, but it didn't do no good.

No arguing with that one either. Bounce. Bounce. Bounce.

I read about newborn sleep in a dozen books, on Pinterest pages, and in three times as many articles. The sleep cycles, the need for feeding, how quickly breast milk calories are burned over formula calories. I'm still at a loss as to what's going on with Ester.

This is the curse you deserve from the God you abandoned.

The tears burn my eyes, but I blink them back even as I fear the truth. That it is me. This child hates the look of me, my smell, the taste of my breast refused by her tiny, perfect mouth. I want to be a good mother more than anything. I do not accept this failure.

My whirling mind realizes it's the only sound other than my bouncing. Ester is quiet; the voice is quiet. When my pulse is almost normal again, I breathe in the stillness of my bedroom.

The flashes of morning sun through the blinds remind me that our bedroom has too much white, like celebrity teeth. Bounce. Bounce. Bounce.

I glare at the white marble bedside tables, the mirrored white cabinets, and white upholstered headboard. I'm a coward. I was afraid of revealing that I don't belong. Those colors, those patterns, those pieces of furniture aren't worth a home like this.

Jack didn't care. He only needed to say, *You know, babe, let's go kelly green or chartreuse.* It didn't cross his mind that I didn't know what I was doing. That every bedroom I'd ever had was sparse and bare and ignorable. So the first time I really tried resulted in our bedroom having the charm and authenticity of veneers.

You don't belong here.

He'll realize you're trash and dump you.

My gaze roams over the room again, seeking to anchor me to this idyllic New England life. But all I find is agreement that this room is Exhibit One that I am a fraud. Bounce. Bounce. Bounce. Bounce.

After easing off the exercise ball, I place a sleeping Ester in the (white) bassinet on my side of the bed. I retreat down the hallway toward the room where I spend most of my time, the nursery.

I analyze everything, seeking to quell my uneasiness. First, the gray walls with pink accent stripes are adorable and not totally cliché. The white wood glider with a gray chevron pattern is derivative of every *Pottery Barn Kids* catalog, but Jack liked it (miracle!), and I couldn't justify the cost of custom. A matching white wood changing table gives the room a finished look. My toes curl into the plush faux-sheep-wool rug that will be cozy for tummy time and a soft landing for early unsure steps.

Surely this is the kind of nursery a good mom would have.

No photos on your walls.

Changing pad isn't secured to the table.

She'll be needing three-month clothes soon.

Other moms, good moms, they'd have it done.

You don't love her enough.

"You're crying again, Dev," Jack says from the door, in his soft way, the way that's meant to make me feel connected. The tone works to pull me out of darkness and back into our lives. I can still hear his words that brought me back at the hospital: "Do you want to hold our daughter?"

Now in our home, returned to our life, his voice is strange. Like a language I used to speak but forgot.

I take the tissue he offers. "Just the blues." I used to hate crying, but I've discovered its real cathartic pleasure.

"Is it the baby?" he asks. "Belina?"

At the mention of my dead friend's name, I nod. It's easier to blame my sadness on what I lost instead of what I gained.

We are quiet, assessing each other, and the contrast is a fresh wound. He's showered and relaxed and standing in the doorway. I'm smelly and uneasy and slumped on the twin bed in Ester's room.

"Will you rest today?" Jack asks. The subtext to the question is our home's tidiness. Near spotlessness, actually.

"It needed to be done." I hear my formal tone, a crutch. It's not that I'm trying to avoid sounding like a Kansas hayseed. I'm not intimidated by his local private school education, which had roughly the same yearly tuition as our Georgetown undergrad and law school. But I don't like to remind him of our differences unless it's relevant.

"Ester needs a clean home," I say with a weak smile. It's not the first time I've used her as an excuse for my behavior. Not the last.

He raises his eyebrows, his large forehead punctuating the annoyance. He doesn't want to argue. Ever, actually, which I've always appreciated. But I wish he'd say what he wants me to do. Ignore the laundry and the soap scum and pretend this house isn't covered in germs waiting to infect our NICU baby.

Even before Ester, I cleaned. This is our home. You make time for what you care about. It's easy for him to take it for granted because he's always had love in his home.

I keep myself from saying any of that because I recognize the thread of crazy, and it's daily work lately to keep it from unspooling in front of him. "I'll take it easy today."

But you still won't be better.

Rest never healed the wicked.

He kisses my forehead as I reach over to feel the soft sleeve of his dark-navy suit. I lean back and note the red silk tie, his power combo.

"Big meeting?" I smile in the way I used to, which says I understand.

"We've got a new public relations consultant," he says. "He's going to tell us everything we're doing wrong."

"It'll be a short meeting," I say.

"Doubtful."

"A come to Jesus before you're all crucified?"

His laugh surprises me. It's been a while since I made him laugh. "That's about right," he says. "It might be late. I'm sorry."

I try to hide my disappointment that his work is shifting back to normal. I want to keep this real conversation going. But it's not a surprise. I could feel him pulling away the past week. Watching his phone more than me. That's who we were once. Who he still is.

I try to remember that person, how we'd fall into bed, exhausted but still buzzing from full days of difficult decisions, reaching for each other. I need him so much after a lifetime of not wanting to need anyone. "Lunch ordered in?" I ask with what feels like a smile.

He scratches at the short black hairs on the back of his neck. "And dinner."

Here is the root of the root. I'll be by myself all day and evening for the first time since we've been home with Ester. For the eight weeks I was in the hospital, much of it semiconscious, Jack was there as I drifted—hours, days passed. He was always curled in the uncomfortable pleather chair in the corner, watching, waiting, hardly moving himself. We've been home three weeks, and he's continued to go into work late, leave early.

"You've been out of the office too much," I say. "That's the problem."

Jack gives a big shrug. "What matters is us. If the ten other people working for the mayor can't keep things running, that's on them."

I don't agree, and in his heart, he can't either. The mayor hired Jack as chief of staff to turn things around. It's not easy to be a probusiness Democrat in a town that went Bernie over Hillary. He has a big job that needs a focused leader, first in and last out. The fact that they're bringing in a consultant, certainly expensive, means it is more serious than he is letting on.

His failure is your fault.

You've never deserved him.

"What is it?" he asks, hazel eyes wide with worry. "The baby?"

I shake my head no and smile, though it's work. He's the last person who can know about the voice, and yet he's the only person I'd ever trust enough to help.

He twists one of my fuzzy curls and lightly pulls it before tucking it behind my ear. "I'll text when I'm coming home. If you need me at all . . ."

This conversation wakes my pride, steels something formerly mushy within me. I want to be closer to who I was before. For both of us. "There is something I need to do."

"What's that?" he asks, surprised.

I head to the changing table and almost reach for a folder I hid in a drawer. It contains four articles about Belina's murder, those I managed to save from the paper without Jack noticing.

You would think of that now.

Terrible mother, not caring for your baby.

This is where trouble always starts for you, girlie.

I refold onesies until my nerve is back. "I have to check on Alec," I say about my friend. Technically, our friend.

"Not today," Jack says, softly but firmly. "They're still investigating Belina's . . . case."

"He didn't respond to my texts. All my calls have gone to voice mail," I say. "Something isn't right."

Jack's jaw rolls side to side, his tick when he's trying to solve a problem. "Okay," he says and leaves. He returns with a present, wrapped in an old Sunday *Times*. "I was saving this for the weekend."

I run my finger along the paper's creases before slowly peeling off the tape. Inside is a long strip of fabric in a gray chevron pattern. It's soft and has a flex to it. "A baby wrap?"

"There's a YouTube video on how to do it," Jack says with his typical confidence. "You should start walking again. You miss it."

My muscles ache for the activity, but my mind whirls in alarm. "I'm not sure."

"The baby will be safe, covered completely by the wrap."

He thinks you're fat.

You've never been his type.

Now you're repulsive.

Tears burn, but I blink them back. I'm still wearing my maternity jeans because my C-section scar is only now healed over. The soft material of the band is all I can stand against the raw incision.

"Dev, listen. There's always a reason not to do something."

I hate it when he sounds like a crappy Tony Robbins, but he's right. I miss my long walks through the East Side streets and along Blackstone Boulevard. But the cracked sidewalks are too bumpy for the stroller. Or at least that's what I theorize because I haven't left our home. Yet.

"She'll be safe against your chest," he says too eagerly. "You need to walk again."

I want the truth to be that I will walk because I want to do it. But it's actually that I'd bounce on a pogo stick to bring back a sliver of my old self.

She's long gone, girlie.

This pathetic lump is all that's left.

As a tear falls, I hear Ester in the bedroom. "Oh no. She's up," I say, but Jack takes my arm.

"I got her," he says. "Let's try the wrap, please. The video says wearing calms them down."

I want to argue but let him leave the room instead. Her cries soften as I hear him pick her up. She's quiet when he walks into the nursery. The sight of her in his arms, their twin black hair, releases some kind of maternal hormone in my brain, and I can breathe again.

"Let me put her down," he says. "We'll get the wrap on you first."

She almost killed you.

He wishes she would have.

Not the first person to love you and then wish you were dead.

"She'll wake up," I say too loudly.

He dips his forehead, as if stepping into a windstorm, and continues with his plan. As he eases her into the crib, she does not cry. My fingers flex to check to be sure she's breathing. She always cries when I put her in the crib.

Jack is grinning victoriously as he faces me. "Okay?" he asks.

I can only nod.

"First step is like a tube top," he begins as he finds the center and wraps the fabric across my chest. "Then cross it in the back. Pull it over your shoulders like a parachute. Then tuck each side through the tube top." The fabric not wrapped around me only just touches the floor. "It needs to be tight," he says as he's pulling. "For her head and neck support."

I purse my lips as if he's told me something new. As if there's a corner of Pinterest and mom blogs and local "kangaroo care" Facebook groups I haven't analyzed for the leading ways to baby wear. I made notes, observing moms and nannies wearing babies (ring sling versus soft wrap versus carrier versus carrier with insert).

Jack may have guessed as much, but he knew the most relevant fact: I hadn't pulled the trigger on a carrier.

In the long mirror across the room, I watch him finish tying the wrap as efficiently as his double Windsor. My heart aches with gratitude.

"Okay, now for baby girl." He hurries over to Ester, still quiet in the crib. He doesn't bounce her but is gentle.

He's going to drop her.

Her tiny skull will crack open on this cheap rug.

"Bend over a touch, babe." He directs me slightly forward so the tube top becomes a pouch. He slides Ester against me, and my arms come around her small body.

He tightens the fabric and wraps it around my waist a few times before finishing with a knot.

I take a deep breath, so relieved to have her close. "This is nice," I whisper. I snuggle her against my breasts, regretting I didn't pump as soon as I got her to nap.

"You're ready," he says as if assuring us both. He gently slides an organic cotton knit hat over her black hair. "Wear your maternity coat, and zip her up."

He's impressed me with his present, a solution for how I can finally check on Alec. My chest warms at the idea of Jack caring about me. It never stops being a surprise.

I keep my arms protectively wrapped around Ester, so she's able to nuzzle into my chest. I bend my neck to make sure I can kiss the top of her head, one of a dozen safety tips I remember.

I stare at both of us in the mirror. Jack watches me, likely wondering if I'll do something odd. The kind of behavior that will lead him to make excuses for missing the big meeting and stay with me. A week or two ago, I'd have been oblivious to his attention. I'm getting better. A bit more sleep, and who knows? Maybe the voice will leave too.

I step toward the hallway. "Help me into my coat?"

He is close behind and keeps a steady hand on my back as we ease down the stairs as if they're covered in ice. My C-section scar burns, but I don't let on. The real pain is when we reach the landing where there's a blank spot on the wall. Ester's birth photo should be there, both Jack and I proud but exhausted, beaming at the camera. But with the emergency surgery, her NICU stay, and my long recovery, it's blank. I couldn't even muster the energy for two-month photos.

You don't love her like a real mother would.

I wipe the tears as Jack's back is turned. He faces me, holding out my long jewel-green mohair coat. It's a little big because I bought it with pregnancy in mind even though I wasn't pregnant at the time. I spent more than I should have, but it'd been so easy to picture the shape of my pregnant stomach beneath the soft, fuzzy fabric.

Jack leads me toward the back steps until we're through the sunporch and into the winter air, cold and cleansing. He drops the spare key in one of the many empty flowerpots.

I can't move.

I took Ester out for fresh air once but decided against it and hurried back inside our "oven house" as Jack calls it, since I now keep it at a cozy seventy-four degrees.

No one wants to see you make your baby cry.

"You should get a latte," Jack says. "Go see Cynthia at Chip."

I've been avoiding my good friend and her bakery, and that will have to continue for now. "That's not where I'm going."

"Yeah." His head dips to the left as if I've punched him.

"Alec is our friend," I say. "He's mourning Belina too."

Jack's mouth is slightly open. His tongue taps against the back of his teeth. It's a tell that there's a lot he's not saying, likely can't because updates on Belina's investigation would have been given in confidence during a briefing with his boss, the mayor. "The investigation is almost over," he says finally.

"Then it won't hurt to check on Alec." I hope Jack sees the old me. Realizes she's still here.

"We'll talk tonight." He kisses my forehead before hurrying to the garage.

Leaving his wife and baby.

This is the best part of his day.

I scrunch my chapped lips into my teeth until I draw blood.

Enough.

"We've got work to do," I say to Ester. With a cautious first step, testing our weight together, I hurry toward Blackstone Boulevard.

Chapter 3

The bank sign on Hope Street says it's just above freezing, and I open my coat to double-check that every inch of Ester is covered for our walk. Her arms and legs are beneath the fabric, and her cozy hat is pulled down, covering most of her soft black curls. I slowly zip my coat back up.

You took this tiny baby from her home.

Worried more about your fat ass than your baby freezing to death.

I push myself to walk faster, hoping to exhaust the voice and the rising panic at the thought of Belina's death.

Because Ester's cries aren't the only thing keeping me awake at night. The radio voice from the operating room before I was put under plays in a constant loop during every dark hour: "Murder rocks the East Side of Providence tonight. A woman, identified by exclusive sources as twenty-seven-year-old Belina Cabrala, has been found at Swan Point Cemetery off Blackstone Boulevard."

A week after I was out of the hospital, Jack agreed to talk about Belina. I had a nap and then a shower and felt as if I could focus on something other than Ester. She was asleep in the living room for her late-afternoon nap. We shared a beer and finally spoke like two adults for the first time since she was born. Jack had saved some articles from the paper, which I've since underlined and analyzed, hiding them all in Ester's room.

We sat in silence as I read over them, searching for answers in the few facts: At approximately 7:30 p.m., Belina was stabbed in the chest inside a mausoleum at Swan Point Cemetery. Her body was dragged to the river, where her right arm was cut, most of her blood drained. A cemetery guard found her shortly after. There were no witnesses. No suspects. Jack added only that the mayor needed an arrest.

You could have done something.

I hold Ester tighter, trying unsuccessfully to focus on her instead of my grief. I see Belina everywhere on Hope Street, one of the main roads on the East Side of Providence. "That's capital *E* and *S*," Belina would say as she rolled her large brown eyes.

I made her laugh when I told her the story of when Jack and I moved here, newlyweds fresh from our ten years in DC. I was ready to jump into being a Rhode Islander. The cab driver asked where we were headed. I proudly said, "East Side," because it made me feel local. Jack cringed.

The cabbie quirked his thin lips and said, "East Side, huh? Good for you."

Belina explained that in Rhode Island, *good for you* (pronounced as one word: guh-fa-yoo) basically means *go fuck yourself.* "Just say you live in Providence now, if anyone asks," she said with a smirk.

Assumed snobbery aside, I loved strolling with Belina through the neighborhood. I'd grown up in what I'd classify as a ghost town, a former mining metropolis long abandoned by the companies that took anything valuable from the land and didn't even bother to clean up after. All that was left were people too stubborn and poor to leave. But Providence and our East Side house are the opposite. Not only is our home a charming butter-yellow Cape Cod, but it's only two blocks from quirky local shops and packed restaurants. A place with a pulse and vibrancy. A place worth living and raising a family.

I cross Hope Street, heading toward Blackstone Boulevard, both large streets that run parallel to each other with a swath of neighborhood blocks in between. Closer to Hope Street in our section of the East Side, homes are somewhat more affordable. It's easy to picture the happy families in them, front yards cluttered with bikes and red plastic wagons and water tables abandoned for the winter.

They've got real love in their homes.

Mothers who know how to take care of babies.

Babies that don't cry all the time.

I pause at the turn I'd usually make to head toward Swan Point Cemetery. After the moment by the dogwood there, when I realized Belina was the new nanny for my friend Alec's son, we took a walk together. She asked me a lot of questions about her new employer. My friendship with him went back to college.

After a while, she revealed a few things about herself.

She'd taken the job nannying Alec's son, Emmett, because it was time to change. Not *for* a change. It was time *to* change.

I nodded as if she'd hardly said anything, but the words were powerful. They were key to who I'd become. What I'd had to do.

Then I asked what else she'd done for work.

"I was raised in Newport but not fancy. I worked in boutiques on Thayer Street. Was a hostess for a while. What you'd expect of a college dropout. Smart enough to talk to rich people but not enough to become one. I did finally get away. From my mom. From that gossipy town." Then she said softly, "I should have finished college."

That was when I knew: We were the same because we had wanted to be different. We wanted more.

On the surface, we might appear to be poor social climbers trying to make it up a few rungs of the ladder. But it's not about money, not that type of wealth. It's about people with fully lived lives, artistic points of reference, and happy Sunday plans with smart, boisterous families. Playing the piano at Christmas. Making a real cheese soufflé and arguing about a review in the *New Yorker*. That's the "more" worth leaving your mother behind in Newport for. Worth never looking back at your parents and their abandoned Kansas town.

College is a passport for people like us, people who want to *be* different. When we aren't born with much and need more than a shitty high school education to get somewhere else. The difference between Belina and me is that I made it out. She had still been treading water, focused on the sunny shore of "more."

Being a nanny for a family on the East Side must have felt like progress. She was certainly good at it. But she was still on the outside. What would she have done to get inside?

Nothing worse than you did.

You should be dead. Not her.

I rub a shaking hand along Ester's back as the road slopes steeply. If we'd had a snow or ice storm, no way I'd be able to brave the sidewalk. But the sun is shining, and I'm breaking a sweat when I'm only a few blocks from Blackstone Boulevard. Now I'm close to my end point and where the real money lives.

The streets are wider and the yards precisely landscaped; rarely is a hedge unshaped, a lawn not the perfect inch and a half. Slate roofs for the oversize English cottages and stucco turrets with leaded windows for the Tudors and thick columns lining the grand porches of Georgian Colonials.

They'll see trash like you coming a mile away.

I unzip my coat but keep most of Ester protected from the cool breeze. Tipping my head back, I blink into the sun as I near my destination. The moment echoes in my mind, and I see Belina warming her face a dozen times.

I stand on the corner of Cole and Ogden, breathing fast, not sure what I should say to Alec. I can't cross to his house. It's too easy to see Belina hurrying out the door, pushing the stroller with Emmett. She'd wave my way with an extra coffee or smoothie she'd made for us. I often wondered if she needed these walks together as much as I did.

My reverie is interrupted by an older lady power walking past with three Chihuahuas. With a wicked curve of her wrist, she hurls a neon-blue plastic poop bag onto Alec's lawn. Her bag is not alone. There are dozens of poop bags, all kinds, in fact, from white CVS to purple biodegradable, littering the unkempt landscape like malformed croquet balls.

"Oh my God," I say, almost unable to believe what I can see. Unable to imagine why a neighbor strolling by would drop shit on his lawn.

The large wooden front door flies open, and Alec shuffles into the yard. He's carrying a small wastebasket and starts picking up the bags.

Still shocked, I hurry across the street. "Hey, Alec."

"Devon," he says, stumbling at the fence. "You had the baby already?"

He'll see what a terrible mother you are.

What an awful child you've had.

"Her name is Ester." I glance down as my chest seizes at the prospect of Alec seeing her, judging us both for her crying or not being as big as normal newborns.

My fingers stroke up Ester's covered back to the hat pulled down over her dark hair. My touch confirms she's fully wrapped and protected from judgmental eyes. I relax slightly at how safe she is against me.

"You should have called," Alec says without enough enthusiasm for me to believe him.

I'm not surprised Jack didn't tell him. I only texted Alec to check in, hoping he'd share something about what was happening with Belina's case. "Would have dropped off your Up-All-Night-Dorito-Nacho-Supreme?" I tease with a joke from our college days.

"Saved us from plenty of hangovers," he says with a grin, letting out a pleased little sigh that quickly disappears. "I don't think I've smiled since . . ."

I see some tears in his eyes. "How's Emmett?" I quickly ask about his son.

"He's okay," Alec says as if that were the wrong question.

I nod toward the yard because I can't not ask. "What on earth is with the shit bags?"

His gaze drops to the ground. I take a step back and really study him. He's in a cinched bathrobe and looks like he hasn't shaved in days. His face is gaunt and his eyes bloodshot with purple rings from sleeplessness. He steps toward me, trembling, an intensity radiating from wide eyes. "I didn't do it."

"What?" I shake my head. "What are you talking about?"

"Belina . . . they think . . ." Alec's long fingers cover his face, and he begins to cry, something I've never seen. After a few sobs, he swears and wipes the tears on the sleeve of his robe.

"No," I stammer. "You would never . . ."

Pulling me close, he releases a whisper-sob. "Everyone thinks I killed her."

Chapter 4

I remember the feel of Belina's skin the day she died. Her touch was delicate like the dogwood bloom, and the olive color of her fingers contrasted with my own, pale and freckled. Her last day on earth, I held her hand on a bench. We were as quiet and ominous as the tombstones around us in Swan Point Cemetery. The place I first met her and now the last place I'd ever see her. The place she was murdered.

It should have been you.

The way Alec cries into my shoulder, I wonder if he also knew Belina's touch, shared the generosity of skin against skin. Alec and I have a friendship that goes back a decade, but still I can't ask.

"Who said you killed her?" I ask, incredulous, glaring at the bags of poop. I know what it's like to feel stares. To experience the heat of embarrassment every time you step outside your house and the feeling barely subsiding when you're in.

Alec slowly rubs his forehead against my shoulder, something he hasn't done since he was drunk at college. "You know I'd never hurt her . . . She is . . . was . . . so remarkable."

I've seen Alec upset plenty, but he's usually quick to rebound. Ready with a joke and an offer to buy a drink, which is important for someone who screws up a lot. But we've never been anywhere close to a situation like this.

Oh, but you have.

Blood on the pillow.
Knife in your hand.
How he screamed.
How you ran.

I met Alec before Jack, my first day at Georgetown University. He plopped down next to me in the back of a class full of girls with good highlights and Coach bags and guys who knew each other from lacrosse. All I could think was that everyone could see through me, smell the Kansas bumpkin who came from trash and who'd always be trash.

Nothing has changed.

Alec elbowed me, whispered for a pen and paper with an apathetic laugh. He never knew, but my hands were shaking under the desk. My nails dug so deep into one palm that I could feel the blood. I was about to stand up and leave and likely never return. But I stayed.

He asked me to go out with him and some friends that night, but I said thanks but no thanks.

"Come on, daddy-o," he said. "Don't be a—" He paused and made a square with his pointer fingers.

I laughed and asked what the hell he was doing.

He smacked his forehead with his hand. "You haven't seen *Pulp Fiction*? Come on, Kansas. We're watching it right now!"

And we did. We even danced like John Travolta and Uma Thurman after the fifth replay of their "Twist" contest scene. I'd never fallen so platonically in love with someone so quickly in my life.

Alec's music and movie selections were epic. In my small town, the closest theater was almost an hour away, and I didn't have a car. Even the movie rental place was three towns over. Alec wasn't shy about helping me catch up with the real world. A place I'd never dared to imagine I'd really belong.

"You just *have* to know Radiohead," he said. "How can you talk to anyone without an opinion on *Pablo Honey* versus *Kid A*?"

Alec did end up getting me to go out that night after the movie. He already knew so many people, bartenders, a professor who summered in Newport near where he grew up. The evening was a swirl of jokes and shots and stories ending on a punch line. He kept bringing up *Pulp Fiction* so I could easily join in. I watched him carefully, wanting to be like Alec.

He took me to parties, bought dinner while I forced him to study, and most important, introduced me to Jack. They were complete opposites but also the only two guys from their Providence prep school to go to Georgetown. The logistics made a friendship that wouldn't have been there otherwise.

Freshman year, the three of us were always together, exploring DC, crashing parties, and following that with all-night movie marathons. That first Christmas, Alec bought Jack and me great tickets to Radiohead. It was the first gift I could remember getting that meant anything to me. I didn't tell Alec that, of course. How I savored every moment of that night. Held tight to the thousand moments of a freshman year full of freedom and joy I never imagined were possible. All because of Alec.

But sophomore year, I was changing again. Wanting more. Jack and I studied regularly, already focused on what it'd take to get into a good law school. The more we were in the library, the less we saw of Alec.

Then Alec's LSAT wasn't strong enough for him to stay with Jack and me for Georgetown Law. He returned to Rhode Island for the only school that accepted him, Roger Williams. A perfectly fine option, but it created more distance. After starting our careers in DC, Jack and I got married and moved to Rhode Island. I hoped our friendship with Alec would start again.

But we had all changed. There were occasional drinks, and Alec pitched us a few investment opportunities but never followed up. I helped him get an investor for one of his ideas but never heard anything about it.

I side-hug him tighter, my fingers digging into the bathrobe. Knowing Belina rekindled my friendship with Alec. Not to what it was in college, but he was back in my life again. I was grateful.

Alec pulls away from my shoulder, his whole body sagging. "No one understands," he says in a cracked whisper, as if it's our secret.

The front door flies open, and Alec's wife, Misha, stomps onto the front porch. Her wide eyes snap from him to me. Hands on hips, she's a sentry in yoga pants. "Can you two do this inside?"

Misha will know you're a terrible mother.

That your child cries all the time because this is the child you deserve.

Shrill little baby.

Evil like her mother.

I consider coming back later, not wanting Misha's judgmental stares on Ester and me. I picture my exit as I trace the outline of Ester's arms and legs hidden within the soft cocoon of the wrap beneath my coat.

Alec whispers, "Please, Devie," a nickname from college that warms me to my core, making me feel like the cool kid has called me over to his table.

You didn't deserve his friendship.

You used him to get to Jack.

One more rung up the ladder.

Alec sulks over to the last few poop bags in the yard. It's so familiar, the grit of shame, that I follow him, mustering a nod at Misha, who leads us inside.

She's always wrestled for control. We first met her during law school when we'd come back to Providence to visit Jack's family. We grabbed a last-minute drink with Alec and his new girlfriend. Misha barely said hello before she began bragging about the huge house her parents had bought. The expensive trip she'd taken Alec on and the next one she had planned. Then she nagged us into joining them for dinner somewhere Jack and I couldn't afford.

While it would have been easy to assume she was just some rich snob, I could see there was more. The need to be seen as wealthy, to throw money into every conversation, meant she hadn't always been living that way.

At their wedding reception, Alec confirmed as much. He drunkenly told me he mostly married Misha for her new money and that Misha was getting his "good" family name out of the deal. That was the side of Alec I liked to ignore. The privileged Newport golden boy who took everything for granted. Alec had a melancholy streak, so I hoped he was only feeling sorry for himself. That he did really love Misha. That he hadn't taken love for granted like so much else in his life. I didn't bring it up in the sober light of day.

We follow Misha through the entryway as she makes a few comments about Ester and how tough babies are and how I should get *good* help. I bite down my response ("Help that isn't murdered?") because Alec flinches as she says it.

Misha knows you need help because you were never meant to be a mother.

Even a bad mother knows that much.

We stand in their sleek kitchen overlooking the sunken living room. What did Belina say?

"Copy and paste from any HGTV Dream Home. They don't have the money for a real decorator, so Misha faked it, like everything else."

This house is worth north of one million, so the money point stuck out. My brain typically files most details like that away for later. I also wonder how Belina knew about their finances. Maybe her nannying checks bounced?

Misha heads toward the back sliding door, where I can see their large city-issued trash can. She dumps the wastebasket into it and leaves it outside before returning to the kitchen to wash her hands, murmuring about East Side assholes.

She digs in a drawer and pops a coffee pod into the Keurig. Misha is in her lululemon uniform, complete with a low-cut workout shirt that shows her high, fake breasts.

Dressing like that might keep her husband's head from turning but not yours.

You don't have her body.

The voice knows my insecurities. I once had a little vanity about my naturally slender shape, but even that feels obsolete, sharp edges and pleasing curves now mushy. Even the opportunity to have larger breasts is lost. They are feed bags, swollen with milk for Ester and dotted with painful blisters from pumping.

I hand my coat to Alec and think of how my body does not feel like my own. My mind invaded by the voice and breasts full of milk my baby rejects and stomach scarred from the emergency surgery that saved us both. I hate myself for these thoughts. I want to be a woman who sees herself as strong because of what she's endured. My body a tribute to the child wrapped against my chest.

At least you're alive, you ungrateful bitch.

I heave at the double punch of guilt rising in my chest, threatening to burst through my eyes. Ester begins to cry, and I bounce quickly as Alec crosses the room. Misha ignores my efforts as she's busy with her coffee. I watch them both for any reaction, and they spare me the judgmental looks.

They hear proof you were never meant to do this.

Finally, the crying stops, and I rush over. "I'm so sorry. She isn't sleeping at night, and I'm just trying to—"

Alec blinks at me as if mystified. "We get it," he says. "Emmett was a handful too."

I relax a little and see Misha nodding. "It gets easier. Especially if you get help."

"I don't need help," I say too loudly. "Sorry."

Misha is smirking, that knowing look mothers who are on the other side of newborn life like to give the rest of us new-mom zombies.

"How are you doing?" I ask Alec calmly, approaching him where he's slumped over the counter.

"We're managing," Misha answers. "That asshole detective keeps coming after Alec, but there's not enough evidence."

Not exactly a ringing endorsement, but I nod as if it's a certainty.

Misha's chin is in the air, her arms posed to the leanest lines. "Our new nanny is old and boring, which is who I should have hired in the first place. I'll never let you make those kinds of decisions again," she says to Alec. "Hot nannies are a plague with people like us," she explains to me, though I don't think I'm included in the "us."

Likely she's lumping herself in with Ben Affleck and Jennifer Garner types.

Is Misha trying to imply Alec and Belina were sleeping together? I begin again. "Why do people think you killed Belina?"

"The East Side is full of assholes." Misha punctuates the point by taking a loud sip of coffee. "We're moving to Newport the second I can get this dump market ready and—"

"I'm the only suspect," Alec says in a rush, frustration in his voice. "My lawyer says they don't have enough to arrest me. Yet."

"What do you think happened?" I ask Alec.

"She was probably meeting some boyfriend at the cemetery who killed her," Misha answers. "Men kill women like that."

"Kill women *like what*?" I snap.

"You've always been such a feminazi, Devon," Misha says coolly, blinking her artificial lashes at me a few times as if she knows me. As if she was at Georgetown with us. As if she was more than Alec's Newport townie girlfriend whose parents came into money in time for her to lock him down.

You're an even bigger fraud.

A townie is a step up from white trash.

"Can you explain what you mean, Misha?" I say as nicely as I can, feeling guilty for my razor-wire thoughts.

"Belina was flirty," she says. "Attractive for a Portuguese girl. I mean, it's exotic to rich men with skinny blonde wives—"

"Stop it," Alec murmurs. "You didn't know her. Even if she was raising our child."

"Like hell she was," Misha says, spitting each word.

"She's dead," he says to the marble countertop. "Have some decency."

Misha's eyebrows rise despite the Botox shine of her forehead. "That's perfect. You worry about the reputation of the dead nanny. I'll worry how we're going to make the mortgage without you working. It's not like we can draw unemployment—"

"Stop it," he says, louder this time.

"What's going on with work?" I ask him. I pressured Jack's uncle Cal to help Alec get a grant a few years ago. I hoped it worked out but didn't really check.

You knew he'd fail.

"Nothing is going on," Misha says. "That's the problem. Another worthless idea like all the others."

I glare at her. "Misha, that's awful—"

"It's fine, Devon," Alec says. "I'll be in jail soon enough. She can finally run back to her parents."

"Maybe so," Misha says softly, her gaze cast toward Alec, but he doesn't notice.

It'd be easy to dismiss Misha as vapid or superficial, but I've always seen through her posturing. Because like Belina and me, she also set her sights on being someone else. Or at least, having the lifestyle to fit her attitude.

You're jealous she's succeeded: good mother, hot wife, perfect life.

You'll never see one of those.

I watch Misha fiddle with her hair, pulling too hard at where her split ends used to be before she could afford regular cuts and colors and blowouts. She grew up poor, like me. When we first met, she told me stories after too many glasses of chardonnay. But when she was at Rhode Island College, her parents made a pile on some family property along the new interstate, and suddenly she was wealthy and looking to climb. It took a few years for her to make it into Alec's circles, but soon she had the life she'd dreamed of: East Side address.

I can't imagine how difficult it is, staring down being a single parent with nothing but an incarcerated husband and a mortgage. Your whole life disintegrating into something worse than what you had before. Worse than you ever thought possible.

I lived with that kind of change as a girl. Saw how truth altered the faces of my parents each time they saw me, a reminder of my accusations. I harnessed my fear of that life to get away from it. Away from that awful town full of people who looked the other way at the sight of me. Fear was the key to razing my life to make way for something new.

But what Misha and Alec have here is different. Misha is afraid of losing this life, which very much includes Alec, chairing galas, and VIP access to wine tastings on expansive Newport mansion lawns. It's a life worth saving because it's what she built. And there's Emmett, who would know the regret and shame. Of the life they will lose if Alec goes away and Misha starts over.

As if you could help.

"How many times have you been questioned?" I say to Alec. "Did the police search the house?"

"Searched everything," Alec says. "They found Belina's blood in the trunk of the car."

"Jesus, Alec," I whisper. "How?"

"The stroller," Misha says too quickly. "There was blood on the stroller and the floor of the trunk. I'm sure she mentioned cutting her arm when she put it in there."

Her voice goes up, the way it does when conversation turns to college classes, and she's overcompensating for her two-year degree.

"Hi, Devie!"

I shift toward the boy's voice behind me. "Emmett," I say as he springs into the room. I loved seeing him regularly for the past six months Belina and I were friends. He's a little taller, his hair freshly cut, the curls still unruly, which I appreciate as a fellow curly-haired redhead. He's in khakis and a red polo half-zip sweater, a preppy male version of Annie. "How are you, bud?"

"Good," he says. He's a smart three, direct and always observing. "We're going to the library. For story hour. Do you want to go? You love story hour!"

I went several times with him and Belina, and I swallow thickly before I can answer. "Maybe next time."

"Okay," he says, shifting from foot to foot and back again. "Belina won't go. She's gone."

"I'm sorry," I say, my voice shaking.

"Oh yeah. She's in heaven. She has a new family." Emmett pulls at the thick collar of his sweater. "And there's angels, right, Dada? They have big wings."

I keep smiling, though I'm slightly horrified that even in her afterlife she's looking after other people's children. "That means she can watch over you," I say finally.

"And Dada?"

"No," Misha says sternly from across the room. "She's busy with the angel babies."

"She loves babies," Emmett says to me. "Is that your baby?"

"Yes, her name is Ester. She's sleeping."

That dead woman would want you far from Emmett.

She always knew you'd make a terrible mother.

Now you're proving how right she was to everyone.

Alec comes over and picks up his son, hugging him tight.

"Belina could have watched her," Emmett says, wistful at the missed opportunity.

I nearly pull Ester out of her wrap so I can snuggle her close. Tears burn as I recognize their new nanny, Frances. She hurries into the room with a coat, backpack, and toy truck. She watched the Morris twins before they went to Jewish Community Day School in the fall. She would be at the same parks where Belina took Emmett. I often tagged along to observe children and parents, especially mothers, in action. Frances and I would exchange a look or two when Belina told us the latest Misha story. But there were good stories Belina shared about Alec as a father, which made me proud of him. Perhaps that was enough to persuade Frances to work for them.

"Ester has arrived," I say to her. "Early."

"I told you it'd all be fine," Frances says, leaning close. "Is she sleeping? Can I see her?"

She'll start crying, and Frances will know you're a fraud.

She'll tell all the other nannies, who will tell all the other mothers.

You're cooked, girlie.

She's lightly running a finger on Ester's soft hat, and I pull back with intense panic. "Next time," I say. "She's not a good sleeper. Her days and nights are confused, I think."

Frances gives me a sympathetic tip of the head as she adjusts her grip on the backpack, shoving the toy car inside. "She'll grow out of it. Takes time."

"He's going to be late," Misha says from across the room. "Love you, Emmett."

His round face turns to his mother. I see the longing. The wish of love given differently, more.

Ester will look at you the same way.

You're never gonna be what she needs.

"I miss her too," Frances says to me. She reaches into her coat pocket and hands me a tissue from a small pack. I'm embarrassed to be crying again and can only nod. She squeezes my hand before returning to Emmett. "Let's get your coat on, boss."

Alec helps his son into his blue plaid Patagonia puffer, then crouches down to zip it up and hug him again.

Emmett nuzzles into the embrace, then takes Frances's hand. His grin is toothy and wide, the glow from time with his dad lingering. "See ya, Devie. Bye, Devie's baby!"

He hops to the entryway. Frances laughs lightly as he drags her along for the ride.

The door slams, and I don't hesitate, putting myself squarely in Alec's face. "You cannot go to jail. It will destroy him."

His lower jaw sticks out, then quivers. "I know," he mumbles as Misha lets out an exasperated grunt.

This sad-sack man is my friend, but that doesn't change the times he's frustrated me too. I know why I love him as a friend. How he helped me more than survive college but really thrive. Find happiness and freedom that on some level I hadn't thought I deserved. If I'm honest, I sometimes think he was my friend because I had no qualms about helping him with his homework, all his homework.

But maybe that's not fair. There are complex reasons for the friends we choose and when we choose them or they choose us. Perhaps I meant as much to Alec as he meant to me.

He's always been open with me. I've seen heartbroken Alec at least a dozen times. Inactive Alec more times than I can count. From missed dinner reservations to ignored girlfriends to his senior thesis, he was always bumbling through, making it all work somehow. Honestly, he drives Jack crazy. But I owe my present life to this crying man accused of murder. Somehow, knowing Alec as I do, his current situation doesn't feel as shocking as it should.

Standing next to him, I squeeze his hand. "Have the detectives told you anything?"

"You know how they build cases," he says.

He's right. Detectives aren't even forthcoming with witnesses, let alone suspects. Alec won't know anything until he's behind bars and learning it from his lawyer.

Misha narrows her eyes at him from across the counter. "His alibi is the problem," she says. "He was getting drunk at Ivy Tavern, but no one remembers him there. He paid cash for once in his life. The cop cameras on Hope Street were malfunctioning. It's Alec's word against, well, no one's."

Alec licks at his bottom lip, the sweat on his forehead a sheen in the pendant light over the counter. It's as if we're taking the bar again, and he's as unprepared as before. Knowing he'll fail but not being able to stop himself from doing what's expected, believing it will all be okay.

Ester begins to stir and make those small, prescream noises. "I need to feed her," I say, taking a step back. "Can we talk later?"

He hears her.

He knows she's waking up scared of her terrible mother.

"Let me get your coat," Alec says and follows me to the door.

He helps me into it, and his hand lingers on my arm. We stand in the dark entryway. I bounce Ester, trying to get her to sleep a bit more.

He takes a deep breath. "Can you do anything? You worked some tough cases in DC, right?"

You got run outta that job.

I could have helped him. Once. But every edge of reality is fuzzy. The control over my emotions tenuous. "Having this baby . . . it's been difficult," I say. "I'm not sleeping . . . she cries a lot. We both do."

"They're going to arrest me," he says. "That damn blood."

"The blood could be circumstantial," I hear myself say, old gears from my first job in DC, which dealt with criminal evidence, turning suddenly in my mind. "If they don't have a good motive." I pause, waiting for him to look me in the eyes. "You weren't sleeping with Belina?"

He glances away, across the sunken living room at Misha. Her back to us in the kitchen. "I didn't cheat . . . I cared about her, but it wasn't like, you know, an affair kind of thing." Alec finds my gaze again. "I'd never hurt her."

Belina didn't mention anything inappropriate about Alec. She hardly mentioned him at all, other than a few stories about what a great father he was. She asked me lots of questions about him, our friendship. But I thought she was only curious about her employer.

Were you even looking that hard?

So obsessed with your pregnancy you ignored the truth.

"It's the loneliness that's hardest," he says. "People staring. I hate leaving the house. But I hate having to stay in."

I take his hand, the understanding a groundswell in my chest. "I saw Belina," I say finally, out loud for the first time. "The day she was killed. She wanted to meet up that afternoon. My contractions started right after. I walked around until evening, trying to work through it, until I collapsed. I almost died having Ester. Then Belina did."

"Oh my God," he says, his eyes wide. "The same day? I didn't know you almost . . . that it was so serious."

He knows it should have been you.

The wrong life was taken.

You never should have lived.

Alec lets out a puff of breath. "But you saw Belina that day? Did she say anything about me?" he asks with hope, not fear.

I shake my head because it was a strange conversation. The whole interaction was fractured and fuzzy after the trauma of what followed.

"You should talk to the police," Alec says. "They didn't seem to know much about what she did on that last day. Or any day, really."

He's right. I may be one of the last people to see her alive. And when we met, I could sense something was wrong.

Alec is frowning at my silence. "Was she upset?"

"Yeah," I whisper. "I think she knew something was going to happen."

Alec squeezes his eyes shut, and his chin crinkles. "Why did this happen to us?"

I picture the bench where we sat, skin against skin. I see her glance at the river before she carried a clinging Emmett toward his afternoon story time. But there was something else. My fingers curl at the memory, not of touching her skin but of what was left behind on the bench we'd shared.

"What is it?" Alec whispers. "What did she say to you?"

It wasn't words. Her day planner. She left it behind, and I didn't notice until she was gone. The ER nurse bagged the yellow book with my purse. It should still be in there.

"I can help you," I say with a certainty I don't have but will need to resurrect.

"How?" he whispers.

"Trust me," I say because I don't have time to take his hand. Belina is reaching out for mine.

Chapter 5

What a terrible friend.

Forgetting that dead woman's journal.

You'll never be able to help Alec.

Never keep this baby alive.

I kick over empty flowerpots outside the sunporch, desperate to find the back door key. Ester is screaming, a wail made worse outside. I can almost feel the neighbors glaring out their windows, wondering why I can't keep her happy. Their fingers itching to call Jack or maybe child services.

At last the key falls to the concrete with a tinny clink, and I shudder back tears. I gently squat to the ground, holding Ester tight against me. Key in hand, I hurry up the stairs. The glass door slams behind me as I move swiftly toward the living room.

Ignoring my tight nerves at the prospect of unwrapping her, I arrange several pillows into a nest on the floor. I untie the knot Jack made at my waist with one hand, pressing the other hand against Ester. The fabric slowly unwinds from my body as her wail reaches a new volume. I jump at the piercing sound, bobble her, but recover, clutching her tight in my trembling arms.

You should drop her.

Let this all be over.

I gasp, surprised by how the voice is coming after her now too. I tell myself it doesn't matter, that I won't listen. I whisper the refusal against Ester's cool cheek. We can fight this together.

After I stop shaking, I gently lay her onto the pillows. Jack usually handles the bottles and left one ready in the refrigerator. After I warm it, she drinks greedily. She's not much of a burper, but I bounce her a few times, getting her settled, calming us both.

I take Ester upstairs, and it's twenty minutes of bouncing on the exercise ball before we're both calm. I lay her in the bassinet asleep, but she won't stay quiet for long. I stare at her perfect little face, my heart catching from the fear and love that blooms within me now. I hurry down the stairs. My breasts ache to be pumped. The sinuous pain brings guilt at my inability to nurse.

I decide to endure the needing-to-nurse pain and scramble to the hallway closet. I toss out umbrellas and old shoes and coats we don't wear until I find the purse I had in the hospital. Jack got my wallet out, and it didn't occur to me that there was anything else I'd need. My fingers find sunglasses, ChapStick, a half-eaten KIND bar, and loose receipts before I feel the hard spine of a narrow book.

My hands shake so much that I stop. I take long deep breaths and lean my back against the cool plaster wall. I focus on the blank space where our family photo should be.

You can't even take a picture. No way in hell you can help this dead woman.

Clutching Belina's planner to my chest, I remember the last time I saw her or would ever see her.

I woke early from light cramps, my mind already spinning about something being wrong. I was relieved to get a text from Belina to meet her at Swan Point Cemetery that afternoon. We'd walked there a lot in the six months we'd been friends. As I waited for her and Emmett, I stared at the forest along the great stone wall that creates a border down to the Providence River. The sloping hills covered in gigantic sycamores and dogwoods and maples and oaks. It's not a normal burial ground, more of a sanctuary for nature and remembrance. The graves are art, some small and thin, dating back to the Revolutionary War. Others are monuments, obelisks, and great mausoleums. Former governors and the oldest Rhode Island families are buried with war generals and the writer H. P. Lovecraft.

I was reminding myself that my child and I were on this side of the grave when I saw her pushing Emmett. I waddled over, and we strolled down an outer road toward the river.

I told her about the cramps, and she nodded as if understanding. We stopped at one of the largest graves near the water. It's all white granite with gigantic benches on either side of an enormous angel cast in dark bronze.

She tipped her head, reveling in that late-in-the-day sunshine. "There's a new moon tonight," she said. "Everything will be purged."

I turned to her. "What do you mean?"

"All the curses hidden in the moon's shadow come out," she said with a smile. "Have you been cursed?"

"Yes," I said, not feeling like being teased. "My grandfather. On his deathbed."

"*Oh, meu Deus,*" she whispered in Portuguese. "Your own blood."

I heard his curse, a garbled hiss under the erratic beep of the heart monitor installed in my mother's house for him by hospice. "I don't believe in curses," I said.

Her gaze roamed my belly. "Go to the doctor." She curled her arm around her own flat stomach. "As soon as you leave here. No one is safe tonight."

I'm not a big believer in superstition or religion or whatever it was that made Belina so often speak of God and curses and blood. But I could hear the pain in her voice, regret even. She hardly moved as my hand slipped over hers. I squeezed her long fingers, her olive skin chilled against my slightly swollen, warm hands. I leaned my head back like hers, both of us searching for some sun.

In the quiet cemetery, a great canopy of trees above us, I felt what I thought was her loneliness. "Do you want to talk about it?" I asked.

She shook her head once, sharply, but then her face softened. "I'm tying up loose ends under the new moon."

"What loose ends?"

"Ask me tomorrow." She pulled away and stepped onto the bench; she climbed one step, using the giant angel statue's wing for balance. She stared at the river, her head following the banks all the way to the edge of the cemetery and back up to where a lone mausoleum is built into the hill.

Of course, I didn't know it then, but it's where she would be murdered.

But you knew something was wrong.

Too fixated on yourself.

You never really cared about her.

If you did, she'd still be alive.

Belina jumped down and landed in front of me. "Call the doctor," she said again.

Those were the last words she'd ever speak to me. I watched her check on Emmett, who was waking up from his afternoon nap in his stroller. She rubbed his cheek where the strap had given him a red spot.

I was consumed by her premonition. Maybe that's why I didn't think much about how she pulled Emmett out of his stroller, whispering in Portuguese, which she wasn't supposed to do because Misha insisted on English only. She kissed the top of his head, lingering on the reddish-blond curls. He snuggled into her neck, still dozing. She could have easily slipped him back into the stroller, but she pulled him close, her gaze on the river. She slowly pushed the stroller with one hand, the other tight around Emmett, who clung to her.

I wanted to hug her goodbye, but silence remained between us.

Perhaps we both sensed the other was about to bleed.

I stared at where she'd been looking during our conversation, but then the first of what would be hours of cramps seized me.

After the first cramp passed, my shaking hand fell to the stone bench in relief and touched something. I looked down to see Belina's yellow day planner.

I didn't forget. I didn't have a chance to remember.

I stare down at my hands, steady now, ready to find the truth. I flip open the rectangular cover and see she wrote her name. My fingers trace each loop and letter of *Belina Cabrala* and back again. She took it with her everywhere, scribbling a few words at a time. She said she made notes for Alec and Misha, but that never really made sense to me, knowing them as I do.

I turn to the first page. It's from eighteen months ago and begins with AM for Alec Mathers and MM for Misha Mathers:

> Nanny Day 1
>
> Monday: AM sleeps until noon. Leaves to get coffee and watches TV. MM gave me a quick tour, shared E's schedule, and was gone all day.
>
> Tuesday: AM doesn't get dressed until noon. Says he's going out. MM is gone to spin class. I don't see her or AM until 7:00 p.m. when I leave.

The journal continues like that for one month. Then something changes.

> Monday: E finally eats peas with his lunch, add more butter and less cheese. AM responsive to my idea. Takes the meeting with CF. Need to meet CF at CCH to talk after.

It seems as if Belina set up that meeting between Alec and this new name, CF. I scan through more of the usual until the following month.

> Monday: Alec takes us out on his boat. E is so happy. Alec offers me coffee with whiskey. He shaved and took my suggestion on new shoes. Said something about young boyfriends. I assure him I don't have one. Showed E how to cast a fishing line. He's never looked so handsome.

I notice there is no more AM but Alec. Something has changed. Maybe a lot, maybe a little.

I flip to the last entry, the day she was murdered. It's a to-do list.

> Friday: Transfer $. Library with E. Tell Alec. Find Devon. Meet with Ⓐ & CF at SP.

I freeze at Ⓐ—an *A* with a circle—being at the meeting at SP (Swan Point, I assume, where she was killed). Could Ⓐ be her new code for Alec? Is he lying that he has no idea what happened to her? That he was drunk at a bar when she was killed?

"Tell Alec" as well as Ⓐ could mean they are two separate people.

Perhaps this Ⓐ person and CF were there, and even if they didn't do it, they are witnesses.

I have to find them.

The pain in my breasts shifts from uncomfortable to excruciating. I take the planner with me to the glider in the corner of the living room. I quickly unbutton my shirt, sliding out of it and into the sports bra–like pump that allows me to be hands free.

A good mother wouldn't have to stop to pump but could just nurse.

A good baby, right with the Lord, would be able to nurse.

As I click the button for the pump to begin, I picture Belina's body by the river. My breathing, hot and angry, speeds up with the sound and pressure of the pump, faster and faster.

She wrote *Find Devon*. She met me at the cemetery but didn't tell me anything. She left me only her planner, filled with small clues about her life from the past eighteen months when she worked for Alec. She needed my help, even if she couldn't ask, then or now.

What help could you be?

I haven't been any help so far. But she sought me out the day of this meeting, likely knowing there was real danger. She left me evidence that could clear Alec and find the real killers.

You'll never be able to do it.

Belina brought me into the center of this investigation. I will prove that one of her last choices was the right one.

Chapter 6

Ester's cry freezes my confidence, and I hiss, "Damn it," because I'm only halfway done pumping. I gently unscrew the milk bottles from the pump and twist the yellow lids on top with the steadiness of someone defusing a bomb.

You wasted time on Belina's planner, and now your baby will starve.

I get out of the pumping bra and snap the buttons on my shirt. There's still an ache in my left breast, but I can't handle the crying, so sharp and loud despite being a floor away. I take the stairs two at a time. First, I move her black-and-white-patterned bouncer from the nursery to my office and then rush to my bedroom, where she's wailing in the bassinet. I take a deep fortifying breath and begin bouncing her. Up and down the hallway, I hum "Twinkle Twinkle Little Star" fourteen times before we're both calm.

In my office, I strap her into the bouncer and spin the little mobile she likes to watch. I adjust the mirror that hangs over her sweet face so she can see what I see. Her father's black hair. My green eyes. The nose that's less prominent than mine and perfect.

You're the only one who sees her that way.

She's the worst thing that ever happened to your husband.

She's a stain on his family name.

A name you don't deserve.

I leave her to stare at the mobile and do a full turn in my office. I stop in front of the gigantic dry-erase board on the wall across from my desk. Half is dedicated to sleeping solutions, and the other half is labeled *Anderson Indictment*. My obsessiveness nicely complemented my most recent specialty as a lawyer: working with accountants to identify and prosecute fraud. Teaming up with CPAs, the tax people, I pored through data about the businesses my clients were suing. The Anderson case was my last one before I took time off in my first trimester because I'd started spotting. The doctor wasn't worried, but Jack and I were.

You gave up that job because you were bored with the right side of the law.

It's true I wanted to focus my time investigating motherhood. I began with books, reading nearly every one in our local library, then continued to online forums, mom blogs, and Pinterest pages. Thanks to Belina's friendship, I received the most valuable resource: firsthand observation. I spent hours in the company of parents, grandparents, and nannies at tot lots, story times, library trips, and music classes.

Little good that did.

Such an investigation may sound obsessive, but that's how I'm wired. When I was building fraud cases, I had to find the right information to fit the legal strategy. I needed CPAs as a sort of Rosetta Stone to translate the math into English. Then I'd put that into legal terms to support the case. My specialty was digging deep into the psychology of a business.

I had great success with a simple three-pronged approach called the Fraud Triangle. That's how I managed the Anderson case. I took each possible suspect and dug up the answers to three key questions: was there pressure to commit a crime, motivation to do it, and rationalization of how to live with it?

To some people it must have seemed boring poring over numbers, bank accounts, and tax history. Maybe a credit card statement or two. But it wasn't to me. I saw it as a language, and while I don't consider myself Saint Jerome, turning the Bible Latin, there were a few times I almost brought the courtroom to Jesus.

You must be outside your mind, girlie, if you think you could do that again.

I crouch down, pressing on my temples, willing the voice to stop so I can focus. Helping Alec will require more than deciding between a soft wrap and a ring sling. It requires the Anderson-indictment me. A version I carefully constructed to have a challenging but manageable job with plenty of time to build the home I always wanted.

Recalling that version of myself, I picture her process, how well she operated. I swipe the eraser across the letters, my pulse pounding as I clean the board. I line up my markers and write each area of inquiry in a different color:

BODY
SUSPECT(S)
ALEC (alibi)
TIME LINE

I do a quick LexisNexis search, thankful my account is still active from the previous job. I search Belina's name and run Swan Point as a cross-reference if some coverage didn't include her. My first question: Why is Alec the only suspect?

I'm surprised to see the most coverage is from TheHaleReport.com, which has only one owner, operator, and reporter: Phillip Hale. His blog had been inactive as far as I knew. And my knowledge came from being the one who shut him down.

I half grin at the image of him looking all "serious reporter" on the blog's header. Something kicks in my gut, but I scroll instead of letting in the guilt. Not yet.

Phillip has a photo from Belina's freshman year of college at Salve Regina in Newport. She's pictured in tight jeans and a flowy top, talking to a professor. She's smiling wide, obviously aware of the photo. One commenter (Oysterdigger77) wrote that she was "probably fucking the whole class." Some sickos say worse than that, but I skim the rest.

The next article was posted the following morning in the *Providence Daily*, the main local paper, playing catch-up. It doesn't report anything new other than the standard "looking into it" from the police communications officer. It runs the same freshman-year photo of Belina, with credit to TheHaleReport.com. There are many more comments on its coverage, mostly racist trolls blaming her murder on "them immigrants, blacks, or Mexicans." I grew up around plenty of racists in Kansas. I thought in liberal New England, I'd see less of it, but the worst of people grow everywhere.

My disgust with the human race continues with comments about how hot she is and how that probably got her killed. I can't ignore it now, noting the chatter.

Maybe she did ask for it.

Maybe you're too stupid to see what your friend really was.

There are slams against the East Side because the police got here so quickly. In other neighborhoods, it would have taken them at least twice as long to get to the scene. A few people theorize that gay prostitutes who supposedly use those woods should be suspects. A dozen insist any woman alone at night is asking for it.

I return to the in-depth coverage from TheHaleReport.com about Belina. *Ms. Cabrala was from Newport, Rhode Island, a graduate of Saint George's Academy, an elite prep school. She attended Salve Regina University in Newport until her sophomore year. Cabrala held hostessing and office jobs.*

Alec Mathers, her employer, is described as an entrepreneur in the fishing industry. His business employs recently incarcerated men to give them skills and a paycheck. Misha Mathers is a stay-at-home mom and had employed Cabrala as the full-time nanny for their son, Emmett, three, for the past eighteen months.

I shake my head at the last line because it's structured for judgment toward Misha. I didn't take Phillip Hale for someone looking for the cheap shot. I'd know because I took a few at him. And he never gave them back.

Not yet.

In his next major article, Phillip publishes Belina's private Instagram photos. She didn't have many: five selfies and three of Emmett from a distance. Someone leaked them or hacked them, and I make a note.

The story explains how Alec had clicked the little red heart on all of them. There are no photos on his Instagram page. Most of the other accounts Alec follows are for local restaurants or boating.

But Phillip's lead picture that day and for days to come was a selfie Belina had taken with Alec and Emmett on Alec's boat. There's sunlight and a corner of a sail behind the three of them, all smiling, especially Emmett. Her caption: *With my boys #newport #goodlife #boafortuna #saudade.*

I side-eye her use of "my boys," since they're not. But my gaze returns to her effervescent smile, and my heart wrenches. I don't want to think about her smile now—embalmer's choice—rotting in a dark casket beneath the earth.

I focus on my task and google her *saudade* hashtag. The word doesn't have an English equivalent, but it's about longing for a point in time. Not necessarily a time that's happened or will ever occur. A quote from a Portuguese writer, Manuel de Melo, pops up. He says *saudade* is "a pleasure you suffer, an ailment you enjoy."

Neither Alec nor Belina appear to be suffering in that moment, but perhaps she knew pain waited for them back on land.

The alt-weekly newspaper, the *Cthulu*, named after H. P. Lovecraft, takes all Phillip has written and adds nonattributed quotes from around the neighborhood.

The dead nanny basically raised that kid. I never saw the mom around.

The killer is inside that fancy East Side house.

The kid seemed to love her more than his own parents.

I'm not a Misha apologist, but as a mother, I cringe at the remarks. The coldness of people when a family is in crisis. But I do wonder if Misha was jealous of the closeness between Belina and Emmett. Or the relationship between Alec and Belina. Had she seen the Instagram pictures?

The unattributed quotes were picked up in other articles as "neighborhood perceptions," whatever that means. For a couple news cycles in the first week, national tabloids ran Phillip's articles, adding the "hot nanny" quotes and photos. Going viral meant Phillip had little control over the coverage. That was when he changed gears.

Phillip is featured in a special edition of *Good Day RI*. This half-hour news talk show normally includes local interests: a chef sharing her shrimp scampi recipe or an anchor stomping grapes at the South County wine festival. But two weeks after the unsolved murder, Phillip appears to have pitched a whole show focused on the murder, with him in the driver's seat.

I click on the video and turn up the volume. After the lead-in, Phillip is sitting in the guest chair, looking sharp in his dark suit and hipster glasses. I watch *Good Day RI* regularly, the cohosts smiley and upbeat, the man bald and woman blonde, both white. It's not every day they have a black male guest join them and even rarer that it's someone breaking news about a local murder.

Ester begins to whine, and I hurry over to rock her bouncer. She'll need to be fed soon, but I get her calm enough to continue.

Phillip runs through the evidence, teasing the breaking news of a tape. But first there's footage of the Mathers home, three stories and imposing, before the video shows the other large houses along Cole Avenue. Then there's a long shot of Belina's house, which I've never seen. Her apartment is located on the west side of Hope, close to busy North Main Street. Phillip explains to non–Rhode Islanders, national producers in particular, the subtext East Siders already know.

The shot pans to more weathered and less pristine places. "The closer you get to North Main, there are fewer single-family homes. Instead houses are split, floor by floor, into apartments."

Phillip wants to be clear that Belina was a renter. She was pretty but poor, working for a family in the right kind of East Side neighborhood while she lived on the wrong side of Hope Street.

The male anchor is full of theories, noting on the map how a boat could have come up the river if the cemetery were closed. They've obviously never been there. There are at least a half dozen ways someone could get to where Belina was murdered, including two walking paths. But, yeah, maybe a boat.

The blonde anchor asks, with a deep, serious voice, who would want to harm a nanny. That's the moment I see something click for Phillip. He needs a villain.

"If she had a lot of boyfriends, as some suggest," he begins, pushing his black-framed glasses up his nose, "one of them may have been jealous."

I nearly throw my computer. It's bad enough that internet trolls are lying about Belina and Alec, but we certainly don't need our journalists gossiping on air. Phillip knows better.

You're so arrogant to assume you know anything at all.

On to the last segment, with the breaking news of a tape. Working with the media was a small part of being an attorney in DC, particularly when I was working a high-profile case. Best guess, this tape got Phillip the meeting with the *Good Day RI* executive producer. But the end goal would be to parlay this local half-hour segment into an advertisement for national news producers about what an excellent guest Phillip Hale could be. This could be very good news for both of us.

I'm impressed with this move. Phillip may have been forced out of the media game for a little while, relegated to being a basement blogger with a few hundred clicks a week, but now he is back.

He'll come for you too.

After a short lead-in, the video plays. It's dark, and the time stamp reads 6:07 p.m. The footage is slightly grainy and mostly dark colors, giving the effect of *The Blair Witch Project*. If Phillip had somehow been given the choice of full-color HD, he'd still have gone with this version.

There is a woman in the distance at the center of the shot. She strolls across the frame toward a side road. I'm holding my breath because I don't need to see her face to know how she stands, the way she tosses her long hair as it blows in the wind.

And you'll never see her again.

Phillip's voice-over begins, his tone serious and solemn. Neither anchor interrupts; it's now his show.

"Belina Cabrala entered Swan Point Cemetery on the East Side of Providence after it was closed for the night. She wandered alone in the growing dark. Here we see Belina walking toward a gazebo that overlooks the river. It's a quarter mile from where she will be murdered within hours."

Murdered and alone.

You could have done something once.

She trusted the wrong person.

The camera zooms closer, and she is standing at the center of the gazebo. Her silhouette is dark against the setting sun's brightness, fading into the long line of the riverbank in the distance. Her hair continues to blow in the wind until she tucks it inside the jacket she's wearing. It's oversize on her shoulders, and I know she didn't have it on when I saw her that afternoon. In fact, I've never seen her in it before. It was so warm that day. Why wear it? I see her nuzzle the shoulder, and then it clicks. That's Alec's jacket.

Phillip continues. "We'll never know her final thoughts before she met her death. Belina seemed to have had a lonely life or, at the very least, a mysterious one. Most of her life was in Newport, living with her mother off and on while her father was never in the picture. Her social media had no photos of friends, and none have come forward since her death. Some say she had many boyfriends, but they also remain elusive. Who would a young woman meet in a secluded cemetery after dark? What kind of encounter did she expect? Why would they need such privacy?"

I roll my eyes at his lazy reporting, the "hot nanny" narrative being picked up even by him.

The footage continues, and Belina turns to face the camera, her jaw set, her eyes determined as if she's made a choice. She stands up straighter, heading toward the river. Where she'll die.

She wanted your help.

You didn't even try to stop her.

Tears slide down my cheeks, and I have to hold my breath to get control. I fight these emotions. Fight this voice. Ester and exhaustion give them dominion again.

It takes a bit of focused breathing, but I'm back to the video. The segment cuts to the wide-eyed anchors, visions of New England Emmy Awards dancing in their heads. Phillip, in his nice suit and tie, hipster glasses, and deprecating grin, played this all just right.

I head to my whiteboard and add *Phillip* to my growing list of areas of inquiry. But not as a suspect. As my only way forward.

Across a bridge you burned.

Before I return to my desk, I text Phillip, asking to meet. Preferably at our old spot.

Chapter 7

It's completely dark in the house when I open my eyes, which are burning from too little sleep. A key is turning in the back door lock, and Jack's shoes echo on the hardwood floor.

He'll know what you've been up to.

Breaking your promise.

Obsessing over cases again.

I slowly sit up on the couch in the living room, where I moved to give Ester a bottle. She fell asleep on my chest, and I joined her soon after.

I whisper for him to be quiet as he turns on a lamp. His shoes thump onto the floor, and he heads over to us. After first kissing my forehead, he gently takes Ester and disappears upstairs. Most evenings, he puts her to bed. She falls asleep much easier for him. If only she'd stay that way for more than a couple hours at a time.

It's almost eight p.m., a little late for dinner, but Jack texted he'd be hungry, and I said we'd make something together.

I head to the kitchen because cooking is the right place to channel my anxiety about Alec. It's also where Jack and I fight, and that's coming too.

I turn on the lights to illuminate our kitchen, nicely updated but not especially big or modern. Everything is within a few steps, except the small alcove with a table and two chairs. I can see an older Ester there whizzing through her math homework, a brother and maybe a sister pestering her as they fight over the last slice of carrot cake, freshly baked.

Belina will never have that family.

You could have helped her, but you didn't.

I stare at the ceiling light, blinking back tears, trying to focus on how to bring up Alec's problems. With him in mind, I ask Alexa to play Radiohead, *Kid A*.

As the soft opening beats of "Everything in Its Right Place" thrum, I take the garlic from the window ledge. I crack off five large cloves and smack each of them harder than required with the side of a large knife before slicing them thin. What I don't use in the sauce I'll drop into butter I'm melting for the garlic bread.

I fill our spaghetti pot with water. Jack walks into the room as I turn up the flame. He's changed into sweatpants and a ratty Georgetown hoodie. When I saw him in it for the first time, we were in law school, and he showed up at my apartment in the sweatshirt, then brand new, bright navy-blue with letters white and crisp. I rolled my eyes, explained wearing your own college's shirt is like going to a concert with the band's shirt on.

He frowned, and I said, "Anyway, what's the big deal? It's not like we're at Harvard."

That got a laugh, which was my aim.

"My uncle Cal sent it, so I have to wear it."

"But he'll never know," I said. "He's all the way up in Providence."

Jack shrugged one shoulder, his cheeks flushing a little as he said, "Yeah, but I'll know."

I never teased him about it again. I'd have married him in it.

Jack steps into the kitchen and kisses my cheek before heading over to the wine fridge.

"We're cooking together, huh?" he says on a pause. Then he pulls out the Chianti we first tried during our honeymoon in Italy, and we grin at each other.

"We are cooking," I say, handing him the corkscrew. "And talking about Alec."

He sighs and opens the wine before taking two glasses out of the cabinet to fill them. He hands me one, and we raise them at each other and both take long sips.

He wishes you were your old self.

We only fight while cooking. We've done this many times, chopping together while airing grievances or a slight that we can't let go. Working side by side, stirring and tasting together. Somehow, putting together a meal, helping each other chop or season, talking things through, and finally sitting down with our shared victory makes a peaceful table.

I'd like to claim the idea as mine, but it's something Jack observed growing up, from his uncle Cal, who's very "involved" in Rhode Island politics. Uncle Cal would invite opponents or conspirators over to his house to cook, drink, and eat together until eventually the guest acquiesced to whatever was on his agenda. In fact, Uncle Cal cooked with me once, when we first moved here, convinced me to take on a couple cases for him. Over lamb chops, he confessed he needed someone like me.

Uncle Cal cut into his bloody-as-hell lamb and said, "You've got three things I need." He held up a pinky. "The myopic obsession of a prosecutor." He chewed a bite, and the ring finger followed. "The ability to follow the money, also very important, but not as important as"—he lifted his middle finger to indicate number three—"very few scruples."

I started to protest, genuinely disagreeing, but he silenced me with the hand still displaying the three fingers.

"These characteristics are the only reason I gave Jack my blessing to marry you. We can make him governor at the very least."

"The suspense is killing me," Jack says, bringing me back to him. He tops off my wine. "How's Alec?"

"About as good as the prime suspect could be." I set the glass down. "You could have said."

He swallows thickly and starts peeling the onions. I hand him the large knife I used on the garlic. He's halfway done chopping before he pauses and sets the knife down. "This case is breaking my heart."

He needs you.

You're pushing him away.

Just like before.

I straighten up, crossing my arms. "Then why don't you help him?"

"Because I don't know if he's innocent, Dev."

"If you talked to him," I say softly, remembering the exhaustion, the anguish on Alec's face. "If you looked into his eyes."

He shakes his head. "I can't get involved. The detective on the case is a smart man. He'll find the right person."

I roll my eyes. "That's a pretty naive view."

"Is it?" He begins chopping again. "Hey, Mayor, you know the murder investigation grabbing all the headlines and making us look inept? Mind if we pressure the cops to stop looking at the prime suspect? He's an old college buddy of mine."

"Alec is really alone," I begin, picturing him on the lawn with the wastebasket. "Everyone is against him. He steps out of his house, and there are bags of shit on his lawn."

"I noticed that on my run the other morning," Jack says quietly. He slides the diced pieces into the bowl with the garlic. "I understand why that would strike a nerve. Alec's situation is not yours."

I take a shaky breath and dump the bowl into the pan. The garlic and onions sizzle in the olive oil. Of course Alec's situation is different than what I faced as a girl, but there are similar threads through both. The isolation and feeling of being ostracized. "We're both innocent," I say.

Are you so sure?

Were you really innocent?

Why were you the only one they wanted to leave?

"Devon." Jack takes my elbow, pulling me close. "They found Alec's DNA at the crime scene and on her coat."

I think back to Phillip's video and how surprised I was that she was wearing a bulky coat on that warm night. "I've never seen her wearing it before." I throw my hunch out there. "I think it's Alec's."

His eyebrows go up. "How do you know what jacket she had on?"

"I saw her wearing it on the video Phillip played on *Good Day RI*."

"Christ," he says and heads over to the refrigerator. He gets out the two packages of meat. "Did you review all the coverage?"

Instead of waiting for an answer he knows, he rips open the white paper and dumps the meat into a bowl. "There's too much evidence. You can't start digging . . . not like last time."

You're breaking what little was mended.

He should have left you crazy and jobless in DC.

"Alec told me about the blood in the trunk," I say too sharply, realizing I'm hurt he kept so much from me. I take a deep breath to keep myself from saying something nasty. I add chopped mushrooms to the sizzling skillet. "Misha said Belina scraped her arm on the stroller when she was putting it in the trunk."

"Who's naive now?" he says. He shoves up his sleeves to knead the chopped Portuguese sausage with the hamburger meat.

"The detective," I say as if I haven't researched the lead investigator, Detective Frank Ramos, as thoroughly as possible this evening. After I sent a text to Phillip, I even called an old contact at the police department. He said Detective Ramos was a twenty-year veteran who kept his head down. He'd hardly worked any murder cases until catching this one. "The detective is dragging it out. He doesn't like Alec for it."

The little phrase feels good hanging in the air. It's something cops would say when I worked at the Sex Offense and Domestic Violence Section of Washington, DC's US Attorney's Office. I interned there all through law school, and it was the only job I applied for after graduation. I understood how detectives worked. Why the good ones would drag their feet in an investigation when something wasn't right. Go back and find more witnesses. Interview the suspect again. So the charges would stick. So the right person would go to jail.

The charges didn't always stick. Our office was infamous for not taking as many cases to trial as we should have. "He said / she said" bureaucratic bullshit. After watching rapist after rapist after child molester never even see the inside of a courtroom, I began to take the burden of proof and "beyond a reasonable doubt" into my own hands.

As if someone like you could make a difference.

When your whole life is nothing but paying for sins that can never be forgiven.

It started small, getting someone to hack into the computers, steal a few bank records. But then I needed more. So I started stalking violent offenders out on bail to seedy motels. Sleeping in my car outside an accused pedophile's home. Harassing bowling buddies and joining Bible study to find more witnesses or corroborate the victim's testimony.

Justice at any cost, including my safety and sanity, proved too much. And after my boss refused to move forward with prosecuting a human sex-trafficking ring, I leaked confidential information to the press. No one else had access to those files. I knew it'd be my job on the line, but I didn't care. What's a career when you see a room of abused women chained to the floor? Have to look them in the eyes, see that familiar broken gaze, and say you don't have enough evidence to prosecute?

I was almost disbarred. Jack convinced me to leave my dream / waking nightmare job that would certainly destroy me.

He should have left you then.

He regrets it now.

Regrets this whole awful life you've built.

"We have to have lines and to stay within them," Jack insisted. I promised I always would.

So we got married, Jack got a great job as chief of staff for the mayor's office, and we moved to Providence. I started doing freelance business fraud cases, like the Anderson indictment. And until I started working for Uncle Cal, life was as normal and happy as I'd ever experienced.

You'll never experience it again.

I finish stirring the drained pasta into the sauce, thinking of all I've gained, not just postcollege but from Kansas forward. I can keep to the lines Jack drew for us, to preserve the life we have since built.

We sit down at the eat-in kitchen table. The plates of pasta steam as we swirl noodles and take a few quiet bites.

I set down my fork. "I met Belina the afternoon before she died." I pause as he stops eating. "She left me her day planner full of notes. It was in my hospital stuff, and I forgot until today."

He wipes his mouth with a napkin. "Notes about what?"

My heart is heavy with love and guilt. He doesn't immediately demand I give it to the detective, even though that's obviously what I should do. I hope he still respects my decisions, even when they're different than his.

You're not deserving of his trust.

You don't deserve anything good.

I leave the kitchen and return with Belina's planner. His brown eyes go wide as I hand it to him. "Look at the last page," I say. "The day she was murdered."

He angles his head forward, flips through the planner, and finds the page. "Transfer money. Library with E. Tell Alec. Find Devon." He flashes a concerned glance at me before continuing, "Meet with *A* and CF at SP. Jesus, is *A* with a circle Alec?"

"Read it again," I say but manage to wait only a few seconds. "She writes 'tell Alec,' but when listing who she's meeting with, it's two other names. Why would she change the code midlist?"

"Why have a code at all?" he says, flipping back through a few pages. "She's a nanny."

I nod, relieved he's trying to understand. "I'll give the journal to the detective. He'll need my statement, since I saw her that afternoon. But I've got to have the rest of the week to finish my analysis. To develop a theory."

"There were a couple of hairs from Misha at the crime scene," he says. "That makes sense with what you said about the coat."

"I can do this," I say, meaning it, wanting it to be true. "I need time to put an alternative theory together."

You're just embarrassing yourself.

Embarrassing him.

Jack scratches at the back of his neck. "Okay," he says finally. "What if you tell the detective about the planner at one of Uncle Cal's happy hours?"

Uncle Cal hosts big schmoozy and boozy events at his house a few times a year. Detective Ramos's bosses would be there, and hopefully, it'd communicate that he should give me a pass on withholding the evidence. And make him more open to us working together to find the real killer. "When is the next one?" I ask, liking the idea.

"Friday," Jack says. "I thought if the walk went well . . ."

So he has his own plans. "The wrap was so I could go hands free with a martini."

"That's a thought," he says. "Or we get a sitter."

I shake my head. "No, it's too soon."

"There's a nice lady from the office, Gillian. She's a grandma type. I'll forward her resume and references. You can check her out as thoroughly as you want. As long as it's legal."

I slice him a glare, though it's a point well taken. "I'll think about it."

"Imagine a shower and your old clothes? We'd talk to adults and be our former selves. It has to happen at some point."

I try to tamp down the nasty words about how he's been his old self this whole time.

You're the one who can't adjust.

You're the problem.

"What if you talked to your mom group about it?" he says.

That is the generous term. It is group therapy that started in the hospital. And I hate it. "It takes too much . . . time," I say, starting to eat again to avoid the topic.

He knows you're not doing well.

"If you're going to . . . help Alec," Jack continues, "you need more support. Please."

"That's your price?" I ask.

He shakes his head, but I'm right. "I'll talk to Uncle Cal and get the detective there," he says. "I understand why this is important to you. It's important to me too."

The bread beeps, and I stand, running my hand across his before heading to the stove. I open the door, and heat warms my face. I rest the pan on a pot holder on the counter. I hear him pouring another glass of wine. I slice the bread and coat the steamy side with large swaths of buttery garlic.

"How many spreadsheets have you made so far?" he asks behind me, nuzzling my temple.

He hasn't teased me about my process in so long. This is as close to normal as we've been since Ester. I smile up at him, and the frisson curls in my stomach. He raises one eyebrow, the playful look that asks: *Upstairs?*

It'd be our first time together since the baby. I let the idea linger and lick my lips to respond but freeze.

Ester is crying. "She's up."

His face falls, but he recovers, finishing the wine.

"Sorry," I say, even though it's not my fault. Or maybe it's all my fault.

He wants his old life back.

You pushed him to start a family and ruined his life.

"You got her?" he asks, though he's not really asking.

"Of course," I say too brightly, rushing toward the fridge to grab her milk. "Finish dinner without me. The pasta is *al dente*," I add in my terrible Italian accent.

It's a joke from our honeymoon, but he doesn't smile.

Chapter 8

Friday, December 9

My head snaps up from my desk at Ester's wail, a four a.m. call to arms. I rush to get her from the bassinet in the bedroom. Jack continues to lightly snore through the activity, and I resist the urge to shove him awake.

You wanted this before either of you were ready.

Before you deserved to be a mother.

Ester shouldn't be hungry, so I bounce her for a while in the lamplight of my office as dawn catches up to our restless night. She's docile on her play mat, and I leave her there, content, for a few minutes at least. I rub my eyes, focusing on the spreadsheet on my computer. I click through the tabs, delaying my final review of Belina's planner. It's been five days of analysis since I remembered the yellow book stashed in my hospital bag. Since I promised Alec I'd help him. Since I tried to find my new self.

Five days of failure.

Five days of being selfish.

Taking time away from your too-tiny baby.

For what?

I can't put it off any longer. Now I must decide on a theory about her murder. One that will get Detective Ramos's cooperation at the happy hour tonight. One that will save Alec's life.

I start at the first tab focused on time, inputting eighteen months of entries, her entire time employed as a nanny. I reviewed and categorized each day, noted who Belina saw, where, what she did, and anything unusual or different from other entries. It's a rough approximation, but I need data.

I haven't cracked the code, and the voice is right. I feel like I've failed already.

You were never going to succeed.

I click over to my computer file with every photo I could find of her. I stare at the Instagram shot of her along Blackstone Boulevard. She captioned it "the best walks are with friends." I'd taken that photo.

It took one afternoon with Belina, seeing her care for Emmett, to realize she was different. Ninety percent of nannies are too calm. Their subtext always, *This isn't my child.* They want their charges safe, sure, but the sunshades aren't always pulled down enough to block the glare. The scraped knees not attended to as fast as a mother or father would.

But Belina nurtured Emmett. She worried over every cough. Swooped in instantly with each stumble. I first noticed her planner because she logged details about Emmett's day.

"What kinds of things matter?" I asked, rubbing a contented hand over my slight baby bump.

"How he laughs on the swings. Which slide is too fast and scares him. What snacks he ate all of and which were left on the bench for the birds."

But now I have her planner. I've spent the past week with her words, and the only thing I'm sure of is that she was lying.

Like recognizing like.

Belina's day planner is in a language new to me but familiar enough. Some sentences in the planner are the language of a caregiver: "Peas with cheese; big slide too scary; playhouse board is loose on north side." But after reading and analyzing, I believe the real purpose, and what comprises 72 percent of this journal, is notes about Alec and meetings she had with CF.

Back at the whiteboard, under her name, I write *WHY NANNY?* And then:

1. "NEEDED A CHANGE" (FROM WHAT?);

2. INTERLOPER;

3. HOME WRECKER;

4. JUST A JOB.

There's a balance to drawing conclusions and moving forward with a theory. I'm going at a faster pace because I must.

I decide the notes about Emmett were for Belina. So I disregard those, hiding them in the spreadsheet. What's left are the meeting notes and code names I have yet to break. I sort the data by the code to see every note about every person and group theme by theme. I search for patterns and apply the fraud triangle.

You'll never be that good again.

I click and sort.

Who is CF to Belina? To Alec? To Ⓐ?

Click. Click.

I search the time line. She met with CF as soon as she had the job. Met with him regularly. Then Alec met with him.

Click. Click.

Is there pressure to commit a crime? Did CF ask Belina to watch Alec? To inform on him?

Click.

What would be her motivation to work for CF? Money? Usefulness?

Click.

How did she live with it? If she did care about Alec, her feelings growing, was there guilt? Resentment? Was she living a lie?

Was it fraud? Was she a fraud?

You should know.

I flip through the pages of her journal, running my finger over her final sentence:

> Friday: Transfer $. Library with E. Tell Alec.
> Find Devon. Meet with Ⓐ & CF at SP.

I'm stuck on "transfer money." I need to know what money. To whom? My gut says Alec knows a lot more than he's telling.

After swiping the eraser across the whiteboard, I write my theory about Belina: *spy*.

I reach for my phone to text Phillip again because he hasn't responded all week. I linger over the words and settle on: **We must talk. Please. It will be different this time.**

There is no bubble that indicates he's responding. I doubt the little check mark that says the text was received. It's likely he's blocked me. If that's the case, this reaffirms what I have to do. Where I have to go.

"Ready?" Jack calls from downstairs.

I glance at Ester in time to hear her cry as if she senses my anxiety. I pick her up and whisper that it's going to be okay. I bounce her, humming a country song I used to listen to as a girl back in Kansas.

Finally, we're both quiet, and I get us dressed before heading downstairs. Jack's in the kitchen with coffee in a travel mug.

"Let me drive you," he says as he hands me the cup.

It's possible he doesn't trust that I'll go to "mom group." But more likely, he knows it's my first time in the car with Ester since we left the hospital. I don't like either thought. I bounce Ester, running my hands along her green outfit with ruffles on the bottom. "I can drive myself."

Jack swallows thickly, and the curve of his lips presses together.

He doesn't trust you anymore.

I hand him Ester and pack the larger travel diaper bag for the first time. The list of the top twenty must-haves from various mom blogs rolls through my mind. Ten minutes later, I return to him in the kitchen. Ester is slumped in the crook of his arm as he sips coffee with the other hand.

"Careful," I snap, letting my nerves out on this silly situation. "You could burn her."

"I've got it," he says, defensive as I quickly take her back into my arms.

I nuzzle her as anxiety punches my gut until it finally deflates into embarrassment. "I'm sorry," I say. "I'm nervous."

He raises his eyebrows.

"No. I'll drive myself."

He bows his head to the side as if he knew I'd say that. "Call me when you're back. Tell Dr. Lauren hello."

I kiss him on his smoothly shaven cheek before he can notice my eyes filling with tears.

I really do hate lying to him.

Chapter 9

From the rearview mirror, I see Jack with his hand in the air and a relieved smile as if I'm actually doing what I said I would. But I have to see Cynthia to apologize for how I failed her and find out if she'll trust me again.

What kind of friend are you?

One friend dead.

The other hates you.

Ester wails in the back seat. I head toward Hope Street in the direction of the Day Hospital for postpartum women, where Jack thinks I have an appointment.

After a half mile, I turn back, toward Chip Bakery. I'm about to take the left into the small lot, but I can't press the gas to cross both lanes of traffic. My foot won't move at the idea of being hit on Ester's side. I can see how the back door would cave into her car seat, tearing her body apart, and I can see it as real as her sitting there now.

A car horn blasts, and I push the gas without looking as another car pulls around me. I scream and swerve, barely missing the huge truck. I overcorrect, and I'm going too fast, and I run up onto the concrete curb with a loud thud.

"Shit!" I say as we slam forward. I reverse into the spot and shove the gear into park. Ester continues to cry, and my breath comes in quick white puffs. I forgot to turn on the heat. No wonder Ester is so upset. I blast us both with the warm air. A minute passes, a few more. I feel wet tears streaming down my neck before I realize I'm crying.

I don't want Cynthia seeing me this upset, but I hardly have a choice.

She'll know you're hearing me again.

You were stupid to tell her about me before.

Dumping my purse onto the passenger seat, I rummage for some makeup, a brush, anything to seem more together than I actually am.

I use my fingers and a pencil to tame my frizzed hair into a high bun. I have some old lipstick that's too pink for my coloring that I put on anyway and a little Blistex over it for shine. My eyes are red with purple circles that paint spackle couldn't cover underneath.

At least I put on a clean shirt. My maternity pants look cheap because they are.

It's embarrassing you're still wearing them.

Cynthia will be ashamed to know you.

Ester's cries are becoming frantic. I read that most new babies hate the car seat, so it shouldn't be a surprise she's screaming. But it's still frustrating. I try to keep my voice kind and even as I clench the steering wheel.

"I'm coming, baby girl. It's okay."

I pull the wrap out of the diaper bag. I wore Ester around the house this week as I worked. She calms down when she's next to me. We both do.

After turning off the car, I head over to her side. I stand in the snow as the wind pulls at the wrap, and I quickly have her on my chest, every inch covered by fabric and secure against me. With her cotton hat in place, I take a deep inhale of baby powder and detergent.

The sun is bright in the cold stillness of early winter days. I breathe it, listen to the quiet, and try to feel a little better staring into the windows of the busy coffee shop. Cynthia opened Chip Bakery right after Jack and I moved to town. I usually spent several hours a day working at a table in the corner, enjoying the noises of customers over the silence of my home office.

Cynthia is so disappointed in you.

You're not welcome anymore.

Ester begins to scream again. I worry that she's hot somehow and unzip her more. I shush while taking her hat off, letting her face feel more air.

A mother with her baby in a stroller passes us but halts midstep. Her eyes widen, and her back stiffens at the sight of us. As if her baby never cries. As if her blankets piled into the fancy bassinet stroller with wind protection are so much better. As if there's something wrong with Ester. Or me.

She knows a mother like you would have an evil child.

Ceaseless crying.

Too small to love.

My eyes burn with tears, from the wind and the voice. I begin to hum and bounce, heading down the block and back while I wait for Ester to sleep. I cannot give in to what I hear. She is not a monster. My sins are not hers. I must stay focused and move forward, or I will drown us both.

Minutes pass, and the cool air seems to have calmed us. I zip my coat tight with Ester finally sleeping against me. I try to shrug off that mother's expression, her mom shaming, which I read about many times but haven't really experienced before.

Better get used to it, girlie.

No one will love your child.

Just like no one could ever really love you.

I force myself to head toward Chip Bakery and focus on my apology to Cynthia and convincing her to contact Phillip.

Chip is the only coffee shop in the heart of Hope Village, the main shopping area along the commercial blocks of Hope Street. This was strategic. Cynthia's capstone at Harvard Business School was to identify the most profitable venture using her credit line, skill set, and connections. She graduated with honors and brought her capstone to life, opening a coffee shop on the East Side of Providence.

It is more than coffee, actually. She took the concept of cheese boards and added house-made desserts paired with slightly bitter, locally sourced coffee. It's as if she's saying, "Make no mistake. This place is worthy of your precious East Side."

I take a deep, satisfied breath at her success. The expanded menu was the perfect upsell, more than tripling profits over the past two years. I helped her run the numbers after she found out about my legal work with accounting firms.

But her business hit a plateau, and she needs a liquor license and a second location to take things to the next level. I know that because I pushed her to apply for a grant through Uncle Cal's Economic Development Council.

She had a lot of hesitation. The fact that Uncle Cal and her brother had clashed, to put it mildly. I'd been in the middle of it, and I had forced Phillip out of the blogger business for a while. I didn't regret it, but I wished it had been different.

No matter the history, I did help Alec get one of these grants. I could help her. And so she trusted me and put herself and her business out there and applied for the grant.

But this time, it isn't working out. She barely made the second round. None of the councilmembers have visited Chip. They aren't taking her seriously because she's alone. But I promised her she wouldn't be.

You never deserved her friendship.

Ester is still asleep as I head toward Chip. An older couple in matchy puff vests holds the door for me, smiling as I pass. The place is packed. Staff swirl around the customers, who are stuffing their mouths with chocolate ganache and espresso. Everyone is in New England casual: skinny jeans, yoga pants, ill-fitting khakis, maybe a blazer or cable-knit sweater. Conversations echo about the latest play at Trinity Rep or how bad the roads are already this winter.

Cynthia is easy to spot, steady among the chaos in her spotless white silk shirt and tan slacks. She puts her hand on the back of a customer's metal chair as he tells her something that seems complimentary. She doesn't fully smile, but her eyes brighten. As the owner, she'll let you buy her coffee and her cakes, and that entitles you to quality but not more. It's common to see her nod with acknowledgment, but she's not a pleaser, which is the opposite of my midwest upbringing. I admired her immediately.

That said, she usually smiles at me. But not today.

As Cynthia's gaze locks with mine, I remember another characteristic: When she frowns, her eyes go wide. It's as if she's trying to see even more of what you're doing wrong.

Looking me over, she frowns as deeply as I've ever seen.

She's going to kick you out.

Like she should have done a long time ago.

She stops by the counter, likely ordering me something, and I'm able to put on what I hope is a brave face.

"You're here," Cynthia says, taking my hands, stretching them wide. "Look at you, mother warrior woman, wearing that baby."

There's no trace of anger or disappointment. That's worse. She's blaming herself instead of me.

"You told Jack to buy the wrap," I guess as I kiss her quickly on the cheek. She isn't a hugger.

"I may have texted him the idea. You only mentioned baby wearing twenty times or so." She steps back, still frowning. "I haven't seen you since the hospital."

"I'm good," I say in the same voice I use with Jack. "The nights are long and full of terrors, but I'm surviving."

She's not a baby person but smiles at sleeping Ester. "Your order is up. Come on."

She leads me to a corner table in a section that's closed. We sit down and have privacy.

To keep your evil baby away from her customers.

A barista brings a cappuccino and a glass of sparkling water. Sitting on the edge of the chair, I manage to balance Ester in her sleeping position without much disturbance. After a beat, I find my courage. "Sorry I didn't call you after. It's been hard . . . adjusting to everything."

"Hey, it's fine. You needed R & R."

"Yeah," I say.

"You've got that look," she says. "Let's hear it."

"The grant," I say. "I left you high and dry."

She shakes her head once. "I don't care about that," she says. "I built this business on my own. I can do the same with the next one."

"I know you can," I say. The fact remains I really pushed Cynthia to apply for the grant. She argued the only way anyone gets it is through serious politics, which wasn't her thing. But it was my thing. I told her if she put herself out there, I'd make sure she was covered. But she wasn't.

She is on the short list because she's smart and has a great plan. But she has the lowest scores because I wasn't able to work my angles with Uncle Cal. It was insider politics and white boys' club nonsense. "I overpromised and underdelivered."

"You were in the hospital," she says. "I honestly have barely thought about it."

"Really?" I say with a grin and sit forward. "Uncle Cal is having his big holiday happy hour tonight."

"Oh," she says, a little flush at her neck. "I hadn't heard."

"You could come and work the Council," I say. "One last shot."

"None of them have been in," she says. Her gaze shifts toward her staff, hurrying around the noisy room.

"It's not you," I say, hating myself even more. "It's all the stupid reasons you didn't want to apply for the grant in the first place. But I can help now."

Her stare is back on me, and it's unconvinced, which is fair.

But she also has to weigh an evening of ass-kissing Uncle Cal types over her need for the local endorsement and support. Coffee isn't getting cheaper. The liquor license is tied up in serious red tape. The banks will have heard about her not quite getting the green light.

Winning the grant clears the way for her second location. She'd not only get the major upsell of booze, but she could buy it at a reasonable cost with her new connections. This holiday happy hour will likely have all the members of the Economic Development Council. Or at least those who are in Uncle Cal's good graces. In other words, the important ones.

You'll just fail her again.

It should be easier for Cynthia. She's a well-educated, successful business owner, but as a black female she has to work harder in one month than most of the people at that party will in their whole lives. It certainly isn't fair. But I'm not a teenager anymore, so I don't spend a lot of time thinking about fair. Not when I can actually do something about it.

Her gaze returns to mine. "I want that grant."

I run my hand down Ester's back. "You deserve it. Let me try to help. Again."

She should never trust you.

No one should trust you.

She nods, and I can see some relief. She was holding back her disappointment. We're silent briefly, sipping our coffees, but then it's time to pivot.

"You've got that look again," she says.

"It's your brother." I dig into the diaper bag and grab my cell phone out of the side pocket to pull up the article. I hand it to her.

Cynthia glances at the headline on the screen, *Blogger Breaks Hot Nanny Murder*. "Phillip's getting attention again," she says. "He says this story could be his Amanda Knox. National byline or book deal."

"He's reporting rumors. Like that Belina was a slut who got herself killed."

"He said that?" Cynthia's mouth ticks up, but then she shakes it off. "Forget it, Dev. I'm not getting involved."

"Did you go to the funeral?"

"No, we were short staffed and really . . ." Cynthia pauses to breathe deeply. "She liked double espressos and ordered Emmett a mostly water apple juice. That was about the extent of our relationship."

"What if this happened to me? Or you?"

"Phillip needs this story." She refolds her white cloth napkin. "He was talking about moving back in with our folks before this heated up."

I like how much Cynthia watches out for her younger brother. When I forced Phillip to quit pursuing the Economic Development Council lead on Uncle Cal by basically blackmailing Phillip, she didn't get angry. Or at least, she said she understood why I did it. That I was trying to protect Phillip.

And maybe that's part of why I pushed the Economic Development Council grant. Thinking if she took my help, then everything would be forgiven.

"I want him to have this story," I say. "With Belina's side of it. Not as some hot nanny slut. Which is incredibly sexist by the way."

"It is," Cynthia says.

"He's rebuilding his reputation on fake news and misogyny. I thought better of him." I shift forward in my seat, putting my hand on Ester's back to be sure I don't bump her against the table. "I can help him."

"You burned that bridge," Cynthia says, a protectiveness flashing in her eyes. "His sources dried up. He didn't work for almost a year. It cost him a lot."

"It would have cost Phillip a lot more if I hadn't stopped him," I say. "He went after Uncle Cal. That's never ended well for anyone."

"I want to stay out of it," she says.

"It's a little late for that."

She sits back in her chair. "Is this happy hour invite conditional on my cooperation?"

I continue patting Ester. "Does it have to be?"

"What do you want?"

"Text Phillip to meet me."

"Why?" she says. "Really, Devon. Why?"

She knows you don't have what it takes anymore.

"I will solve this murder," I say. "Belina wanted me to help her."

Her brown eyes go wide for a moment, her anger giving way to alarm. "What does Jack say?"

"Go to group therapy," I say too quickly, too emphatically. "I'm supposed to be there now."

"You lied to Jack?" She sighs but reaches across the table, squeezes my hand. "That doesn't sound like you."

"I can't tell him how much I hate it," I whisper. "Can't stand how he'd look at me."

"Go easy on yourself. Maybe getting involved in this investigation right now isn't—"

"It is the best thing," I say, pulling back from her. "For me. Right now." I swipe a tear, clearing my throat, trying to tamp down how kindness almost breaks me. "I used to be able to do this. Phillip and I were good at it."

But you chose Cal over him.

"Why don't I call Jack?" Cynthia says, handing me a tissue. "He'll understand."

She doesn't know what those words mean. What I'd have to admit to Jack. To myself. What I could lose.

I shove the tissue into my pocket. I am stronger than this voice. Stronger than the headlines that parrot what trolls and gossips are saying about Belina. Stronger than whoever thought they had the right to take her life.

I find Cynthia's frowning gaze and begin. "Text Phillip that I've got Belina's planner. We have to meet today. Now, if possible. If you reach out, he'll listen."

"He's still angry," she says gently. "He's a long way from forgiving you."

"I don't need forgiveness," I say. "We can help each other. We were really good together once."

"Dev, I don't think now—"

"I'll get you the invite to the happy hour. You can still get that grant."

She swears under her breath. "This white woman privilege shit gets a pass because I love you." She shakes her head lightly, pulls out her phone, and starts texting as she talks. "I'm not doing it for the invite. I'm doing it because you asked. That's how friendship works."

She hates you now.

While she texts Phillip, I send a quick email to Uncle Cal, asking him to add Cynthia to his guest list.

Cynthia's phone buzzes. She shows me the texts.

Cynthia: Dev needs help.

Phillip: No.

Cynthia: I need you to do this. Please.

Phillip: Swan Point in half hour. By the river.

Chapter 10

I pack the memos I wrote after studying Belina's planner. The theories are hopefully strong enough to convince Detective Ramos that Alec is innocent. I drop them into my old messenger bag along with a bottle of breast milk and changing supplies. Tapping my finger on a copy of Belina's journal, I'm unsure if I should bring it for Phillip, if I can trust him. He may hate me for slamming the brakes on his career. I'm ready to explain myself. Ready to let him see it doesn't have to be over between us. We can still help each other.

You'll just use him again.

As I walk toward Swan Point Cemetery, I review my strategy, ordering my tactics from friendly to aggressive. I pass by Alec's house, and it's quiet. I snatch two bags of poop from the lawn and throw them into a trash can along the boulevard jogging path.

I go faster than I should and have to pause, almost breathless, huffing by the red mums wilting in a semicircle at the cemetery's entrance. Huge boulders loom with letters spelling *Swan Point* in bronze that has turned a magnificent green with age.

I wipe sweat from my heated face, perspiration dripping between my swollen breasts. But I don't dare unzip my coat. Ester could chill and get sick and end up in the hospital.

What if she's too hot?

You're smothering her.

What kind of mother walks this far in the winter?

A terrible mother.

I adjust her knit hat. One side of her face is cool but not cold. The cheek against my body is warm. I hurry along the asphalt road, nearing where the tape showed Belina's final moments.

The wind picks up by the river, whipping my long coat against my jeans. I trudge through the muddy grass, avoiding headstones, toward the large wooden gazebo. I stand at its center, and with the trees bare, I can see all the way to the river.

My mind flashes images from the video of Belina there in the dark, tombstones all around, completely alone at the end. I imagine her in the water, cold and drained of blood, body abandoned, eyes open in darkness.

My vision blurs, the panic attack completely cutting off my air. Even though I haven't had one since I was a girl, I remember to stick out my hands. But there is Ester now, and I shift to clutch her instead, falling onto my bottom with a thud. My head reels back until it connects with the corner of a bench.

There's pain, but I can focus only on Ester, my hands searching her. She's silent, shockingly so, and I wonder if somehow I hurt her. I breathe and breathe and breathe until I see stars, then the blurry ground, and finally reality.

Standing up, I brace myself against a beam and check her until it rouses her awake. She begins to cry.

You're the same weak little girl.

I whisper how sorry I am to Ester, fighting the pain in my chest from the attack and my own terror that they've returned. I bounce us both around and around the gazebo for maybe a half hour. I'm connected only to her, not time or place, until finally, we're calm.

I know why I used to have blackouts. I told myself they don't have to be so terrible. Sometimes your mind must leave. It's better to go away, and when I returned, it was all over, buried deep.

I shouldn't be surprised or as scared as I am that the blackouts have returned. They've been back before, while I was in DC. Jack knows about them. But I guess I hoped it'd be only the voice. That I'd have to deal with only one terrible thing from my past at a time.

You're getting exactly what you deserve.

But I'm not a terrorized girl or an obsessed DC lawyer. I'm a mother, and it's only Ester and me here in the cemetery. I'm not sure why all the old reasons must return with the new. What my mind is trying to hide. What it thinks I should forget.

Blotting the tears from my face with the edge of my coat, I force myself to remember Belina. Remember why I must find out the truth. And that I need Phillip's help.

On unsteady legs, I follow the path Belina took. It's less than a quarter mile until I reach Cynthia's old VW sedan parked at the top of the hill. She gave it to Phillip when she upgraded to her BMW. I see my face in the car window reflection, blotchy from tears and yet pale from almost passing out.

I spot him first, sitting down on a bench near the crypt where Belina was murdered, stabbed once, deeply, in the chest. According to Phillip's reporting, she bled profusely before her body was dragged down the hill to the muddy riverbank. There the killer cut open her right arm in diamond patterns. Some of her skin was taken by the knife, some by the water, like most of her blood.

Phillip will never trust you again.

You threatened him for trying to tell the truth.

My chest tightens, still sore from my attack. I have to get it together. Phillip needs to see me as a capable partner, not a sobbing, emotionally unstable liability.

He glances up as I approach, puts his phone away, and waves. He's in his reporter uniform, head-to-toe black, the slacks and dress shirt, skinny tie, and plastic-rimmed glasses. His hair and beard are all the same short length.

The Hale frown quickly appears. "Are you all right?" he asks, alarmed, as if he can see that I blacked out. That my mind was fighting with my consciousness to escape. It's not as bad as it used to be in DC. Or when I was a girl. But it's not good, that's for sure.

"I'm fine," I say too brightly.

"Hold still. You're bleeding." He pulls a handkerchief from his pocket.

His face nears mine, and there's kindness and concern in his dark-brown eyes. He touches the cloth to my forehead and wipes blood along my hairline. He continues to dab along my scalp, all the way to the back of my head. We're silent, except for the sound of our breath mingling. He puts pressure on a sore spot, and I hiss, but he continues his focused attention.

After dabbing a few more times, he nods once and steps back. "The bleeding stopped," he says, refolding the handkerchief to a clean side. He wipes a few tears from my cheeks. I didn't even realize they were there.

I want to say, *I'm not doing well.* I want to say, *Help me.* I only mumble, "Thanks."

He hands me the cloth, and I brush it over my cheeks. He takes a long step back. Straightens his sleeves and clears his throat. "How did that happen?"

"I slipped earlier," I say. "At the gazebo. We're fine."

"Good," he says. "The baby—"

"Ester," I offer. "She's fine. Sleeping now. We both had a cry."

"I can see that," he says. "Well, I'm here. What do you want?"

"I need your help," I say. "I don't think Alec killed Belina."

"Okay," he says, scratching at his temple, a tell that he's annoyed. "I hear an arrest is imminent."

"I'm speaking with Detective Ramos in a few hours."

He crosses his arms. "You're being vague."

I sigh because he really doesn't miss much. "Meeting him at Uncle Cal's house," I say.

The anger flashes, but he swallows it. He nods until he's regained his composure. "You have some grapes, Devon."

"I know he caused us a lot of pain—"

"Pain? That man is a pox."

"He's family."

Phillip laughs. "He's your husband's uncle, not yours."

"Beggars can't be choosers."

"Please." He steps closer, lowering his voice. "When I agreed to work with you, I didn't know it'd be him pulling the strings. He set us up to take out his enemies until finally I became one."

"The people you and I went after were criminals," I say. "The FBI carted their offices out of the Providence statehouse in boxes marked *evidence*."

"But they were very specifically Cal Burges's enemies," Phillip says loudly, his voice reverberating. "He had you dig up dirt on his enemies and leak it to me to report it. Now he's the only kingmaker left in this state. That was his plan, and it only worked because of us. Don't say it's because he's family, and we were fighting bad guys."

"You benefitted plenty from our work," I say. "That regional Peabody still on your desk?"

He blinks at Ester, the anger warring with some uneasiness, and then takes a step closer. "You're damn lucky we didn't get caught. Your hacking and blackmail was dangerous to both of us."

I shake my head at his indignation. "You sure as hell never asked or complained."

"Wow," he says. "This was a mistake. Do you need a ride home?"

I adjust Ester's hat, hearing her shift as if she's sensing the tension. "I didn't choose Uncle Cal over you."

He looks up at the canopy of bare trees, as if that's where patience lives.

"I protected you both," I say, getting to the heart of my betrayal.

You protected yourself.

Phillip and I worked great together. I did dig up dirt on people that Uncle Cal asked me to look into. Those Rhode Island politicians were so corrupt it was hardly work at all. Phillip was suddenly the hottest reporter in town. He was even talking book deal. But then one of Uncle Cal's enemies wised up on our arrangement. He sent Phillip some information about the Economic Development Council being a front for money laundering. Uncle Cal swore it wasn't him and that he'd force anyone involved to resign.

Stupid enough to believe him.

I wasn't worried about the money laundering. But I was terrified of what would happen if Phillip took on Uncle Cal. It was suicide. I also believed Uncle Cal, that it was a mistake. Not something to ruin the good name of his Council as well as his own.

Tried to have it both ways.

Ended up with nothing.

I dug up a little dirt on Phillip. Found some lightly plagiarized texts from his college newspaper days. I told him I'd use them if he didn't back off Uncle Cal. Word got out that he dropped his investigation into Uncle Cal. Made him seem like a puppet. All his sources dried up. He was back to being a basement blogger. Until Belina.

You're gonna wreck his life all over again.

"I didn't use it," I say, referencing the plagiarized articles that were more accident than ethical breech. "It kept you both from destroying the other. It was my only move."

His shoulders relax a little, and he nods. He hasn't forgiven me, but he's not trying to make a beeline for his car. I wore him down, which is good. But he doesn't seem closer to working with me.

"Things are different now," I begin. "Jack has never liked how Uncle Cal does things. I promised him I was done crossing those lines."

"Great," he says. "But here you are, bleeding in the middle of Swan Point. Getting yourself involved in a murder investigation? You don't see where this will lead?"

"Belina was my friend," I say. "So is Alec. I know he didn't do it."

"How do you *know*?"

"Belina left me her day planner." I pause to enjoy how his expression changes, the hunger for the story surfacing. "It's eighteen months of legally obtained data about her time working for the Mathers."

"And the day she was murdered?"

I pat my messenger bag. "She used a code, but the meeting in Swan Point is noted. Alec wasn't there, based on her own hand."

I pause to let his mind imagine that headline. How he'd pitch it to a national producer.

"She wrote about who she was meeting?" he asks, measuring each word.

"She did," I say, recalling my whiteboard and the three letters, *spy*. "I believe she was working for someone else. The angle isn't 'hot nanny.' She brought some business idea to Alec. There was someone else involved. Maybe someone she was working for, pulling the strings?"

"Who?"

"I don't know yet. But Belina was meeting with people to discuss Alec as soon as she took the job."

"Alec seems like . . ." He pauses, and I see where he's going.

"A privileged dipshit?" I offer.

He laughs. "Look, he's your friend. So was Belina. There's a lot of bias there, Devon. Maybe he's not so innocent? Maybe she's not either."

"It's not him," I say. "And I don't care what she did. She didn't deserve to die. And not alone, cut up—" My throat cuts off the air. Tears burn. I swear and dab at my eyes. "I'm so mad."

"Okay," he says softly. "I understand." He gives me a minute before continuing. "Let's talk about this planner. Did you take it directly to the police?"

"I'll tell Detective Ramos all this tonight."

He stares up at the trees again, but this time, his gaze darts back and forth as if he's calculating how he can legally break this news before I take it to the detective.

"I saw her the afternoon she died," I say, offering a solution. "I can give you that account firsthand right now."

How could you do this to him again?

"That could help me," he says, running his fingers along his short beard, lightly scraping at his chin. "What's it going to cost me?"

"The slut-shaming narrative needs to be changed. It's untrue and distracting."

He nods, waiting for the rest.

"You have to share everything you've got as soon as you get it. I'm going to rebuild this case from the ground up."

He raises an eyebrow. "Quid pro quo, Clarice?"

I laugh lightly, but he's serious. "Two-way street. You'll be breaking more news than Rachel Maddow in the first hundred days of a Republican presidency." Ester starts to shift, and I bounce a little. "We're better together."

He agrees. I can see it, but he's not convinced. "I'm not a partner person anymore."

"Listen, I'm sorry for what happened, for what I did. But I need you, and you need me."

"Do I?"

"Phillip," I begin, switching to a tactic I hoped I wouldn't need. "Your articles have decreased in shares, likes, and comments every day for the past two weeks. Even your big scoop that Alec was going to be arrested was only Tweeted by Huffington Post. They didn't even do a write-up. You need my information to stay relevant. I need your brain and sources."

He's shaking his head, but he knows it's true. I see him running through the scenarios, weighing how we once worked together with how little he trusts me now.

"You're sure with all this baby stuff"—he pauses to nod down at Ester—"you've got the . . . time?"

He can see how worthless you are.

You're embarrassing yourself.

"I've got time, Phillip," I say. "But does it really matter? You need this story."

"Yeah, Devon, it does matter."

"I'm good," I say softly.

Right back to the lies.

"This is not a yes." He clears his throat, wiggling his Harvard ring on his right ring finger. "I want the day-of murder details right now."

"You got it," I say. "You can call your *Dateline* producer as soon as we're done. I'll walk you through everything."

"And the planner?"

"A copy is in my bag," I say, sure that handing it over is the right move. Or my only move, as if there's much of a difference. "Take it with you. But don't post anything without talking to me first."

"My condition," he says, "is you don't make deals with Cal or anyone behind my back."

"I'm done with all that," I say. "We can solve Belina's murder the right way."

He frowns sharply, taking another handkerchief out of his pocket. "Let's try it for a week," he says softly, almost to himself. He dabs at my hairline again. "Please don't make me regret this."

"You won't," I say, relief easing the constriction in my chest.

I tell him about my interaction with Belina on her last day in detail, how she was distracted and clingy with Emmett.

He takes notes and records my testimony. He asks several questions, particularly about Belina's state of mind. He's working on something.

"When can I break this?" he asks.

"Tonight," I say. "After I share the planner with Detective Ramos."

The delay should cover me for any obstruction of justice threats.

"We need to figure out who those mystery meetings were with," he says slowly. "I called Belina's mother right after it happened. She sounded drunk at nine a.m. and was rambling. She said her daughter was trying to catch a big fish."

"What does that mean?"

"Maybe an affair? I couldn't get a lot out of her."

"I'll talk to her," I say.

He nods, but I see his mind is somewhere else. "Can you get some rest before your happy hour tonight?"

He says it softly, a tone typical in 90 percent of my interactions since having Ester. A tone I resent 100 percent of the time.

"I will," I say. "Break the story tonight at five forty-five on the dot."

"Okay," he says. "Let me know how it goes with Detective Ramos. He's yet to take my call."

"You got it," I say, but it's Uncle Cal who is the real first test between us.

Chapter 11

It's the witching hour. Two words that strike fear into the heart of every new parent. I read extensively about the phenomenon but am unprepared for Ester's jag of crying in the late afternoon when my nerves are already spent.

After two hours of failing to soothe Ester, I am a possessed form, thighs burning, tears in both our eyes as I obsessively bounce on the workout ball to exorcise these wails from my child.

You were never meant to be a mother.

If she had a different mother, she'd never cry at all.

Another half hour passes, and she's quiet, sleeping deeply in my arms. I try to think of my meeting at the cemetery with Phillip, his prescient warning that I get some rest, because right now, I'm too wrung out for the happy hour.

There is a soft knock at the front door, and my whole body clenches in fear of more cries. But Ester remains sleeping. I debate ignoring it, no visitor or Amazon Prime package worth her waking.

I roll off the ball to a standing position but continue bouncing movements up and down on weak legs. I open the front door, staring through the half-fogged-over glass. There's a smiling older woman at my front door. She takes a sip of her to-go coffee cup from Chip and has three days' worth of the *Providence Journal* under her arm.

"I'm ya sitter, Gilly," she says. "Got ya papers."

Gillian O'Bryan is a central casting grandmother. I read her resume, called three references, but it's her smart eyes that ease some of my worry about leaving Ester.

"Jack sent me over early," she says in a whisper. "Get ya a nap and shower." She pulls the glass door open and shoos me into the house. "Here go ya papers." She pauses to drop them onto the entryway table. "Now, let me hold the little love."

I can't move.

Ester has been with only Jack or me since we left the NICU. She usually sleeps from five p.m. to eight p.m.—the length of the party—so I'm not completely terrified about leaving her. My panic is more subdued, like realizing you've run a red light but survived.

The smart-eyed woman is glancing around my living room, which looks like a garage sale, or tag sale, as they say in New England. To prepare for her arrival, I set up from most effective to least: the rocking bassinet, mamaRoo, cheap bouncer seat, play mat, and tummy time pillow. Any of these could be solutions when Ester begins crying.

She lifts her out of my tired arms, and the relief is sharp, causing me to grab the edge of the couch for support.

She's safer with a stranger than you.

"The bottles are in the fridge," I say in my chipper voice. "You don't need to heat them up."

She smiles at me in a way that says, *You're fucking crazy, but let's continue pretending you're not.*

"Your references had such nice things to say," I try to say casually, though it sounds like a question.

"I've raised five of my own. Help with nine grandchildren." She pats Ester's back with a placating smile. "Why don't ya go upstairs? Have yourself a nice nap and long shower."

I take the stairs two at a time.

You don't even know her, you shitty mother.

The words roll through my mind as I drop onto the bed. I set my phone alarm for one hour, and even those terrible but true words don't keep me awake. They are my lullaby.

Shitty mother.

Shitty mother.

Shitty mother . . . mother . . . mother . . . mother.

I awake to my chirping phone alarm. The heaviness of sleep is rich, and I savor it. Burying my cheek into the pillow, I stretch and wallow in the mental evenness from rest.

Gilly's voice carries from downstairs. Quietly opening the door, I listen.

"She's fine, Jack," she says softly.

I hope he's asking about Ester, but I doubt it.

"She's exhausted all right. I checked on her. She's sleepin'."

He's tired of caring for you.

He's sent someone else to do it because you're not worth his time.

I swallow thickly, the sleep giving me the strength not to cry. I am balanced or at least not wholly unstable. I resist checking on Ester. Instead, I pump and then head for the shower.

The hot water quickly steams our small master bathroom. I hesitate because it's going to hurt.

Wrapping my arms over my bare breasts, I step into the shower back first. A little spray still scalds the three blisters I have on my left nipple from pumping. No matter how much lanolin ointment I apply, they keep getting worse.

I shampoo my hair three times. I'm dizzy with the freedom that if Ester cries, I don't have to dart out, dripping, cold, and frustrated. I shave the forest that's grown on my legs, reminding myself that tonight is important. I used to live for important.

Minutes later, I stare at my red face in the steamed mirror. It's the best shower I've ever had. I'm a new life form, scrubbed and defurred. My face shines from the fancy exfoliant I haven't used since learning I was pregnant. I'd read chemicals we use from hair dye and face wash could somehow reach the baby growing inside me.

Taking my time, I blow-dry my hair so my curls are defined and controlled. My feet are warm against the cool wooden floors in the bedroom. I retie my robe and sit at my vanity. There's a glass of chilled white wine waiting. Gilly is a little too good.

I'll have another drink at Uncle Cal's, so I'm going to pump and dump when I get home, even though research says that's unnecessary. Because I worry that next year the research will say something else.

Sipping the wine, I put on my makeup and run through my questions for the detective.

I select a red skirt and cream silk blouse. I pull on high-heeled black leather boots that haven't been worn since last winter.

My heels echo against the stairs as I descend a woman reborn. Gillian has Ester in the mamaRoo and MSNBC on at a low volume.

"Look at ya," she says and puts the TV on mute.

"Thank you for the wine," I say. "Sorry I ran off. I'm not myself."

"Dontcha worry," she says.

She's still smiling at me when I recall where she works, Phillip's warnings still fresh in my head. "You've been one of Uncle Cal's assistants for . . . ?"

"First job and only job," she says. "We joke we'll both be carried out feet first, ya know."

I manage a laugh.

"Jack's on his way home." She glances at her watch. "Should be here now if traffic's not too bad."

It feels like she is pushing me to leave. "I'll grab my purse so I'm ready."

Upstairs, I stand in my office but hesitate. But if I don't do this, I'll think of nothing else. I grab my computer and all the documents, along with Belina's planner. I shove them in my wall safe and reset the code. Jack texts that he's outside, but I've still got to walk Gillian through the house.

I hurry back with my small red purse and throw on my coat. "Can I show you a few things?"

"Sure," she says and mutes the TV again. She clears her throat as if to tamp her impatience.

I show her around the house: the bottles, the thermostat setting (Post-it), contact information (second Post-it), the stack of diapers, creams, extra clothes, and how various bouncers work best for Ester.

Jack arrives through the back door at some point and is standing in his jacket with the bottle of wine we're taking. He watches me walk her through everything again (but for a slightly different scenario—tummy troubles versus hunger versus separation anxiety).

Their gazes go from me to each other and back. I feel them wishing I'd stop talking.

Jack regrets bringing you before you're even there.

I leave them in the living room for the kitchen, where I do something I haven't done since my DC job: pop a Xanax.

You'll damage Ester with this drug, you weak failure.

I'm pumping and dumping already, I counter. The truth is my new mother's skin won't work for this happy hour; it's too raw, too exposed, and too vulnerable. I drink some water and take a few deep breaths.

Enough.

The antianxiety effect kicks in quickly, as it always has for me. The nap, the shower, my handsome husband waiting to take me away, it all bubbles over my worry.

I open the purse I haven't used in months and tap my fingers against an old lipstick, powder, and blush, conjuring the woman who once used them.

Striding into the hall, I find Jack and Gilly waiting for me. He seems relieved, as if he recognizes my effort.

"We'll be home later," I say as casually as I can and take his arm. "Text Jack if anything comes up."

That last sentence costs me something. I read on one mom blog to set limits on how often you text a babysitter. Every hour, maybe. They'll text if something happens. No news is good news, etc. But to give Jack all the power is essential. I would stare at the screen all night, constantly checking to see if I missed the vibration of a text.

We go too fast down Hope Street in Jack's silver two-door Audi, but we're running late because of me, so I'm not about to say anything. Uncle Cal's home is located on a very nice block off Blackstone Boulevard.

After Jack's mother died when he was a boy, he spent a lot of time over at Uncle Cal's house. Jack's father was busy working to keep his four boys in Catholic school and refused any financial help. But he encouraged his sons to spend time with their successful and important uncle Cal. Jack, in particular, would have dinner there or catch a Brown University football game with him at the stadium down the street.

We spent time with Uncle Cal before moving to Providence. We visited him in Boston for a Sox game, where we had box seats. He'd visit DC often, taking us both to dinner, giving me the third degree, which I enjoyed. Despite seeing their close relationship, it still surprised the hell out of me when he gave us a house in Providence as our wedding gift.

It wasn't keys to a place unseen, only a card with two qualifiers. Under 400K and on the east side of Hope Street.

We actually bought on the west side of Hope (by two blocks), but he was so happy about Jack's job as chief of staff for the mayor he didn't mention it. He even bumped up our budget because I'd fallen in love with the formal dining room of our home. Uncle Cal said: "It's what family does." I'd never realized that was possible for me.

Jack squeezes my hand before shifting into a higher gear. "I'm glad we're doing this."

"We needed time to ourselves," I say, even though we'll barely see each other tonight.

He'll be too embarrassed to stay close.

We park along the hill that's a block from Uncle Cal's house. Both sides of the street are already full of guests' cars. As he's gotten older, Uncle Cal's Friday happy hours aren't as frequent anymore, making them all the more popular and exclusive. When Jack was a kid, he served drinks and snipped cigars for the guests. That's a pretty old-school political machine for formative years, but Jack's actually a progressive guy. What it did do is create a connection between him and Uncle Cal that can forgive almost anything.

But he'll never forgive you.

Jack turns off the car but doesn't reach for the door, so we sit in silence. I know what he wants to ask, so I save time. "I'm not working with Uncle Cal," I say. "He only did me a favor, adding Cynthia to the guest list."

"Cynthia?"

"I want her to get that Economic Development grant," I say.

"Is that it?" he asks, probably hearing something in my voice that says it's not.

"Cynthia got Phillip to meet with me to talk about Belina." I shift in the seat. "We're going to help each other again."

"All right." Jack stretches back, pulling me close. "It's good that you want to work," he says, brushing some hair behind my ear. "But not the kind of work that will make things . . . difficult."

I almost smile at that last word. Difficult. God, he's cute. "You mean me going to federal prison? Obstruction of justice?"

He inhales sharply but covers it with a grin. "That would be quite *difficult*."

"Quite," I say. This moment is close to how we were before Ester. The teasing mixed with the truth.

It's all pretend now.

Just like your marriage.

Break it, then fake it.

Before I can reach for the door, he grabs my wrist, gently shifting me back to face him. "High road, right? Not too much stress? You promised."

I kiss him softly, and he smiles against my lips as I pull back but not too far. "I still promise."

You still lie.

Our car doors slam in the cold air, and for a few seconds, I'm as whole as I've been in months. But then I notice a few leaves on the trees, orange and red stragglers, floating onto the smooth black pavement. Today is Ester's real due date.

I can almost feel the blood on my legs at the thought of those bright-yellow leaves taunting me through the ambulance's back glass. Everything was wrong.

It'll never be right again.

"Coming?" Jack says with a concerned smile.

"I was noticing the houses. I forgot how pretty they are," I say in a rush, grabbing his hand too tight.

I try to make the lie true and focus on each large and expensive home we pass along Hazard Road. Oversize Capes and brick Tudors and even a stucco. There are split-rail fences and charming stone walls, each lawn professionally cultivated. Our house is far nicer than the one I grew up in, but I've adjusted to feeling like it's ours. A home on Hazard Road, where a million is the price of entry, is a place I'll never belong.

Uncle Cal's house is dark stone with a turret on the front. It was built in the 1940s and has lots of charm amid the size. It's a favorite with neighborhood children, especially the girls who like to think there's a princess living there. Not quite. Uncle Cal's house is the largest, which is impressive since no one really knows what he does.

But he's got an office in city hall, four doors down from the mayor's. He's had the same title for twenty years, public works commissioner.

His crown jewel, the Economic Development Council, is all he focuses on now. It helped Alec, and hopefully it'll help Cynthia too.

You don't have what it takes to help her.

Jack's hand in mine, I focus on the lamplights shining bright. My boot heels click against the pavement, and the tendons in my feet are already tight from not being in ballet flats or UGGs. I pull my wrap tight around my shoulders and wish I'd remembered hose for this red skirt. It's not short, but there's a breeze.

Stupid hick doesn't even know to wear hose in December.

"You're sure you're okay?" Jack asks as we near the house. I was squeezing his hand.

"Nervous," I say, which is mostly true. There are a lot of people in there who know my history with Uncle Cal.

From one failure to the next.

I check my phone to see I've got one hour until I need to have Detective Ramos right where I want him.

You'll never pull it off.

"Keep your head up," Jack says, which I don't like. I do not need to be handled.

At the moment, anyway.

"You look frightened." Jack squeezes my hand, which is still in his as he glances through the lead-paned window. "They're more scared of you."

He's grinning like it's a joke. Like there's not a room full of people who know me. Know that I helped get Uncle Cal's political enemies thrown in jail. That I used Phillip Hale to get them there. And they must assume that, with the snap of Uncle Cal's fingers, Phillip and I stopped investigating. We both stepped back. Until now.

Chapter 12

Jack opens the front door to Uncle Cal's house, and the voices roll over us. The person manning the entry quickly shuts the door, and we stand by a small fireplace as he gets a tag for our checked coats. I use the delay to put on my confident mask as if I'm not an exhausted mother who has barely had a nonmom conversation in two months. I'm someone who belongs in this room. I'm someone who can help solve a murder.

No one wants you here.

The entryway leads to a large double parlor with wood-paneled walls and paintings of dogs and ships. It's exactly what I'd pictured even before I stepped inside. A huge fireplace blazes on the wall opposite the windows. People are already flushed from the heat and martinis. Two men are out on the back patio, the distinct orange glow of lit cigars blinking in the darkness.

You're not in that club anymore.

I set a small smile on my face and glance around for Uncle Cal. Not that we need to rush over. He'll find us when the time is right. Or find Jack anyway. He's been distant from me since learning about Phillip's move against him and my threats to keep them from going after each other.

I'd never thought besting Uncle Cal would be so simple, but it was because Phillip, again, had done great work. The Economic Development Council did have some ties to money laundering. Not any connected to Uncle Cal. But close enough that it would have looked bad if Phillip had run the story. Likely would have gotten the whole Council shut down. Ruined Uncle Cal's reputation and the good they were doing for small businesses in a state that doesn't make that easy. Businesses like Cynthia's.

In the end, I came over to Uncle Cal's house; made chicken fried steak with him, like my grandma taught me; and told him the truth: We were done working together, and he was leaving Phillip alone. Phillip would, in turn, leave Uncle Cal and the Council alone. He agreed, and neither of us ate the chicken fried steak.

He used you.

You're too stupid to see it.

Then my pregnancy. Specifically, Ester and I are taking all Jack's time when he should be focusing on his career and building political connections. Uncle Cal never married, never had children—that I knew of, anyway. He made only one comment that our starting a family was sooner than he'd expected.

We obviously bought a large home, one he paid for, and had mentioned kids before. Jack loves having three older brothers and even hinted that maybe five would be ideal. I am open to it. I have no number, only an idealized vision of bread baking and math homework and stinky hockey equipment and piano scales and a dog chomping on a book report. A house as full as our lives. With a crying infant and a voice back in my head, I've never felt further from that home.

Keep dreaming, girlie.

There's nothing inside you that deserves that life.

Enough.

I see Detective Ramos is in the corner by himself, trying not to look uncomfortable. The track lighting reflects off his shaved head. He shifts in his suit, buy-one-get-one-free bad, loose despite his tall, muscular frame. His tie is nice, matching his light-brown eyes. Dollars to doughnuts his wife bought that tie.

But I can't start with him. People are watching me, and making a beeline would show my hand. Plus, there is a timing issue. My punch line is Phillip breaking the story about a friend meeting Belina on the afternoon she died. Something the police didn't catch.

He'll never work with you.

What value could you possibly bring?

My tongue is thick in my mouth, and I need to warm up before seeing the detective.

I find Cynthia in the corner, chatting up a pasty white guy who's on the Economic Development Council with Uncle Cal.

I hover so I can hear her at work. The man is on the Council because he's a big Democratic donor, not because he's smart or particularly good at business.

"Tell me about my ROI," he says with some spittle on the corner of his mouth.

ROI is a phrase stupid people think makes them sound smart. One of a hundred reasons I was glad to leave DC. It's full of people smugly dropping acronyms into happy-hour conversations.

Cynthia makes surprised sounds like this old white dude is really imparting some pearls of wisdom on this young black woman.

"If ya open more locations," he says as if he's Sam Walton thinking up the superstore, "the money comes in faster."

Cynthia blinks because that's not true. But she doesn't give him a *Well, when I was getting my MBA at Harvard.* Instead she nods and says, "Oh yeah?" with a bit of Rhode Island on it.

She's not the only one. The Rhody accent floats through the room, *W*s becoming *R*s and *R*s drowned by *A*s. It makes me feel like I'm in a Mark Wahlberg movie or an episode of *Family Guy*. But it also reminds me (and anyone with the accent) that I'm not one of them.

"I'll give that some thought," she says to something I missed. The man glances down her white blouse. She's wearing gray trousers: tailored but not tight. She's beautiful but doesn't have to advertise it.

"I'm looking forward to reading your comments on my application to the Council," Cynthia says after his gaze makes it back to her eyes. "There's a lot I can learn from you."

His face lights up, the pudgy bulldog thinking he sees a bone.

I feel some guilt. He seems genuine, smiling at Cynthia as if he's helped her. This guy is probably a loving husband and kind grandfather. I am judging him because he glanced at her boobs and wanted to feel smart.

He pats her arm, and she does a good job not recoiling, which is what I do anytime an older man suddenly touches me. Some habits will die only with you.

"You're very articulate," he says. "Be sure to smile, and you'll do fine."

Poof. The guilt is gone.

"Your smile coach is here!" I flash a wide one for both of them.

"Mrs. Burges," the man says with his eyes bulging. "You had the baby? Congratulations."

"Thanks," I say.

He's blinking rapidly. "Are you here . . . for work?" He shoots Cynthia a look. "Are you working on Council matters?"

"What matters?" I ask, torturing him a little. Letting him worry I'm going rogue, digging into his businesses and boys' clubs for ties back to the Council.

"I . . . don't know . . ." He takes a deep breath. "It's all beyond reproach."

"Good for you," I say with a nod. "I'm sure fantastic businesses like Chip Bakery will thrive with your support."

His face falls. "Oh. Yes, yes, of course."

Cynthia shakes his hand, and he nearly runs away from us both.

"That went well," I say, watching him whisper to another board member.

"Pretty sure that was coercion." Cynthia sets her untouched glass of white wine down on a passing waiter's tray. "But probably got his vote, so thanks?"

"Sure, I'll take it," I say. "How many members of the Council do you have left?"

"Most of them." She glances in the direction of the other two applicants working the room, same as her. I see doubt in her gaze and then resolve.

"Your business plan is by far the best," I say.

"You can't control everything," she says. "You're as bad as Cal."

I see her confidence slip. "What's going on?"

"I got a really high bid yesterday from a coffee distributor," she says. "It's all state monopoly nonsense. This grant will save me so much time. The 'She's okay' stamp of approval."

I touch her arm because it's not fucking fair. But who wants to have that conversation for the hundredth time. Not when she lives it. Not when she's doing everything she can to overcome it. Double standard is the only standard Cynthia has known.

And you're only making things worse.

She will never forgive you this time.

"How'd it go with Phil?" she asks.

"Tacit gentleman's agreement," I say. "He's a forgiving person, so that's always going to hold him back."

"What's your plan while you're here?" she asks.

"Avoiding most of these people," I say.

"Who are you really here to see?"

It is good I'm not married to Cynthia because she never lets anything slide. That's why Jack and I work. He's smart but stays in his lane and respects mine.

"I had Uncle Cal invite the detective working Belina's murder." I nod toward him lurking behind his captain.

I can see she is holding back some real talk. It's possible she wants to scare me off this to focus on Ester or maybe myself. But she isn't going to discourage me either because I am helping Phillip. "The detective doesn't look chatty," she says.

"I'll take him a martini and see what happens."

"Twenty says he doesn't drink."

"Not willingly, that's for sure. But I'm pretty good at persuading babies to take their bottles."

She smiles, but it's fake. "Good luck." She glances at her Rolex. "Phil said he's breaking something around—"

"In twenty minutes."

She's surprised, and then an eyebrow arches. "Anyway, after it, he's got a call with a producer from *Dateline*."

She is warning me. "I'm not going to screw him over."

"Okay," she says. "I'll see you on the next lap."

I move to Jack, squeezing his arm as he nods me toward the bar and continues his chat with a newly elected state representative. The rep is one of several dozen faces I recognize from these happy hours, or fund-raisers for the mayor, or the evening news. Politics always feels small, even in DC, but in Rhode Island, it's a petri dish.

Behind the large bar at the center of the room, Uncle Cal sees me coming. He nods away a donor from South County and steps around his station to give me a quick kiss on the cheek.

"You look lovely," he says, smelling of his spicy cologne, cinnamon gum, and gin. "How's everything at home?"

"Ester is wonderful. I'll bring her by soon."

He doesn't want to see her.

Witness what a terrible mother you are.

Be reminded that his nephew married trash.

"Great, great," he says. "What's Jack got you working on?"

"Having a good time. Thank you for inviting Detective Ramos. And Cynthia."

"I was happy to do it," he says. "I have a favor of my own, if you're up for it."

I like that Uncle Cal doesn't fiddle fuck around. "Anything for family."

"It's related to Detective Ramos," he says, pouring Belvedere Citrus vodka, my favorite, into the shaker. He's the only one who makes martinis at his party. "I assume his invitation relates to the murdered woman?"

"Yes," I say. "Belina was a friend."

"I didn't realize." He pauses but only for a beat. "I'm sorry."

"Alec is a friend too, as you know." I pushed for Alec to get an Economic Development Council grant, the first given. It was right before we moved to Providence, and it meant I owed Uncle Cal a big favor, which he more than collected.

"Alec is my problem," he says. "One you gave me."

"We're hardly even," I say. Uncle Cal's "favor" for Alec's nomination started with my investigating some information he'd gotten about the Rhode Island Speaker of the House, who had been tired of Uncle Cal's strong-arm in the state. Phillip joined me, and that was our first case together, leading to the Speaker being thrown in jail. Phillip and I kept working the information from Uncle Cal, exposing corrupt members of the statehouse. Until Phillip got his own information on Uncle Cal. And they nearly blew each other up.

"I can't have that clod sullying the Council's name," he says. "You need to get a handle on the situation and fix it."

"I don't think he's guilty," I say but can tell that's not the issue. "What do you want me to do?"

"I need to know about his business," he says. "Alec blew through that grant like a frat boy on a bender. He was taking money from questionable places. We didn't renew and cut all ties. But we're still connected."

I rub a tense knot in my neck, feeling unsurprised but deeply disappointed in Alec. Loyalty has always been a blind spot for me. Something I craved in every relationship, often giving it too freely because I felt it so rarely as a child. But loyalty is not free, and often, you pay for the sins twice.

"I'm sorry about Alec," I say. "I shouldn't have recommended him for the grant. But I'm out of the excavation business."

You don't want to be.

You won't be satisfied until you've ruined everything.

"I have the file already. You only need to fill in what's missing." He takes his time spraying my glass with vermouth and shaking the vodka, the ice cracking loudly.

I showed my hand by asking the detective to come, so he thinks I owe him. Maybe I do. "I've got a good start," I say. "I don't need to get into his financial history." Even as I say it, I hear the lie.

"Is Phillip helping you?" he asks in the tone that says he knows the answer.

"Yes."

"Then you're hardly retired. If you can work with him again, you can certainly do me this small favor." He pauses and stops the shaker to stare me down, which after all these years and many stares still rattles me. "Everything you'd be reviewing is legally obtained."

"Is it?" I don't hide the flash of temper. "We got close to serious trouble last time."

"From what I know of this case, you're headed in the same direction. That's a certainty."

"What does that mean?"

He gives me a pitying look and turns on his Italian loafers toward a fresh rack of glasses. Done with our conversation for now, he's certain to be redrawing battle plans. I decide to table a talk about Cynthia's application.

He knows you can't do this right.

He'll use you again like you deserve.

He pours a second martini into a glass.

"The detective isn't a pushover," Uncle Cal says. "I'd play it straight."

"Thank you," I say, meaning it, as he hands me the drinks.

He looks over my shoulder at the next person in line. The detective is watching us. He's close to the wall, awkward beside an antique chair not meant for sitting. His bosses are nearby, the police chief and captain. That's normal this time of year for them, working the room for future bond ballots and budget line items now that the election is over. But I've never seen a detective at one of these parties.

"Detective Ramos," I say brightly. "Thanks for joining on such short notice."

"I do what I'm told," he says with a tight nod.

Those five words sum up Detective Ramos's ethos as far as I can tell. He's had a nearly perfect career, according to media coverage and another detective I worked with during the Uncle Cal days, whom I spoke to on the phone earlier this week. Detective Ramos does his work, keeps his head down and his name mostly out of the paper. He closes cases at a high rate but isn't assigned many outside the standard low-level drug offenses and breaking and entering. No high-profile political stings. No homicide investigations except open-and-shut cases with suspects arrested at the scene.

He's been on the force for twenty years, the last fifteen as a detective. This case is a career anomaly with one exception. He was almost fired his first year on the job. He made some connected guys mad about the crooked (but effective) ex-mayor's downtown land deal, tying a murder back to them. He was yanked off the case, thrown on parking ticket duty, and eventually returned to the detective desk.

"You need a drink. Otherwise, it looks like you're working," I say.

He frowns at me but takes the martini. "Not my kind of party."

"Sorry for bringing you here."

He draws back an iota. "You?"

I let him sit with that a moment. To most people here, I'm Jack's wife, Uncle Cal's niece by marriage. But he needs to understand I am much more. "How's the murder investigation going?"

He stares at me in a way that says he's not giving in that easy.

You can't do this.

Go hide behind your husband.

"Belina Cabrala?" I pause. No response. "She's your first murder case that's not open and shut since you caught your first body. So, yeah, that one."

He scowls and clears his throat. "What do you want to know?"

"As much as you can tell me."

His lips thin as he glances around. He tries to readjust the martini in his hand, but he's not holding it right. He pinches the bottom of the delicate stem, and a few drops slosh. "It's an ongoing investigation. I can't tell you anything," he says with some annoyance. "*Good Day RI* had a special with some blogger."

"Phillip Hale," I supply.

"Yeah. Plenty to keep housewives of the East Side busy."

"I'm not rubbernecking, Detective. She was my friend."

He sticks out his wide jaw. "First I've heard of it."

"We hung out while she watched Emmett. Alec is a friend of mine going back to freshman year at Georgetown. This case is personal."

"Continue."

"I know you suspect Alec. The DNA fibers at the crime scene are a good lead. Misha says the blood is from an accident. Not airtight, but a jury might want to agree. More than that, he doesn't fit. It's clearly not a crime of passion."

"Clearly?" he mocks.

"She wasn't sleeping with him," I continue.

"That so?" he says. "You girls like to giggle and gab about him?"

I smile at him, the really shiny one as if he were the smartest goddamn guy in the whole world. I lean over and whisper, "What would your wife say if you spoke to her like that?"

He clears his throat, the smirk disappearing. "She'd tell me to go fuck myself."

"Then we're in agreement."

He glances at his martini, trying to keep the drink from sloshing again. "Why do you think they weren't sleeping together?"

"I have her day planner," I say and steel myself for a bluff. "It doesn't read like an affair took place."

"Excuse me." He steps close to me. "*You* have her planner? Alec mentioned she kept notes, but we hadn't found it."

"I saw her in the afternoon on the day she died," I say. "She left it behind for me. I don't think it was an accident. She knew she was in danger. She kept staring toward the river."

His lower jaw works a few circles. "You withheld this evidence, Ms. Burges?"

"More of an interlude," I say. "Don't you want to know who she met with that night?"

"She names them?" he says, too loud. Several people turn in our direction.

"She was meeting two people at Swan Point. There's an *A* with a circle—not how she indicates Alec. The second person is labeled CF, who she'd been meeting with since she started nannying."

At the second initials, I see recognition in his eyes, but he shifts, and his martini sloshes again, and he curses. He wants to smash the glass. I can see the rage. I know it.

You're screwing this up.

Everyone is whispering about you.

They can't believe you're here failing again.

I slip the martini from his fingers, raising an eyebrow toward a waiter who immediately hurries over, taking it from me. Detective Ramos is seeing me now, for the first time.

"She didn't meet Alec for a graveyard tryst," I say. "I hate to blow up your theory, but it's true."

"Your husband's boss would disagree."

"The mayor has a budget to sign next week that did include a line item for increasing the police department's discretionary budget. A high-profile homicide investigation that's wide open suddenly closing would help. I get it. But it'll be a short-term win because Alec's not guilty."

He sees through you.

"Why now?" he says. "Why withhold evidence until today? That's a jailable offense in Rhode Island."

I like the threat, even if there's no way in hell a DA would bring that weak sauce in front of a judge. But the detective is listening.

"I honestly didn't remember she'd left it," I say. "I also almost died a few hours later. I went into labor, detached placenta."

"I'm sorry," he says, demeanor softening. "My wife is twenty-eight weeks."

I half smile at him, the connection of children creating an understanding, realizing our passports have stamps from the same terrifying and wonderful country. "I didn't remember Belina left the journal until recently. I analyzed the data. I have a theory."

"I'm not interested in your theories, Ms. Burges," Detective Ramos says. "I need you to come in right away to give a statement and hand over this crucial evidence."

"I'm a lawyer who puts complicated financial cases together. I used to try violent crimes in DC. I can help you."

He doesn't seem impressed by the bravado. "I'm going to trust the evidence. Not a Real Housewife of the East Side."

I smile at that. "Your wife makes you watch Bravo."

"Nightly," he says flatly. "Tomorrow morning, eight a.m."

I hear the urgency. "How close are you to an arrest?"

"Very."

You're finished before you even begin.

My chest tightens. "Not until you see my analysis and the journal."

"Be there," he says, not hiding his annoyance. "Or I'll send a cruiser."

I hear his phone buzzing and step close. "Phillip Hale, the blogger you mentioned, he's breaking that Belina met with a friend the afternoon of her murder. A friend who hasn't been interviewed by the police. Yet. Reasonable doubt is like voting, Detective. Do it early, and do it often."

He cracks his neck to the left, grinding his jaw. "You don't want to do this. I don't care who your husband works for. I don't care who your uncle is."

"If you arrest Alec, it will blow up in your face," I say. "You'll be dreaming of parking ticket duty when it's all through."

His mouth drops open before tightening. I turn on my heel and smile as if it's been pleasant conversation number three. I pulled a cheap shot at the end, but he surprised me with how little time I had to help Alec.

He'll be arrested within the week. I see Emmett crying in his mother's stiff arms as another person he loves is taken away.

I stand in the hallway at the back of the house. It's dark, and no one is around. I put my arms around my shoulders, breathing deeply, picturing myself calm and collected.

The detective sees what a worthless piece of trash you are.

He'll never listen to someone like you.

The dark pull starts to swirl, a drain in the bathtub, offering to take me with it. It could all be over so easily. I close my eyes, picturing the hollowed-out chat mine down the road from where I grew up. The dark water that could swallow all my pain a hundred feet below. I chose to keep going.

"Too much too soon?"

Uncle Cal's voice snaps me out of rural Kansas and back to the life I've built in Providence. "No," I say. "I'm tired. Ester doesn't sleep."

"Makes two of us," he says. "Or three, I guess."

He sounds a bit awkward, which is unusual. I want to ask him if it's a waste of time for me to try to help Belina. To hear that I'm strong enough and smart enough. But I'm not a twelve-year-old girl crying over the edge of an abandoned mine. I made it out because I am strong, and I am smart. "I promised Jack I'd give it up."

"I know," Uncle Cal says. "You sent over your files and boxes."

After I stopped Phillip from writing about Uncle Cal and kept Uncle Cal from going after Phillip, I packed everything that led me to that place, pitting family against my partner. Not to mention most of what I'd dug up was through illegal sources and methods. "All of it belongs here, with you."

"You could have destroyed them," he says. "Says something."

"It says I'm done." I cross my arms, posturing.

"Jack will never know. He has you and me to work behind the scenes. Do what needs to be done. You're good at this work."

"At moral indiscretion?" I say.

"An understanding that justice is not a truth universal. It's a side you choose to uphold and pursue at all costs."

I don't disagree with anything Uncle Cal says, and that's the problem. I believe in my justice and my sense of right and wrong. But I can't trust myself any more than I can trust him. "I'm choosing Jack."

No better lies than the ones we tell ourselves.

"But what about your dead friend? Is one little promise to Jack worth injustice?" He steps closer. "I thought of a compromise."

"How unusual."

"I'll consider Cynthia's application fully. Get the right press involved. All aboveboard but with a touch of . . ." He waves his hand a few times in the air. "Finesse."

"That would be appreciated," I say, the relief sharp. "What's the cost?"

"A simple review of Alec's application for the grant and shoddy follow-up reports. Mostly public information and all freely given."

"To the Council," I say. "Not me."

"He's your friend. You're the reason he got the grant."

"I don't owe you anything anymore."

"Perhaps," he says, "but you still owe me after your blackmail threat."

I did that to help Phillip. Told Uncle Cal that if he went after Phillip, then I'd leak all the dirt on the Council. Then I made Phillip swear off Uncle Cal under threat of ruining his reputation about that college plagiarism. It cost me my relationship with Phillip. And I swore to Jack I wouldn't work for Uncle Cal again. I did it to save Uncle Cal and Phillip both. Gave up work I was damn good at. These points mattered to me, though, not Uncle Cal.

"Click those shoes, Dorothy. No place like home that I gave you."

A Kansas joke. He really is desperate. In fact, this is a full-court press. Close to begging, as far as Uncle Cal is concerned. "You're that worried about your reputation?" I ask.

"Reputation?" He grimaces. "That's the wrong word. It's my legacy. My Council is cresting right when I am. Alec is a buffoon, but that also makes him dangerous. I don't trust anyone else to find out the truth."

I hate to see Uncle Cal like this, his back against the wall. I also wonder, if it's that important, perhaps it's information I need to know too. To protect Alec or possibly find ties to Belina. "I will tell Jack I'm helping you," I say. "And Phillip."

His forehead wrinkles, then a smirk. "This is the game, you know. The one you wanted to play. The rules never change."

"But I changed," I say.

"Whatever you need to tell yourself."

"The folder is already on my desk?" I guess.

"Gillian has a copy. Just in case."

Of course she does. "I'll get back to you."

He waves his arms in a mock hallelujah and turns on his heel. I return to the party to hug Cynthia goodbye, whispering I've got good news so she knows I helped her with Uncle Cal. Finally. I give Jack the signal it's time to go.

I need more information before meeting with Detective Ramos. It'll take me the night to sort through the financial data and dig more into Alec's life to be sure there aren't any connections to Belina's death.

And you know there will be.

Chapter 13

Saturday, December 10

There are three missed calls from Detective Ramos by the time I pull into the Newport Polo grounds. I text that I'll come by the station this afternoon to give my statement. I had the journal couriered to his office. He has plenty to keep him busy until I get there.

One year ago, Belina wrote in her planner that she attended this charity match with Emmett to watch Alec play while Misha was on a spa-cation. Today, I texted Alec to confirm he was going again and asked to see him. He tried to push me off until tomorrow, but that's not going to work. As Detective Ramos hinted, I am running out of time. It is now or never to get the truth about Alec's business and any connections to Belina. And I don't mind annoying Alec by crashing this party among his Newport set.

He needs to face this situation. To see everything that can be taken away if he doesn't start helping me.

It's warm for December, sunny and forty-five degrees, as if God himself donated a beautiful day for this polo match fund-raiser.

I am dressed like new money: a bright pink-and-white Lilly Pulitzer dress I snagged during its After Party Sale, a navy blazer from my DC lawyer days, and Cynthia's slightly-too-small-for-me nude Louboutin heels. The shoes are ridiculous to wear to a polo match, but here I am, standing on the balls of my feet to keep from sinking into the thick browning grass, determined not to ruin them.

Lipstick on a pig, girlie.

You look like trash no matter what you're wearing.

I'm late because it was hard to leave Ester with Jack. There was relief on Jack's face as I kissed him goodbye.

If you don't come back, it'll be the best day of his life.

I ignore my panic at the voice's direct hit and take in the Newport Polo grounds. Like most of New England, there's a lineage here going back to the Pilgrims. The ancient linden trees and fieldstone walls surround brand-new Mercedes and Audis and Land Rovers with black-and-white NPT POLO stickers on their bumpers.

I pass the cheaper seats where you can bring a blanket and cop a squat in front of the field. I loop past the vendors selling cocktails and NPT half zips. Next it's old money, a few dozen tables where people can bring in their own shrimp cocktail and famous crab avocado dip.

Once I reach the VIP tent, I head up the few stairs leading to the wooden deck. I wink at a young man checking the tickets and wave toward an empty space among the tables and chairs and heat lamps.

Everyone knows you don't belong.

He glances at my breasts, my cleavage a new tool I didn't experience before Ester. He doesn't stop me.

I march toward a corner table where three middle-aged men are dressed in bright pants with sweaters layered under blazers. There are similar facsimiles all over the room, and it's a few seconds before I spot Alec. He and two older women are the only ones with butts in chairs. He's slumped over, shotgunning champagne and forlornly watching the players and horses warming up on the field.

I was too emotional at his house five days ago. I didn't ask the right questions. Now with more information, I need to go hard at Alec.

There are no poop bags being launched at him, but it's clear there's a stench. Groups of people glance his way and whisper. Even the two older ladies across from him are basically clutching their pearls at his presence. Misha avoids him, in the corner with friends who are equally tan and blonde and thin.

I start to approach Alec but pause when someone gets there first. He's lean in a well-cut suit, his wavy hair brushed back casually. He grips Alec's shoulder with a wiry intensity, bends down, and whispers. Alec laughs a little while shaking his head, a light in his gaze as he smiles at the man.

This charmer sets down a dark drink and goes in for what appears to be another joke. Alec notices me, and his face falls. I wave and head over.

You're not good enough to pull this off.

"Hey there." I bend down and kiss his cheek, feeling Misha and her gaggle of friends watching. "How are you?"

"What are you doing here? I said I'd meet you later next week." His gaze darts around. "Oh my God, is Cal here?"

I let him squirm before answering. "No," I say finally with a smirk. "We missed you at his holiday happy hour, though."

Alec lets out a breath. "I doubt that."

"Listen." I drape the chain of my purse on the back of the folding chair next to him and sit down. "I've got some information you need to hear. Now."

The stranger, still there, leans into Alec. "I just cheered up my boy."

Alec smiles, but there is something off.

"Your *boy* is in trouble, and it's closing in fast," I say. "Give us a minute?"

The guy blinks slowly, and I recognize he's assessing. He thinks I have money. That's the point of this outfit and the expensive purse I got as a law school graduation gift from Uncle Cal.

"I'm Ricky Cardin, Alec's business partner," he says. "You are?"

A partner is news to me. Not that I knew much about his business until last night. "His college buddy."

"Good for you," Ricky says.

"She knew Belina." Alec takes a fast slurp of the dark drink.

Ricky lets out a light whistle. "So sorry," he says.

"Thank you," I say. "Can we have a minute alone?"

"Sure, sure," Ricky says, waving his hands. "What are you drinking, miss?"

"Mrs. Burges," I say. "White wine spritzer, please. Take your time."

Ricky gives me a nod and then heads toward the bar.

"Alec." I put my hands on the arm gripping his drink. "The police are coming for you. You have to help me figure out what happened."

"Jesus, Devon, not here," he snaps. He scrubs his face up to his hairline and back. "I don't know who killed her. Or how my DNA was there. She had on my jacket—"

"I know," I cut off his rising voice, not needing to hear more of the same. He's agitated and defensive. The detectives will have him twisted up and confessing in an hour, maybe less. "Why was she wearing your jacket? Did you give it to her?"

"No," he says softly. "But I never minded when she borrowed it."

"She did that a lot?"

"Sure, if she didn't bring hers. Kinda nice to give her something she needed."

I don't roll my eyes, which is no small feat. This isn't about their relationship, whatever it was, right now. I think back to the earliest entries of Belina's planner. "Who did Belina set up the meeting with? A month after she started working for you."

He pales. "How the hell did you know that?"

"Answer me, Alec."

"I really don't remember." He sniffs and sips his drink.

"You always were the worst liar," I say, ignoring his glare. "What did you talk about the day she died?" I ask, referencing her planner and the task to "tell Alec."

"Emmett had some overdue books. Um, she finished some other work for me." Alec takes a sip of his drink. "Nothing much to it."

Nothing much? When someone tells me how to interpret his or her statement, I assume the opposite. "What work?"

"She does our accounting. For the business. She did it at her last job."

"Really?" I scan through our conversations, trying to recall any hints of our connection. She certainly knew I was in her field. We even talked about some of my clients. Perhaps she didn't want me to know what she was doing. "What did she do? Payroll? Taxes?"

"Sure, and kept our numbers straight week to week."

"Did you pay her for it?" I ask. "That's a lot of extra work."

"She liked it," he says meekly.

"You were taking advantage of her," I say and wish I didn't. He turns from me, sullenly sips his drink.

This is where Belina connected to Alec's business and why Uncle Cal, predictably, isn't wrong to be concerned.

I spent my mostly sleepless night reading through information on Alec's grant, while wearing Ester, trying to keep her calm and quiet. Alec's grant from Uncle Cal's Economic Development Council funded his new commercial fishing business, which trained people recently released from prison to be commercial fishermen. It was an all-cash business, revenue based on a set number of fishing licenses Alec had been granted, twenty of them, thanks in large part to the doors opened by receiving an Economic Development grant.

Every commercial boat in Rhode Island must have a license to fish and sell what they catch. It's tightly regulated by the New England fishing board. The day's worth of fish is usually paid for in cash. Money that's collected by Alec, who then distributes it to his twenty captains. While Alec's business didn't grow past the initial twenty licenses, his profits continued to increase by thousands of dollars each month. That's a big red flag.

Pouting time is over for Alec.

You want him to be something he's not.

Spoiled rich boy you helped all along.

You're the sucker.

"I looked into your company's financials," I say.

Alec's sullen face snaps my way. "Why the hell did you do that?"

"Because you asked for my help," I say evenly. "This is what my help looks like."

"I want you to find who killed Belina," he says. "I don't need you and your tornado brain digging around my business."

I forgot that was what he'd called me in college when he needed help, asking for my tornado brain to figure out what'd be on his calculus final. At the time, I'd taken it as a compliment with a nod to Kansas roots. But maybe it was a judgment.

You're an unnatural disaster.

First smart thing he's come up with in his whole life.

"Oh my God, Devon," he says with a gasp. I know the question before he asks it. "Did Cal tell you to do this? That old bastard needs to stay away from me."

"That's not how the world works, Alec." I lean into his personal space. "Your whole business started because I vouched for you to Uncle Cal. If I'm going to help you, I will need to assess what exactly you've done."

He blows out a bratty breath. "Whatever, Devon."

I almost laugh, but I'm too annoyed. Instead I'd rather twist. "Where was the additional money coming from for your business? Not your boats. The slight increases in fish prices do not correlate with your profit increases."

"Why does it matter?"

"Everything matters."

I let him huff and puff. It's classic Alec to think I'd just trust whatever he said. To not put together that with my background, of course

I'd dig into his finances. Perhaps he just wanted me to fix everything like college. Share notes he couldn't be bothered to take. Write the paper for him, even though I wasn't in the class. Take his online tests. Help his study group. Ask my new uncle-in-law for a favor, even though Alec wasn't prepared.

Loyalty made you a joke.

You're only worth using.

"My business has nothing to do with Belina's death," Alec says in a long breath, the anger evaporating. "I have nothing to do with Belina's death. I need you to help me. Not make things worse."

"Do you have the documents she prepared for you?"

"Um, yeah. The police wanted them. There's nothing there. It's a lot of numbers."

"I'll manage," I say. "Just forward what you sent to the police."

"Fine." Alec flips his dark hair in that preppy, privileged way and reaches for his phone. After a few clicks, he puts it back in his pocket.

My phone buzzes in my purse, and I check it to be sure he sent it. I'm also relieved Jack hasn't texted about something wrong with Ester.

"Misha is staring daggers," Ricky says behind us.

Alec starts to stand. "I should—"

I rise enough to push him into his seat. "Sit down, Alec."

"You can sit down too," he says to Ricky.

I start to argue but stop when I see Misha air-kissing friends goodbye. I don't have time to argue, and it's possible since Ricky is a business partner, he'd have information Alec won't give. Out of options, I press forward. "I have Belina's day planner." I say it plain, but there's plenty of subtext. "She recorded a lot of information about you, Alec."

He grimaces. "Like what?"

"She told you something important the day she was murdered." I scoot my elbow on the table until it meets his forearm. "What did she say?"

"What I told you. It was about Emmett's books being due. Some accounting stuff. I didn't see her again. Not ever again."

"This could be your break," Ricky says, patting Alec's shoulder. "Does the planner have any names of who she was meeting?"

"There's a code that I haven't broken yet."

"Oh my God," Alec says, sitting up. "Did she say she was meeting with me?"

"No, it's not you."

Alec's face is pale. "Did you hand it over to that detective? Get him to investigate?"

"Yes," I say. "I also have to give a statement. He'll pick apart our friendship and look for dirt that would stick with a jury. If you don't tell me everything, I can't help you."

"I don't know what to say," he yells.

I freeze at the outburst. He's so close to breaking.

"We'll help you, man," Ricky says. "Take a breath, okay?"

"Oh shit," Alec whispers, something catching his eye across the room.

Ricky's gaze goes to where Alec is looking. They both sit up straighter, glance at the other.

"I gotta get outta here," Alec says.

Misha makes her way toward us, and Alec points toward the exit.

"Tell me what happens with the detective," Alec says to me, nod ding goodbye to Ricky, and hurries to catch Misha.

And just like that, you've failed again.

I grit my teeth and turn toward where Misha left. Her so-called friends are already tossing each other dramatic, wide-eyed looks. I want to linger there and understand better what Misha's up against. How much she cares about preserving her life as is.

But that's not why I'm here, not where the evidence is pointing. It's Alec that matters. What he's done and what he's hiding.

I find the people who made him run. There's a good-looking Hispanic man with his focused gaze on us. He's next to an older man, who is also very well dressed.

"Did those men spook Alec?" I ask Ricky.

He makes a clicking noise. "They're newcomers to the fishing game. Jealous of what we've got."

"All right," I say, letting it go for now. "I'll need your phone number."

"Business or pleasure, Mrs. Burges?"

I know Ricky then, in that moment. He's good looking but a fuckup. Probably still does coke even though he's in his midthirties. He's smarter than all his friends and likes it that way.

He's a lot like my younger brother. In all the best and worst ways.

You led him to those ways.

"I'm joking," he says, likely not able to read my stare.

"Really?"

"I want to help Alec," Ricky says. "You've got a great lead with this planner. However I can help, I will."

I have fifteen questions outlined in my mind. But I don't trust him to give me a straight answer. Not yet. The smart ones are always a lot of work, but I can crack him.

No one is cracking today except you.

Ricky holds out his arm for me, and I take it. He leads us to the only bar set up in the tent. He nods at the bartender, and two martinis arrive. I'm not going to drink a whole martini before giving a police statement, but I raise the glass.

Ricky smiles, glancing at my purse. "You're not a real Newport girl," he says after his sip, which is much longer than mine. "Though you're dressed pretty close."

I set the drink down. "That so?"

"The purse," he says. "Too new to be vintage and too old to be fashionable. You're pretending. Like me."

"That's quite an admission."

"Back when I was just driving a fishing boat, I'd spend half a day's wages on a decent ticket to come here. I like pretending. *Great Gatsby* syndrome or something, right?"

I appreciate the confessional angle he's running. Trying to quickly befriend me, getting us on the same page. I'll have to play my own game, flirt to keep him wondering if I'll let him fuck me or get money out of me or both. That's my angle to keep him interested while I dig.

You have no idea what you're doing.

He knows it too.

"Fitting in is a good skill," I say, "if you don't like where you're at." I glance around at the people in the VIP tent, all born exactly where they want to be. Maybe they want to marry a little better or upgrade the summer home but nothing that would make them frauds.

Like you.

You don't belong here.

We all see it.

"That's why I wanted to work with Alec," Ricky says. "He's a little bit pretender, little bit genuine article."

"Don't tell Misha that," I say, taking another sip, even though I shouldn't.

"She figured it out. Alec used to ride in these matches. Was pretty damn good. He'd take side action to keep the lights on in his parents' big place over in Newport. Gotta respect hustle."

I did, in fact, but obviously Ricky was doing a little hustling of his own.

"Marrying well also helps," I say.

"I noticed you got a quality ring."

"My husband loves real vintage," I say. "And I love big diamonds."

This isn't true, but I can see it's what Ricky expects to hear. If he knows what a woman's purse is worth, he certainly knows a thing or two about what big diamonds mean.

I lean toward him. "So Alec brought you into the business?" It must have been a recent change. Ricky wasn't in the grant application or any of the subsequent reports Alec filed with the Economic Development Council, which I went through last night.

"We met two years ago," Ricky says. "He needed help, and I liked his shine."

"What's your role in the business?"

"My role," he says mockingly, perfectly articulated without any Rhode Island accent. "I'm in charge of the holy trinity: boats, captains, and fishing licenses." He counts each off on a finger in front of his cocky grin. "I keep the coffers full. Or I used to anyway."

"Do you handle the books?" I ask.

"No way," he says. "The money is Alec's thing."

I wonder if Ricky is pushing the money troubles onto Alec. "Were you friendly with Belina?"

Ricky's face doesn't move, which is different than previous statements, as if he's trying to lie well. "I saw her around."

She didn't make any notations of a Ricky or RC. "You have a nickname?" I ask.

"Nothing I'd say to a lady," he says. "What's your first name, Mrs. Burges?"

"Devon."

"How close were you with Belina?"

"Friends," I say, "but I'm learning she kept a lot to herself."

Because you were the terrible friend.

"Like what?" he asks.

"Maybe a boyfriend in Newport," I say, thinking of Phillip's lead from Belina's mom. "Heard anything like that?"

"He'd have to be rich."

"What do you mean?"

He pulls the toothpick out of his drink and slides the olive off. "Her mom was basically"—he pauses to pop the olive into his mouth—"well, the sidepiece of Newport. End of the eighties and early nineties. Belina learned from the best."

"You're suggesting Belina was a prostitute?"

"Naw, not at all." Ricky drops the toothpick onto the bar. "She understood hustle. She didn't have a lot of opportunity growing up. She made the most of what she had. Just like her mom."

"But you met her only a few times?"

"Newport is a small town."

"Did you introduce Belina to Alec?"

He shakes his head. "It was separate but worked out well for everyone." He pauses, glancing around the room. "Until things dried up. No one saw that coming."

"You're in financial trouble," I say.

Smile lines crease around his bright-blue eyes. "We made enough for me, but I don't have an East Side wife with Newport expectations."

The phrase comes out too quickly. He is trying to chat me up instead of talk. "The amount of money your twenty boats generate does not explain your revenue."

He shrugs. "It was a real division of labor in that I was the labor."

"Who did what?"

"Alec had the grant money from that committee. The fancy schools and degrees. The last name. He handled the money and investors. I've got the accent and experience, so I dealt mostly with the captains and boats." He grimaces, his focus landing behind me. "We got company."

The handsome younger man who made Alec nervous heads our way with another guy, someone I hadn't noticed. The two of them are muttering in Spanish, and mine is terrible, but I pick up a few phrases, mostly *gringo asshole*.

"Hey, Miguel," Ricky says. "Let me buy you a free drink."

The guy I think the comment is directed at cracks his neck to the side as if trying to keep his temper under control. "I've learned even something free has a price from you," Miguel says. "You a friend of Ricky's?" he asks me.

They'll see right through you.

This is all going to fall apart.

"New acquaintance," I say. "Devon Burges."

He nods as if recognizing my last name. "Nice to meet you." Miguel's teeth are perfect veneers, and I think of my bedroom furniture. His shorter friend has less polish, a laziness to his appearance: the poorly fitting suit, the undone tie, the sleeves shoved up to his elbows. He wants people to know he doesn't give a flying fuck about their polo lifestyle.

Miguel, however, seems to like being under the VIP tent. He's got a perfectly cut suit similar to the older man in the corner. They all have the same high forehead, thick black hair, and pointed jaw. I'm guessing this is a family affair.

There's a ping in my memory from the journal. Two weeks before her death, Belina met with a Miguel. And this one is already connected to Alec and Ricky. "That's a nice suit," I say.

"I only wear it around white people," he says with his one-hundred-watt smile. "It's flashy and plays into everyone thinking I'm a drug kingpin. What else could a brown guy do?"

"They probably wish you were," I say. "Plenty of takers in this crowd."

Miguel laughs and wags a finger in my direction.

"I hate that drug shit," says the shorter one. "I hope the place gets raided."

"This is my cousin, Thomas," Miguel says.

Ricky is at my back, effectively crowded out of the conversation, which is maybe a good thing with the way Thomas keeps looking at him, anger narrowing his eyes. Ricky starts loudly chatting with a woman two seats down.

"You were talking to Alec," Miguel says, putting himself a step closer to me.

"We went to Georgetown together."

"Ah," Miguel says. "My father, Vicente Rossa, is a friend of Cal Burges. He's your husband's uncle?"

"He is," I say, realizing I met Vicente before at one of Uncle Cal's happy hours. He is a self-made multimillionaire, having built a security business that monitors most of the East Side.

"I've got a lot to live up to," Miguel says. "But I'm well on my way."

Thomas looks at Ricky, who is working on a second martini. He raises it with a wide grin, continuing his Gatsby impression, and returns to the woman.

"We're getting our own group together to start in the fishing industry," Miguel says.

"I was thinking of investing an inheritance I came into recently," I lie. "My great-uncle loved to deep sea fish in Florida. I thought it'd be good to honor him and make a little money."

"I'm sorry for your loss," Miguel says. His gaze narrows, more calculating than sympathetic. "We could show you around our docks. Discuss some exciting opportunities."

"It'd need to be soon," I say.

"Not a problem," Miguel says.

Thomas orders a Manhattan, finishes it quickly, and orders another one. Miguel widens his eyes at the bartender, who just laughs. No doubt he doesn't get paid enough to argue with a man hell bent on getting drunk in the VIP tent.

I get Miguel's number in time to watch Ricky finish his drink as he ambles over to us. "Fellas," he says, his words slurred. "Don't we have a boat deal to discuss?"

I try to hide my surprise that they're doing business together. They seem to barely be able to be in the same room. Of course a bad deal may be why Alec ran.

"You're a fucking cheat," says Thomas. "That boat won't be worth half of what we have to spend on repairs."

"Back luck," Ricky says and winks at Thomas.

"Leave it alone," Miguel says to Thomas. "We're here to watch my nephew." He nods out toward the polo players racing up and down the field in red shirts and white pants. "Let's not make the situation worse."

"Or we can make it much, much worse," Thomas says as he spits on the ground an inch from Ricky's shoe.

Ricky laughs, staring down at him. "Vicente seems well," he says. "Nice of him to let you out of the van." He leans toward me. "They're basically cable guys."

"I will never be embarrassed of working for a living," says Miguel.

Ricky leers, the cockiness roiling off him. "Your father did all the work," he says. "Or at least got rich paying people next to nothing to do it."

Thomas lunges for Ricky, and the punch is fast and hard, if a little high on the nose.

The room explodes, and I'm off my seat, Miguel pulling me away from the action. The small bar crowd swells as Thomas kicks Ricky in the ribs and then stomach. Thomas jerks up his leg, positioning his shoe above Ricky's face. Miguel takes the opportunity to shove his cousin back, yanking at his jacket, and it requires effort, even as he's unbalanced.

Vicente, watching from the corner, stands and buttons his jacket, looking annoyed but not surprised. He casually strides across the tent, bypassing the chaos. A security guard hustles in as Miguel drags Thomas out the back of the tent.

The guard helps Ricky onto a stool, shoving some bar napkins into his hand. His nose is bleeding down his face and onto his suit jacket. He leans back, dabbing at it calmly.

I rush over beside him. "Towel with ice," I say to the bartender. "Clean one, if you've got it."

"How thoughtful," Ricky says to me. "Whiskey back with that."

The nonplussed bartender hands me the towel before sliding over the whiskey.

Ricky shoots it immediately. "Watch your dress," he says as I hand him the towel, blood spattering as he adjusts the ice-filled rag onto his nose.

"Deserve it?" I ask. The room is settling down, attention turning back to the match.

"I always deserve it," he says through the towel.

"Was that just about a boat deal?" I ask.

"Probably a couple other things," he says.

We're silent until the bleeding stops. I pull the rag off his face and clean up some of the blood around his nose.

"Hey, Devon," he says when I'm done. "You need info on our business. I'll do my best to help. We gotta keep Alec outta jail."

"We will," I say, uncertain if we're lying or delusional or both.

"Have a whiskey with me?" He presses the back of his hand under his nose, hissing at the contact as he swipes a trickle of blood.

I realize I'm very late to meet Detective Ramos. "I have to go." I hesitate, squeezing my nails into my palm. "You going to be okay?"

He smirks from behind the bloody rag as if my kindness is surprising. "Want to meet Monday?"

"Yeah," I say. "I do."

I make it to the police station by noon. As I step out of my car, I see a few drops of Ricky's blood on my dress. I button my jacket and hope no one notices. I've got enough to explain as it is.

Chapter 14

Look where we are again, girlie.

I ignore the voice and check my phone outside the police station. Jack texted that Ester is sleeping, and I can take all the time I need. He's hoping my handing over the planner and being interviewed will mean the end of my involvement. And maybe it should, but he knows better.

I open the glass door to the police station and freeze. Even though it's been twenty years, the terror from the first time I visited one returns. The weight of the memory saps my nerve, as jarring as the scent of Mr. Clean on wooden pews or Conway Twitty crooning through an AM radio. The detonation of my worst memories from childhood.

I manage to move and hurry to a folding chair in the station's entryway. I drop onto it, not the woman in her Newport Polo best but a girl of ten who just sneaked out of church and walked four miles to the police station across town. My heels throb from remembered pain, how they were scraped and blistering from my Walmart clearance patent loafers, bleeding through my thin white socks with the ruffles on top.

The feel of the blood down my heel, wetting my sole, reminded me of one of the only movies I'd ever seen, Grimm's *Cinderella*, on a school outing to the movie theater on the last day of fourth grade. The stepsisters cut off their toes to fit into the glass slipper. A bird that witnesses their fraud warns the prince: *Coo-coo, there's blood in her shoe.* There is justice. After the first mile, I was glad for the blood. Glad for the pain. Glad for the bird's refrain that I said over and over. *Coo-coo, there's blood in her shoe.*

I stare down at my shoes, not clearance from Walmart but Louboutins Cynthia let me borrow. I am steadier staring at her kindness, imagining her intelligence and strength reactivating my own. I count a few breaths, and once they're steady, I head toward the small line at security, which is cleared quickly.

A short-haired woman behind the U-shaped intake desk motions me forward. "Ya here for Ramos," she says, not asking, and picks up the phone before I answer with a nod. "Come get 'er."

I step to the side, and a man with a stack of parking tickets takes my place. Detective Ramos gives me a half wave as he approaches. "Back this way," he says.

I met with cops all the time while working sex crime cases in DC. But I'm not on the clean, legal side of things here. I'm the girl with blood in her shoes no one wants to believe.

No one will believe you here either.

But you won't be a lying girl.

You'll be a woman in prison.

We hurry down several hallways, a couple people glancing at me as we pass them. I pull my coat tight and try to focus on how I want this interview to go.

There's another long hallway before we come to a door marked number two. It's clean with a wooden table in the middle and two metal chairs on each side. Belina's yellow planner is in a bag at the center with a photocopy of the whole planner. I know that's what it is because the first page has Belina's cursive name staring at me. Next to it are copies of the three memos I wrote.

He thinks they're a joke.

"My boss is angry about that blogger's post," he says as we sit. "It was not a good look, as they say on *Real Housewives*."

I smirk at the joke. Seems he's trying to play nice. For now. "His name is Phillip Hale," I say. "He's going to be interviewed on *Dateline* tonight. Likely, your boss won't like that much either."

Detective Ramos swears under his breath and then pulls a recorder out of his pocket. "You know how this goes?"

"I do," I say and lean toward the recorder as he presses the red button. "My name is Devony Anne Burges of 225 Lawrence Street in Providence. The evidence I've handed over to Detective Frank Ramos is a yellow day planner that belonged to Belina Cabrala. It came into my possession the afternoon before she was murdered, September 30."

The day you should have died.

Detective Ramos clears his throat. "Ms. Burges told me that she'd forgotten she had the journal. She handed it over to the police when she remembered approximately three months after it was given to her."

"Correct," I say and briefly explain my traumatic labor and how the journal was put away with my discarded possessions from the ER.

Detective Ramos has a pen and small notepad that remains blank, which is good. I read hundreds, maybe thousands of statements. I know to keep it brief and to focus on knowledge within my experience. But now, the real questions will begin.

"Tell me about your friendship with Alec Mathers," he says.

You let him use you.

Because that's all you're good for.

"We were classmates at Georgetown University all four years. We were friends, ate together, studied together. I didn't know anyone when I moved to DC, so I appreciated his friendship."

"Did you date?"

"No. He introduced me to my husband."

Worst mistake of his life.

"Were you friends after you and your husband moved to Providence?"

"Not like we were in college."

"Why's that?"

You're a terrible friend.

I take my time to answer honestly, as much for myself as Detective Ramos. "We were both married and building careers. Mine in law, and he had various projects as an entrepreneur."

"Your uncle Cal helped him with that?" he says.

"Yes, the Economic Development Council," I say. "He got their first grant. For a new business idea right after we moved here. It was almost three years ago."

"Did you know Belina then as well?"

I ignore his question for a moment because I realize that when Belina started working for Alec, that was also when Ricky got involved in his business. And the Council got into some trouble. It was all around then, but I hadn't put that together.

Because you're focused on finding Alec innocent.

Alec's not innocent.

Just like you.

"I met Belina six months ago," I say. "It was a coincidence. I saw Alec's son, Emmett, in his stroller and approached her. I still cared about Alec even though we weren't as close. I appreciated Belina's friendship. It came easy, but the two aren't related."

"When was the last time you saw Alec?"

"This morning, at the Newport Polo charity match."

"Cold for polo," he says.

"Any excuse to wear fur."

He ignores me and presses on. "Did you discuss Belina's murder?"

"Yes, we talked about Belina's involvement in Alec's fishing business. I also shared that she'd left her day planner for me. I told him she didn't indicate that she was meeting Alec the night she was killed. She listed two other people."

"Left it for you?" He frowns. "Couldn't she have just forgotten the planner?"

"I think the meeting that night, possibly the danger involved, was on her mind. First, she kept looking toward the spot where she'd eventually be killed." I pause to let that sit. "The place where she'd meet with the two nicknames in her book. *A* with a circle and CF. In the dozens of times I've seen her with the planner, she's never left it behind. She's never left anything, in fact. Not a sippy cup or toy and certainly not something that important. She left it for me in case something went wrong."

He doesn't believe you.

He knows you're crazy.

"Back to Alec," he says. "Did you see them interacting?"

"Yes, he was usually home when I'd meet her there. We'd chat occasionally."

"Ms. Burges," he says, tone shifting, some condescension in it. "I reviewed the day planner, and it's clear what was happening. Belina and Alec were in a relationship."

He got there faster than I expected. Likely because it's the only angle that makes Alec's motive for murder stick. "I have no firsthand knowledge relevant to your question," I say.

After opening the journal to a dog-eared page, he begins to read. "'Alec brought me soup. He wasn't mad when he caught the flu too.'" He clears his throat and flips again. "'Alec finally bought a blue suit, and his eyes are so beautiful.'" And flips again. "'The boat ride with Alec was everything I needed.'" He crosses his arms, the sleeves too long and arms too tight. "Sound like normal employer-employee feelings?"

"I have no firsthand knowledge relevant to your question," I repeat. It was a gamble to let the detective see this planner. Maybe I should have kept it hidden. But I thought with the memos, maybe, he'd see that they were only friends as Alec said.

No stopping stupid like yours.

"Alec spent several hours each morning and sixty-three afternoons with Belina and Emmett in the past six months," Detective Ramos continues. "His son still naps two of those hours in the afternoon, according to Belina's own notes. You think they were watching Bravo?"

I don't respond to the joke because this question is the opposite. I know Detective Ramos needs this evidence and some eyewitness testimony of their relationship. Otherwise, the DA will have a tough sell.

"That's not enough for a conviction," I say.

"Let's try this a different way," he says as if he's picturing someone reading this transcript aloud to a jury. "Belina was leaving her position as a nanny. She'd sent her resume around and accepted a new job. Did you know that?"

I shake my head, trying not to give away my shock. "I didn't."

"Alec was angry, got blackout drunk as he's already admitted. They had a confrontation, and he killed her. His DNA is at the scene. Her blood is in his car. I got a captain on the dock says he had a black eye the day after. Her knuckles were bruised. Did you know that?"

You're all guilty.

Take away the baby.

Lock her up.

I want to lay my head on the table to think, but I can almost see the germs in the old wood. Nail scrapes and handcuff scratches. I try to regroup. "You don't have the murder weapon," I say. "And your motive is thin."

"Not as thin as it was. Thanks to the planner."

"That's not why Belina left it behind," I say, sharper than I should. "She wanted to catch the real killers. This is lazy police work."

"Tell me about your memos."

He's cutting me some slack. Or trying to push me to act crazier. Either way, I can't stop. "The first memo details Belina's movements over the past eighteen months. The second summarizes why I don't believe Alec was listed as meeting Belina that night and couldn't be the killer. The third is about the *A* with a circle and CF, who were supposed to be there. I think she was working for one or both of them."

It's a lot of guessing, but I feel good about why Alec shouldn't be a suspect. That memo is strongest, and if Detective Ramos is serious about finding the killer versus closing the case, he'll at least look into who Ⓐ and CF are.

That detective sees your memos are nonsense.

"You don't think Alec is the *A* with a circle?" he asks as he scans the second memo.

"She wrote his name out. Why change it to *A* with a circle? Also, her meetings with that person don't fit with Alec's schedule."

"You know his schedule?"

"She met with CF in Newport from the very beginning of her nannying job. Thirteen meetings were noted. She also introduced CF to Alec. Later, there's *A* with a circle, but she also notes leaving Emmett with Alec. They're two different people. We need to find out who."

He turns off the recorder, spinning it around a few times. Then he picks up the charts I made and flips through them. "These are pretty good," he says. "I talked to a guy at the FBI you worked with a while back to bust the Rhode Island Speaker of the House."

He is likely talking about Agent Max Fincher, but I don't ask because that's not the most interesting thing he's revealed. "The FBI is involved?"

"These memos seem like decent guesses," he says, ignoring my question as he taps the stack. "I'm sure big corporations paid you a lot to poke holes into cases. But this is a murder investigation."

My ego wants to go into my work in DC, but that's not what matters. "If Belina was working for someone else, likely CF, we need to know. We need to talk to them. They were supposed to be there the night she was murdered."

"I have a suspect with DNA at the crime scene, the victim's DNA in his locked car, and a motive that's already playing in the media. We're understaffed. There's no money for overtime."

"How do you think your budget will look when the mayor has to explain an overturned conviction of the most prominent murder in twenty years?"

"He's guilty."

You're the only one stupid enough to believe otherwise.

Letting him use you.

Ignoring your tiny crying baby for this nonsense.

"But there's a chance he's not. He doesn't feel right for this crime." I pause as he frowns as if I've hit a nerve. "Alec has a four-year-old son."

"I know." Ramos shifts in his chair. "I appreciate your efforts and the planner. But I see this information another way."

"What way?"

"There's intimacy."

Shit.

"I've seen guys nicer than Alec do some terrible things," he says. "If he was drunk, maybe he can plea to manslaughter. I'm sorry."

"There are other suspects," I say in a rush. "I analyzed Alec's financial data. What he emailed you, plus his application and reporting for his small-business grant. Alec was running an all-cash nonprofit. He had business ties to the fishing industry. He was trying to organize the captains. Maybe he was framed?"

He crosses his arms. "Framed for murder?"

I want to cringe, but I push forward, ignoring the sound of the panic in my voice, how hard I'm gripping the edge of the table. "Why else would there be blood in the car when she was murdered in the cemetery? The killer sliced her arm and drained enough to plant later."

"Whoever killed her had access to his car?" he says slowly, kindly.

"Phillip had reported the alarm was broken," I say not slowly, not kindly. "His source at the police department said it could have been for several weeks. If the killer planned to do it, he may have even dismantled it. Popped the lock and dumped the blood that night."

"Or," he says in a soft tone, "Alec killed her."

Voices begin in my head, but they are not from my broken mom-brain voice but echoes repeating from a real terrible day. I slide my hands over my ears, but it doesn't stop. I'm the girl again, but instead of a police station, it's a courtroom. The defense attorney's voice, the southern Kansas drawl with a hint of aw-shucks, reverberates every nerve.

The speech begins: "Ladies and gentlemen, we have a sad case of he said, she said. A pillar of this community, a preacher whose reputation is for givin' back to us all, is being accused of a terrible crime. But worse, the accuser—"

I fight through the sinkhole in my chest that opens up with these memories and draws me down deep. Quickly the rage kicks in, and I claw my way back to it, not an erratic violence but a precise and focused need to destroy. It hasn't lessened over the years. My hatred is always there, burning bright and hot, whether I'm a young girl hiding in the corner of the courtroom or a lawyer obsessing over a long-shot case or a new mother barely keeping it together in a police station.

Detective Ramos is hiding something. Everyone is. I think of how his face changed when I said *CF* at Uncle Cal's happy hour. "You know who CF is, don't you?"

"Devon, can you listen? There are things about Belina and Alec you don't realize. Things that make a good case. I understand why you want to help him. But women are killed by men who love them every day."

"A first-year law student could convince a jury that there's reasonable doubt in this case." I explode out of my chair, all that anger burning bright. "Imagine Alec on the stand, crying about Belina and how much he loves his son. No weapon, no motive, just a few vague diary entries and neighborhood gossip."

Despite my shouting, Detective Ramos is calm. I imagine it's the look he gives some methed-out tweaker with a box cutter.

"Damn it," I whisper more to myself than him. He's not going to listen. He's going to use the planner against Alec.

You were always going to fail.

Detective Ramos stands and heads to the door. "An officer can give you a ride home. Or I can call Jack."

The tears begin, but I stop them quickly. "Are you arresting Alec tonight?"

"He's the only suspect." He taps a knuckle on the door as if summoning a dog.

"Who is CF?" I ask, not obeying.

"I don't need to explain anything to you," he says. "Thank you for your time."

I shrug on my coat before calmly picking up my purse and letting the sound of my heels reverberate across the room. "No need to thank me now." I pause in the doorway, putting myself in his face. "Save it for when I solve your case and catch the actual killer."

It's good I'm a short drive to Phillip's place on the West Side. If Detective Ramos isn't interested in the truth, it's time to take Belina's case to the court of public opinion.

Chapter 15

I'm driving too fast as I think through the meeting with Phillip. It took several hours, but we have a plan. He's uploading the journal to his website, which is gaining views by the thousands, thanks in large part to a HuffPost link. He will tease the memos and post them after his *Dateline* interview tomorrow morning. We have to start creating reasonable doubt, pointing toward the mysterious CF and Ⓐ and not Alec.

That's our focus now, reasonable doubt, planting suspicion before the jury is even picked. Because Alec is going to be arrested. I can't stop it. He's going to jail.

You both should be.

In the corner of my eye, I see the particular white shine of a police SUV and slam on my brakes because I'm going ten over.

You shouldn't be driving.

You shouldn't be allowed to do anything.

I whip into a parking lot on North Main to hopefully avoid a ticket and head toward the green-and-white glowing Starbucks sign. Relieved it's still open at nine p.m.—God bless the USA—I order a large latte from the drive-through and pull into a space to pump and dump.

If you loved Ester, you'd drop the milk by the house.

Selfish bitch.

Tears start as I plug in the car pump. It's less effective and takes twice as long, but my breasts are on fire. I drop my head back as the relief begins, but my heart is raw. Today is the longest I've been away from Ester, and it hurts so much I can't imagine doing it again.

I check my texts and reread Jack's check-in message that everything is fine. He wants to know more about the interview and where I am, but I don't know how to respond. I type, delete, and settle on: Made things worse. Have to warn Alec now.

I start my car and get another text from Phillip. He heard from a contact that a judge signed off on the arrest warrant. It is happening within the hour.

My tires squeal as I leave the lot, turning too fast back onto North Main, not seeing a huge oil truck crossing. The driver lays on the horn as I swerve, the headlights bright in my eyes as we avoid the crash.

I can't stop my hands from trembling against the steering wheel. Turning onto Olney Street, I slow down. I'm edging toward unstable and take small breaths to get my heart rate under control. My vision blurs. I'm nearing another blackout. I keep breathing.

Coo-coo, there's blood in her shoe.

I will make this right with Alec. Or as right as I can before he's hauled off to jail.

As I take the turn onto Cole Avenue, my brain shifts to keep up with my heartbeat, both going too fast. Questions and fears are stacking up as I struggle to catch my breath. This is my last chance to find out what Alec is hiding, if I'm going to save him from himself.

Save him from you.

As I bump the curb, my front tires roll a little onto their perfect lawn. I don't correct it and quickly get out, glancing down the block for police cars. The streetlights are bright, and it's quiet for now.

I knock on the Matherses' door, and unfortunately, Misha answers. She puts a hand on a cocked hip. "Alec doesn't want to talk. He's putting Emmett to sleep."

"The police will be here soon," I say, my throat tight. "They're going to arrest Alec."

She frowns as much as she can with all her Botox. "They find something?"

I don't admit, yet, that I provided this new evidence. "I have to see him now."

"What's going on?" Alec says behind her with a yawn. "Devon, I don't want to get into it again."

Misha shifts back so I can deliver the news. Alec is in a faded Newport Polo shirt, sleepy and disheveled. I repress the urge to hug him. "They're arresting you tonight. I don't know when but soon."

His head knocks back, but there's some relief in his eyes. Now he knows. "Okay," he says. "The detective told you?"

"Why did you speak with a detective?" Misha snaps. "Come in, and explain what the hell is going on."

Alec lets out a big sigh and leads us to the sunken living room. I don't take off my coat but instead just launch into the awful truth.

"When I met Belina the afternoon she was killed," I begin, "she left behind her yellow planner. I analyzed the data and presented a theory about why Alec is *not* the killer to Detective Ramos. But he's not interested." I pause to shift from Misha to Alec. "He believes the planner contains motive for the case against you."

He runs a hand behind his neck, pinching at it for several moments. "What now?"

"No," Misha says. "I want to see a copy."

Ruin her life too, while you're at it.

I pull a copy of the journal I made in my office from my bag. She snatches it and drops onto the end of the leather sofa opposite Alec. She slips off her UGG house shoes and tucks her feet under her.

I hand Alec a second copy. At first there's a small smile as he begins reading Belina's words, but then tears form in his eyes.

"What'll hurt him that's in this journal?" Misha asks.

I swallow thickly, unsure if this will lead to broken dishes or a yawn. "Belina writes about Alec in a way that makes their relationship seem romantic."

"*That girl* had a crush on him," Misha says. "He can't help what she wrote."

"I agree it's a thin motive, but in combination with the jacket, DNA at the scene, blood in his car, and no one confirming the alibi . . . it doesn't look good."

A red flush spreads up Misha's neck as she begins to read an entry aloud: "'Today Alec brought me purple violets from the playground. We tied them in love knots with Emmett.'" She flips another page and taps the passage with a long manicured nail before she reads it. "'I'm so glad Alec wore the blue tie to our meeting. It's perfect for his eyes.'"

Misha loudly flips through the pages, small gasps followed by glares. "You took her to the polo charity match last year?" she hisses. "We had just talked about creating distance. She is . . . was clearly infatuated." Ripping the page from the binder clip, she crumples it into her hand. "Your vanity is disgusting." She throws the wadded paper at him.

She stands up, the flush fully reaching her face. "You swore you didn't fuck her."

He picks up the wadded piece of paper, smoothing it on his knee. "It wasn't like that."

"Why does she write about you like this? Why would she *care* about *you*?" Her expression softens at her harsh words, possibly some regret there, but she doesn't apologize.

He's on his feet, holding the paper up as if it's evidence. "She brought something special to this house. Something we were missing."

"Oh, really?" Misha crosses her arms. "What was that?"

"She was nice to me, okay? Interested in our son. It was *refreshing*."

Misha's jaw drops. "How dare you say that to me."

"You act like she didn't matter, but it's not true. She mattered a lot."

Misha trails her fingers across her mouth, but I can still see her quivering chin. "Now you decide to find some backbone?" she says calmly, recovering. "Over her?"

"Yes," he says with a childish stamp of the foot. "Goddamn it, she mattered."

Misha shows no reaction to his outburst. "How about throwing some of that courage into your businesses? My father doesn't want to pay our mortgage again."

"You'll be fine," he says. "You know how to climb your way out of anything."

Misha closes the distance between them and slaps his face. I step toward Alec. "That's enough," I say. "We need to work together. Figure out who really killed her."

This is your fault.

You led Alec down this road.

You've ruined his life.

That's all you do.

Misha's eyes are full of tears. She raises her hands, and he flinches, but she gently touches his cheeks. "Do you want to do this alone?" she whispers.

His whole body slackens at the question. "No," he whispers. "Please. Help me."

She inhales deeply and pulls back from him. She turns to me. "What do you need?"

"Alec," I say and wait until he turns from Misha to me. "If you'll look at the last page, there are two initials for whoever Belina was meeting at Swan Point the night of her murder. CF and *A* with a circle. Does that mean anything to you?"

He stills, fumbling the paper. "I told you," he says too loudly. "I have no idea."

"The police are going to ask you the same question," I say. "Work on your lie, if you're going to try it with them too."

"I don't know who killed her." He walks over to the bar to pour himself a large whiskey.

"You're a good man, a wonderful father," I begin, needing some drama to light a fire under his ass. "But this is the moment you choose if you're going to fight for your family. For this life you've built. Tell me the truth so I can help you."

"I have," he says before taking a long drink. "She was our nanny. I cared about her, and she's dead."

You could have helped her.

This is all your fault.

Before I can respond, my phone buzzes in my pocket. Phillip texts: Cops there in 20. Big show. Media en route.

I squeeze the phone in my hand, scanning the room as I put my next steps together. Alec's not answering my questions, and I need to focus on what I can get before the press and police arrive.

"The detectives are on their way," I say.

"I'll call our lawyer," Misha says, picking up her cell phone and heading into the kitchen.

I slide up to Alec at the bar. "They're going to turn your house upside down. I need to look at your computer."

He sets his drink down. "It wasn't supposed to be this way."

"Write down any email addresses and passwords." He writes down his passwords, and I leave him alone, heading for his office. I have to access as much data as possible before the police get here and take it.

His office is small but organized. Each month's financials are in a binder on a bookshelf. I flip through a few pages, and everything seems to be in good order. I think of the chaos of his dorm room and am surprised. But if Belina was really running the show, this may be more her space than his.

I open his laptop and enter the password, EMMETTANDBELINA. Doubt Alec shared that with Misha.

The photo of Alec, Emmett, and Belina on the boat is the background image. I don't have time to get nostalgic. I pull a flash drive out of my bag, one of several I keep on me, and begin uploading as much data as I can.

The mirroring process takes a few minutes, so I head back to the living room.

Before I reach Alec, Misha hurries into the living room. "The lawyer is coming from north of Boston," she says. "He's not going to make it in time."

Alec swears under his breath but doesn't leave his drink.

"Please, what do we do?" Misha says to me. "You have to stay and help. You owe us that."

As if you could help.

"I can stay," I say. "Look, Alec, the police are going to cuff you. They'll walk you down the sidewalk for the press, who will certainly be on your lawn. You have to shower, shave, and put on a clean white shirt."

He turns to Misha. "I can't say goodbye to him. It's too hard."

"Emmett knows you love him," she says so softly. I feel like an intruder for the first time. "This is temporary." She takes his hand. "Let's find you some appropriate clothes."

"Phillip Hale, the blogger, he's going to post Belina's planner," I say to them before they leave. "With my theories, to begin creating reasonable doubt. But if there's anything you can tell me about Belina or someone who would want to hurt her . . . or you."

"My business wasn't all on the books," he says. "She helped me with numbers, had a few connections. Once Uncle Cal dropped me, I needed capital. Ricky had ideas. There were some other investors . . ."

"Who?"

"Stay out of all that. Really, it's not important."

He leaves before I can argue. I pick up the pages of the journal Misha scattered, returning both copies to my bag.

It's only a few minutes before Alec returns with Misha. She's out of her yoga gear and in winter-white slacks and a pink top. We gather in the entry room with the floral wallpaper. Everything is quiet and almost calm. Then headlights beam, and the quiet ends with the sound of vehicles driving too fast down the street.

"It's the media," I say, not needing to look. "They'll set up, and the police will be right behind them."

Misha crosses her arms, her Alex and Ani bangles clinking. "Should I say something to the press? Like they do on TV?"

Alec touches her arm. "No, honey, you can't—"

"Yes, she can and should," I say, surprised at her offer. "It'll cut down the time the media plays the footage of you in cuffs. Sound bites from a tearful wife could make a big difference."

"I can do that," Misha says coolly. "What do I say?"

"Talk about his innocence. Mention your sadness for Belina's family and how important she was to your own. The media will ask if you're cooperating, and you insist you've done everything asked."

"What about the memos you mentioned? The journal?" she asks.

"Yes." I smile at her, which is not exactly appropriate at this time, but it's an impressive suggestion. "Send viewers to TheHaleReport.com for proof of Alec's innocence and clues to the real killers. Offer a ten-thousand-dollar reward for any information about the real killer."

She inhales sharply at the money but doesn't argue. Alec is watching her closely, but he's not arguing either. "You should wear a blazer," she says to him. "The navy Brooks Brothers."

After pulling it out of the hallway closet, she opens it so he can slip his arms inside. She runs her manicured nails along the shoulders, picking off a few pieces of lint that I don't see. They lean toward each other, not touching but reaching out.

Wanting to give them some privacy, I peer through a narrow window by the door. The news crews are hustling, the cords and lights and cameras being set up. As the red and blue lights flood the entryway where we stand, every camera light outside turns on, lenses following the silent police cars—no sirens in this neighborhood—as they block off the driveway.

"This is it," he says calmly, as if finally accepting what's about to happen.

"I'm sorry," I say. My eyes burn, but it'd be selfish to cry.

This is your fault.

Alec's jaw is set, eyes focused. His gaze goes toward the hallway where Emmett sleeps. "Help them," he says to me. "But don't—"

A knock on the door cuts him off.

"Showtime." Misha opens the door to let Detective Ramos and two officers with empty boxes inside.

"Alec Mathers, you're under arrest for the murder of Belina Cabrala." Detective Ramos's assertive gaze is narrowed when he sees me. An officer reads Alec his rights as Detective Ramos cuffs him.

"Some advice," Detective Ramos says to Alec as he shifts him toward the door. "Don't say anything to the press."

"He's not." Misha steps close to the detective. "Now get the hell out of my way so I can."

Chapter 16

I watch Misha leave the gaggle of reporters and stride back into the house. She breezes past me and heads toward the kitchen. I should leave, but I won't. I haven't gotten what I need from her.

I text Uncle Cal that we need to meet, then text Jack to let him know I'll be even later than I said. It's all I can do not to run home. I lean my forehead against the window, my breath warming the cold glass. I've seen people arrested plenty but never a friend, someone I've made dinner for and shared countless laughs with. Someone who knew me when no one else did.

I head back to Alec's office, where I'd taken my flash drive with a mirror copy of his computer before the police confiscated his hard drive. They took a few binders of data with them but not all of them. I open one labeled *contracts*, which is thinner than the others. There's only one inside, signed by someone with a chicken scratch signature from Venantius Ventures based in Jamestown, Rhode Island. It tripled the number of fishing licenses Alec had from four to twelve. It was executed six months after Belina started working as their nanny.

I hear Emmett cough through the wall and then Misha's heels in the hallway. I take a photo of the contract with my phone and head toward the hallway. She's leaning against the doorframe, her thin shape illuminated by a night-light projecting stars all around the room. I stand next to her and see Emmett in the corner of his toddler bed. I remember that my arrival woke Alec, and he had been sleeping there. It's easy to picture the two of them together. Emmett with his arm slung over his dad. Alec snuggled against his son's red curly hair.

But that's not real. Emmett is alone, and the half of his bed where his father slept next to him is cold and will remain that way.

He's never coming back.

You're not good enough to help him.

Misha touches my shoulder, and I realize there are tears on my cheeks. She shuts the door, and we head toward the kitchen, where she starts opening cabinets and then the freezer. The lights are out, and I can see only her silhouette, which now includes a bottle of wine and two glasses. She opens the back-porch slider with her thin hip, and I follow. She turns on a heat lamp and sits down in one of two folding chairs, the patio furniture in winter covers.

I pull the glass door shut and watch Misha reach into her Moncler puffer to pull out a pack of Parliament 100s. I haven't seen that brand since I left Kansas. Those smokers are usually women covered in baby oil, tanning along the river, where people go tubing or noodling for fish. The river was brown from mud and mined minerals resurfacing after the excavation businesses went bust.

You thought you were too good for those women.

Too good for that town.

"Like ice wine?" Misha asks, motioning to the ground where there's a stemless glass filled to the brim. "It's sweet but goes down smooth."

"Perfect," I say, sitting and taking a grateful sip and then another. "You did great out there." She was sympathetic, tearful, which seemed sincere, and she mentioned Phillip's blog.

"I hope it helps," she says, her tone as if that's the last help she'll offer. She takes a deep inhale on her cigarette before sending smoke up in the air.

We're quiet as we sip our wine. It's sweeter than a Coke but freezing cold. The silence isn't easy, and I search the backyard for anything to break it. I notice a red light along the roofline in the corner of the porch. "Is that a camera?" I ask.

"Yeah," she says, sounding like she forgot it was there. "Alec installed it when he had to store our boat in the yard. The neighbors loved that."

"Did you look at the footage?" I ask.

"He said there wasn't anything on there." Misha glances at the camera again. "It's all on his computer."

I hadn't thought about private security systems in the area. Maybe that could lead to more information about Belina and who followed her into the cemetery.

"How's . . . Emma?" she asks.

"Ester," I say. "Beautiful but not sleeping much. Being a mom is different than I expected."

She nods, stares straight ahead. "I have a good momma. Dumb but good. Cares a lot. I sometimes think I've got that formula backwards."

I smile to myself because there is this insightful streak that I really appreciate about Misha. "If you're worried about it," I say, "you're probably doing better than you think."

"Does your mom give you good advice?" she asks with kindness in her voice.

But the voice in my head merely replays my mother's words.

Get outta here, girlie.

You're cursed by the devil.

Don't you ever come back again.

"I don't speak to my parents," I say.

"How awful," she says and glances toward Emmett's window. Her face pales in the back-porch lights.

"Are you okay?" I ask.

"This kind of thing . . . ," she says softly, glaring into the darkness of their perfectly manicured backyard. "When I was younger and my family was still poor, we lived in a two-bedroom shithole. Drug dealers on our corner. Everyone into something they shouldn't be." She takes a long inhale. "But this kind of thing . . . this thing . . . doesn't happen to me *now*. Not with this husband at this address. My family got lucky with that money coming, but what the hell does that matter now? I might as well be married to the dealer on our old block. At least he had real hustle. What good does it do now?"

"Better lawyer," I offer.

She doesn't respond but crosses her legs. I see the outline of her thighs, thinner than I remember. It takes real focus to stay that skinny. Her frame seems like it could be twenty pounds heavier, and she works out all the time and eats very little to keep it that way.

It reminds me she's got a strong will. When her mind is set, on being the thinnest friend, on marrying a name to match her new money, she does it. At the moment, I feel that will turning against me and Alec.

"Are you going to stick with him?" It's one thing to cry for the press. It's another to stay in a marriage you don't want. In a life you'd never choose.

The life Jack has now.

The life you forced on him.

She stabs her cigarette into the iron arm of the chair and lights another. "I don't know. Alec has screwed up plenty. That's part of the deal, I know. But can I forgive this . . . or ever trust him again . . ."

The disappointment is sharp in my gut. "He needs you."

"Alec needs everybody," she says. "If I lived one day of my life the way he lives all of his, then this house of cards would have come down a long time ago."

"What do you mean?" I ask.

"That keeping up appearances and getting bills paid on time is serious work. I can't just bumblefuck my way through it like my husband."

Nothing to argue with there. "Do you believe him?"

She half grins into her wine. "Yeah," she says. "He really did come home drunk the night she was killed. He was loud, covered in pizza grease, but still looking for chips."

"Cool Ranch Doritos?" I say, remembering college.

She nods, not seeming amused. "He had a black eye too." She clears her throat and takes a puff. "He didn't remember how he got it."

I see an awful flash of Belina trying to fend him off. I dismiss the worry and take another sip of the too-sweet wine.

All you have left are lies.

"Our son deserves to know his parents." Misha pauses to slice me a look, and I don't resent her for it. I feel the same about Ester. Wanting more for her than the little I had. "Emmett will have a good address and the right schools and a great college and a fan-fucking-tastic life," Misha says, punctuating her point with her cigarette in one hand, waving her almost empty wineglass in the other. "A lot of my life I was hungry. He will never know that feeling."

"It's difficult changing your life," I say.

You didn't change one bit.

You're the same selfish person.

Misha reaches for the wine, fills the glass to the top again. "I have to step carefully now. I'm too much to handle for most rich men. My age and expectations make me more a first wife, rather than a second or third."

I set down my wine, not wanting to have a loose tongue too. "Don't give up on Alec."

"I don't need your advice," she says as she drops onto the back of the chair.

A hostile witness I could handle. "Tell me about his business, and I'll leave you to this bottle of too-sweet wine."

She snickers. "What about it?"

"You've made some remarks about money trouble. Did your family cut you off?"

"How dare you—"

"I watched my friend and your husband get carted off in the back of a police car. We're far past the point of indignation. I'm here to help him. I suggest you take a crack at it yourself."

"Belina got herself killed. We're caught in the middle."

She stands up for her next cigarette, and I have only an instant of regret before I get in her face. "If Alec's business is as crooked as I'm gathering, you're in the shit, Misha. There will be no house or car to sell, no furniture to sit on, no Dorothy Williams boutique dresses to snag a new husband. Even that wedding ring you keep so sparkling will be sold at a police auction."

I hear her swallow thickly before taking a long shallow breath. "We aren't broke. Alec's business was slowing down because the feds were digging into things."

"What things?" I say.

"All the licenses and cash. The fishing business is volatile. Alec made some mistakes."

"In what way?"

"Payments had to be distributed to these captains regularly. Thousands a week that Alec managed. Cash for the fish, gas, docking the boats. It got to be too much. Belina was helping because it was her idea but—"

"This business was her idea," I say softly, and she doesn't appear surprised. "Did she bring the Venantius Ventures contract?"

Her jaw pops out, gaze suddenly angry. "Where the hell did you come across that name?"

"There's a contract with them in Alec's office."

She lets out an exasperated breath. "Alec said you were digging around. You need to listen to me. Don't you dare bring me into anything with him."

"Him?" I say. "Who is him?"

"This is no joke, Devon. Alec owes some serious money to some bad people. You do not want to be the one asking questions about this business."

I'm stunned she and Alec don't see what this kind of motive would mean. Or maybe they do see, but they're too scared to do anything about it. I take a step toward Misha. "Tell me who Alec and Belina worked with. I'm going to find out anyway."

She waves me back, wobbling as she does it. "We're done here." She picks up her glass, drops the pack of cigarettes, and leaves them. "The lawyer is with Alec. I've gotta check in."

I need more time, more pressure points to dig into the money that's owed. And to find out to whom. "I'm the only way Emmett grows up with a father not in prison. Think about who you're really protecting."

Misha strides over to the sliding glass door, heaves it open. "I know exactly who I'm protecting."

Chapter 17

In the dark of Ester's room, the radiator hisses softly along with her sound machine. I lie on the floor, next to her crib. It's almost midnight, and she'll be crying soon. I don't want to wake up Jack, whom I found asleep on the couch with ESPN on mute. He was waiting up, and I'm not ready to talk.

To tell him you're wrong about everything.

The voice is right. I've got a gnawing feeling in my stomach, painful and real as a loose tooth. This happens from time to time when I'm working on a difficult case. I am doing something wrong.

I wiggle my wrist through the slats in the crib, running my fingers lightly over Ester's chest. I picture our breaths together, mingling across our bodies. I put a shaking hand over my heartbeat and feel it beating with hers. At last comes the focus.

I concentrate on Alec and the contract. These are all my areas of expertise, so I'm in luck. My glance at his monthly financials confirmed the money problems are business related and likely illegal. All that cash is a dead giveaway. The profits increasing even when they shouldn't. The ties to the Economic Development Council. It all points to a difficult conversation I need to have with Uncle Cal.

My mind returns to the fact that it seems as if Belina brought some idea to Alec. Before he met her, his business was small and financially unsuccessful. A few months after she started working for him, and likely arranged the meeting with CF, Alec's cash flow began increasing substantially.

I have to recalibrate how I view her in this investigation. She's not just the victim but the link.

Used by everyone.

Even you.

The real question now is who she knew who could bring Alec this kind of high-risk/high-reward deal.

Just because she's dead doesn't mean she's innocent.

Just because he was your friend doesn't mean he is anymore.

The voice is right there. If I make this about helping Alec, or even Emmett, I'm going to miss facts and ignore others. This cannot be for them. It cannot be for Belina.

My phone buzzes in my pocket. Phillip texts that CNN has booked him after *Dateline*. He's giving them the theory about CF and Ⓐ. This is his big break, the national exposure we need to start finding answers. He's drafting the talking points, and I'll review them later. He knows I'm not sleeping.

I go into my office, turn on the desk lamp, and open my laptop. I type *Venantius Ventures*. The home page says it's the largest commercial seafood supplier in New England and, subsequently, the country. That makes sense, considering Alec's business.

I check the staff page, and the first photo is a headshot labeled *Stefano Venantius, founder and CEO*. He's got a full head of silver hair, dark eyes, and a bright-white smile. His name is familiar, and I know I've seen it before.

I open my phone and zoom in on the photo I took of the signature from the only contract in Alec's office. It definitely starts with an *S*, so this may be one of the "bad people" Misha warned me about.

I google Stefano, and there are dozens of photos from society events and puff piece write-ups, like him holding a fishing pole to commemorate the purchase of his fiftieth boat. Several pages later is a photo from five years ago with a very tan Stefano standing in the center of his employees. In the back I see a familiar half grin. Her long black hair is draped over one bare shoulder in her strapless red top.

"There you are, Belina," I whisper.

I click back to Stefano's corporate bio and note he was a founding member of Uncle Cal's Economic Development Council. He served only one year. I think back to what Phillip had on Uncle Cal. The bank account linking money laundering to his committee. I didn't know at the time the account was connected to Alec, since all I saw were account numbers.

You didn't want to look.

You just wanted it all to go away.

But this time line matches. It's possible only Stefano cleaned money through Alec's business, sure. It's also possible Uncle Cal lied to me when I confronted him with Phillip's information. That he's remained in business with Alec. Or at least started it up again.

Either way, Alec would have already heard of Stefano, if Belina brought him to meet her new employer. And then she started taking care of Alec's financials. Potentially telling CF everything.

Perhaps I should feel some sense of betrayal about my friendship with Belina. She peppered me with questions about my accounting background, never offering her own. Made it seem she was just a hostess from Newport looking for a change. Not someone working an angle on my friend.

Like recognizes like.

The stairs creak, and Jack is standing behind me.

He wishes you'd never come home.

"I watched the arrest," he says. "The mayor called too. We've got a seven a.m. debrief."

"I can take Ester tomorrow," I say, not wanting to leave her again.

"Let me see if Gillian has time to help you," he says. "How's Misha?"

"About what you'd expect," I say. "I screwed up."

"How?"

"The planner. I gave Detective Ramos what he needed to make the alibi stick."

"I'm sorry," he says, putting a hand on my shoulder, rubbing at a knot. "Maybe you should take a break?"

Before he leaves you and your crying-nonstop baby.

"It's not over," I say. "Belina's planner is still an asset. I can make this work." I flinch at how defensive I sound. After waiting ten seconds, I turn my chair to face him. "I tried to do it the right way. That was my mistake."

He lets out an exasperated sigh, shaking his head as if he were expecting this all along. "Now what? The wrong way?"

"My way." I hope he'll leave it at that because I want to get back to work. He doesn't respond, so I continue. "I need to push harder. Force the killer out."

"This feels like betrayal," he says. He stares at my computer, and then his gaze lands back on me. "It's not only hacking, if that's what you're planning. Or the fact that you'll lie. Work with dangerous people." He pauses, but I don't contradict him. "It's that you won't be here. In our home. The place you swore you wanted us to build and live in and have a normal life together. We know how this goes. How it ends. You said you didn't want that anymore."

He's right, of course. When I was prosecuting cases in DC, I was gone all the time, barely sleeping or eating, nothing but the job. I almost lost him. Lost the life I had always wanted but never thought possible. The life I was living right now.

"I will be here," I say. "I am here. For you and Ester."

So many lies.

Then as if she heard me, she begins to cry. "Oh no. That's her—"

"I got it." He closes his eyes, drawing in a long breath, fighting something I hope isn't tears because I can't take it. "Uncle Cal's here," he says quietly and then leaves for the hallway leading to the nursery.

I smell the cigar before I open the back-porch door. I see Uncle Cal's outline, the expensive overcoat and leather gloves, puffing away in the dark like Tony Soprano. I throw a blanket around my shoulders and head outside.

"Thank you for coming over," I say, hearing my exhaustion.

Maybe Uncle Cal hears it too. He motions for me to sit down, but I shake him off. I remain at the top of the few stairs, away from where he stands on the dead grass. "Alec was arrested despite my best efforts."

"Are your efforts over?"

"No," I begin, not completely sure how hard to twist. "I analyzed your information from when Alec got the grant. It's partial at best."

"And?"

"I also reviewed emails Alec sent to the police," I say. "It's pretty basic but plenty to guess what's really going on."

"What's that?" he says and lets out a long puff of smoke.

"You and a few other board members were washing money through Alec's failing business. It's what Phillip accused you of the last time we worked together. I dropped it because you said you fired the people involved."

He coughs, and I realize it's a laugh. "Even after all these times working together, you surprise me."

"Am I wrong?"

"No, you're not. I thought we'd hid it better."

"You hid it fine," I say. "But it's a cash-based business with a relatively stable gross income, and then suddenly there are large infusions unrelated to expenses. The fact that your Economic Development Council gave Alec the cash with zero oversight was another red flag. Plus, I know you."

"Alec was only useful as a patsy," he says, matter of fact. "I realized that after I gave him the grant. Something you foisted on me."

With so few people who like you, it's no wonder your loyalty is so dumb and blind.

I'm culpable. He's right. I felt bad that Jack and I never invested with Alec. That I'd let our friendship lapse. So when Alec asked me for the favor, I did it as much to alleviate my own guilt as help him.

This is your fault.

"But the money laundering did stop," he says. "I stopped it."

"I want your real files, not just those that make Alec look guilty. Start with every member of your board."

"You think a board member could have been involved in that girl's murder?"

"Her name was Belina," I say, even though he damn well knows. "Start with Stefano Venantius. One of your board members the first year. When you gave Alec that grant. Who resigned after serving only one year."

"Forced to resign," Uncle Cal corrects. "Alec's not smart enough to pull off any long-term scheme. Stefano is not as smart as I thought if he started dithering with Alec again."

But it wouldn't have been just Alec. "Belina worked for Stefano before she worked for Alec," I say. "I think she set up the meeting a year and a half ago when she started working for Alec."

"Really?"

"Or," I say, still unsure, "Stefano had her work for Alec. Luring him in, as it were." Uncle Cal chuckles at the lame joke, and that reminds me of what Phillip mentioned. "Belina's mother told Phillip Belina was involved with a big fish, like literally, I guess."

"It wouldn't surprise me if she and Stefano were seeing each other," Uncle Cal says. He pauses, looking at the glowing end of his cigar. "*Big fish* is an interesting term. Stefano has a nickname. No one says it to his face."

"What is it?"

"The Codfather," Uncle Cal says.

I laugh at first because that's a pretty solid nickname. But then my brain clicks. "Oh my God," I whisper and steady myself against the back door. "He's CF. She met him the whole time she worked for Alec. He was supposed to meet her the night she was killed at Swan Point."

"Now wait," Uncle Cal says. "That's a tremendous accusation."

"It's only an accusation now," I say. "Give me time."

He steps toward me and looks up. "I'm not handing over ammunition against a man like that to just anyone. You bring a knife to a gunfight with Stefano, and you'll feel the bullet and the blade."

"What do you suggest?"

"If you will really go after him, not this half-assed walking the line bullshit, then I'll give you everything you need."

You're going to betray everyone again.

You'll lose the home you never deserved.

"It can't be like before," I say. "This isn't about your political enemies who happen to also be crooked. This is about real, honest justice. To make sure whoever killed Belina rots in jail for the rest of their life."

"Whatever you need to tell yourself."

"Listen," I snap and step down one stair, getting in his face. "The work we did to put those corrupt opponents of yours in jail . . . we're lucky we didn't join them."

You should have.

You still can.

He pulls back and glances around. The closest streetlight isn't working, so the stars are vivid above us. I pull my blanket tighter, longing for my bed with Jack next to me.

He'll be out of it soon enough.

"Do you know why I consider Jack my son?" he asks, taking a long drag on his cigar before continuing. "He's my son because of you."

Trepidation blooms in my chest, an awful weight warning me that I don't want to hear what's next.

"We marry our parents, Devon. Jack married you. You are nothing like my brother. Jack's caring but simple-living father. You're nothing like his strong but hyperreligious late mother."

"This is ridiculous," I say. I put my hand on the back door. "I'm going inside."

He takes my arm, pulling me down a step. We're so close the cigar smoke wafts between us and stings my eyes. "Jack is my son because he married you."

I pull away, stumbling back up the stair. "You and I are not the same."

"It's a compliment as much as an insult. The sooner you understand your role, what you must do, the quicker we'll have Jack in the governor's seat. How else could I stomach my beloved nephew marrying some nobody from Kansas?"

He's never been more right.

You're trash that doesn't belong with someone like Jack.

"I'm good for him," I say weakly.

"I'm not in the good and bad business. Neither are you." He releases his serpentine smile. "You're what he *needs*. Now be who you are and build a real case against Stefano. Your way. The way that gets things done."

His words are echoes of mine to Jack earlier. This is the only way forward. "Can I borrow Gillian tomorrow?" I ask, and he nods.

I lean back on the door, staring up at the clear night sky, ignoring how easy this sell was for him.

"Send my files back," I say, referencing the box I gave him after we professionally parted before Ester was born. There was dirt on every political leader in the state. And also the dirt on Uncle Cal and his Economic Development Council that Phillip almost published and I buried. "And send my knife."

Chapter 18

Monday, December 12

Ester's midnight cries begin, and I'm almost relieved to have something simple to do. She was with Jack downstairs all day Sunday so I could go through the files Uncle Cal sent over. Doing my own research. I focus on her, calming us both as I bounce on the exercise ball.

What kind of mother ignores her child this long?

Ester is back asleep in her crib after only twenty minutes, a new record, as if she senses my change. The commitment I've made to Uncle Cal. The promise I've broken to Jack and Phillip. The person I've become again. Likely the person who was always there, reposed beneath the surface of my skin like Ester once was, protected by hard scars and the kind of anger that never goes away.

I slip out of her room and avoid the creaking floorboards on the way to my office. Standing in the dark, with only a sliver of moonlight and the glow of my phone, I smile. Back to work.

My phone buzzes because I didn't put it on silent, hoping for this call. I may have left my brother behind, but he's always come through for me. At least when I pay him.

"Hello there," I answer.

"Hey, sis," Derek says, slightly slurring his words.

This is your fault.

"Hey yourself," I say. I estimate ten to thirteen minutes of lucidity from him. "How did the research go?"

"Pretty good," he says. "I was wired most of the night."

Likely speed or meth to start things off, then some kind of opioid to bring it all down. I hope it's not heroin again. No one gets that many lives. But I don't say anything because it's all been said, all been tried, all failed. I doubt he likes many of my choices either, but here we are, breaking the law together again.

This is your fault.

"That Alec guy's files were easy," he says with the dramatic tap of his finger on the keyboard. "Just took some poking around in the banks and accounts to see who was sending the money. Nothing major."

"Good," I say, waiting for the file to come through. I hear at least ten of the dogs he's collected yapping at something. Living in the country is good for his drug habit. Good for his fear of people and the anxiety that comes with having to interact with them. Good for his depression. It is also good for his inability to turn away a stray, from dogs to feral cats. "You doing okay?" I ask finally, unable to stand the quiet once the dogs settle.

"Yup, yup." He pauses, and it's as if I can hear the drugged-out gears clicking. "Oh," he says. "You know Jack hasn't called since the hospital. How are you . . . doing with everything?"

"Ester's not sleeping at night," I say. "But holding her feels like a second chance for the kind of life . . . you know, we didn't have."

"Huh," Derek says. "Jack said you were pretty bad for a while. Voices come back?"

Tell him how broken you are.

He knows anyway.

I glance around my office as if someone could have heard him say it. Or heard the voice. But it's just the two of us, and suddenly I want to be honest. "Yes," I whisper.

"Best to ignore them," he says, as if it's possible. There's another long pause. "Tell Jack about it?"

He'll leave you.

He'll take Ester.

You'd be alone again.

Just like you deserve.

"No," I say. "I can't. He's dealt with enough."

"So have you."

I know he's not just talking about almost dying in labor. It goes so far back between us, and if I'm not careful, I'll feel this room change into my bedroom as a girl. Hear the sound of a body shifting at the edge of my twin bed. The springs creaking. The metal of a buckle.

"I'm not . . . defined by what happened," I say too quickly. "Even if we'd had it perfect, I'd still be me." It's all the reassurance I can muster.

"You always been you," he says. "But I still wonder—"

"Well, don't," I say. Derek doesn't need to be reminded of my problems and shoot up an extra time because of them. The computer dings that I have a new message. "Ah, got it." I quickly open the encrypted folder analyzing Alec's bank records and the data I copied from his computer. "Tell me what stood out?"

He clears his throat, and I hear the rattle of a collar as he scratches whatever creature is in his lap. "Alec's living on credit cards and lump payments every month from a shell corporation located out of Portugal."

"Stefano Venantius tied to it?"

"Presto," he says, though he means bingo. "He's three degrees removed but close enough."

I scan the numbers, the language easiest for me to understand. I look at the first lump payment of $10,000 from Stefano's account to Alec. Then, one month later, Alec transfers $60,000 back to Stefano. Because Stefano owns the boats, it could be justified as rent. But I've been researching the fishing business, and the amounts don't add up. I need to understand what the boats brought in that could cover a money transfer of that high of an amount.

There's another payment through a company I remember from Phillip's file about Uncle Cal. That's where the Council has been trying to wash some money. Only thousands per month versus Stefano's tens of thousands. Then I see a shocking number from six months ago.

"I can't believe Stefano gave Alec a half-million dollars," I say.

"Alec only transferred back two hundred thousand," Derek says.

The transfer was the night before Belina was murdered.

"I need you to look into Belina's bank account too," I say. "In her journal, the day she died, she said she was transferring money. I need to know to who. And why."

"The 'who' I can handle."

As I hear him start to click, I begin looking through the bank records Derek was able to steal and connect to other accounts. It's a lot of vendors, gas, boating equipment. I see one of Stefano's corporations is listed as owner of one property on the East Side but close to North Main. "He owns Belina's apartment building."

"She hasn't paid a lick of rent for five years," he says. "Not that there's anything wrong with that."

We both laugh a little. I picture him in the abandoned farmhouse, almost a half hour from anyone else. I haven't been there since he moved in a few years ago, but in high school it was my go-to spot. I could smoke weed or give hand jobs or whatever my current boyfriend was into. It was total privacy with a hint of rebellion, my ideal setting back then.

What a slut.

Your family knew.

You don't deserve someone like Jack.

One of the last times I went there was during a lightning storm with this hot college dropout. We were on the porch, drinking vodka and Snapple, watching the flashes across the sky light up all that flat land. Some other high school freshmen joined us and threw their empties against the side of the house. I yelled at them because even though no one lived there, someone once had. Someone might again. I wished I could. Ever since I was eight, every time I walked down my block and saw my grandfather's car parked in the driveway and tried not to throw up. I'd have given anything to live in that abandoned house. And now, my brother did.

It's all your fault.

I take a minute to breathe through the sickness the memory brings, waiting for the anger. It arrives with a few tears, and I wipe them away and dig into the spreadsheet. It doesn't take long for a theory to emerge.

"Okay," I begin, "Belina starts working for Stefano's company as an accountant even though she's a college dropout." I close my eyes as I pull at stray thoughts. "Possibly having an affair with him. Then she leaves her accounting job to work for the Mathers family. But she meets with CF, a.k.a. Stefano, right after taking the job. Keeps detailed notes about Alec. Stefano pays for her place. Two months after she starts, Alec starts getting deposits from Stefano's shell company."

"She never stopped working for Stefano," Derek says.

"That's my guess too."

"This Alec guy pretty dumb?" Derek asks because it looks that way. His books, personal and business, are a mess.

"Dumb enough to listen to the wrong people," I say on a sigh.

I open the complete file Uncle Cal sent over. It shows Alec's business had a loss that first and only year of the grant. With things going poorly for Alec, he was vulnerable to the money-laundering scheme. To keeping up appearances.

To making his little nanny girlfriend happy.

And her boyfriend Stefano happy.

Line by line, I see Alec received regular cash payments, anywhere from a few thousand to tens of thousands. Likely, it's an advance for the larger amount of money that Alec would clean.

If Belina set this up, I'm impressed. My guess is the dirty money would come to Alec in a cooler or whatever. Meanwhile, Alec gets weekly cash payments from buyers for the fish his captains bring in. It's thousands each week, and he deducts a small amount for the boat rentals, gas, or whatever. Then he gives the captains cash but not the cash from the fish buyers. He gives them the dirty cash. Scattered among the captains, much of it likely not even deposited in a bank, it would be difficult to trace. Then the clean cash is deposited into the bank, sent back to Stefano as payment for the boats or whatever.

I keep thinking of the first item on Belina's to-do list, "transfer money." I notice Alec paid off his mortgage with a huge chunk of that half-million dollars. He also sent Misha to the spa. And paid six months on his leased BMW. I doubt that's what Stefano would have wanted him to do with his money. But it doesn't look like Belina transferred the money to Alec.

I see where Derek stopped his research, right at the Stefano data. He never minds hacking civilians, but when someone is good enough to really hide their money, he'll stop. I'll have to push him later.

You use him, even though he's got nothing left.

Worst kind of sister.

He should have stopped talking to you like everyone else.

"This is a big help," I say. "Can you dig into Belina's accounts too?"

"Yeah," he says. "Send me the deets, sis."

"Sure," I say. "Five thousand for your time on this? Another grand for Belina's info?"

"Sounds about right," he says. "About right, right."

Repeating words means it's not long now until he passes out.

"You seeing the family for Christmas?" I ask, trying not to sound like I care.

"Naw, better company here."

While I legally emancipated myself from my parents as a teenager to get as far away as fast as I could, Derek played the long game. He was twenty-five when he left without a word. He moved outside their town but hardly ever speaks to them. "I'll fly you out if you'd even want to stay—"

"Can't board my cats," he says. "Too mean."

He'd also need to smuggle a lot of drugs up his ass. "Sure," I say, not offering to visit either. "Thanks again."

He grunts, and I hear the slack-jawed inhale of the doped up. There's a little rumble in the back of his throat. I listen to him breathe. In and out, snore and wheeze. That sound is one of my few happy memories as a girl.

I close my eyes as he breathes. I hear his knock on my door, sleeping bag in hand. He was six, I was almost eight, and he noticed my light was on. I couldn't sleep in the dark anymore. We didn't need to say why, both of us knowing, him the witness and me the victim. He saved my life that night and every one that followed until I learned how to put a lock on my door. But even when I felt like no one could physically come into my room, I had to live in that house. Without Derek, I never would have survived.

"I love you," I say, even though he's passed out. He's the only person I say it to at the end of a call, including Jack. But each goodbye with Derek feels like the last one we'll ever have.

All your fault.

Chapter 19

I'm still awake in the early hours, my brain unable to slow down even as I ache for sleep. I spent the past twenty-four hours preparing for today. My recent legal work rarely required this level of attention, but when I was working for Uncle Cal, it was late nights and digging until dawn. I slipped into some dangerous old habits.

I won't let that happen again. There are two lines of demarcation that I overcame to reach this point. At both edges I almost lost my life and my mind—first as a girl in Kansas and later a lawyer in DC. Now in Providence, I have a life worth living. I cannot go back.

Downstairs I order my files and put them in my messenger bag. I drop in Miguel's business plan for his fishing enterprise. He sent it after I'd doctored some fake financial documents to prove I was a whale of a potential investor and signed a nondisclosure agreement. The plan is light on details, but nothing seems amiss or hidden. The opposite of Alec's files.

It's not only with Miguel that I get to play pretend today. First, a trip to see Belina's mom to highlight my friendship and simple Kansas roots. If she's a townie like Ricky said, the fancy East Sider persona won't help me. I'll save that for my meeting with Miguel after.

I hear Jack in the shower and go check on Ester. I bounced her through a lot of the night to keep her quiet so I could concentrate. I get her changed, and her diaper bag is packed just as Gillian arrives. She says she doesn't mind coming along, but I can see she'd rather watch Ester at the house again.

Everyone sees how crazy you are.

I have to have Ester close. When she's away from me, she's a phantom limb, throwing off my focus, pulling me back when I need to be present.

We get into my SUV and hit the road. Gillian hums to Ester, who seems to like it, finally stopping her wailing. The silence and extra help releases calm, something I haven't felt in days, weeks maybe.

We zoom down 95. Already all eight lanes are crowded as we pass the Providence River and dozens of tankers and cranes in the port. There are billboards for DUI lawyers and Cardi's Furniture before I pass the iconic Big Blue Bug, supposedly the world's largest artificial insect. The pest control mascot is wrapped in Christmas lights with a glowing Rudolph nose.

There's not much else to look at until the South County exit toward Newport. The shift is immediate, trees swapped for billboards, the sky seeming wider as we head in the direction of the ocean.

My phone alarm beeps, which means it's time to turn on Phillip's interview.

The *TODAY Show* is broadcast live on Sirius radio. I press a couple buttons until I hear his voice, keeping the volume low so as to not disturb Ester.

"Yes, Leslie, I don't believe the right man has been arrested. Belina's day planner, which we released last night on TheHaleReport.com, indicates two other suspects were meeting her at the cemetery."

Leslie clears her throat before she begins. "But the suspect arrested, Alec Mathers, had DNA evidence at the crime scene. The victim's blood was in his car. Supposedly they had a relationship."

"She was wearing his jacket at the scene," Phillip says in his conspiratorial tone. "His wife, Misha, said that the blood, which was in the trunk, was a result of a scrape from the stroller earlier that day."

"Seems a little convenient," Leslie rightly says.

You're setting him up to fail again.

Phillip lets out a friendly laugh. "Look, it's possible it was planted. Why else drain her arm in that way? Alec's car alarm wasn't working, was possibly disabled by someone. My source at the cemetery says none of their cameras have footage of anyone other than Belina walking from the gazebo to where she was murdered. And yet a vial's worth of blood is splattered in the trunk of his car, which was not at the scene?"

"On your website, you said you're tracking down two other people Belina was supposed to have met with at the time she was killed?"

"We are. And we're learning who Belina really was as a person. Not just how neighborhood gossips perceived her but her family and friends. A woman is dead, and all the media can focus on is how attractive she was and whether she wore yoga pants to run errands."

"We'll all be watching as your investigation into this murder continues," Leslie says. "Phillip has agreed to be an exclusive NBC correspondent as he uncovers breaking news about this shocking crime haunting New England."

I smile at that revelation, a last-minute negotiation, I'm sure. It puts more pressure on what I'm doing today. We have to keep up the drumbeat of evidence and reasonable doubt.

It's all going down in flames, girlie.

Speeding away from the mainland, I head toward the first bridge to the island of Jamestown, where I'll be stopping soon enough. Stefano's fishing business and ships are based out of that town's port. Alec docked his boat and tried to organize the captains with Ricky from there. That trip could wait only a day.

I cross the second bridge to Aquidneck Island, home of the tawny town of Newport. The large bridge, a blue cousin to the Golden Gate, is an appropriate gateway to the seaside town with colonial architecture and million-dollar yachts.

Once I'm off the highway, I take the long way. I cruise along Ocean Avenue and the large private homes before turning onto Belmont. Across expansive lawns and behind ornate gates are gigantic mansions that once belonged to Vanderbilts or Astors. They're now maintained by the Newport Historical Society, so people in Steelers T-shirts and fanny packs can shuffle through the doors and listen to audio tours about great wealth and great divides.

Not that I can judge. There weren't even any two-story houses in my Kansas town.

The GPS takes me off the main road to streets crowded with houses chopped into rentals. The screen door to Tina Cabrala's first-floor apartment is propped open with boxes, though the front door is shut.

"You don't mind waiting?" I ask Gillian after I put the car in park.

"Do what ya need to do, hon."

How could you leave her again?

In the car, outside, in this neighborhood.

What a terrible mother.

I glance back to be sure Ester is still sleeping, even after the car stopped. She's peaceful, and I grab my purse and a bottle of wine I swiped from our refrigerator.

Sometimes it's intuition. Back in DC, I knew to take off my engagement ring and look forlornly at the balding guy at the end of the bar who would buy me a drink and tell me about his recently arrested buddy. Other days, it's listening for small details. Once Belina made a joke that her mom liked pinot grigio more than her own daughter. She laughed, but it stuck. Most details do for me. It's a survival thing. Clawing at every scrap you can get in case it matters.

To get to the doorstep, I cross over two boxes and a lamp with a torn animal-print shade. I press the doorbell, but it doesn't work. There are two people talking inside, male and female, and their voices drop off at my cop knock on the door. I hear a back door slam.

The woman who appears looks nothing like Belina. She has that tight-faced, 1980s plastic surgery skin. Her breasts are large and too high, age spots and freckles dotting along the tan cleavage zipped into a short leather jacket with a dingy fur collar. She looks me up and down, her gaze landing on the bottle of white wine in my hand. "Yeah?"

"Hi, Tina. I'm Devon. I was a friend of your daughter's. I'm so sorry for your loss."

She rakes her long nails through her overpermed hair, squeezing her eyes tight and then opening them with a purse of the lips. "Whaddya want?"

"Have you been watching the news about the recent developments?" I ask. "See Phillip Hale on *Good Day RI*?"

She sticks her nose in the air. "That black fella? Yeah, he was pretty good."

"He's a smart guy," I say. "I'm working with him on her case. Can I ask you some questions?"

She crosses her arms, leaning against the doorframe, several stacked bangles clanking. "I thought you were friends."

"Belina didn't share much with me," I say. "Please, I'll be quick."

"I don't got much time," she says. "My boyfriend will be back soon to haul what's left. We're moving outta this shitbox."

"I'll help," I say with my brightest smile. "I'm a very organized person."

"I did just getta manicure," she says. "Gel kind, ya know. Pretty expensive. Be nice to keep it."

I am glad she can see through her pain to get her nails done. Inside the apartment, there isn't much left other than a pile of clothes on the bed and a few pots and pans in open cabinets.

"It's not much to raise a kid," she says, swiping some crumbs off the counter. "We made it work. The new place is better. A real house, not too far from the water."

"Good for you," I say with a little Rhode Island on it.

She wrinkles her nose at the phrase. "It's not exactly on Ocean Drive."

"You want me to start here?" I ask, stepping toward the pile of clothes on the bed. She nods, and I fold a few gauzy tops, stuffing them into the black garbage bag lying on the floor. "Cute stuff," I lie.

She doesn't respond as she rummages through open boxes. She pulls out a corkscrew and coffee mug. "You want some?" she asks.

"No thanks," I say. Anyone who drinks white wine before nine a.m. does not want to share.

I fold and pack her Forever 21 wardrobe while she finishes the drink almost as quickly as she poured it into the Flo's Clam Shack mug.

This is the future you deserve.

White trash is all you'll ever be.

"Belina didn't come around much after she moved to Providence," she says, voice more relaxed.

"Why's that?"

She shrugs and pours the second glass, bottle now half gone. "She helped me with bills. Thought that gave her the right to treat me how she did."

"How was that?"

"She didn't want no advice, for a start. She had opportunities, rich men interested in her. She's pretty and smart, not a typical combination around here. She had two years of college. I told her where to work to meet men who'd help her. But she did what she wanted."

"Where did you want her to work?"

"Places with people who had money," she says flatly. "Why else do people like us live in a place like Newport?"

After tying a knot in the garbage bag, I pick up another one and shake air into it before folding more clothes. "Sounds like you wanted her to be the way they're describing her in the news."

She laughs at that, a throaty rumble I can imagine floating my way at a dingy hotel bar with a little caress of the shoulder and vodka martini. "Belina was always good at numbers. Wanted to have the power-suit lifestyle. I bought her a Coach briefcase, nice one secondhand. She said it was too flashy for her job."

"Venantius Ventures?" I ask.

"That's the place." She takes a long drink. "Her attitude started when she went to her fancy high school, Saint George's in Middletown."

"That must have been expensive," I say.

"I did what I could. She got a scholarship and thought her shit didn't stink from then on."

"What about her friends there?"

"They went to college. Good places not around here. Massachusetts or Maine or whatevah. I don't think many of them were around. At the end of the day, she's a townie. Boys liked Belina. That's the only reason those rich bitches cared."

Sounds like that dead woman never had any real friends.

She probably never saw you coming.

Selfish bitch like you just blended right in.

"Why'd she drop out?" I ask.

She shrugs again, eyes me suspiciously. "You go to college?"

I shake my head, sharing the half lie. "My parents wouldn't pay for it. I did just fine."

"That's what I told her. Lots of ways to make it in this world." She gestures as if we are standing in one of the mansions, and she's a tour guide for the social climber.

"What did she tell you about her time at Venantius Ventures?" I ask.

She turns from my question and becomes very interested in packing a drawer. "Not much." My patience wanes with each paper clip, old coupon, and rubber band she moves into a beat-up box.

"Belina left her day planner with me the day she died." I pause as Tina's gaze snaps in my direction. "You're not in it anywhere."

Trying to break her heart too?

As if she hasn't suffered enough.

Her thin red lips form an O. She doesn't look happy about it. "Well, who she got in there?"

"Code names," I say. "CF and *A* with a circle around it."

Her watery eyes go wide, but then she snaps back into her too-relaxed stare. "Don't mean nothing to me," she says, and I'm sure she knows that CF is Stefano.

"What about the place she met CF. She called it CCH?" I ask.

The same recognition widens her eyes, but she shakes her head. Before I can press her on that point, a truck door slams outside.

"Shit, Lee's back already." Tina stashes the empty bottle behind a small table. "Come help me dump these drawers into the trash bags. I was supposed to be done by now."

I hold the bag while she empties one drawer, and the back door flies open.

"Goddamn it, Tina," says a short but wide-shouldered man with a long face and intense, bulging eyes. He's wearing a ratty Narragansett Beer T-shirt, even though it may snow tonight. His jeans are tight and paint spattered. "Who the hell are you?"

Tina shrinks at his words, batting her goopy eyelashes. "She's working with that black reporter to find out who killed my Belina."

He snickers. "Good luck with that."

"What do you mean?" I ask.

"I been Tina's boyfriend off and on for a whole year, and I hardly met that stuck-up girl," he says. "She came to Tina's birthday for about five minutes. A real bitch move."

"She was my daughter," Tina says softly but with some heat. "I won't have you talking trash—"

Lee steps toward Tina and me. "I ain't saying nothing worse than you did. Now she got herself killed she's Saint Belina."

Tina shows no response to the accusation. "How'd she get herself killed?" I ask.

"Meeting some guy in a cemetery?" He shakes his head, scoffing as if I've just fallen off the proverbial turnip truck. "Asking for it."

"You sonofabitch," Tina says in a slur of words, smashing her coffee cup into the ground. "If you got such a problem with her, don't spend her goddamn money."

Rage flares the veins of his neck like wires being pulled by the fists clenched at his side. "Don't you test me, Tina. I'm in no mood."

I take Tina's arm. "Belina left you money?"

"About a hundred grand," Lee says. "We deserve every penny."

The tempers are good. I see my angle. "You paying estate taxes on it?" I ask.

"It's not like that," Lee says.

"Where did the money come from?" I ask. "The truth."

"Give me a cigarette, Lee," Tina says. "We're not getting the deposit to this dump back anyway."

She lights two and steps around the broken mug in her gold heels. She hands the second one to Lee and remains next to him.

"It was a gift from an admirer," she says.

"That big fish," I guess.

"You don't want to mess with this guy," Tina says on an exhale.

"You don't want to mess with a federal audit," I say. "If you don't pay estate taxes. Probably forty percent between Uncle Sam and Rhode Island. You haven't spent it all?"

"He dumped it right in my account," she says. "Belina worked for him. It was some kinda policy he had."

"We went through enough with that girl." Lee points the cigarette at me, and ash falls on the floor. "This government ain't seeing a lick. Say what you want and get out."

"What was the relationship between Stefano and Belina?" I ask Tina.

"Her business," she says.

"You should leave him out of it," Lee says. "He did right by her as far as I'm concerned. Most men would have tapped it and run."

"Cool it, Lee," Tina snaps.

"What do you mean?" I say to him.

He looks Tina over, as if wanting to see the hurt he's about to inflict. "Belina stalked Stefano for a while."

"You got no right," Tina says.

Lee continues his antagonizing stare. "There was a restraining order."

How did you miss that?

I didn't think to look at Belina's record. "When?" I say.

"Right before she took that job at his boatyard," Lee says. "Guess they made up."

Tina heads over to the metal sink, ashing into it. "Few years ago."

"Why did he give you this money?" I ask. "Their relationship?"

"He's married," Lee says. "Doubt divorce would be cheap if it got out."

"You don't know shit," Tina says, swallowing thickly, her too-tight face giving way to wrinkles down her neck. "Stefano sent a condolence note that said he transferred money and hoped it helped. He's a good man."

Lee starts to laugh. "You gotta crush on him, Tina. Think he'd want the mom after he had the daughter."

"What the fuck do you know?" Tina screams.

Lee takes a step toward her, and she backs up nearer to me. "I know that having that money means a lot more to us than having her around."

Tina pivots away from him and finds my eyes. There's a lot of shame beneath the anger, and I head over to a dirty window to give her some space. My car is still running, and I see Gillian's shape in the passenger window. After another few seconds of quiet, I approach Tina. "Did you save any of your daughter's things?" I ask softly.

Tina sniffs, and there are tears in the corners of her eyes. It could be the smoke, but there are circles too. Grief lines around her eyes and mouth made prominent in her thick makeup.

"Anything left in her room?" I ask.

Lee steps close to me. "Couple boxes," he says. "We're not bringing her stuff with us. No point. Want me to take you back there?"

"I'll do it," Tina says, shoving him back.

Lee nods toward a closed door. "Be quick about it."

It's easy to be quick about it because there are only two plastic tubs. No jewelry box with "Once Upon a Dream" playing as the blonde ballerina twirls. No posters of boy bands or celeb crushes. No trophies or medals or artwork or science projects.

It's mostly books, different than my collection growing up. I read classics and literary fiction, anything that would make me East Coast smarter and set me apart from my classmates.

What good that did.

You're still just stupid trash.

I flip the first lid and see some clothes and cheap necklaces but mostly books and brochures, a mix of local information—from guidebooks to hotels and restaurants—then accounting books, and a few romance novels. The second tub is a lot of magical realism, authors like Jorge Luis Borges, Isabel Allende, and Toni Morrison.

I grab *One Hundred Years of Solitude* because I've never read it but always meant to, and it looks well worn. There're scribbles and underlined passages.

After putting the book in my bag, I begin to flip through other volumes. There are a few more with inscriptions, and I take photos of them on my phone. The handwriting looks the same, and I start to see the chart I'll make from this data when I'm home. My guess is they're gifts from Stefano, but I'll use the contract from Alec's office to compare the handwriting.

There are a few folders at the bottom with pay stubs and tax information. I see two different bank accounts listed and stuff the papers in the book I plan to take.

"Find anything?" Tina asks from the doorway. She's got her coffee mug again, which explains why they left me alone for so long.

"Not much," I say. "Did the police take anything?"

"Naw," she says. "I didn't even tell them about these boxes. Think they're better than me 'cause they got a badge. Fuck the police."

Tina digs into the first box to find a glittery top. "I'm taking this one. Bought it for her one Christmas with the last twenty bucks I had." She runs a shiny red nail along the cheap-looking fabric and pulls out a faded tag. "She never wanted to be like me. Don't know how a daughter can hate a mother like that."

I do know, but I just put the books back on top of the loose papers. "What did her room look like as a girl?"

Tina lights another cigarette. "About like this. Never had much clutter or care."

It sounds a lot like my room growing up. Perhaps she also never considered this her home, just a way station until she was able to get out.

But did you really leave it behind?

Tina's face softens, and her lips purse as if she's remembered something. She steps toward the largest box and digs around. "She had this one since she was a girl." She hands me the thin volume. "It meant a lot to her."

"Portuguese folktales," I say, reading the cover. The title font is in thick scroll script over a turbulent ocean, a single boat trying to survive the waters. "Mind if I borrow it?"

Tina tosses her head as if indifferent, as if I'm not asking for something her dead daughter loved. She holds tight to the sparkle sweater. "Like Lee said," she says, blinking her clumpy, spider-leg lashes to hide the tears, her voice thick. "Better to leave it here."

If I had more time, I'd pick a few more things to remember Belina by. Learn about her by sorting through what little is left. But Miguel will be waiting, and finding her murderer seems like a much better tribute.

Chapter 20

I watch Gillian push Ester in the stroller after she made an excuse to find a cup of coffee while I use the car pump. I send Derek a photo of Belina's tax and bank account information. The relief is sharp when he responds immediately, alive to hack another day.

It'd be better if you were both dead.

From the rearview mirror, I see Gillian and Ester go into a cozy tea shop. I move forward, mentally going over my next set of objectives as I put the pumped milk away. I'm a half hour early to meet Miguel Rossa at the mostly empty boatyard in Newport. I get out of the car and head toward the edge of the parking lot. The sun shimmers on the water like fish scales, and I shade my gaze until I find Miguel in front of a large fishing boat, yelling into his phone.

"It's another thirty grand?" He glares up at the pale-blue sky. "I'll have to talk to my father. He's not going to like it. Hello? Hello?"

He curses a few times at the phone, then jams it into his pocket. Miguel circles the boat, staring down the vessel as if it had just hung up on him.

I keep myself from falling into an old trap, watching secretly, and instead step onto the wooden dock. My boots echo, jeans tucked into them. I snap up the collar of my green maternity coat, my best coat, as I lower my head into the wind.

You'll never pull this off.

Miguel is still muttering to himself as I walk up. "Boat giving you problems?" I ask, guessing the actual problem is Ricky and the boat he sold Miguel.

His slouched posture rights, and he turns with a bright smile. "Early bird," he says, reaching a black-gloved hand my way. "Let's not worry about it. Life lesson on being careful who you trust." We shake hands quickly, and he gestures farther down the dock. "The boat worth seeing is this way."

There aren't many boats left, the season long past. Most are either covered in plastic and dry-docked or, in the case of the yachts worth millions, sailed toward warmer waters. All that remain are a few fishing boats, and we're not talking New England charmers with engines guided by hand. These are year-round fishing boats, the souped-up 4x4 extended cabs of the sea. The one Miguel is guiding me toward is in the thirty-six-footer range, all nose, shining white like the ass of an angel, covered with steel rails and three stacked platforms over the main cabin with a large satellite on top. All Tony Soprano versus Moby Dick.

I can tell he's about to give me the hard sell: invest in a portion of this boat and get a percentage of the fishing net profits.

"Here she is," he says. "For a fifty-one percent stake, you can rename her."

It's an expensive boat, something to show off to investors. I smirk at the blue letters painted on the side. "*Flounder Pounder* will be tough to top."

He laughs, and I see a bit of tension relax his shoulders beneath his navy cashmere coat. "The season starts in April."

"You want a dozen boats and captains," I say, quoting the brochure. "Doesn't that require each boat to have a fishing license for the quantity of fish they catch each day? Are there licenses available right now?" I ask, knowing the answer is no.

The fishing boat licenses are notoriously difficult to acquire. Alec got a few of his through Uncle Cal's connections and then later, based on the contract I found, more from Stefano. Even with the increases in profits from those licenses, Alec still often made two and three times what he should.

"There will be more licenses on the market soon enough," Miguel says too quickly. "I have it on good authority. At least a dozen."

He quotes the exact number that Alec and Ricky manage for Stefano, according to the grant paperwork Uncle Cal gave me. "You think you can get them all?" I ask.

"I need twelve this year," he says. "We prove our model and show that a Rossa business can succeed in this industry. Then we'll expand even more. Now back to you, my early investor, called angel investors"—he pauses to wink—"you will have the first pick of the highest-profit boats and most senior captains."

"If I'm going to invest," I say, not returning his grin, "I need more details. To understand if you're market ready."

"Of course," Miguel says. "Let's get out of the wind. I'll show you the nice accommodations below deck."

That's where the good girls go.

Down.

Down.

Down.

Everyone will hear.

No one will stop him.

"I can't," I say, my heart spiking as my breath crystalizes into a heavy lump at the center of my chest. The boat around me is fading, and I see a small bed and dark-paneled walls and smell candy-sweet warm breath over me.

I feel Miguel take my elbow, firm and steady, bringing me back. I breathe deep, the cold air loosening the weight on my chest. Bringing me back to this deck, my shoes, my coat. I am here. I am here with a purpose.

"Small spaces . . . I can't breathe there . . ."

"Of course. You're claustrophobic?" he says with sympathetic bravado.

I nod quickly, relieved he's supplied the lie because he'll never get the truth. "Above deck is fine," I whisper. "As long as I can see the sky."

He helps me aboard, lingering on my elbow as we walk the deck. "She goes twenty-eight knots," he says finally, "which is—"

"Thirty-two point two miles per hour," I finish.

He smiles as if it's a parlor trick. As if I haven't spent hours researching boats, the New England and Rhode Island fishing industries, and related marketplaces. I want to understand this business. Determine where Alec went wrong. And who helped get him there. "I need dollar amounts," I say.

He sighs, and some of the charm fades. "With each license, we can earn five hundred dollars per day after expenses," he says. "You multiply that by seven days a week, fifty-two weeks per year, and you've got . . ." He pauses.

"It's one hundred eighty-two thousand dollars per boat per year," I say. "Almost two point two million your first year." I don't subtract the estimated 40 to 60 percent that new fishing ventures usually lose their first year.

"There's weather and employee training and turnover, but yeah." He pauses to grin. "It's a good start."

"Are there other ways to make money?" I say with a half grin. "Not on the books?"

Miguel looks me up and down. "We're not doing anything like that," he says. "My father built his business fairly. It's hard enough to do this within the law. Being outside of it creates more problems than benefits."

"Good," I say, impressed. "I wanted to check, since our main competitor has a reputation for working outside those laws."

A place you know well.

He shrugs, another person not wanting to even say Stefano's name.

"Do you want to see what our captains will use?" Miguel opens two large benches filled with new-looking fishing gear. There are already fishing rods in the four holders on each corner of the boat. "This is my favorite," he says. He pulls out a lure that's as large as a crib mobile, but instead of planets or butterflies or fuzzy sheep, there are three layers of octopus-like tentacles, silver and reflective, with hooks on each end. It spins in the wind, catching the sunlight as he hooks it on to the closest pole. "This is better than chum," he says. "Man's outsmarted nature."

"Really?" I say. "And you can see the schools of fish as they pass by," I say, referencing what I read. "Chartplotters, GPS, color sounder, and forty-eight-mile digital HD color radar?"

He shrugs again, but I can tell he's impressed.

"You didn't outsmart," I say playfully. "You're cheating."

He waggles his finger, then returns to the bench. He pulls out more large contraptions, one with balls on the ends to feed the electronic sensors of the boat. Finally, the show-and-tell is done.

"Tell me about your initial investment," I say. "Your father put up all the capital so far?"

"He and a few friends," Miguel says. "I'll pay them back within five years. None of that will come from your profits."

"He'll be an investor with me?" I say. "I looked into him. He's made quite a name with his security company."

"Monitors most of the East Side, downtown Providence, Newport, and Jamestown," Miguel says.

"Why not work for him?"

"I did for ten years, but building a successful fishing business is in our blood. It's not just the Portuguese and Italians who have the connection to the sea. My father traces our family line back to Spanish explorers." He puts his hands on his hips, staring out at the ocean.

I like this part of the pitch, the history and pageantry. It's easy to picture his ancestors as explorers at the behest of Queen Isabella, on the heels of Christopher Columbus. But as far as an actual business proposition, there's a very big issue.

"Where will you get the fishing licenses?" I ask.

"I'm working on it," he says, that grin again.

"My investment will be contingent on the full twelve licenses and captains being secured."

The conquistador pose falls. "My job is to worry about those details."

"It's not a detail," I say. "It's an essential fact."

"A very complicated matter."

He knows you're too stupid to understand.

He sees right through your game.

"Miguel, I'm looking for a partner. If we can't begin this relationship openly and honestly, then I see no reason to continue it." I nod curtly at him and stand.

"Wait," he says quickly. "You're right that as of now, there aren't enough commercial licenses to make our business profitable. But there are other factors."

"Such as?" I press.

"Between us . . . Ricky can help," Miguel begins. "Alec has always been the one who said no to this partnership and expanding. But Ricky brought me this opportunity. He may have screwed me on the boat, but Alec is no longer in a position to say no. They can't afford their licenses and won't be able to keep their group of captains together. Both will be on the market soon. We're first in line to get them."

I'm not surprised Ricky is already putting another deal together. Even if it's basically profiting from Belina's murder. "You're so sure Alec's going away for murder?"

"If you know him, I don't want to insult you," Miguel begins but then pauses as if needing to shift the topic. "Listen, I hear there's another large block of licenses coming onto the market. Not immediately but by next season. If we have one good year, we can make a play for those."

"How significant?"

"We'll be able to buy one of those," he says, pointing to a large yacht, in the million-dollar range.

Even the largest boat groups have only a few dozen licenses. A yacht like that would cost millions. There is only one person with that large a block: Stefano.

"This conversation has been very promising," I say, meaning it.

Miguel has a lot to gain with Alec's murder conviction. It's something I suspected and am glad to confirm. But more valuable, he's alerted me to a new issue: Stefano is in some serious trouble—legal, financial, personal, or all three.

Chapter 21

I'm relieved to find Gillian in the car with Ester, and as I get inside, I warm my fingers against the hot air blasting through the vents. Wiping my window with my sleeve, I watch Miguel hurry across the dock into the parking lot. The wheels of his black Mercedes squeak while a loud bass rattles the tinted windows. I rub my hands over my eyes, wondering if I've really found a new suspect.

You think pointing your fingers will amount to anything.

You've already failed.

You're just too stupid to see it.

"What was his deal?" Gillian asks from the back seat.

I tap my fingers on the steering wheel. She works for Uncle Cal, so of course I can't trust her. But at the same time, if she's worked for him this long, she's probably forgotten more than I'll ever know about Rhode Island. "Miguel wants to start a fishing business. Like Stefano Venantius. Know anything about him?"

She stares out the window. "Not somebody I socialize with."

"What do you think it'd take for Stefano to give up his commercial fishing licenses?" I ask. "Sell his business?"

"Divorce, jail, or body bag," she says matter of factly.

"Divorce?" I say.

"Wife gets half," she says. "Breaks things up, don't ya think?"

My phone rings, and I answer quickly when I see the name. "Ricky?"

"Devon Burges," Ricky says. "Can't stay away from a man with a shiny rod and reel?"

"How the hell do you know that?"

"Easy, tiger," he says. "If you step outside your car and look back at the docks you just left, you'll see me waving like an idiot."

I throw open my door and climb onto the doorframe to better see the water. Ricky is on the dock, wildly swooping both arms. He's beside a commercial fishing boat, a real one, mostly rusted steel with hefty nets hanging off the side. Less flashy than what Miguel was trying to convince me to invest in.

"I see you," I say into the phone.

"Come on over," he says. "I smell like fish, but I can make a Bloody Mary that'll curl your toes."

"A little early for a drink."

"Black sea bass sushi," he says. "Only touched the ocean and air before my cooler of ice."

Something about black sea bass pings from my research, but I'm too surprised that he's here to place it. "Were you following me?"

He laughs. "What an ego, Mrs. Burges. This is my dock. You'll find me here around this time every morning."

"Oh," I say, feeling stupid. Getting down from the car, I give Gillian a just-a-minute wave and shut the door. "I was about to drive around Newport," I say, leaning against the car.

"Looking for what?"

I hesitate because there's nothing about this guy that I trust. But I also don't have a lot of time. "Belina had a code in her journal. A place she'd go."

"What kind?"

"Initials," I say. "CCH."

"Too easy," he says. "Clarke Cooke House right across the parking lot on Bannister's Wharf."

You're too stupid to see what's right in front of you.

"I've got a friend and my daughter in the car," I say. "Why don't I meet you in the middle and say hi?"

"Yeah, sure," he says.

We put our phones away, still watching each other. I tell Gillian I'll be right back and head toward the dock entrance. I feel a flush spread up my chest as we walk toward each other. Something about Ricky reminds me of the aloof guys from high school. The type who'd sneak Skoal tobacco chew in the back of class and spit it on the floor when the teacher wasn't looking. The kind of restless boys whose attention I was constantly trying to get.

"Hi, Mrs. Burges," he says with a shit-eating grin. He's in dark-tan fishing overalls and waders. "Fancy seeing you here."

"You do smell like fish." I wrinkle my nose at the smell, not actually disliking the mix of plastic lures and blood and sweat and cold ocean air.

"Captains are giving me trouble," he says. "They like Alec better, so if we're going to make ends meet, I'm back to fishing my limit," he says, a faint blush. "It'll be tough to keep the business going with Alec away."

"I'm sorry," I say.

That tugs at something much deeper than high school crushes. My brother also has odd jobs in addition to hacking, putting cash together week by week to afford his drugs and cat food.

"Forgetaboutit," he says with too much of an accent. "Alec, on the other hand, may not."

"I'm working on it," I say.

"What's with the CCH code?" he asks. "Are there others I can help with?" He puts his hands in his pockets.

"Not really," I lie. I want to confide in Ricky, but I don't fully understand his motives and role in Belina's life and death. Plus, he lied to me about Stefano. Or at least didn't admit they were working together. That most of their business was because of his fishing licenses. I want to hear the truth. "Who paid you and Alec?"

Ricky runs his fingers through his dark wavy hair, scratching at the scalp as if trying to remove leftover sea salt. "Couple streams of income. There one particularly on your mind?"

I shiver, glance toward his boat. "Venantius Ventures?"

Ricky doesn't respond as the wind kicks up, pulling at my curly hair, causing my eyes to water.

He sees you're too stupid for this work.

You're wasting his time.

He's laughing at you.

He's using you.

Like everyone.

I start to explain that I've read Alec's financial documents, traced the offshore accounts, wanting to prove myself when no one has doubted me. But instead, I focus and get to the point. "He's your only source of income."

"Underestimating pretty women always bites me in the ass," he says. "Yeah, I work for him." Pauses to sniff and clear his throat.

"What about Belina? Did she know Stefano?"

"Biblically know him?" Ricky asks.

"However."

"Yeah, she did, once upon a time, at least." He pulls at the strap on his overalls. "Stefano owns most of the fishing industry around here. That means I'm not in a position to screw with either of them. You know what I mean?"

It is heavy-handed, but I leave it because he seems to be opening up. "Can you share information? I won't draw you into this . . . unless you're involved."

It is a weak reverse psychology play, but Ricky lets me have it. "I'm happy to help you, Devon, but Alec is who really matters. Personally and to our business."

"I met Belina's mother this morning."

Ricky makes a clicking noise from the side of his mouth. "She's a mess, huh?"

I knew women like Tina growing up. Working every angle to get an inch, usually a Sisyphean pursuit, but sometimes it meant rent was paid. School clothes bought. Doing what had to be done no matter how they were judged. My respect for them was tempered by a fear I could become one. "Stefano paid Tina one hundred grand."

Ricky's mouth falls open; he breathes deeply, the swoosh of it speeding up. "Why?" he says sharply.

"She said it was a kind of insurance policy."

"That bastard never does something for nothing unless it's a stab in the back." He stares out toward the boats, his the junkiest, the rust and faded number on the side. "I'm sure Tina's a pig in shit about it."

I don't mention Tina's tears or the look on her face as she stood in Belina's bedroom. "What's worth that kind of money to Stefano?" I ask.

"Tina is a hustler," Ricky says. "I wouldn't put it past her or Lee to blackmail Stefano."

"You know Lee too?"

"Sure," Ricky says. "He's useful in lowlife circles. I've employed him from time to time."

"How lowlife?" I ask.

"Murder kind, you mean?" Ricky licks the corner of his mouth. "You really see the worst in people."

"I met Lee," I say. "Not much imagination required."

"I can ask around, see if Lee's been bragging about the money. Or knew about his payday before Belina was murdered." Ricky smiles as if proud of himself. "I'm kinda getting into this."

"Sherlock on a ship," I say flatly.

"No ship, Sherlock?"

We both laugh a little more than required. "Did you sell Miguel a bad boat?" I ask, more curious than judgmental.

"I told him why the price was so good. If he didn't look into what it'd take to fix it up, I'm hardly gonna feel bad." Ricky crosses his arms, taking a step closer to me. His eyes are bright as if he's really sharing something that matters to him. Something I'll understand. "People like Miguel," he begins softly. "People like Alec, for that matter. They don't understand what it means to work for something you want. They're treated special by their parents and East Side schools and Ivy League colleges. They expect the world to do the same. Over and over they expect it. And when the world isn't handed to them, it's a shock."

He doesn't sound mad. In fact, I feel as if he's giving me a tip on a horse race. "You and Belina understood that?"

"Sure," he says. "She was one of those wisteria women."

It takes me a minute to connect what he means to the blooming vine. "She was a beautiful climber."

"Bingo," he says. "Two years younger than me in high school. Didn't know her, but I saw her."

I then focus back on Ricky's relationships. "How did this business with Alec begin?"

"I met Alec at a polo event. We hit it off. He had the idea."

"From Belina?" I ask.

He frowns. "I'm not sure. Kinda weird to take business advice from the nanny."

"What about working with a rival?" I say. "Miguel seems to think you've all but signed a contract. Alec wouldn't like that."

He whistles and shakes his head. "You really get people to talk, huh?"

"Pressure points," I say, enjoying his praise a little too much. I hear a baby crying, and I freeze. "I need to check on my daughter."

"I'll walk you," he says, almost gallant covered in fish guts.

She's dying in that car.

You left her with a stranger, and it will all be your fault.

I don't wait for him as I hurry across the parking lot. Reaching the passenger side of the car, I see Ester's not crying but asleep in her seat.

She's not breathing.

Gillian sees me and smiles, then returns to her newspaper. I let myself feel that deep relief that everything is okay. I head back toward Ricky, who is watching me. "Sorry," I say.

"I don't know why people have kids," he mutters.

"Why do people do anything?" I say, my gaze snapping back toward the car. "I wanted to have a real family."

He raises his eyebrows, his tan forehead crinkling. "Not a good home life?"

You're so obvious.

Everyone sees the stains.

"That's an understatement," I say, pulling my coat tighter. "We can have a pity party contest next time."

Ricky flashes a half grin, and my brother's smile appears in my mind.

"Bad shit happens all the time. The end of the story is what matters," he says, taking a step backward. "No matter how bad we had it, we're not in jail."

"Not yet," I say to his cocky grin before he turns toward his truck. He hauls his cooler over to his pickup and drives away with a wave.

"Feel like an early lunch?" I ask Gillian when I get in the car. I stare across the parking lot at Clarke Cooke House, ready to uncover the Newport Belina and see if that version could have gotten her killed.

Chapter 22

Clarke Cooke House is classic New England charming, two stories of white clapboard and large windows with evergreen shutters decorated with red Christmas bows. A deck sits off the back, covered by plastic flapping in the cold ocean wind. Like everything in Newport, CCH is built for summer, so during quiet winter months, they batten down and pray for locals. Christmas shoppers are a respite, but even today, the cobblestone streets leading down the wharf's narrow, pedestrian-only road are mostly empty.

Gillian remains overseer of Ester, keeping her covered with a breathable blanket in the stroller we wheel into the restaurant's quiet waiting area.

I put my and Gillian's coats on the rack next to where the pretty hostess is stationed. I push the stroller to a table in the corner of the main dining room.

"I'll join in a bit," I say to Gillian.

The hostess looks about a day over eighteen, so I don't bother showing her the picture of Belina. Instead, I head toward the back. In a separate room, the main bar is a long L shape near a dozen tables, all with a view of the water and a few inexpensive boats people didn't bother to dry-dock for the winter.

There's a middle-aged couple chatting at the far end of the bar, near the large glass window with the best view of the docks. I sit at the opposite end, hearing the bartender humming from the back before I see him.

He's a handsome guy with neatly combed gray hair. His bright-green eyes assess me quickly before shifting attention to the other customers. He drops their check and heads back to me. "Sorry for the wait," he says, returning his gaze my way. "Keg kicked. What can I get you?"

"Hot toddy would be great."

"Brandy or bourbon?"

"Wild Turkey is fine," I say, letting my white trash show.

He nods, dropping a napkin in front of me. It has the CCH logo, which features a mermaid with her tail split and curling, like an anchor. "What's her story?" I ask as he fills a glass mug with a shot of whiskey and then pours hot water.

"That's our girl, Melusina," he says and sets my drink down. "We had her before Starbucks."

I realize he's right; the corporate coffee chain does sport a green version of her on its logo. "Why her?" I ask.

He glances down at the couple at the end of the bar, both still chatting and beers mostly full. "She's beautiful but cursed with a dual nature. It's the waist down that gets her into trouble." He pauses to shake his head, a faint blush on his cheeks. "I don't mean it like that. She turns into this serpent when she bathes. When men discover she's not what they thought, she shifts into a dragon and burns them to death. She wins, in the end. But is always alone."

"Sounds a bit sexist," I say.

"Yeah, most old stories are," he says. "I gotta check in the back for some lemons. Sit tight."

I sip the drink with just honey, whiskey, and hot water, not minding the strong taste. The bartender returns, squeezes a lemon in my drink. The couple at the end, who now have their Newport map out, leave some cash and exit quickly. The bartender picks up the money and grumbles as he puts it into the drawer.

"Off-season tourists not the best tippers?" I say.

He laughs and drops some change into his pocket. "I didn't say it."

"I remember. I worked as a server in Providence for almost ten years," I lie. He has a Rhode Island accent, and because of it, there's a 99 percent chance that he's lived and worked only in Newport.

He nods as if we have a bond. "I've been in Newport and Jamestown off and on for about thirty years," he says. "Pete."

"Devon," I say.

You use everyone.

"This state is such a funny place," he says. "I probably talk to more people from Spain than Providence."

"People won't drive across town for the best Italian on the East Coast," I say with a Rhode Islander's authority. "Newport might as well be the dark side of the moon."

He waggles a finger at me. "You holiday shopping? Couple nice stores havin' some sales."

"Nope," I say. "A friend of mine used to come here. I was wondering if you'd recognize her."

I pull out my phone and show him a picture of Belina from her Instagram account.

He looks at me as if I'm telling a joke. "That's the girl who was murdered."

"You remember her?" I ask and take a sip, trying to seem casual.

He picks up a glass from the washing area under the bar as if it were screaming for his attention. After beginning to dry it with a towel, he finally sets it down. "You a cop?"

"She was a friend of mine," I say. "They arrested the wrong person. I'm trying to figure out who really killed her."

Pete whistles. "I've heard a lot behind this bar, but nothing like that."

"Ever heard of someone taking a restraining order out against her?" I ask.

Pete's eyes widen, then focus, and I relax at his resistance. This detour isn't a waste of time.

"They've got the wrong guy for her murder," I continue. "He's sitting in jail right now. His wife and kid at home because the police won't dig around on . . . the guy who would have taken out that restraining order. Someone she met here often."

"Look, I still see . . . *him* a lot. I don't want word to get around. For a lot of reasons."

I'm not surprised Pete doesn't want to say Stefano's name. "The restraining order. What do you know about it?"

Pete's gaze makes a full circle of the room. It's just us, but he pauses and leans close. "About three years ago . . . this guy . . . he thought she was around too much. Popping up at his job after she didn't work there. She'd drive by his house. Run into his wife and daughter when they were out shopping. He threatened to file a restraining order. Or at least that's what he told me one night when I asked where she'd been lately. He was pretty drunk but told me and the manager to keep her out if she showed up."

I know from Belina's journal that she did meet Stefano, or CF, as of two weeks before her murder. "But she did come back. She was here with him right before, actually."

"Yeah, guess he got over it." Pete sighs, and I feel a little guilty, but it's not going to stop me.

"Were they sleeping together?" I ask. "Was he worried about his marriage? Maybe his wife knew?"

"I really don't know. For a while, he seemed uncomfortable around me. Happens sometimes with regulars who drink too much one night. They stay away, embarrassed. I didn't think much of it."

"When they came back after, did their relationship seem different?"

He shrugs. "He'd get his private table with her. I didn't listen."

"You watch people all day and night," I say. "You don't remember any details?"

He leans closer. "I don't want what I say spread around and ending up on TV."

So he is following it closely. "Are you one of those bartenders who thinks if he kisses enough ass, some rich guy will come through on drunken promises to take you up the ladder with them?"

"It's not like that with him," he says.

"Then what do you remember about her? About them?"

"She seemed into him," he says softly. "Hung on every word. Always dressed up. Trying hard, I guess you could say. She didn't drink much but always kept on me to refill his glass full. She wanted him to have fun. Or keep having fun, I guess. They always left together."

"Does he have a lot of girlfriends?"

"Not anymore," Pete says. "He used to really chase ladies way back when. Brought a few here. But Belina was his regular for a long time."

I try to picture Belina here, dressed up and flirting, trying to keep this married man's attention as he's watching over his shoulder for his wife.

Just another whore.

She doesn't deserve justice.

Neither of you do.

"When's the last time he was here?" I ask.

His shoulders relax as if he knows we're almost done. "Every Wednesday. Mass in the morning, buck a shuck for lunch after."

"Thanks, Pete." I pull out my wallet and pay. "I have a weird question." Ricky's sushi offer still niggles in my mind. "Do you have black sea bass on the menu?"

He shakes his head. "No way. Damn government regulations keep fishermen from getting it this time of year. We can't until the spring. Throw you in jail for it, if you can believe it."

"Why would someone fish it if they can't sell it?"

"Black market pays triple, maybe more." Pete leans close. "You're looking in the right direction for that too."

Chapter 23

The car ride back from Newport is quiet except for Gillian's soft singing, which seems to calm Ester. It's a welcome distraction from my guilt about having my baby in the car most of the day. When we turn off the highway onto North Main Street, Gillian stops singing, but the car isn't silent.

What kind of mother coops her baby up?

Doesn't do tummy time?

She'll never sit up or pull up or crawl or walk.

You were never meant to be a mother.

"What songs are those?" I ask, desperate for distraction. I like the melancholy lyrics, wife leaving a candle in the window for her sailor husband or desperate crew crashing their ship into rocks.

"Sea shanty songs," she says. "My grandpa worked the docks, and they'd sing them while havin' a pint at home. They go back further. Them old songs were a way the masters kept the rhythm of work goin' on a ship. Anything for the bottom line."

We grin at each other in the rearview mirror before I focus back on the road. "Did Jack tell you I'm trying to find out who killed my friend? And help another friend arrested for it?"

"Mm-hmm," she says as she's adjusting Ester's blanket. "Nothing much surprises me anymore."

"Looks like my friend was seeing Stefano." I glance back for a reaction, but she doesn't give one. "I was thinking about what you said, about how expensive divorce would be."

"Lots of things are expensive," she says. "Not always about money. At least not deep down."

Her comment sits heavy on my chest, deflating the progress I've made. When there's money involved—possibly the main motivator for framing Alec—both Miguel and Ricky could be suspects. It's more digging, more guessing, more lies. Before Newport, I was so sure it was Stefano.

You shouldn't be sure of anything.

I drop Gillian off at her condo in Wayland Square only a mile or so from our house. I offer to pay for her time, but she waves me off as she collects her purse and zips her coat.

"Naw, I'm all set. Not every Monday lunch I get a lobstah roll that fancy," she says with a chuckle. "Puttin' celery peels on top." She pauses at the door handle. "About your friend. People are a mystery, even to themselves. Usually, in the worst ways. Just be ready for that, ya know."

I thank her again and wait as she hurries toward the entry door. It started lightly snowing when we left Newport, and it's picking up.

You wasted her time.

You're making everything worse.

I turn the wipers up a notch more than they need to be and start toward home. Ester begins to cry, as if she can read my thoughts, hear the voice, and she agrees.

I try to hum a sea shanty song, and it's lame, doesn't rhyme, and she keeps crying.

She hates the sound of your voice.

She wishes she was still with Gillian.

I count to one hundred, thinking of all the time I've spent with Ester. Refuting the voice's point. I'm calm by fifty, and Ester has fallen asleep by one hundred.

Back home, I carry her in the infant car seat, which is relatively light. The house is still. Jack texted he'd likely be late tonight. Again.

I leave Ester sleeping in the living room after checking to be sure she's comfortable. I hear her soft snore, a light and puttering version of Jack's.

In my office, I put on my hands-free pump and start to work.

I write *Alec* and *Stefano* on my whiteboard and draw a long line in between them. I dial Phillip, putting in my Bluetooth, feeling more like myself despite the pumping.

"Hey," Phillip says. "How'd it go?"

"We're getting there." I can hear the distinct rumble of the train. "Where you headed?"

"Back home," he says. "But the *TODAY Show* producer wants to work on a Stefano exposé ASAP. We'll wait for evidence before airing, of course."

"Sure," I say, but my gut sinks. "We need to be careful. It's a 'You come at the king, you best not miss' situation."

"Is that from *The Wire*?" Phillip says with a laugh. "Are you Omar or McNulty?"

"All right," I say. "Every person I spoke to today, Tina; her boyfriend, Lee; Miguel; Ricky; and the bartender at Clarke Cooke House—"

"Ah, that's CCH," Phillip interrupts. "How'd you figure it out?"

"Ricky," I say. "He was at the dock this morning too. My point is everyone is afraid of Stefano."

"That's good for us," Phillip says. "What'd you think of Miguel?"

"He has a lot to gain with Alec in jail," I say. "He hinted that Stefano might be in some kind of trouble."

"Really?"

"The kind that would put his fishing licenses—that's tens of millions of dollars—up for grabs."

"Wow," Phillip says with the enthusiasm he used to share with me when we were digging into a Rhode Island politician. He's in a good mood and rightly so. The *TODAY Show* interview went great. His Twitter feed was blowing up last I checked. I'm sure his inbox is full of media requests.

"Stefano paid Tina one hundred thousand dollars after Belina was murdered," I say. "He said it was an insurance policy, but not the kind you pay taxes on."

Phillip whistles into the phone. "What's worth that kind of money?"

I refrain from saying that it's the hundred-thousand-dollar question. "I don't know."

There's a rustle of fabric, like Phillip's on the move. A door slams, and a metal lock clicks. He's just locked himself in the train bathroom. "Okay, let's talk it through," he says. "Belina is cooking the books for Stefano. He moves her over to Alec's business so he can start washing money there. She's getting paid as the nanny, doing that work, and then also watching Alec for Stefano. Then there's the relationship complications. Belina was likely having an affair with Stefano. Maybe with Alec."

"I don't—"

"Fine," he says. "Maybe Stefano is unhappy with her work. She doesn't have great control over Alec, who spends that big chunk of money instead of washing it. Belina hides it from Stefano. He kills Belina and frames Alec."

"Sure," I say. "But we're pretty far from proving any of that. Good TV can also make a good libel lawsuit."

"But they're cleaning money connected to Stefano. The crimes must be linked." Phillip hasn't asked how I found out about the laundered money. Likely he knows it's Uncle Cal and hacking. But like last time, he's enjoying success too much to ask.

"The motive is weak," I say, staring at my board. "Would Stefano kill Belina because she was threatening him? Maybe about the affair, but I'd say business is what matters." I think of Uncle Cal, how "legacy" means so much to people of a certain age and personality.

"Alec was in the middle," Phillip says. "Easy enough to frame. What about Miguel?"

"Miguel needs the licenses Alec and Ricky managed," I say. "Then he's got his eyes on Stefano."

"Ambitious," Phillip says. "But that's hardly a crime."

"Stefano doesn't strike me as a person to give those up without a nasty fight."

"Can we get more information from Miguel?" Phillip asks.

"We better," I say. "His father's security company monitors most of the East Side. If there's footage of Alec to create a real alibi, he's our only chance."

"Damn," Phillip mutters. "Amtrak stopped." An announcer comes on, saying they're clearing the track as fast as they can. "Well, I'm not going anywhere, so let's keep going. What happened with Ricky?"

"He's looking into Tina's boyfriend, Lee," I say. "If Lee knew there'd be a payday with Belina's death, that's motive."

"And the bartender?"

I want to keep the stalking private, but that's what the old me did. "Belina was stalking Stefano for a while. Lee said it, and the bartender confirmed it. But they made up, and she took the job with Alec and Misha."

"What can I post on TheHaleReport.com now?" he asks.

"Let's humanize Belina a bit more. I'll email you some details from Tina. Notes from books she had growing up. I'm sure you'll know what to do."

"That's good," he says. "Oh, I forgot. The producer said a PR person from the Providence Police Department will be on tomorrow."

They're feeling the pressure. "I'm sure it'll be a female, probably blonde and white."

"Without a doubt," he says. "I'll push on Belina's business ties and background with Stefano."

"Phillip, you can't mention him by name."

"I won't, but I'll allude. So *they* know *we* know."

You're doing it all wrong again.

You're going to ruin Phillip's reputation again.

Cynthia will hate you again.

This time, no one will forgive you.

"Hey, Devon," Phillip says, his voice sounding hesitant. "Alec's bail hearing is tomorrow."

I hear the implication. "We need him to post," I say for him. "They don't have enough for a bond in their bank account. Maybe Misha's parents will help?"

We're silent, aware that we're getting to the heart of this conversation.

"What will it take for Alec to flip on Stefano?" Phillip asks finally.

"I don't know," I say quietly, thinking that that's the real one-hundred-thousand-dollar question. "We need Alec to explain the payoffs and why they stopped. Money laundering may just be the beginning."

"But if Stefano killed Belina," Phillip says, "Alec has to cooperate, right? He loved her."

It is what Phillip needs for his *TODAY Show* producer, but I am not so sure it is true.

I get the sinking feeling in my stomach that I'm guessing instead of verifying when I hear Ester crying. I glance at the time and realize I should have already given her an evening bottle. I want to feed her before Jack gets home and I leave again.

"Hope your train starts moving," I say. "I'll say hi to Cynthia for you. I need her to charm some alibi information out of the Hope Street bartenders."

I feed Ester upstairs, and as I get her settled on her mat, I hear Jack downstairs. He stomps the snow off his boots and soon after finds us upstairs in the nursery. I pick up Ester, cuddling her against my chest, and follow him to the bedroom so he can change out of his work clothes.

He wishes you were already gone.

Wishes you'd never come back.

"You're going to see Cynthia?" he asks, referencing the text I sent earlier.

"I'm working on Alec's alibi," I say. "If he was getting drunk on Hope Street, someone saw him."

"Cynthia knows everyone," he says.

I sense the day is still heavy on his mind. "How was work?"

"Phillip's interview didn't help," he says. He exchanges his tie and collared shirt for his Georgetown Law hoodie.

I'm torn: I want to apologize because his day was difficult, but I want him to tell me he's proud I made it that way. "We're not slowing down."

"I know," he says, tired. "I want this to be over."

I place Ester in her bassinet. I stride around to the foot of the bed to pull him into me. He inhales before I kiss him deeply for the first time since Ester. I'm greedy for the taste of him, restless to close a little of the distance. I picture what our evening could be, me curled next to him on the couch, discussing his meetings, sharing how good Ester was with Gillian today. We could order meatball subs from Sandwich Hut delivery and open a bottle of Sangiovese. We could be together, enjoy each other, connect.

I don't pull away from the kiss. He does.

"You better get going," he says softly. "Is anyone else meeting you there?"

"No," I lie.

Chapter 24

The evening crowd is gathered at Chip. A few families, but mostly people in their work clothes having a coffee and snack before heading off to dinner. This time of day frustrates Cynthia because she's leaving money on the table by not having a liquor license. A lot of money.

The person I'm meeting could make that issue go away.

I spot Cynthia toward the back, showing someone how the register works. She finishes her point and then strides my way.

Her gaze darts over the room, and she seems satisfied, though uneasy. "Your uncle has been sitting in his car for a half hour," she says, cutting me a look.

I wave at Uncle Cal through the glass door, but he doesn't get out of the car.

"Real quick," I begin. "Can you talk to anyone you know at Ivy Tavern who can confirm Alec's alibi? The police didn't get anything. My guess is their staff don't want it getting around that drunk patrons are ratted out to cops."

"Or maybe they don't care that much about some rich guy on the East Side?"

I nod, her reasoning sounding more likely. "Do you mind digging?"

"No problem," Cynthia says. She brushes a tangle of my hair behind my ear. "Are you sleeping?"

I start to lie but stop myself. "Not really."

She takes my hand, squeezes it, then holds our hands together. "Not everyone can be saved."

She'll tell Jack.

You're going to lose everything.

"I can't leave it alone," I say. "It's too close to things that matter."

She inhales, pulling me closer. "You see so much of yourself in people. Find connections that aren't . . . exactly there. I know it's from a good place, but . . . be careful."

I hug her quickly, not sure how to refute what she's said because it feels true. I see Uncle Cal getting out of the car and pull back. "Thank you."

He knocks snow off his shiny loafers on the side of his Mercedes. Buttoning his long double-breasted tan coat, he strides toward us.

Cynthia tips her chin at the manager across the room, who quickly straightens the counter case.

"It looks great," I assure her, but she doesn't react.

"The Council meets in one week," she says. "The financials don't work for my second location without their support."

She's never admitted that before, though it's something I suspected. "You're going to do this."

She touches my hand one more time, lightly, and I can still feel a tremor. It's as nervous as I've ever seen her. "I'll get him seated," she says. "Can you check in with the kitchen?"

I head over to the assistant manager, waving at a couple of people I recognize in the back of the kitchen. "Hey, Lila," I say. "Got a special order for you."

"Good to see ya, Devon." Lila crosses in front of a metal table with a lump of floury dough resting on it. She's a whiz at pastries, which is good, since she's got a sleeve of pie tattoos on both arms. "What d'they want?" she asks.

"Creamy cheeses, grass fed, and dark chocolate. He likes espresso too, with a drop of whole foam on top. Lemon peel on the side. Any herbal notes that would pair with a martini, basically."

Lila moves quickly, and I don't hover. Cynthia takes Uncle Cal's coat and escorts him to a seat in the corner but still in the window. There are empty tables around. The table she leads him to is marked with a **RESERVED** sign. She points out a few things on the menu, laughs at a joke, and then Lila hands me the board. The chocolates, cheeses, and espresso are served on a thin slice of oak cut in the shape of Rhode Island. It's beautifully done, exactly what he'd want, but I hesitate.

You're going to fail her again.

You're going to fail Uncle Cal and Jack and Ester.

All you've ever done is fail.

I take one step and then another. Uncle Cal raises his neat eyebrows as I approach. "Are you my food taster?" he asks.

Cynthia lets out another generous laugh and leaves us to our table. Uncle Cal flips over the menu.

"No booze," I say. "Real shame."

"Gotta know someone to get a license," he says without a whiff of sarcasm.

I don't take the bait and pull out the folder I put together. "Here's everything I've compiled on Alec's business that's tied to your Economic Development Council."

He takes the document and quickly scans it. "All related to Stefano?"

"He was only on the board one year, and yet he continued his ties to Alec's business. His offshore corporation is easy to link to the payments Alec has been receiving, washing through his fishing business and then back again."

Uncle Cal lets out a long breath. "I asked Stefano to resign as soon as it came to light."

"I almost ruined Phillip's career over the truth," I say, referencing the information Phillip received about the Council. The information I blackmailed him not to use.

Uncle Cal runs the lemon slice along the edge of his espresso cup. "The band is back together. And we've been able to continue the EDC's important work. That may extend all the way to this very shop."

I lean forward. "See that it does."

He smirks at me as a person who hasn't taken an order in thirty years would. "What else is on your mind?"

"Tell me about the fishing industry," I say. "What do you know of the Rossa family?"

"An immigrant builds a security empire from the ground up to become a wealthy businessman and community leader. An American success story."

"And his son, Miguel?"

He scoops some savory herb jam onto a cracker with a soft brie. "You're acquainted?" he asks before putting the whole bit in his mouth.

"He thinks I'm an investor in his new business. Miguel wants to build a business that rivals Venantius Ventures."

Uncle Cal wipes his mouth before answering. "There are a limited number of fishing licenses. I don't see any more coming onto the market."

I watch him take another bite, this one ganache with espresso cream. "Miguel says he's going to get Alec's licenses. And by next season, Stefano's."

Uncle Cal chuckles. "New money confidence," he says.

"Is he completely delusional?" I ask.

He sips his espresso as if really considering the question. "If he and Alec had a deal, it's possible. But Stefano is a warrior. He'll die on his sword."

"What's that mean?"

Uncle Cal chews slowly, his stare incredulous. "His business is worth over one hundred million dollars. Maybe two, depending on any other enterprises."

You're missing everything that matters.

I lean back in my chair, surprised at this valuation. His offshore account that paid Alec is a fraction of that amount. That kind of money may be worth killing someone. "How would Stefano lose those fishing licenses to Miguel?"

He raises a shoulder, his suit looking baggier than normal. "Must I do all the work? Weren't you creative once?"

"Blackmail for the money laundering," I say. "Or forfeiting them due to an FBI-level arrest. Or divorce. Wife gets half so he liquidates."

Uncle Cal waves at Cynthia and stands. "Or all three," he says. "Wouldn't that be something?"

He's pulling your strings.

Playing you like a fiddle, busted or not.

"And the black market fishing?" I say, thinking of what the bartender said and what Ricky was likely doing. Maybe he and Alec had been doing it all along. "Selling high-value fish under the table?"

"Fish, coolers of cash. A boat is very convenient for all kinds of dark deeds."

I stand up too, handing him the folder but not letting go. "Will she get the grant?"

"I never liked Starbucks," he says with a grin, pulling it from me. "But remember as you dig, my EDC can't go down with Stefano."

Chapter 25

Wednesday, December 14

"You're sure this is right?" I ask Derek for the third time. He sounds fairly lucid, but I still can't believe we got lucky enough to directly tie Belina's last day to Stefano.

"She transferred one hundred thousand to him the morning she died," he says.

"It can't be a coincidence that's what Tina was paid," I say.

"It's like Belina paid her mom's own hush money," Derek says. "That's messed up."

"Yeah," I say. "She'd never sent Stefano money before. Not from this account anyway."

It was a newer account, one she opened after taking the nannying job. "How did she get his bank details?" I ask. "She must have reached out that day."

"It's pretty random based on how she spends her money," he says. "She's cheaper than me."

We both know where Derek spends his money. Drugs and organic cat food. But instead of needling him, so to speak, I click through Belina's expenses. She was frugal to the point of spending only a few hundred dollars a month on food and the occasional trip to Savers thrift store.

I probably should have talked to Derek a little longer, but I am restless to meet Stefano. To finally see this person at the heart of Belina's murder.

Gillian is already with Ester, happy to come over and babysit once Jack left for work. He asked where I am going but nothing more.

He knows you'll just lie.

I drive in silence; the sun is already bright and full in the sky over the Newport Bridge, even though it's only seven a.m. I'm cutting it close to make the morning mass at Saint Mary's. Pete the bartender's casual comment about Stefano attending every Wednesday is too convenient to ignore.

I eek through a yellow traffic light, passing Thames Street, the main shopping drag, before turning into the Saint Mary's parking lot.

Place should burst into flames with you darkening its door.

Evil mother having an evil baby.

My snow boots crunch against the two inches of slush still on the ground as I lean into the wind. Saint Mary's is Gothic Revival, a stunning reddish brownstone that's almost pink in the morning sun. I pause to stare up at the tall narrow tower beside the main entrance. Even though this is a beautiful church hundreds of miles from the one I grew up in, a heavy sickness settles into my bones.

I shrug out of my coat, feeling stares that aren't there. My thighs begin to itch as if I'm back in my yellow Easter dress. I can hear my grandfather's voice, thundering scripture all the way to Derek and me in the back pew, my mother in the choir, father passing out programs at the door.

Smoothing the front of my olive-green dress, I remind myself who I am and who I chose never to be again. I pull the knockoff Burberry wrap tight around my shoulders more for comfort than warmth. The ladies' restroom is right by the door. I could go inside and throw up before I sit down. My stomach full of acid and memories of powerlessness; it'd take only a few seconds.

Instead, I make the sign of the cross and bend a knee, entering like a Catholic, though I was raised Southern Baptist. The organ music begins on a high note, the perfect dramatic soundtrack for the stone archways and glowing stained glass above us. I remain behind the back pew as the procession begins. The boy carrying the gold cross goes first, and two candle bearers follow. An older man holds a Bible rigid, and the priest swings the incense behind him.

The fires of hell will be welcoming you soon enough.

I don't believe in hell, so the voice's threat is empty. It's the hell people can create for you on earth that terrifies me.

I pretend to study the program. The church appears to be a popular spot for wealthy Catholic Newporters, based on the cars in the parking lot, but it's a shrinking group; I count only twelve families. Saint Mary's does have the distinction of a local history worth touting: JFK and Jackie were married here. If the church leaders were smart, they'd see the appetite for the liberal nostalgia and cash in with tours and tote bags and Kennedy wedding toppers.

My gaze lingers on a thick crop of silver-white hair above a tan neck and crisp white collar poking out of a suit. Stefano's shoulder almost touches the thin woman next to him. She has a good haircut and a silvery-blonde dye job. The back of another blonde's head matches with photos I've seen of their daughter, who is only a few years younger than Belina.

If Belina was stalking him, she probably saw the family together like this, in church or maybe a restaurant. Did she feel guilty for hurting the family with an affair? Jealous that Stefano had this family with someone else?

It's too late now.

You're embarrassing yourself.

I don't know what I'm looking for, but I keep staring. Belina cared for this man. Spent the last years of her life working for him, seeing him socially, and likely, breaking the law for him.

I move to their side of the church but sit a couple of rows back and over. They're in line with the priest, so staring will be easy to cover.

Stefano watches the priest like he's paid for the robes and sacraments himself, which is likely. He glances at his wife, nods at his daughter as if checking on a ship's sails. He casually drapes an arm behind them as if all is right for now, and he's back to focusing on the priest.

I like watching people when they're relaxed. When they're in a familiar place, hardly registering the expected faces and tastes and smells. Their guards drop quicker, and their natural rhythms emerge.

I saw it with Alec playing with Emmett, joking with Belina. He is a man who likes to be cared for, to make others love him and be proud of him. As he is full of big ideas and enthusiasm, the attraction is hardly a stretch to understand for someone like her, like us.

Stefano seems like a different personality. He worked day in and day out to build a successful business on the backs of fishermen. He took what he wanted, from women to illegal business deals, all the while going to the same buck-a-shuck lunch at the same bar for twenty years. Alec and Stefano could not be more different, and yet, they're possibly the two men Belina cared about most.

I glance around, seeing one other person alone. He's got a buzz cut and a bad suit, and he probably benches 250. An FBI agent out of central casting, but that's not a guess. His name is Max Fincher. We worked together to put away the Rhode Island Speaker of the House.

He'll laugh at you.

You have no real reason to be here.

I quietly cross to the back of the church and scoot in close next to him. "Found Jesus?"

He glances at me, the slow blink of recognition and alarm. He lets out a deep grumble, a sound of frustration, one he often made around me. "You shouldn't be here," he says, leaning close.

"I have as much a right as you," I say, tucking some errant hair behind my ears. "Rhode Island was founded on religious freedom. Take that, Puritan Masshole."

He smirks because he's a proudly born and bred Boston, Massachusetts, Masshole.

I dig one thumbnail into the other thumb's cuticle. Max always makes me fidgety, chatty, as if it's high school all over again. He's a little too close to the popular dickhead football players I avoided in high school. But I'm happy to do something other than listen to an old white man talking at me from a lectern. "You know Rhode Island was the real birthplace of the American Revolution?"

Max puts one arm over the back of the pew. "Really?"

"We burned the British Army's ship, the *Gaspee*, as a protest six months before your precious tea party. Not sure *Gaspee party* sends the right message, though."

His mouth quirks to hide a grin.

I pause to watch Stefano with his family. As Max's gaze finally makes it there too, I press my luck. "When you arrest him—"

"Who says he's going to be arrested?"

"I'd guess Frank is outside," I say about his partner. "Unmarked car, inhaling an Awful Awful chocolate malt despite the cold temperatures?" I don't blame Frank. The local dessert is nicknamed for being awful big and awful good.

"Dunkin' Cronut, actually," he says.

I frown at him. "A what?"

"It's part croissant, part doughnut. All wicked disgusting."

"Right," I continue, picking at the other thumbnail. "So again, when you guys arrest him, who will take over the fishing licenses?"

He shifts closer, leaning down to my ear. "He knows we're on him. Puckered right up. Arrest at this point is unlikely."

"When?"

"He stopped everything we were tracking cold two months ago." He shakes his head. "If we don't get creative, they'll shut down the whole operation. It's not just the year of work and people who have stuck their necks out to get him. It's that this guy is as guilty as they come."

I hear the frustration in his voice, which is unusual. Max and I had at least a dozen interactions when I was building the first case Uncle Cal gave me as a "Welcome to Providence" gift—or test, as hindsight taught me. No matter the surprise or setback we experienced, Max was a cool customer. Back then, I could really walk the line of leaking information to Phillip but not obstructing justice. Max was quick to accept my methods, focused on the career-making optics of hauling a top Rhode Island political official out of his statehouse office in cuffs. Those were the early, good days, when Uncle Cal's enemies were actual criminals and not just people he wanted out of his way.

You were too stupid to see how he used you.

That's all you're good for.

Use and throw away.

"Operations don't run any quieter." Max rolls the mass program in his hands. "I'm not sure where the leak came from. I even looked at Frank for a desperate minute."

I almost laugh. His partner inhaling the Cronut lives and breathes the FBI. No close family, no expenses, no vacations, just working cases and eating shitty food.

"How many people knew?" I ask.

"No," he says. "I was venting. Drop it."

"Aren't you curious why I'm here?"

"I know why," he says. "Detective Ramos warned me you'd be sniffing around Stefano."

"Did you interview Belina?" I ask, the possibility raising even more questions about what she knew.

"We left her alone. She was too close to him," he says, giving me a look. "Very, very few people knew about our operation."

"Did the Rossas? Miguel? They're positioned to take over these fishing licenses. At least according to Miguel."

"With that much money, there is always someone lined up." He pulls away, putting his elbows on his knees. "Look, Devon, you and Hale dug up some interesting things. Truly. But there's a lot more at stake than Belina's killer."

I want to tell him and his patronizing tone to piss off, but the organ blasts a few notes, and people begin to shift in their pews, preparing to head to the front for the sacrament. I check my phone and see Ricky texted out of the blue. He found evidence leading to Stefano and needs me to bring a flash drive. Good thing I always keep extras.

He texts me an address, and I text back, It's no problem.

Excited about the possibility of evidence against Stefano, I decide to just leave early, conspicuous and all. "Nice to see you, Max," I say and scoot to the end of the pew. "Gotta go see a friend about a boat."

He nods once, tightly, and we both glance toward Stefano. He's standing in the pew, hand on his wife's back, guiding her forward to the Eucharist line. As they step into the aisle, Stefano snaps his gaze to where Max and I sit. His chest rises and falls, even and yet unsettled, his eyes darting back and forth between us.

"That can't be good for you," Max says, cocking his head toward me as I stand.

"See you at buck a shuck," I say. He lets out another deep grumble.

Chapter 26

I drive over the Newport Bridge back toward the mainland and pass the first of two exits into the island of Jamestown. It's a short enough distance that I don't have much time to second-guess myself for chatting with the FBI agent right in front of Stefano. There's not much use in pretending I'm something I'm not. I'd like Stefano angry and unnerved when I confront him.

He's going to chew you up and spit you out, girlie.

Jamestown is the shy younger sister to Newport. A smaller version in every way but with plenty of history and opulence. Edith Wharton's family home is a focal point heading over the bridge. I pass the historic windmill open for tours on the weekends. In the fall, a working farm has an unmanned roadside stand where they trust you to put the right amount of money in the box for the apples or pumpkins. People move to Jamestown for the good elementary school and a friendly, affordably upper-class life on the ocean, if you've got the half million for a fixer-upper.

Another place you don't belong.

I drive along the gentle curve into the downtown area, the ocean ahead and the Newport Bridge over my shoulder. Most of the shops are along Narragansett Avenue, and a couple more are on the marina. Ricky texted that he was in the back of the Conanicut Marine Services.

I park on the street and shut off the car, glancing at my cooler with the milk I pumped in the church bathroom after I left the service. An older couple walks their hobbling lab as a woman pushing a stroller hurries past. My ache for Ester is sharp, but there's also relief that she's not with me, and I can be alone with my work. I double-check that the flash drive is in my purse, get out of the car, and slam the door harder than required.

Conanicut Marine Services is all brick with narrow white doors and two large windows with mannequins wearing what I assume is the latest in New England nautical fashion. I enter the store, and a bell clanks overhead. There's a shih tzu sleeping on her back near boxes of Sperry shoes piled a few steps inside.

"Holiday shoppin'?" says a thin, well-dressed woman behind the counter.

"Meeting a friend here." I try not to seem nervous, though I'm uncertain what exactly Ricky has planned. I brought a flash drive, but I can only guess from there.

I glance around at the mix of high-end yacht wear and sunscreen and Jamestown gear. Deeper into the store, there's a large glass window where several desks hold mountains of paperwork, brochure displays, and images of boats. Ricky is sitting on the desk of a pretty woman. This one is in her fifties and grins at his bullshit charm act.

Getting closer to the door leading to them, I hear her laugh like she means it, as if it's a real pleasure. I get a familiar longing to be a little more like her. Where every move isn't a calculation, but rather I just open my arms and fall, expecting to land somewhere soft every time.

I slip inside the office. Ricky waggles a look my way but keeps chatting.

"So, Ricky, you still busy on boats most evenings?" she asks, shifting over to let me approach.

"Lynelle, Lynelle," he says. "You know I got a thing for married blondes. You better not be flirting, or we'll get in some real trouble."

"Trouble I can handle." She winks at me as I stand next to Ricky. "Is this her?" Her smile matches her laugh, open and delighted as if I've brought her a present.

"This is her," he says. "You're the only one who can talk her out of buying her husband a Zodiac."

"Gotta give the people you love what they want. Life's too short."

I keep my smile in place, not sure what's going on but understanding I need to play along. "Smart lady," I say, looking down at the brochure with a Zodiac fishing boat soaring over waves.

"What can I tell ya about 'em?" Lynelle asks.

"Dig around for us," Ricky asks. "Her husband is a data dork. He'd love all you got on Zodiac."

"Sure, honey," she says. "One second."

As Lynelle swishes toward the back, Ricky nods his head at her desktop computer. "Get it all," he says under his breath.

I bend down and set my handbag on the floor by the computer tower. As I pretend to dig through my bag with one hand, I use the other hand to pull the flash drive out of my coat pocket and plug it into the back of the computer. I shift to see her screen, and the small bubble shows it's compatible.

I sit on the corner of the desk and discreetly use the mouse to make a copy of all her files. If it's a hidden file, then we're out of luck, but Lynelle doesn't strike me as someone very worried about security. I see the symbol that the download is complete. Keeping my eyes across the room, I lean down and take the drive out before dropping it into a side pocket of my purse. I stand back up just as Lynelle returns.

"Here's three years of catalogs," she says, handing me the lean, glossy books. "Bring that husband back here, and we'll get him fixed up."

I thank her, dumping everything into my purse, and shake her hand goodbye, leaving Ricky to chat.

Back in the main store area, I see the small kids' clothes sections, but they don't have three-month sizes.

As if your tiny freak baby would fit.

You don't give her enough milk.

She's probably starving right now.

I leave the baby section immediately and head to the men's. I see a tie with a map of Rhode Island and realize I haven't even thought of what to buy Jack for Christmas.

Rather than try, I zip up my coat and head outside to Narragansett Avenue. I stare down at the end of the road by the water at a veterans' memorial, a dozen flags whipping in the cold ocean wind. December is losing its frosty charm as we near the new year and the real New England winter settles in.

The Conanicut store bell rings behind me, and a lighter clicks. I turn as the cigarette smoke wafts, and I inhale. I quit smoking several years ago, but the smell isn't unpleasant.

Ricky stares at the ocean at the end of the road where my gaze was. He lets his cigarette dangle from his mouth as he zips his jacket. He puts on a black skull cap, his cheekbones and nose looking sharper and prominent, reminding me so much of Derek that I have to step back to keep from hugging him.

His focus darts across the street. "Too early for a beer?"

"They drink red beers out here?" I ask with a grin.

"What the hell's that?"

"Beer and tomato juice," I say. My brother, Derek, would shotgun at least a couple before class, starting as early as middle school.

"The Ganny should be open," Ricky says, and I get that kick of pride from learning a nickname for a local bar. "Let's see what Suze has behind the bar."

I motion for him to lead the way. We cross Narragansett Avenue toward the creatively named Narragansett Café.

Inside it has a stage in the corner and black floors and walls. They display Best of Rhode Island awards for local music and trivia nights. We sit at the bar, and Ricky waves over the bartender, who is in her late sixties. She has dull brown hair with plenty of gray. She's not well dressed like Lynelle, no easy smile but rather the hard, skeptical stare of someone life has said "Fuck you" to more often than not. I like her instantly.

"Who ya got with ya, Ricky? Not from the docks," she says, glancing at my dress and purse.

"Boat investor," I answer. "My name's Devon. I'm from Kansas."

Her lips thin until they're almost invisible. "Guess ya hear plenty of *Wizard of Oz* jokes."

"One more won't hurt."

"I don't tell jokes," she says.

"Got red beer?" I ask.

"No," she says, blinking as she waits.

"Two Gansetts," Ricky says. After she walks away, he leans over. "She likes you."

I'm not in the mood for his charm offense. "Why don't you start at the beginning of why I just copied some woman's hard drive."

"I was dropping off some fish to one of Stefano's captains who was short," he says, animated like he knows his first drink of the day is en route.

"Is that something you normally do?" I ask.

"Not really, but I'm not in a position to say no right now," he says. "This captain asked me to take back a Zodiac to Conanicut. Turns out, Stefano had rented it. Seems Stefano goes night fishing in them."

"Is this a new hobby?" I ask.

He waggles his finger as if I'm on to something. "Stefano rents them regularly once a month. Takes 'em into the Providence River to fish. Close to where Belina was killed."

"I can work with that," I say. Stefano likely won't use his own name, but maybe his phone number or credit card can be traced. It was a good call on the flash drive.

Suze drops the drafts and goes back to washing glasses. Ricky raises his pint.

"Here's to drinking Narragansett beer at the Narragansett Café on Narragansett Avenue." I clink my glass with his and take a small sip. He glances at the clock on the wall. "We should hear about the bail pretty soon."

"Hope Alec is out quickly," I say. "I appreciate the lead, but, Ricky . . ." I pause and glance around. It's quiet except for a local classic rock station wafting from the kitchen. Suze has moved to the back, and there's an old man in the corner booth reading the paper. "I need to know more about your business."

He takes a sip of beer. "Ask me anything, Devon."

You're so stupid to trust this guy.

He's going to use you and spit you out.

Just like you deserve.

I turn my glass and take aim. "Miguel said you two were going to work together. Now that Alec's out of the picture."

Ricky grimaces. "It's not like that."

"But you are working with him. Even though Alec didn't want to."

"Look, we're worse than broke. If I have to bring in more investors, I will. Alec is going to be thanking me if I can save our business. No matter whose cash it is."

"Why can't Stefano help you?" I say, wanting to confirm what the spreadsheets say. That Alec blew through money they were supposed to wash for Stefano.

Ricky takes a long sip, glancing around the room before scooting a little closer. "Alec messed up. He thought he could pay some things down, and the boats would keep making money. But it didn't work out like that."

"Why pay things down now?"

Ricky shrugs, takes a sip. "I just know Stefano is real mad. There's no way he's going to keep buying from us. We gotta . . . diversify."

"How much did Belina know?" I ask, thinking of the one hundred thousand she sent to Stefano. Maybe as a way to help Alec out.

Ricky finishes his beer and stands up to slide behind the bar. He puts the glass in the washer and sits back down with a cocktail straw in his mouth. "She knew we were in trouble," he says as he drapes one elbow over the back of his chair. "But it's Alec, you know. He always figures something out."

"Have you spoken to Stefano since Alec was arrested?" I ask.

Ricky lets out a bitter laugh. "That SOB wouldn't slow his car down if I was crossing the road. He only speaks to Alec. I deal with his captains, if I deal with anyone at all in his precious business."

He runs his thumb along the wooden bar top. It's a deeper pain than I expected. "Why does it matter if Stefano likes you?" I ask.

He chews on the straw. "I grew up . . . admiring him, I guess you could say. My mom, well, she passed when I was young. I worked on boats instead of focusing on school. Read a lot"—he says it quickly, as if I'll think he's dumb otherwise—"but I always wanted to impress him. Big successful guy. It was stupid. Some stuff, well, it takes a while to grow out of it."

And some never do.

Failures follow you everywhere.

Repeating and multiplying.

I keep to my barstool, but I want to embrace him. I feel the pull of sameness, can almost see Derek next to me. If I did hug Ricky, it'd be the same too-skinny ribs and knotted spine. "From what I've seen, he's not worth impressing."

He flinches, then a half smile. "Belina thought he was."

The pain doesn't leave his eyes as he shifts the conversation to her. In fact, there's more. "You cared about her?" I say out loud just as I realize it. "Ricky, tell me the truth."

He rubs his fingers along his chin stubble. "She was never going to stay with a guy like me. But, yeah, we were friendly for a while."

"Did Alec know?" I ask.

He sucks in a breath. "God, no. We never told anyone. She was embarrassed of me. Stefano was the kind of guy she wanted to be seen with all over town. And Alec had a thing for her, but that didn't bother me much."

Ricky is a good-looking guy. Seems to work hard and is pretty charming when he wants to be. "No, maybe she—"

He slices me a glance that says, *You know what I mean*. And I do. My cheeks heat in embarrassment for Ricky. I had a lot of sex in high school but no actual relationships because it seemed the guys just wanted sex, not me, and I took whatever I could get. Not that Belina was using Ricky in that way. I have no idea what she was doing with any of these men. And that is part of the problem. "I'm sorry," I say finally.

"We had this love/hate chemistry, you know. It was fun, but I think she hated herself after."

"You can finish this one." I slide my beer over, and he tosses the straw he's been jawing onto the bar. "So what happened?" I ask.

"What always happens," he says. "I like a girl that's too good for me. She likes someone else." He swallows thickly and doesn't make eye contact, just rubs his knuckle along the rounded edge of the bar.

Something in my gut says to be careful. That all this is a little too stacked for Ricky. But I understand what it feels like not to be good enough. To make your bedroom white because you're too afraid the real colors you want will give away that you're not worth loving.

He's like Derek.

You'll ruin his life too.

The voice hits me just right, knowing who I need to contact. Tears burn my throat as I say goodbye, put a twenty on the bar, and leave Ricky to my beer. But my emotions don't stop me from uploading the marina data onto my laptop from the parking lot and sending it to my brother.

Chapter 27

I'm the first one inside Clarke Cooke House as they open the doors for lunch. I take a seat at the end of the bar. Pete nods my way and makes me a hot toddy with Wild Turkey before dropping a menu.

"He should be here soon," Pete says. "The table in the window is his."

It's five feet from me, and I take a sip, considering if I should move. Once he sees me, and likely ties me to Max in some way, he'll probably "pucker up," as Max put it. I'm hoping as I press him with questions about Belina, he'll get mad. And his anger will reveal something, anything.

I need him to confirm several things for me beyond if he's capable of killing Belina or at least getting someone else to do it. First, the meeting with Belina the night she was killed. Was he at Swan Point? Second, why did Belina transfer him everything in her bank account? Was it the same hundred grand he sent to Tina? And I'm wondering how he heard of the FBI investigation. The timing lines up with Belina's murder.

I push the drink aside because the frustration has me reaching for it. "Can I get just a sparkling water, Pete?"

Reaching into my pocket, I feel the flash drive, but that's not what I'm looking for. I dig deeper and run my fingers along soft organic cotton, one of Ester's knitted shoes that matches her hat. I doubted Gilly would take her outside, so I brought it along. The time away has been difficult. The possibility that she's changing, and I'm missing it.

This is exactly who you promised never to be again.

"You need something from me?" a deep voice says at my back.

I crush the delicate shoe in my hand, my nails poking into my palm through the small knitted gaps. One more breath, and I turn around. "I do need something from you."

He's still in the wealthy businessman armor, but I'm getting a closer look: good haircut for his silver-gray hair, expensive suit, likely a local place like Marc Allen. I can't see his shoes, but I'm sure they're expensive too. But his eyebrows are bushy and too long, like he's not the type to let someone trim them nor is he the sort of person who gets asked.

"Can I buy you a drink?" I ask. "Or a shrimp cocktail?"

His caterpillar eyebrows shoot together. "No one's bought me anything since I was a boy," he says. "But you can watch me have a drink and eat a shrimp cocktail. Though I'm more an oysters and lobster kind of guy."

I stand up, and we're almost the same height. I gesture toward his table, and then he mimics the gesture for me to go first.

"Pete, my regular." He pauses, and Pete stands up straighter. "Make it my Friday regular. Not Wednesday."

We sit down in the window. I look at the view, one long gray dock extending between wood-shingled buildings out toward the ocean. I feel his hard gaze and think of Uncle Cal, unflinching, searching for weakness. I drop back in my seat and return his stare.

"You know Agent Fincher?" Stefano asks, his dark-brown eyes steady on my face.

"A recent acquaintance of yours?" I say and get no reaction. "We've worked together."

He takes the napkin off the table and drops it onto his lap. "Where?"

"Statehouse," I say. "It's been a few years."

"And today was a coincidence?"

"Yes. Seems we're both tracking the same man."

Pete steps over to the table and pops a bottle of Dom. "Two glasses?" he asks, but I shake my head no before Stefano can do the same. He pours, then steps back with the bottle.

"Leave it," Stefano says. "And close off this room."

You'll never beat him.

One way or the other.

This will be your undoing.

Pete is at the bar with the Dom. He scoops ice quick and loud into a silver bucket and drops it off between us at the table. Then pulls a curtain at the two entrance points before slipping out of the room.

"They really care about customer service here," I say.

Stefano leans into the table. "Why don't you start with how you know Agent Fincher."

He's irritated, which is helpful. "I help the FBI from time to time. I'm here because of an employee of yours. Alec Mathers?"

Before he can answer, Pete enters the room, balancing a large silver bowl full of shaved ice with a lobster heaped in the middle. As he places it at the center of the table, I see unshucked oysters and clams and a small knife. Pete leaves the room quickly, and it's quiet.

Stefano picks up the lobster and looks at it end to end. He takes a sniff, shakes it, then, seeming pleased enough, grabs the claw cracker. He begins where most people would, at the main large claw, and gets most of the meat out quickly. It's shiny even before he dunks it into the butter.

But he doesn't eat it. Instead, he puts it on the large plate Pete left. Just where the meat would be in the actual lobster. He continues, cracking and twisting and pulling the meat from the claws. Then he moves on to the body, popping the jagged edges under the belly, flipping up the sides until the large middle portion is free of shell. He plops it onto the plate. It's mesmerizing, like watching a Michelin-starred chef work.

He continues until every edible part of the lobster is outside its shell. After scooting the small silver bowl of butter closer, he dips a knuckle and slurps it down.

I've nearly forgotten my question, but he has not.

"Alec is a protégé of mine. He wasn't much of a fisherman, but he had the right connections to run a business of that kind. He listened, did his best, and I wish him well." Stefano pauses to slurp another knuckle, much more loudly than seems necessary. "Why do you ask?"

"I don't think he killed Belina." I watch him chew, but there's no break. "In fact, I have evidence to the contrary."

Stefano raises a bushy eyebrow. "You've given it to the detective? What's his name? Ramsey?"

"Ramos," I say. "Yes, but it hasn't made a difference."

"Perhaps your evidence isn't very good."

He sees you're a joke.

Reckless, out of your depth.

The last person to help anyone.

I cross my arms as if miffed, but it's a fair point. "Belina kept a day planner. A lot of meetings between you two, including the very last entry. Guess what day that was?"

He stills his hand; the large piece of claw meat drips butter onto the table. "Are you accusing me of . . . hurting her?"

"I'm asking," I say. "Who was in her life. Who she cared about. Who cared about her. Or, maybe didn't care about her as much as she thought."

He dips a meaty chunk, pinkish and floppy, and takes an exaggerated bite. Stefano chews loudly, mouth slightly open. Not like a successful businessman. The armor is slipping. Or maybe it's been a weak façade all along.

"I put a lot on the line, personally, for her," he says.

"You pushed her to work for Alec. To have him work for you. She was a part of his family and ran his business. Seems she put a lot on the line for you."

He chomps loudly and takes a quick sip of Dom. "She made her own mistakes."

"Like working for you?" I say.

He doesn't look up as he grabs the meat of the next claw.

"I spoke to Tina."

"Well, she loves to talk."

"About her dead daughter?"

He drops the last bite of lobster onto his plate with a plop. "Tina tried," he says, leveling a look at me that dares me to contradict him. "Not everyone who is a mother should be one."

He sees you.

He sees you.

We all see you.

That I certainly won't contradict. "And Belina?"

"She did better than most with her situation."

I can't disagree with him there. "You think Alec killed her?" I ask.

He stares out at the water, then focuses back on the oysters and clams remaining in the ice. He picks up the small knife and takes an oyster. He jams it into the side, gently turning until it pops open. "I don't know," he says quietly. "He was going to leave his wife for her. Maybe Belina changed her mind . . ."

I've been staring at the oyster in the shell in his hand, but with that last statement, I find his hard gaze. "How do you know?"

"The way I know anything." He slurps the oyster and drops the shell into the ice. "When someone tells me."

"Alec told you he was leaving Misha? When?"

Stefano cracks into a clam this time, scraping the top and bottom of the shell. "The morning Belina was murdered."

Maybe I should believe that Alec didn't have that kind of relationship with Belina, but I don't.

"Look," Stefano begins. "Alec is a poor rich kid through and through. Expects everything, even though he's really only good at screwing up. Belina kept that business going as long as she could. But what none of us could admit is that Alec is more loser than winner."

"You mean the money," I say. "The half million he blew through?"

"No comment," he says, scowling at the clam he's cutting into.

"Did you get any of the money back?"

"Not yet." Stefano sounds as if that's a temporary issue.

"Not one hundred thousand dollars?"

He looks at me now, I realize, for the first time. "How the hell do you know about that?"

"How does anyone know about anything?" I say, parroting his phrase. "Someone told me."

He sighs deeply, setting down his knife. "Devon," he says, and I almost jump at him knowing my name. "I owe your uncle a few favors. That's why we're having this conversation. But now, it's over."

"What about Alec's partner, Ricky?" I ask. "He says the relationship went bad with him and Alec. Belina knew a lot about—"

"Do not put Ricky and Belina in the same sentence," he hisses, real anger flashing. "I hated that Alec brought Ricky into the business."

"But you still worked with him. I guess money washes all sins?"

He smirks at my phrase, though he doesn't acknowledge that that was basically what they were doing, cleaning his dirty cash through their fishing business. "Ricky is trash," he says. "He comes from trash. Actually, he comes from crazy."

"Crazy," I say. "Who is crazy? His mom?"

"That's none of your business."

"But it's yours?" I say. "Because he works for you? Or was Ricky's mom an employee with benefits too?"

"She killed herself," he says coolly. "That's all I'm saying. He's from crazy, and I should never have done business with him."

I feel a little guilty at bringing up Ricky's mom but not enough to stop. "What did Ricky do to you?"

"This topic is over. As is our conversation." He picks up an oyster and digs into it, popping it open. Then he grins at it and leans it my way.

There's a white speck, pear shaped, floating amid the meat. "Is that a pearl?" I ask.

"It is," he says and scoops it out. He rolls it between his finger and thumb before dropping it into the ramekin with vinegar. "It'll dissolve in a few minutes. Portuguese royalty would drink pearls whenever an explorer left for a great journey."

He presses the flat of the oyster knife onto the pearl, stirs, then presses again, as if making a powder. "Medicine from the old country," he says, and I think of Belina's words when I first met her.

"Purifies the blood," I finish.

His eyes narrow as if he's angered that I know the phrase. He shoots the pearl and vinegar, then wipes his mouth with his sleeve.

The small distraction gone, I'm left with the truth. Alec lied about Stefano and the money laundering. Lied about how he owed a lot of money to a powerful man. How can I go after someone like Stefano with half truths?

You can't.

You were always going to fail.

As he slurps his last oyster, I'm suddenly nauseated by his efficiency with the knife, seeing flashes of Belina's butchered arm.

An easy smile appears at my silence because he must see the truth: I'm outmatched.

He knows what the FBI has and that it's not enough. He knows there's even less than that relating to Belina. He's not going to tearfully admit to killing his girlfriend. He's not going to weepily hand over all his books and confess his evil deeds. Not even when he's caught, hook in mouth, knife at the throat.

Remember what your grandfather taught you.

I see my hand around a knife hidden under my ruffled pillow as I whisper: "Whatever they do to you, if you want to win, you have to do worse."

My grandfather's scream. A slap across my face.

What difference did it make?

Do worse.

I can barely stand, the shaking moving from my hands through my body. I steady myself on the table and back of the chair.

"I will turn you inside out," I whisper. "This is our beginning."

My vision narrows and blurs as I hurry from the room. The blackness is here, but still I hear my feet move.

Do worse.

Do worse.

Do your worst.

Chapter 28

Thursday, December 15

I open my eyes in my bedroom, and I blink at the chandelier above me. The lights are off, but the sun is up. I reach for my phone, and my arm pinches, but I can't feel any scrapes.

My phone tells me it's the next day. I got a full night's sleep. The first time since I had Ester that I slept all night.

My phone also shows several missed calls from Phillip.

I decide to table reality for a moment, taking a deep breath to savor how good a full night's sleep feels. My body is lighter. I stand on my new bird-bone legs.

But then I realize I have no idea how I got here. I must have blacked out. Not like that moment at the cemetery before meeting Phillip. But a real one. Like the DC days. Like when I was a girl.

"Jack," I call out into what sounds like an empty house.

They've finally left you.

There's no response, but I won't let myself panic. Instead, I go to the nursery and pump quickly to relieve the pressure that's built up over the full night's sleep.

I head downstairs, and the tightness of worry eases as I find Ester sleeping in her mamaRoo, the hum of the motor the only sound as Jack watches something on his computer with his headphones on. I put the milk into storage bags and into the freezer and sit next to him on the couch.

He slips off his headphones. "You look better," he says.

"Yeah," I say, not wanting to admit I have no memory of what happened. "How was Ester?" I ask, glancing at her, itching to hold her and hide my face in her neck.

Great, because she was far away from her terrible mother.

"Fine," he says, as if waiting for me to apologize or something.

"Coming home is a little fuzzy." I rub the pinch in my shoulder and feel a Band-Aid I hadn't noticed. "What happened?" My casual tone is too high-pitched, too obvious.

"You scared me," Jack says. "You were ranting about Max and Stefano and hacking into the FBI databases."

"Oh," I say, sinking into the couch.

Jack scoots closer. "I know you hate drugs, but I had to call the doctor to sedate you. So you'd sleep."

"Right," I say as if I remember. "I overdid it in Newport."

His eyes watch me carefully as tension freezes his face. I remember that same terrified expression from when I was in the hospital with Ester. As if I were a skittish deer frozen in front of his speeding car.

"Did you black out?" he asks, real fear in his eyes. And memories. I've blacked out before from stress. But not like this since we moved. Not since I promised I'd change.

I think back to how bad I let it get in DC. One minute I'd be working late in my office, trying like hell to figure out how to convict some rapist or child trafficker. The next minute, I'd find myself buying a drink at the bar where the defendant was known to hang out. Waking up in my car at the corner of the school where he'd stalk young boys. No memory of how I got there. Only knowing it was what my mind thought I needed to do for justice.

But in DC, the voice that's taunting me now didn't come with these blackouts, so at first I thought it'd go away. But as the cases kept growing along with my stress, it was happening more. It scared me enough to tell Jack the truth. About why I would lose time, hours, as a girl. Why the blackouts had returned in DC. I was honest then but not today.

"It wasn't so bad," I say. "I'm feeling better."

His eyes are wide at my lies. No shock or anger but longing for the words to be true. His desire for me to be better is so strong I can almost feel it between us, wrapping me, tethering me, drawing me closer to him and what we once were before.

You'll never be able to go back to the good.

It's only the bad from now on.

"Will you hit pause on the case?" he asks. "For a few days? For me?"

Say the wrong thing.

He's going to leave you.

Say the right thing.

He'll never trust you again.

"I'm close to the truth," I say quietly, pulling back. It's not an answer to his request because I don't have one yet. I don't want to be so upset I have to be sedated.

But none of this is a shock. My mother used to lock me in my room when I got out of control. Of course, she never took the time to understand that being in that room was half of why I'd break.

"You don't have to do it alone," he says.

"I'm not. Phillip is helping. Cynthia is too." I don't mention Uncle Cal because that'd just lead to a fight. "Yesterday was too much. I'll go easier."

He takes my hand. The lines around his eyes seem deeper, new since Ester and the stress we created. "I watched Phillip's *TODAY Show* interview from Swan Point this morning. He's hinting at Stefano's involvement. You need to be careful."

"I saw Stefano yesterday," I say. "Spoke to him, actually. He said Alec was leaving Misha for Belina. It makes sense, if you follow the money. He was paying off all his debts with Stefano's dirty money to start fresh with Belina. Alec has lied about the money. His relationship with Belina. Everything."

Jack nods and clears his throat. "Is it possible . . . if Belina ended up backing out, maybe . . . that Alec could have done it?"

Ester begins to cry before I can answer. "Sorry," I say. "I'll take her for a walk. I need to check in with Cynthia anyway. You can get to work."

I kiss his cheek, and he rubs my wrist gently. "I thought bringing you home with . . . her after the hospital was a good idea. But maybe it was too soon—"

"No," I say too loudly because it's a threat, even if he doesn't mean it that way. "God, no, I'm getting better, Jack. I love you for supporting me. For letting me find my way back to my old self."

The concern in his stare breaks, and I see real pain. "I don't know, Dev," he whispers. "I don't know if I'm doing anything right."

I drop to my knees, ignoring Ester's cries, and put my hands on his cheeks. "Trust me like I trust you."

He nods, clears his throat, forces a little smile. "I'm trying."

You always ruin those who are stupid enough to love you.

Ester's cry is piercing, and I can't ignore her anymore. I kiss his temple, then take her into my arms, inhaling the baby powder scent.

"Everything is okay, baby girl," I say and shush against her soft, cool cheek. "I'm here with you now."

She'd be better if you weren't.

They both would.

I decide to take a little time with Ester and find the book of Portuguese myths Tina gave me. I put Ester in the bouncer and do a quick comparison of Stefano's signature and the inscription on this volume. I scroll through the photos I snapped. It's certainly similar but not definitive proof that the books were gifts to his girlfriend.

Taking up the myths again, I open a few pages. I snuggle Ester onto my chest and begin to softly read stories to us both. There are tales of kings and princes and fairies. Catholic references are woven into the morality portions.

I shift Ester, and the pages fall open to a well-worn spot, the myth of the Adamastor. There are doodles in the margins, *O*s and *D*s colored in. The story is a retelling of an epic poem, *The Lusiads*, which reads like a Greek myth. The Adamastor descends from gods, who he disobeys by falling in love with a nymph. As punishment, he's turned into a jagged, isolated mountain. He spends his banishment trying to destroy the sailors who pass along his waters.

"'Who are you?' whispers a scared explorer to the great monster in the mountain.

"'I am that vast, secret promontory,' says the Adamastor. 'You Portuguese call me the Cape of Storms.'"

I study the circles and loops Belina drew around the letters before deciding it's time to see Cynthia.

After putting Ester in another layer, I throw on a thick sweater and jeans before strapping her onto my chest with the wrap. I slip on my coat and zip it halfway over her. I toe into my snow boots, slinging on the diaper bag, and start walking. I hear Jack getting out of the shower and decide not to open myself up to more questions I can't answer.

There are more lies than truth between you.

He might not be here when you get back.

I head toward Chip and text Phillip on the walk. He responds that he'll meet me at Alec's house in forty-five minutes.

Chip is busy with the lunch crowd, but Cynthia hurries over. She kisses my cheek and scans my face. "Jack called yesterday," she says. "Are you sure you should be . . . out?"

"I'm fine," I say, not sure if it's a lie. "I needed some sleep."

She grins, the pitying one. "Sure."

I'm not in the mood to be placated. "What'd you find out from the owner at the Ivy?"

Cynthia hesitates, and I know it's something good. "Alec was there that night but only for a couple drinks. He left at six p.m., just like they told the police. He was not wasted as he claims—"

"Damn it," I interrupt, desperate. "He keeps lying."

She cocks her head to the side and blinks at me. "May I finish?"

"Sorry."

"He was not wasted at Ivy as he claims because he went next door to Hope Street Pizza Kitchen and got hammered there. He closed the place down."

"So two a.m.?"

"Actually, the waitress, Joanna, helped close and remembers him eating a gyro, so it was more like three a.m."

"The police never questioned her?"

"She was out from knee surgery when the police were there. They only did one round of questioning. The bartender that night left early and didn't remember Alec."

"Oh," I say. "What did the server say?"

"Alec was meeting with one of their regular customers, who is a lawyer," she says. "Care to guess what kind?"

"Divorce," I say.

"The lawyer left after an hour, so he wouldn't have helped with the alibi. But what does help is that Alec kept drinking. He was buying people shots and singing loudly. They just had one other waitress and one bartender working that night and were slammed. But when I showed her Alec's picture, she remembered him."

I grin at Cynthia, refraining from kissing her full on the mouth. "This is amazing," I say. "Truly, you've saved his life."

There's worry in her eyes as if she's wondering if saving Alec's life comes with the price of mine.

"Got a couple to-go coffees?" I ask.

"Soy milk, three Splenda?" she asks, quoting Phillip's usual order.

She doesn't wait for my answer and instead goes behind the counter to quickly make them. I carry them in a tray, lessening the chance that either drips on Ester.

I walk cautiously down Hope Street, where there are several patches of salted sidewalk with ice shining. Even though it's the steepest way, I wind down the well-shoveled and salted sidewalks of Rochambeau Street. Against my chest, Ester sleeps soundly. I feel her breath rise and fall. I can almost hear the soft murmurs echo in my ears.

How dare you bring her into this cold weather.

Everyone will see you're the worst mother.

I stumble at the voice, loud and strong despite the cacophony of wind in my ears. Starting down Cole Avenue, I see Phillip's car outside Alec's house. The smoke from the tailpipe signals Phillip is waiting for me even before I see his outline in the driver's seat.

As I near the car, he shuts it off and steps outside. He makes a big show of pointing to the alarm and activating it with a short beep, beep. "Scary neighborhood," he says with a grin. "You okay?"

I hand him the coffee tray and run my gloved hands along Ester's back. "Let's go."

Phillip leads us up the unshoveled sidewalk. There are footprints everywhere and small round marks where camera tripods were set up. I frown at the poop bags littering the snow.

Phillip knocks, and one of the curtains covering a narrow window by the door flutters opens. I see Misha's cool blue gaze for an instant, and then she's gone. Phillip clears his throat, adjusting his scarf. As he starts to knock again, the lock clicks, and the door opens.

"He's putting Emmett down for a nap," she says. "What do you want?"

"We have evidence that will keep him home," I say. "But we need to speak with him privately."

Her breath stutters, almost sounding huffy, but her eyes are relieved. "Okay."

She shuts the door in our faces, and we stand there, not sure what to do. My anger spikes because she saw Ester and didn't invite us inside.

Minutes pass, and then the door opens again. It's Alec or a version of him. He's thinner, unshaven, and the circles under his eyes are nearing the color of plums. I reach over and give him a side hug, squeezing his arm tight. "I'm glad you're out," I say. "Can we talk?"

"Yeah, yeah," he says, as if he was expecting us. "Out back okay?"

Ester is warm against me and sleeping well, but I want to get her inside. "Seriously?"

"Why don't we sit in my car?" Phillip suggests as a burst of cold wind scatters snow in our faces.

We hurry, and I get there first and open the door to the back seat. I slide inside and scoot forward so Ester has more room to stretch within the wrap. She remains settled as I gently pat her. Alec and Phillip shut the doors to sit up front.

The car starts, heat already cranked to full blast. We sit, warming up, waiting for someone to begin.

"I can't go back," Alec says. He runs his knuckles over the bottom of the passenger window where it's fogging over. "I'll do whatever you say. Please help me."

You aren't capable.

It's all gone too far.

You've ruined everything.

"We will help," Phillip begins, glancing at me in the mirror before continuing. "But we need the truth. All of it."

"Okay," Alec says. "Whatever you want."

I lean forward a bit more. "How did you meet Belina?"

"Ricky introduced us," he says. "She was working for Ricky's boss, Stefano, and wanted a change. Misha had just fired another nanny, and Ricky thought Belina could do it. He'd brought her around to a couple polo matches, and I already liked her. I mean, she put up with Ricky. I just didn't know about her and Stefano. That made it complicated."

"She was dating Ricky and Stefano at the same time?" I ask.

"I don't know if she was dating Ricky. They honestly didn't seem to like each other very much. I only know about her and Stefano because of what happened later."

"The money." Phillip shifts to stare at Alec. "You admit that you were laundering money for Stefano?" he says. "Through your business?"

Alec turns away, and his fingers squeak against the window as he runs them back and forth. "Yeah," he says. "I didn't really have a choice. Stefano presented this opportunity after I got the grant from your uncle." He glances back to me. "I needed cash, and he was so successful. I didn't even realize it was *that* illegal at first."

"Jesus," I whisper, frustrated by that very Alec-like answer, as if it were a silly mistake. Whatever was left of my waning sympathy is gone. "We know you were meeting with your divorce attorney at Hope Street Pizza Kitchen," I say. "Or did that just happen all of a sudden too?"

"Misha will leave me," Alec shouts, and I put my hand on Ester. "I lost Belina," he says, softer, "now Misha. I never thought . . ."

"What happened when you told Stefano you were going to get a divorce?" I ask. "Did he want his money back?"

"Yeah," Alec says. "I spent it to get things cleaned up with Misha. Belina had, you know, projected or whatever, that we'd be able to cover it long term, but things dried up. We had our worst quarter. Suddenly, I owed a half million dollars. But we were going to figure it out."

"Stefano didn't agree?" I ask.

Alec rubs his eye. "He punched me in the face."

"Oh." Phillip shoots me an intrigued look in the mirror. "He's a violent guy?"

"He's basically a thug in a fancy house," Alec says bitterly. "I should have known better."

"I don't think you're as dumb as you're playing," I say. "You knew CF was Stefano. That it's more than likely he killed Belina. You lied. A lot. Why?"

"I'm sorry," he says. "I still can't believe they think I did it. I kept expecting that detective to catch the real killer. How could I ask Misha to support me when I was about to leave her? Bail me out like she did—" He pauses when his voice breaks. "If you can get me out of this . . . please, I can't go back to jail. I can't miss out on my son's life."

"If Stefano sent you a half million in dirty money," I say, "you needed other sources to clean it besides the twelve boats."

"Yeah," Alec says. He slumps his body as if all that he'd been hiding was finally let go. "We used my boat to take coolers to New York regularly."

"Black market fish?" I guess. "Cash?"

"Yeah." Alec begins to fidget. No longer lazing his finger along the glass, he's rubbing his thumbs together, scratching his shoulder, shifting in his seat. "Drugs too."

He's just as dirty as Stefano.

Why protect him now?

Because you're just as guilty.

You're just as bad as the boys.

I frown. "Ricky was with you on these New York runs?"

"Yeah, he brought the idea to Stefano," Alec says. "Once the FBI targeted Stefano's business . . . he needed us more. He had a lot of money to clean and hide. If things got bad."

"You knew about the FBI sniffing around?" I snap. "Stefano told you? When?"

His chin drops, his whole face twisting left as he unsuccessfully holds back tears. "Not Stefano . . . Belina told me, just before she left to meet him that night . . . she told me that she knew the FBI was on to him and maybe us. She was going to give Stefano this money she had saved. And then the three of us . . . Belina and me and Emmett. We were going to start over." Alec puts his head in his hands. "I loved her so much, and now everything is gone."

I suck in a long breath, trailing my fingers along Ester's back. Then I put the hand on Alec, squeezing his now boney shoulder.

"How could I go to jail when I didn't kill her?" His voice is so distant, as if he's speaking only to himself. "My life is over. And she . . . we . . . she was pregnant," he sobs. "Oh God, the baby."

I see it in a flash of memory, how Belina stared at my pregnant stomach that last afternoon I spent with her. Then later in the video, how she wrapped her arms around her waist in the gazebo, wearing Alec's coat, staring at the river where her body would be dumped just a few hours later.

She needed you.

You ignored her.

God punished you both.

God's not done with you, girlie.

"Alec," I whisper, my hand still on him. "You should have told me."

"It was just once," he murmurs. "We didn't want to have an affair. I loved her and told her, and she said she loved me too." His voice is so soft, far away. "That's why I had to move things along so fast. Paying off the mortgage, keeping Misha happy, and working for Stefano more. To get our new life started. Guess it was stupid, but at the time . . ."

"You can still be a father to Emmett," I say, squeezing his shoulder, wanting him to keep fighting. "But you're going to have to admit everything you did for Stefano. Even things that implicate Belina or Ricky."

"I don't want anyone to know about the baby," he says.

I frown, glancing at Phillip. "The detective didn't mention it? Her autopsy would have—"

"He lied about it," he says, sounding disgusted. "They said the baby's not mine. It's an interrogation tactic, right? Assholes."

Before I can respond, my phone buzzes, an alert that lets me know it's an email from my brother. He confirms that the money Belina transferred was to an account belonging to Stefano. And the same account sent the money to Tina. From one payoff to the next.

I find Phillip's stare again in the mirror. "Let's call Agent Fincher."

Chapter 29

The sun has set, and rush hour traffic is quiet. I watched most of it from a small conference room in the US Attorney's Office, where the state's FBI office operates downtown on Dorrance Street. Alec's attorney got there shortly after us. Max interviewed Alec for almost four hours straight.

The attorney did a masterful job negotiating immunity for Alec's testimony against Stefano. It wiped clean any charges against Alec related to the transporting of illegal fish, cash, or drugs. Alec was released without going into protective custody while Max continues to build the case.

I sat next to Alec in that room because he asked me. Squeezed his hand when his voice faltered. Gave him an encouraging nod whenever his scared gaze darted my way. He didn't mention Belina's pregnancy, but now that I know, I recognize his shame. The resentment of our sad shared knowledge. After it was over, with the last look he gave me, I knew he'd never want to see me again.

That's how everyone leaves you.

Full of regret.

Full of shame.

Detective Ramos said they didn't know who the father was. My guess is that'll change once they arrest Stefano and compare his DNA. More motive for him killing Belina.

With Alec's testimony over, he asked Phillip, who'd worked in a small office during the interview, to drive him home. It's almost time for me to walk over to Jack's office, where I left Ester with Gillian. Hopefully, he'll be done for the day and can give me a ride to Uncle Cal's.

Instead of leaving, I find an outlet in the women's bathroom and pump a bottle while deciding I need one more conversation with Max.

I find him in the interrogation room, reviewing his notes. "What part of Stefano are you most interested in?" I ask, hoping that since the immunity deal is done, he can be more open.

He glances up at me and then back to his notes. "The drugs," he says. "Though he may get more time for the black market fish. They do not fuck around at NOAA."

I chuckle. "How about the money laundering?"

"It's tough to prove. We're looking at about . . . fifteen counts so far."

"What if you get a tip? Some anonymous informant?"

Now he laughs a little. "I don't know, Devon. I'd rather find it on my own. The right way."

"Wait until you see it first," I say. "Can you give me anything?"

He nods once, tightly, and I know it'll come from an email account not tied to him. He used it before when I was trying to find something on Phillip to keep him from releasing the money-laundering story about Uncle Cal.

"Thank you," I say and stand up.

"Need a ride?"

"No thanks." I start toward the door and pause. "Do you think Belina told Stefano about the FBI? Or did he tell her?"

Max crosses his arms, his suit coat too tight for his muscles. "No offense, but I'm not sharing anything about the case with anyone besides Frank. I've already lost too much trusting people."

"Trusting who?" I say.

"Doesn't matter anymore," he says. "Thanks to you."

You were wrong about everything.

Jack is outside in the car, and I sit with Ester in the back. He doesn't ask why I was at the FBI. Instead we drive in silence through College Hill, the neighborhood next to ours. My mind can't settle, and then Ester begins to cry. I shush her, hum a sea shanty song I half remember from Gillian.

Jack wants to leave you.

Wants all of this to be over.

To be free of you.

To be free of this terrible child you forced him to have.

"I'm sorry," I say, but he doesn't look angry. He looks so damn sad. After a few seconds, I find my courage. "I need to see Uncle Cal."

He slows down momentarily but then goes faster, up the hill, down the historic narrow Benefit Street, the cobblestone road reverberating the back seat. He continues toward Uncle Cal's house until we're there, sitting in silence.

"I'm not stupid," he says finally. "I know Uncle Cal is pulling the strings. Working some angle you probably don't even see." He sighs, glancing at me in the rearview mirror. "I expected it of him. But you promised it'd be different."

I glance at Ester, who's fallen asleep, and I wonder why I can't change for her. Change for Jack. "I have to help Belina," I say. "What kind of mother would I be if I didn't?"

He drops his head back. "I don't know what to do."

"I can take her in," I say.

"She's fine in here," he snaps, and in the mirror I see him work to gather patience. "Half hour enough time?"

I run my fingers along his arm, but he pulls away. He gets out and pushes his seat forward so I can get out. "Thank you," I say as I stand. I give him a kiss on the cheek, but he looks pained as he returns to the car.

He won't come back.

If he's smart, it's the last time you'll see either of them.

Ringing Uncle Cal's doorbell, I'm unsure what I should say, only that I owe him this visit.

He's not your real uncle.

He's using you because that's all you're worth.

Uncle Cal answers in his work suit, martini in his hand, face a bit surprised.

"I'm coming from Agent Fincher's office," I say. "We need to talk."

Both sides of his jaw flare from a quick grinding of his teeth. He steps back, and I knock my boots against the outside rug, then pull my feet out of them. My wool-socked feet sink into the first of several Moroccan rugs, each likely costing a year's worth of mortgage payments.

Imagine trash like you prancing through his house.

He leads us down the hall toward his study, but a violent cough racks his body. He barely gets his drink onto a console table before doubling over, bracing himself against the wall. My first thought is one of relief that Ester, so susceptible to germs, isn't with me. Feeling guilty, I step toward him and take his elbow, but he pulls away.

His trembling hand searches his pocket. He pulls out a tissue and dabs his twisting lips. After clearing his throat, he goes to put the tissue away, but I see crimson before he can. Germs may not be the issue.

"Is it bronchitis?" I ask.

He shakes his head wearily as if he wishes it were.

I step toward him. "What did the doctor say?"

"What he always says." He leaves the martini, shuffles to his study, and opens the door. "I'm not about to start listening."

"Maybe you should," I say.

"My health, or lack of it, is not up for discussion."

The room is dark except for the cast from an emerald desk lamp. He drops into his wingback chair behind the oversize desk. I really observe him for the first time in a while. He's older, hair thinner, not brushed out as it was at the party last week. His skin is sallow, and I wonder if he's been using makeup. The suit is baggy, as if he has lost weight.

"Will you tell Jack you're sick?" I ask, sitting across from him. "He'll want to know. To help."

He makes a phlegmy growling noise. "That's the last thing I want. From anyone."

My guess is Uncle Cal has lung cancer, and that changes things. "How bad is it?" I ask. "I won't tell Jack, if that's what you want."

"Full of secrets these days," he says, his voice still raspy from the coughing.

"I missed the changes in you," I say. Not to mention all his talk of legacy. His focus on the Council's reputation. It was right there for me to see. "I'm sorry."

He half grins or maybe grimaces. "Why are you here?"

You don't belong here.

You don't belong anywhere.

You should be dead.

Guilt sits within my gut, pulling with it memories of my grandfather, relishing his painful decline in a La-Z-Boy in my mother's living room. "Alec is cooperating with the FBI. He has information on illegal activities Stefano committed. It includes the money laundering, and Max will likely take a hard look at the EDC. I haven't heard your name, but you'll want to protect yourself."

"This ratting on Stefano gets Alec out of the murder charge?" Uncle Cal asks, seeming confused.

"I am getting him out of the murder charge," I say. "He has a real alibi now." I shift in my chair, focusing on my second reason for the visit. "Tomorrow morning, Phillip will air video evidence proving Alec's alibi for the murder. The case will be blown wide open."

He taps a thin finger on his oak desk. "Will Stefano be charged with murder?"

"He's the only other suspect I can see," I say. "There's a long list of reasons he may have killed Belina. She was supposed to manage Alec, but she let him burn through all Stefano's dirty money. Then Belina gave Stefano a hundred grand, to get him to let her go, maybe. I doubt he liked that."

"The licenses will be on the market," he says, more to himself, finally relaxing into his chair. "How soon?"

"Why?" I say. "You looking to invest with Miguel?"

He smiles at me and rests his hands in his lap. "I already did."

I see it now, what else I missed. Uncle Cal wants Stefano to be charged with murder. That's why he wants me on Stefano's trail. He's throwing money in with Miguel and the Rossa family. It is high risk, high reward, and quick turnaround. I am used to Uncle Cal having patience and an unusual appetite for the long game.

Just like that dead girl.

You were too wrapped up in yourself to see death circling.

Another soul touched by you damned to hell.

His breath is a wheeze, soft and rhythmic, answering why he is breaking his normal business pattern. He's out of time.

"Why this risk now?" I ask. "Miguel is unproven, and Stefano is not an easy man to take down. When is enough money actually enough?"

"When Jack is governor," Uncle Cal says quietly.

I laugh, louder than I have in months, maybe years. But when I stop, there's no smile. "He doesn't want to be governor. He's barely keeping it together as chief of staff."

"And whose fault is that?"

A slap in the face would have been easier to take. I swallow thickly, trying to find a way to disagree, but I can't. "He doesn't want it."

"Not yet," Uncle Cal says. "But soon he'll get tired of making the mayor look good. And if I'm not around to raise money, he'll have a nice war chest. That is my real legacy."

So this is his gamble. Invest with Miguel after I suspect Stefano. The licenses could mean millions to early investors. "How long do you have?" I ask.

"This is my last Christmas," Uncle Cal says. "One way or another."

"Miguel could be connected to Belina," I say.

"You've got your man," Uncle Cal says. "Take aim at Stefano, and don't stop until he's behind bars."

Do as you're told, girlie.

Let these men use you up.

Spit you out.

The river waits for you too.

I stand up, tired of his games and gambles. Not when it comes to justice. "Just get your house in order," I say. "I'll do my best to keep Max from your legacy."

I pass the carpets, the expensive paintings, and the turret fireplace warming no one. Jack's car is waiting in the driveway. I hurry inside after he opens his door so I can climb into the back. Ester begins to cry, and I lean over her car seat, trying to soothe her, wiping a few tears of my own.

A snow flurry begins as Jack drives us home. I imagine the conversation we could have if I were honest about Uncle Cal's health. I consider going back on my word as we pull up to our house.

"That's weird," Jack says.

I look at our home. The front door is wide open.

Chapter 30

Jack and I sit with Ester in the locked car, waiting for the police to arrive at our home. There are no lights on. No movement. It's all going to be a silly mistake; I forgot to lock the door on the way out, and the wind blew it open.

You're about to get what you deserve.

Ester begins to cry, a piercing wail from within the confines of the car. I fumble with the diaper bag for the milk I pumped in the FBI bathroom. I make Ester a bottle, take it to her lips, but it spills, and she spits and doesn't seem to want anything from me.

You were never meant to be a mother.

You're reckless and selfish.

Your actions brought an intruder into your home.

I cry with Ester, silent tears, wiping them quickly, so very tired of my emotions being on a hair trigger.

I notice Jack is watching me in the rearview mirror. "Let me take her," he says.

I unbuckle Ester and hand her to him. She's quiet almost immediately.

She hates the feel of your skin.

Smell of your weakness.

She wishes you were dead.

I curl my knees up under my chin, trying to think of things I can do while I wait. Check to see how Phillip's segment is coming along. Confirm the waitress with Alec's alibi will talk on video. I also need to call my brother, to check on the data he analyzed from Jamestown. To see if he found another link to Stefano.

Instead I breathe and breathe and breathe. Someone has broken into my home. The place where my baby sleeps, where my husband and I built a life. It has been violated by someone else.

I don't want to watch the police pick through my drawers and run gloved fingers over shelves. My stomach burns with acid, the bile at war with my mind, which is trying to keep me from throwing up.

But the past is so close lately, with the voice's return.

Come close, girlie.

Be good, girlie.

Lay still.

Pray with me, girlie.

My mind is stuck back in my tiny childhood bedroom, the scene of the "supposed crime." Everything was upended: books scattered, New Kids on the Block poster torn, dolls disheveled, jewelry box broken, and the small diary hidden under my bed taken as evidence. A ballerina figurine I'd painted at Vacation Bible School the summer before was crushed beyond recognition. I threw it all away, even if it wasn't damaged. I never decorated my bedroom again. Not in college, law school, or my first apartment in DC. Not until we created our home in Providence.

You destroy every home.

It's all your fault.

Detective Ramos pulls up next to us in the driveway with two uniformed officers. He nods our way and then hurries inside. Flashlights appear through windows, the first floor, then second. They're in the baby's room the longest, and I can't take it.

"I need to go see," I say, not recognizing my voice.

"It's not safe," Jack says. "Let's wait for Detective Ramos to tell us we can go in."

I know he's right, but I still open my door, and suddenly I'm sprinting to the back door, which is wide open. I try to yell that I'm inside, but my voice falters in the entryway. Every drawer has been pulled out and dumped onto the floor. Every cabinet emptied. Boxes of mac and cheese are mixed with broken dishes and metal pans and takeout menus.

In the hallway, our wedding pictures have been pulled off the wall and smashed onto the ground. The dining room has every chair upturned, every dish smashed, including our wedding china. Even the champagne glasses we bought from where we'd had our first date are tiny shards.

Footsteps thump above, and I'm sure it's the police. The person or people who broke in are gone. Threat made and received.

The living room is almost comically destroyed, like a movie. The couch ripped up, cotton and foam exploded all over the rug. All the DVDs are scattered and out of their cases. The mantel is bare, but it shouldn't be. The fireplace poker is nearby, probably used as a bat against the photos; an empty vase and my collection of succulents in a small terrarium, now all in pieces on the floor.

You've destroyed another home with your lies.

The sickness and shame and guilt are suffocating, but I breathe because I must get to Ester's room.

Lumbering up the stairs, I have to pause several times as my vision narrows, the blackout almost certain, but I safely make it to the landing. I freeze at my office when I see my laptop is gone. I doubt they'd be smart enough to get past the security codes before the hard drive wiped itself clean. But it's possible.

I open the closet door and see my small safe ripped out. They won't get much, but there's a full copy of Belina's journal and some personal things that meant a lot to me. My emancipation paperwork. My sealed court documents. I have scans of them elsewhere, and maybe I should have destroyed them. But I couldn't. They went with me everywhere in that safe.

You may be done with the past, girlie.

We'll never let you go.

I don't even glance into my bedroom, but I open the door to Ester's room. Two uniformed officers and Detective Ramos are gathered around the crib.

They can see the truth.

You don't deserve to be a mother.

"Let me see," I say too loudly.

They're trying to stop me, but I shrug off their gentle touches on my arm. I know Ester is in the car, but her crying fills the room, loud and frantic.

There's a knife in the crib. The entire blade shoved deep into the center of her soft pink sheets.

We're not done with you.

Not until you get what you deserve.

Chapter 31

I'm sitting alone in Ester's glider, rocking softly, staring at the place where the knife was taken out of my daughter's bed and bagged as evidence.

They should have stuck it in you.

I tell myself it's okay.

I can put our house back together, even if it'll never be a home again.

Destroyed your home, then left the ruins.

Who are you to try to build another?

This is what you deserve.

Everything is so familiar. This feeling of helplessness. The intruder in my home.

My grandfather was the worst of intruders. A preacher who roamed Kansas and much of the Midwest because Southern Baptist churches are notoriously autonomous. Like in the Catholic Church, no one mentioned any of the "complaints." They just sent him along to another town, another church, until finally, he had nowhere to go but his tiny hometown.

I told my mom about the first time, and she ignored me, doesn't believe me to this day. I don't know why I kept trying to get her to believe me, believe me, believe me. Maybe it's nature that instills in us an almost infinite amount of forgiveness for our parents. The desperate need to be loved and cared for and kept safe. And even if they fail, maybe the next time. Or the next. Or the next.

It took three years of listening to his sermons until the Sunday he stood on the pulpit and preached about God's justice. There was something about that word, the idea that justice was possible for anyone, whether it be God's or the police's or my parents'. It occurred to me that justice could also be mine, if I did something to get it.

The police were surprised and skeptical. Who would believe a preacher, beloved and local, capable of something so terrible? They took me home and got permission to search our house. I watched them in my room, more men, opening and closing and rummaging. There wasn't anything to find. But they went through it all.

My mom glared at me with each item overturned, hating me even more than either of us thought possible. My father silent and doing what he was told. After the police left, no one helped me with my room. Derek wasn't allowed, and he'd been hiding most of the day anyway. Mom said I should live in filth, since it was all I talked.

I didn't sleep but instead put my room back together, trying to wear the guilt down into exhaustion. Thinking if I did just the right thing, Mom would suddenly understand.

I woke up the next day and was interviewed by a special detective. She brought an assistant district attorney and a counselor. That was where I saw justice, at least some form of it, for the first time. Where adults believed me and tried to put him away.

It didn't work. So I waited. Left home at sixteen, legally emancipated, justice working for me at last. And I didn't come back, except to watch my grandfather die painfully. He cursed me on his deathbed, body rotting away from a spreading stomach cancer. That was the truest form of justice.

I hear Jack's steps and return to this home I've chosen and built with him. But I don't see my fearless partner. Instead, everything about him is slack: his suit, his jaw, the circles under his eyes. He is angry, weary, and there's plenty of worry in his hard stare. He watches me for a few seconds.

"Dev, are you okay?" he asks finally.

"Define *okay*," I say but don't move from the steady rhythm of the chair. "Where's Ester?"

"Sleeping in the car," he says. "There's police everywhere. She's safe."

She'll never be safe with a mother like you.

His shoes thud softly on the carpet, and he puts a hand on the back of the glider, stopping the rocking.

I look up. "This is terrible," I say.

"We're okay," he says softly, not sounding entirely convinced.

He's right. On the list of possible crimes committed against me in retaliation, it's manageable.

"Is Detective Ramos still here?" I ask.

Jack sighs, then crouches down in front of me. "We need to stop. For a day or two."

"That's impossible," I say. "Is he downstairs?"

He reels back, and I see his patience end, even before he realizes it.

"Christ, Dev." He bolts up, starts for the door, but then spins to face me. "What will it take for you to back off? Our house burned to the ground? Belina's murderer on our doorstep?"

"I can't stop," I say simply because it's the truth. He knows this about me. Loved me for it once.

You're turning him into someone he never wanted to be.

You've ruined his life.

You've ruined everything you never deserved.

Jack stomps down the stairs, and I hear some murmuring as the back door slams. I look out Ester's window and see him get back into the car.

I find Detective Ramos on the porch in the dark. The moon is a sliver, and shadows are everywhere. "I'm sorry about your house," he says, not turning around.

"Me too," I say. "But it's not really your fault." I pause, realizing that's not true. "Actually, if you'd arrested the right person, this wouldn't have happened."

He sighs, cracking his neck to one side. "You should get to a hotel," he says. "This will take us all night."

"I know how long it takes." My voice is shrill, terror and memories at my throat. "My computer and the contents of my safe are gone. It was mostly personal, but there was also a copy of Belina's journal."

"We'll need a list of everything," he says.

"I know," I say, again too sharp, too emotional. "Look, we need to talk about the case. Alec's case."

Even now you're obsessed.

You don't deserve this life.

He turns, stepping closer to me with a placating smile. "I'm about to have my second child. My wife has been very enthusiastic about certain . . . aspects of raising our older son. Only organic, all-natural birth and breastfeeding until he can say, 'No thank you; I'll have a beer.'"

I frown but then realize he's making a joke. "Funny," I say.

"Look, she's doing a great job. But sometimes I can see the stress and pressure. From other people. From herself. She's the one with our son, day in and day out. I escape to my job, like Jack does. We get to use nonkid parts of our brain. Go where we want during the day. Not be controlled by this tiny little dictator. We unplug in a way you stay-at-homes don't."

My chest constricts, aching from the truth of what he's saying, but I still want to deflect. "You think I need a vacation?"

He works his jaw. "You've taken this . . . project to help Belina as far as you can. I'm sure it felt nice to use your brain. To think about something other than baby life. You wanted to help a friend."

I keep from calling him a condescending prick but just barely. "I'm about to solve your case. I blew up your entire theory about Alec in one week. So you're welcome, for saving your ass."

"We're not there yet," he says, holding up his hands. "Let me do my job, and you can do yours. To start, you need to take care of yourself."

"That couldn't be any less of your goddamn business," I snap, taking a long inhale to relish what I'm about to tell him. "Tomorrow morning Phillip is going on national television with a one-on-one interview with Alec. He's cooperating with the FBI to build a case against Stefano. That's not a part of Phillip's interview. I'm just telling you."

Detective Ramos curses under his breath and turns to look back outside for a second. "Keep going," he says at last.

"Alec's alibi didn't hold up because you only got half. He did get blackout drunk, as he said, but not at the Ivy Tavern. He went two doors down to Hope Street Pizza Kitchen. The waitress was out for a while from knee surgery. But she remembers him. She'll testify he was there until almost three a.m. And had a black eye. She remembered."

"Why did he lie?"

"He met with a divorce attorney that night. He expected you to find the real killer. So he wouldn't have to admit that he was going to leave Misha and lose them both. But you never did." I stop it there, though I could go on.

But he is guilty.

You're protecting a bad man.

Because you're worse.

"I can't believe my guys missed it," Detective Ramos says.

"She didn't think much about it until we brought it to her attention," I say, not meaning it as an excuse.

He rubs his face with his hand. "What's your theory?"

I picture all the pieces I've managed to uncover, see the threads and theories, and quickly order them from fact to best guess. "Belina is connected to Stefano Venantius. Both work and personal. He rented a boat the night of the murder, and her day planner indicated they were meeting. He's being investigated by the FBI, who were close to charging him with crimes that would put him away for a while. But the day after her murder, Stefano went dark. Likely, she told him about the FBI. Or he knew he'd be watched as a suspect to her murder."

I pause, let him sit with that.

"What I know for sure," I continue, "is that Belina told Alec about the FBI before the meeting where she was murdered. So if she was working with the FBI, perhaps Stefano attacked her. They were linked romantically, but she and Alec were going to try to be together, if Alec left his wife—"

"That's enough," Detective Ramos says, holding his hands up. "We didn't have this conversation. I'm clueless about what you and Phillip are doing on TV or otherwise. And when the DA and my boss come to kick my ass, I'll act like I don't know shit. Which I guess is about right."

"Okay," I say, surprised. "But Stefano—"

"We've questioned him," he says. "He wasn't involved in her death."

Listen to the boys, girlie.

Go where they say.

Do what they want.

Jack steps onto the porch with Ester in the car seat, protected from the night air by a blanket. "Devon, can you get her packed? We should get settled in the hotel."

I know Detective Ramos is going to give Jack an earful, but it doesn't matter.

Every instinct says the bastards who wrecked my home killed Belina. The home I've been trying to build my whole life. This was the exact wrong move if they want me to back off.

Chapter 32

Friday, December 16

The security footage Max emailed me from his anonymous account is thirty seconds long and shows Alec stumbling down Lauriston Street, urinating in a CVS parking lot, and turning onto Cole Avenue toward his home. It's time-stamped 2:55 a.m.

I sent it to Phillip from the hotel last night before I got a few hours of sleep. He's in New York, also up late, working on his segment for the *TODAY Show*. Unlike previous times, he hasn't emailed me notes to look over. I'm telling myself he's busy, but he's always busy. This segment goes beyond our agreement. It'll likely get rebroadcast throughout the day, possibly even lead to a special.

I text him my fear: Keep Stefano out of it. Not enough evidence.

No response.

I curse but do it softly because Ester is sleeping in a Biltmore Hotel–issued crib in the living area of our suite where I'm working. Jack is not the kind of person to get a big room, but we both need space.

You better get used to lots of space.

From Jack.

Revisiting the data Derek sent, I see the link he found, connecting one of the monthly boat rentals to a local account Stefano opened decades ago. I start to text my brother, to say thanks, to tell him about the intruder, to tell him it split open old wounds from our shared past. But he'd be upset, and I can't share like that with him anymore.

I stare at the dates when the boat was rented. It's almost every thirty days and always for twenty-four hours. I look back at Belina's journal: she met with CF each day he rented the boat, a pattern that continued to the night of her murder.

I sort through the data Derek sent about Stefano's accounts. I need to make a case for money laundering that includes Alec's business but leaves out the Economic Development Council.

The commercial break is over, and Phillip's segment is opening the show. He lays out everything we've got to prove Alec is innocent. The video of Alec is particularly sympathetic and a little funny as Phillip makes a joke about CVS not having public bathrooms.

Then it shifts, Phillip sharing about the one on one in his car, how Alec cried about the woman he loved and whose death he's blamed for. There's some simple footage of Alec looking sad and contrite.

"But after we return," says the anchor, "the latest suspect not even the police have uncovered."

"Shit," I say and call Phillip. It goes right to voice mail. I email him to call me immediately. Email the producer to call me immediately. Get put through by the receptionist to the voice mail of anyone I can find on the dial directory.

The segment is as awful as I feared. He includes every last piece of evidence against Stefano: the night fishing boat ride near where Belina was killed, his nickname in the journal, previous working and possibly romantic relationship with Belina, dozens of meetings together, the hundred grand Belina transferred, and his same amount paid to Tina. He even hints at the FBI case as another possible motive.

I put the TV on mute and stare. We've showed our hand completely to Stefano. He's going to bury us. My phone buzzes, and I tell myself not to yell right away.

"I can't believe you did that," I say as calmly as I can. "We had time. You didn't have to do this now."

"Yes, I did," Phillip says. "The producers wanted more than Alec's exoneration. They wanted to know who actually did it. This was it."

"There had to be other opportunities," I say. "Take it to another network."

"There was no time for that," Phillip says. "And . . . Alec told me that Miguel was working with Uncle Cal. That they want Stefano's fishing licenses when he goes to prison. So in the end, aren't we just doing what we always did? Putting ourselves first?"

"I didn't know that," I lie, sort of. "I have only been trying to help Belina—"

"It doesn't matter, Devon," Phillip says, the emotion heavy in his low voice. "I had to make my move."

I should have seen his desperation. He took me back too easily. Went along with every suggestion. He knew he'd never have another chance like this. Maybe that's what Cynthia was trying to tell me. It wasn't just her fear that I'd screw him over again. It was her fear of two people who needed something so badly working together.

Too stupid to see it coming.

Or you let it happen.

Either way, you deserved to get screwed over.

"We're even," I say. "Good luck."

Jack steps out of the bedroom. He's shaved, his suit is clean and pressed, but the circles under his eyes draw the most attention. "Who was that?" he asks.

"Phillip," I say. "We're in some trouble."

"If Stefano isn't guilty—"

"He is," I snap. "Sorry, didn't sleep much."

He nods, but there's no emotion, not real consideration. I wonder if he's in shock from last night. Or if he's been in some form of shock since the night Ester and I almost died. "She's fed," he says. "Gillian will be here in an hour."

I frown at him. I don't plan to leave anytime soon. "Did the police give us the okay to go home?" Perhaps a day of cleaning will help my mind focus on how to really pin down Stefano.

"The mayor wants to see you," he says. "I'm not sure . . . this is my last chance with this job. So please come."

I nod quickly, but Jack waits for more of a response. I'm not sure what to say. I wish I were someone else. Why did you marry me? I told you not to.

Just leave him now.

Leave the baby. She'll be better off.

Leave it all behind.

He picks up his coat, hefts it over his shoulder, and shrugs it together as he buttons it. As if his pockets are full of stones. He doesn't say anything else, which is worse than if he screamed. I've always wondered at what point he'd regret marrying someone like me. Perhaps it's today.

Let him go.

Let everyone go.

Ester begins to cry, so I change her diaper and get her out of her pajamas. Once she's situated in a bouncy chair, I move her near the bathroom and take a shower. She's just outside the door, and I wash and listen for her to get upset. I realize she's been crying less and less. Maybe we're rounding a corner.

One you can't walk back.

I dig out a black dress and the only cardigan I brought over. With heels and some lipstick and undereye concealer, it's all the armor I can slap together in an hour.

Gillian arrives, greeting me with a too-cheerful smile. As if she knows I'm walking into the firing squad, which she might.

I thank her for coming over but leave before any conversation can take place.

I push through the revolving door of our hotel. An icy blast of wind rips at my hair and scorches my bare legs. In my peripheral vision I see past Kennedy Plaza, full of loud bus traffic and a mix of commuters and vagrants.

Leaning into the wind, I cross the street to Providence City Hall. It's exactly how I pictured every city hall. Built in the late 1800s, the exterior is made of pale limestone blocks that shine on this bright winter morning. The iron flourishes are a vibrant weathered green. I hurry up the steps through the entryway, but there's not a big change in temperature inside. It's a large, drafty building, with open staircases rising three floors. My heels click against the mosaic tiles. I hope the sound communicates confidence rather than the trepidation I really feel.

This is where you lose him for good.

You've taken away his home.

His job.

He'll never forgive you.

On the third floor, I approach a large wooden door that reads **MAYOR'S OFFICE.** I knock lightly, and the door swings open. The communications director, Barry Kapps, moves over so I can enter. He's already sweating and nervous but fakes a grin. "This way please, Ms. Burges."

"Thank you, Barry," I say and follow him into the office. Jack is there, sitting rigid in one of the two chairs in front of the mayor's empty desk. I sit in the other, and he doesn't look at me. We both pretend to be really interested in staring at the downtown buildings and the top of the giant decorated holiday tree.

It's a twist in my gut because we don't have a tree this year. Not even for Ester's first Christmas.

Even if you had, it'd have been destroyed, like your home and your life.

My eyes burn with tears, but I'm able to breathe them away. The door opens, and the slow-moving but loud-heeled steps of the mayor tap behind us.

From the corner of my eye, I see a manicured hand squeezing the leather back of my chair.

"Marriage counseling is not my forte," says Mayor Samantha Soriano. "As you well know, I've had three men divorce me."

I smile, even though I've heard the line a dozen times. Her marriages led to us working together after she was elected. Well, one marriage, in particular. Husband number two had photos and several videos that needed to be erased. Thankfully she did not marry him for his smarts. Her motivation was more related to the contents of the photos. The task took less than two days total, with a little help from Derek after my own light breaking and entering.

But now I will have to test the limits of her gratitude. Despite what Phillip has done, I'm not backing down from this case.

The mayor's nails tap on the back of my chair. "How do you see this ending?"

I don't turn around. "This?"

She steps around the chair, leaning onto the front of her desk to face us. Her suit is navy, tailored, and almost tight. "This woman's murder is drowning my administration. I can't get a reporter to ask about anything else. All my statements are defending fuckups of the police, who are fighting me on pension reform. I thought they had the guy who did it. You and the *TODAY Show* tell me differently this morning." She flicks a glance at Jack. "A heads-up would have been nice."

"We're working separate tracks," he says, his voice quiet but firm.

He can't control his own crazy wife.

You make him look like such a sucker.

He's done in this town.

She focuses back on me. "When is this over?"

"As soon as I can get enough evidence against Stefano," I say. "I'm trying to help."

She tilts her blowout to the side toward Jack, giving him a look that says, *Are you fucking kidding me?* He glances up to receive it but doesn't react. "Undermining the police department," she begins, "is not the help I need."

"They screwed up," I say.

She turns on her heel, heading behind her desk as if it's higher ground. Before I lived in DC, I'd had a general respect for elected leaders. I thought they were smart, connected to their voters. But happy hours on Capitol Hill with staffers and a few too-drunk and handsy members of Congress dissuaded me of that notion. Best case, they're smart egomaniacs who want to help people according to their own values. Worst case is sitting in the Oval Office right now.

This mayor is certainly closer to the former, but she'd made a mint on Wall Street before returning to her hometown of Providence, ready to tell us how to live. I feel a bit of pride at the observation because it's about the most Rhode Island thought I've ever had.

But that's not why I'm here. She's going to want me to back off, and that's not an option. "The *TODAY Show* could just be the beginning," I say, bluffing a little. "Phillip Hale will be discussing this case and putting the Providence police and your administration front and center for many, many news cycles. You want my help."

"Unbelievable," she says. She impatiently tips her head toward Jack as if waiting for him to say something, but he only turns back toward the view of the holiday tree. She shakes her head, pursing her lips, putting a hand on a slim hip. "I'm in goddamn union contract negotiations. This distraction could cost the city millions in pension payouts."

"It's much worse than that," I say. "You and Cal started the Economic Development Council. It's about to go down in flames." I pause at the threat. One I don't plan to keep, but she doesn't know that. "If you try to protect Stefano—which, let's be honest here, that's the direction this conversation is heading—you won't survive."

"Detective Ramos told me that Stefano wasn't involved," she says. "He's emphatic, so you see my dilemma."

"You want it both ways," I say. "Stefano is a huge contributor, obviously, but even if it's not murder, he's going to be charged with other crimes. Have FBI Agent Max Fincher in here to brief you on Alec Mathers's deal with them."

She curses and nods toward Jack. "Can we afford to give back Stefano's campaign contributions?"

"It doesn't matter. We have to," he says. "The Republican nominee already paints you as a crooked Hillary liberal. This is exactly what they need."

I stand up, the righteousness of my tone a bit too delicious. "You want me in the middle of this, so I can keep you and Cal out of it."

She leans over her desk. "Are you threatening me?"

Jack will lose his job.

You will lose Jack.

"I'm advising you to back off. We're near the end. I'd prefer the EDC stay intact. You need me to navigate that outcome." I think of Cynthia and what it means to her. Uncle Cal's reputation with whatever time he's got left. How much Jack believes in the mayor and her vision for Providence. How he wants to learn from her and possibly run for office in the future.

"Why are you doing this?" she says.

You ruin everything.

"Because I'm the only one who seems to care about justice. Or is willing to do what it takes to get it."

She puts both hands on her hips now, rearing her head back as if she can't reason with me. Which is correct. "Keep the EDC and my name out of Phillip Hale's mouth." She turns to Jack. "And you—"

Barry bursts in through the door, the pit stains now dark rings. "I'm sorry, Mayor, but it's Stefano Venantius." He pauses to fumble with a remote and aims it toward a TV in the corner. "It's live on the local Fox affiliate and getting picked up national. He's accusing our office of harassment."

Chapter 33

Nothing good comes from a ten a.m. exclusive interview on a Friday. It's intended to drive news cycles all weekend. In Stefano's case, he will likely do that and more.

That's your fault.

He goes nuclear, accusing everyone of harassment: me, Jack, the mayor, the police, Phillip, the FBI. There's even a B-roll package that is polished and ready. My guess is he had a rapid-response PR team get everything loaded after I gave him the tip-off that Phillip and I were nosing around.

That's your fault.

Police footage, nothing I've seen from Max, shows Stefano alone in his boat. It fast-forwards through the evening and into the night, showing him at different places along the river. There are several blocks of time circled in bright red, including one where he was within a mile of the cemetery, but it's positioned as proof. I'm not buying it.

But everyone else is.

Then it cuts to an interview with Tina Cabrala, looking buttoned up and polished. She's tearful and explains how the life insurance policy, which Stefano pays for personally for all his employees, saved her apartment. That Belina had been supporting them, and without Stefano, she'd be on the street. Then Stefano's interview with the friendly blonde anchor who once fell all over herself for Phillip's story. She's looking somber and serious, ready to throw anyone to the wolves for ratings. Stefano ends the interview going after Phillip, saying he is an antibusiness reporter with ties to unsavory sources in the past (my fault).

That's right. It's all your fault.

We sit in the mayor's office for a few quiet seconds, and then the phones start ringing. Office, cell, text alerts, the room erupts as if taken over by technological poltergeists.

Poor schlubby Barry is really sweating now, probably panicked at the thought of drafting the dumpster fire of a press statement while fielding calls from every reporter in New England, possibly beyond.

My phone is buzzing, and I'm sure it's Phillip. Or maybe Max. Or maybe any reporter I worked with during my time with Uncle Cal.

We are in the shit.

The mayor continues to stare at the muted TV and finally speaks by quoting Stefano in the interview. "'Even now, the mayor's chief of staff has employed his wife, a hacker with a *suspicious* legal background, to brief the mayor on how to frame me for these crimes.'"

"I was only *almost* disbarred. Once," I say. "I stalked an accused pedophile to find more evidence against him. Sorry, not sorry."

"I need some distance," she says to me, but then her hard stare finds Jack, arms crossed, standing beside me. "Jack, you're poisoned by association. I need an adviser who isn't a neon sign to my liabilities. You're suspended until we get this under control."

"Mayor," I say, "Jack had nothing to do—"

She holds up her hand, cutting me off. "Get out and fix it."

"I will."

Lie to yourself.

Lie to her.

You don't have what it takes.

Jack gently takes my arm, as if he's been waiting for her to kick us out. I follow, but we don't speak. We walk down the three flights in silence, then cross the street and head over to the entrance of the Biltmore. The wind is bitter cold, and we both shiver but don't move.

"Are you coming upstairs?" he asks. "Please, we need to talk."

I shake my head. "Give me today. We'll talk tonight."

What a terrible mother.

With her terrible child.

He doesn't want to be with your crying freak baby.

Leaving this family you don't deserve to fail again.

He searches my face, and I don't know how to look, what pose or smile or sparkle in my eye will reassure him that I'm capable. That I can still do this, but he has to trust me.

There's anger in his gaze and, I realize, longing. He wants to tell me something, but instead, he turns away, disappears through the door. I grab my phone and see Phillip is one of a dozen people who have called since Stefano went nuclear. I hurry into the parking garage and get into the car before calling him back.

"Devon," he says, his voice a tight panic. "This is bad. My producer thinks NBC might get sued."

I bite back the "I told you so," counting to five until I find, "I'm sorry." We're quiet, and then my brain finally starts to work again. "There's a gap in time while he's on the boat. I think it's possible he still could have met her. Still killed her. When are you back in town?"

"Another hour on the train," he says. "Then I'm never leaving my house again."

"Phillip, this is a setback. Go find Miguel. He's likely at the guesthouse at his father's place on Blackstone and Rochambeau. Tell him he's in the journal. That you're going to drag the Rossa name into this mess if he doesn't give you all the security videos from his father's business related to Belina."

He's paying the price for making a deal with you.

Like a deal with the devil.

As bad as the boys, girlie.

"I don't know, Devon—"

"I'm going to Stefano's house," I say. "I need hard evidence. I need him to confess." I got a few confessions when I was a prosecutor in DC, but they're not easy like on television.

"You'll have to wear a wire," he says as if it's a secret. "Are you sure?"

"Not really," I say. "Find Miguel."

He's quiet, weighing us like when we met at the cemetery. Luckily, we've got nothing to lose.

"Okay," he says. "I'll call you when I get it."

I blast the heat until I can unbutton my shirt and pump. As the pressure in my breasts lessens, I outline my questions and possible tactics to get Stefano to talk.

My big play is revealing that Miguel and Uncle Cal are working against him. That the licenses will certainly be frozen once Alec's testimony goes to the grand jury and Stefano's indictment rolls in. He is cornered. It's over. If I can get him mad enough, I may get lucky, and he will confess. Or attack me. That's why I have the knife in my bag.

Let him stab you.

Your family's better off without you.

After I finish pumping and put the milk in the minicooler, I drive slowly toward Jamestown. My mind is a loop, back and forth, evidence and voice.

This is finally too far.

Jack will leave you.

Ester gone.

Everything gone.

A few blocks from Stefano's house, I pull over. After opening my trunk, I lift up the spare tire and remove a locked kit. Inside are the few things from my past I can't throw away, no matter my promises to Jack. My lockpick kit, a few small tools, and a center punch for breaking into windows, if I'm really desperate and don't mind glass shattering. There's also my knife and a wire kit, a loan from the FBI I never returned.

The transmitter stays in my car, recording what's broadcast from what appears to be an older model iPhone but is actually the wire. There's also a small microphone in my bra as a backup.

I wait in the cold, watching my breath, reminding myself that I'm breathing, that I can help Belina, who is not. It takes an hour of silence, breathing, and thinking to get my mind right. To find my old confidence to approach Stefano.

Phillip finally calls. "I've got the footage of Stefano in the boat," he says. "Are you okay?"

"Nervous," I say. "We're close."

"Miguel had everything. Stefano was right by the cemetery, that missing block of time from his interview. But there's no evidence that he actually got out of the boat to meet her."

"It's enough," I say. "He's hiding something. I'll talk to you soon."

"Wait, Devon—"

I'll call him back as soon as I have the confession. I test the recorder and wire, the one I used with several Rhode Island politicians. I relace it through my bra, test it a few times more. Clear as a bell.

I hear Ester crying and freeze. I whip around and see the empty car seat through the back seat window.

Something has happened.

She needs you.

What a worthless mother.

I try to shrug it off, hurrying the few blocks down the street. The crying follows me, and I am confused, terrified. Her little cry is not the same as the voice. We are not the voice.

I keep scanning the bushes and road and houses on this affluent block, looking for a baby, but no one is there. Perhaps it is someone else's baby. Perhaps the voice is not turning into Ester. I close my eyes, breathing, listening to the bitter wind off the water.

Finally it is quiet. I walk to Stefano's house, large and boxy, mostly windows from the side that can be seen heading over the Jamestown

Bridge. It's stately and wood shingled, and the water views are tough to beat. I'm sure it's what his wife always wanted when she married him thirty years ago. Somewhere to have graduation parties and family cookouts. A place to live and show off.

You can't stop a man like him.

You're too stupid and weak.

Who will believe you?

"Devon Burges," says a man's voice across the lawn. "I thought you'd be coming by."

I jump at his voice, a new kind of terror arriving. My chest tight, I face Stefano, frazzled but unwilling to back down. The wind is strong, and I have to keep myself from adjusting the microphone. "That was a hell of a response," I say as I walk closer. "Well played."

"Thank you," Stefano says. "What's the point of having a PR person on retainer if you don't use her once in a while?"

I'm not in the mood for banter. "Can we talk in the house?" I ask, worried the wind will interfere with the wire.

"I'd rather not," he says. "My wife is taking a nap."

"I hear Agent Fincher has a lot of your financial records," I say. "But he was unfamiliar with accounts tied to Belina and regular boat rentals. Care to discuss?"

His smug smile falls. "This way," he says.

Chapter 34

Stefano leads me through the entryway into his giant kitchen. The Italian marble shines from several soft, dim lights over the counter where the coffee maker is gurgling. The whole first floor is open concept, the dining, living, and family rooms all connected with nothing ahead but sparkling water and a bridge to the mainland.

He pulls out a stool at the counter and gestures for me to sit. He walks over and pours me a cup of coffee. "My wife insists we're civil to everyone in our home." He slides a carton of Rhody Fresh milk over to me.

"Thank you," I say but hesitate.

Breaking bread with the man who killed your friend.

Anything to get what you want.

Blood on both your hands.

"I knew you'd show up," Stefano says. "You finally figured out who was responsible for killing Belina?"

I hold my breath, wanting every syllable on the wire.

He sneers. "You."

I half laugh. "Excuse me?"

"Cal's precious EDC was almost exposed by you and that Hale guy a few years ago. He was all over my ass about it."

"What?" I whisper. My heartbeat speeds up as the wave of panic threatens. Phillip was so close to blowing up Uncle Cal's Council, which created an information arms race. Each tried to destroy the other. I stopped them because I thought it was the right thing to do. I never considered that if I'd just let them all be taken down, Uncle Cal and his Council, including Stefano, that would have stopped Alec's illegal activity. Stopped Belina from working for him.

"Belina would be alive." Stefano spits the words out, the disgust in his tone something I already feel deep in my constricted chest.

As bad as the boys, girlie.

The cup falls from my hand, and I don't react, not even when it shatters. Not even when Stefano scrambles for a rag and I'm watching him on his knees.

"This is goddamn Italian marble," he says.

"I'm sorry," I say, stepping backward. My arguments about justice, about saving Uncle Cal and Phillip from destroying each other, are suddenly light in my hand when weighed against Belina's life. If only I'd let real justice be served. I knew Uncle Cal was guilty. I just didn't want to accept that him going to prison was the right thing. When I could have stopped it all.

Stefano drops the coffee-stained rag and chunks of porcelain into the trash. "You should go."

Was this a tactic? To get me off-balance so I leave him alone? "You were on a boat right by where Belina was murdered. Why?"

He takes a step toward me, the large marble counter still between us. "I'm there every full moon. I like to night fish and watch for bald eagles. I've done it since I was a boy."

"Then you know those waters well," I say.

"I had no reason to kill . . . her."

"The motive they have for Alec is the exact same as you."

He blinks rapidly as if astounded. "Is that so?"

"Detective Ramos can use diary entries by Belina as evidence of your relationship," I say. "There are witnesses putting you both together."

"Not every little thing I do is on the up-and-up. But the idea I'd murder Belina is so offensive—"

"My guess is it leads back to the FBI," I say. "She told you that you were under investigation. She knew what the FBI wanted."

"She told me to protect me," Stefano says, his voice rising. "I would never have hurt her. Certainly not for that."

"She had a lot of boyfriends," I pivot, hating how I sound like an online troll in my desperation. "Alec certainly was ready to blow up his life for her. And Ricky, well, he seemed pretty in love with her."

He pales, hands trembling. "Watch your fucking mouth. She would never go near an ungrateful piece of trash like him. They were . . . they hated each other."

"It's a thin line," I say. "You must have had a suspicion they were screwing—"

"You're wrong—"

I see the anger and jealousy. He's close to breaking. "You're so great she could never look at another man? You must have really been angry when Alec told you he was leaving his wife for her. Let's see, that's three guys she's involved with—"

He smacks his palm flat onto the counter. "Shut your goddamn mouth."

"Belina was scared enough of you to bribe you with everything she'd earned. The hundred thousand you gave to Tina to keep her quiet after you killed her daughter."

"That miserable woman was supposed to keep her mouth shut." He steps toward me. "Something you should consider."

My heart drops at the threat, but I live within the fear and stand up, stepping toward him. "Or what? You'll stab me and frame someone else?"

Let him do it.

It's time.

"You were fine with your girlfriend running away with Alec, an employee?" I say. "One who stole from you? One who is now working against you with the FBI?"

Every vein in Stefano's neck flares, and his face flushes to a purplish red. He tries to control a violent tremble. As if something invisible is holding him back from speaking, something warring within him. Something familiar to me: guilt.

"You can blame me for protecting Uncle Cal," I say, "but whose hands were on the knife? Belina could have told the FBI everything, and you knew it. You had to stop her. Stop her from leaving you. And having your baby."

Stefano's eyes are wide and bulging, and if he's ever had enough rage to stab someone, I'm witnessing it now as he moves toward me, hands out.

Closer, closer, closer.

Let it all end.

It's the only way.

"Stop this," says a woman's angry voice behind me in the kitchen. She is standing in a sleek pantsuit with her hands balled on her hips. "Tell her."

He doesn't seem to register her demand and continues his pace toward me. When he gets here, I know he's attacking. I move closer.

Good, girlie.

"I said stop." The woman's icy tone is so forceful it sounds as if it's always obeyed. "I had to endure this embarrassing secret long enough. He gave Tina that money because he felt guilty for never being there for Belina."

Stefano's face contorts in pain. "Stay out of this, Patty."

"I'm the one who looks foolish," she says. "I let you *try* to be there for her. But all you did was get her mixed up in your dirty business."

"That paid for this house and your—"

His yell is cut off when she holds up one finger, her rage causing her tight face to twitch.

"I've been watching you give that Newport whore money for twenty-seven years," she says. "I doubt poor Belina ever saw a dime."

Shit.

I close my eyes, cheeks heating. I think of the inscriptions in Belina's books from her room. And it's so clear what I missed. They weren't all given in the past few years as part of an affair, but over decades. The first one, the book of myths, had Belina's childish scribbles. Years must have passed, birthdays, Christmases, and she'd kept them all.

"Belina night fished with you," I say, realizing. I see the chart I made of Belina's meetings with CF. There were late ones, scheduled regularly.

"She never arrived," he whispers. "I waited like usual, but . . . she was being murdered in the waters we've fished . . . since she was a girl. I was just sitting there, angry she'd forgotten, but she was . . . dead." Stefano puts his head onto the counter, shoulders slumping, and slowly the sobs begin.

Now I see Belina.

She worked for Stefano all along. Maybe they fell out for a while, but this idea from Ricky to organize the captains brought Belina back to Stefano. She could handle a man like Alec, make him focus and earn Stefano money. She managed the accounts and kept Ricky in check. But then someone told her about the FBI, and she chose to warn Stefano. And to be with Alec.

"Not your girlfriend," I say slowly, an embarrassed burn lighting my skin.

"My daughter," he says loudly, but his voice breaks. "I loved her more than you can imagine."

Patty wraps her arms around her husband, and he cries within her embrace.

You've ruined another life.

There's only one way to stop someone like you.

You should have done it long ago, girlie.

It's time.

He was not the man with his hand on Belina's back, telling her where to go, when to move to the center aisle in church, coming from a place of passion and possession. Instead, Belina was his daughter, building the business, supporting him in any way she could.

"Who knew?" I hear myself say. Stefano looks up at me, eyes angry and red. "Who knew you both went fishing alone on every full moon? That she'd meet you there."

"Tell her," Patty says. "You know who did this."

He stares at Patty, and his face falls. "Just Ricky," he says. "I used his boat sometimes. He would have known where I'd be that night."

I step toward them. "She wrote in her planner that she was meeting you and someone she wrote as *A* with a circle."

He sighs, all the anger and strength gone. "It's a silly joke, a code of sorts. It's from a book of Portuguese fables I gave her as a girl," Stefano says softly, almost trancelike. "The Adamastor was a mythical monster who killed sailors. He tried to throw them off their path, terrifying them and working against them, and yet they'd always return. He is anarchy, but he's necessary for the journey. She loved that story. Always felt sorry for the monster."

"Say it, and let's be done," Patty demands, but Stefano shakes his head like a child. Patty takes a breath and then says, "It's what she called Ricky."

You're as bad as the boys, girlie.

I see the page open in my lap, Ester snuggled on my chest as I read about the Adamastor in her room after visiting Tina. I can see the way young Belina colored in the *O*s and *D*s. How she traced circles around those letters too. All the Adamastor's *A*s had light-penciled circles.

"Does he hate you that much?" I hear myself ask. "Would he really kill someone to frame you? Or Alec?"

Stefano doesn't answer, turns away as if holding his breath to keep back the emotions.

"His mother nearly ruined our business," Patty says. "Took out fake lines of credit and loans and any credit card she could spend. She was really unstable. Accused Stefano of all kinds of awful things. Her husband, Ricky's dad, he worked for us. But he was a deadbeat."

"I helped them plenty—" Stefano says in a low voice, the anger causing me to take a step back.

"It didn't matter," Patty says. "Stefano pressed charges, and she killed herself in prison. Ricky had lots of chances with foster families, but the apple doesn't fall far, you know."

You know it more than anything.

You've ruined everything.

Again.

I mumble goodbyes, sorrys, excuses and hurry to leave them to their grief and anger.

Heartbreaker.

Life taker.

You deserve to die.

I'm halfway down the block, almost to where I parked, when I stumble forward, falling onto my knees. Shame cycles through every blood vessel, pulsing with my inadequacy to solve this case, my arrogance that Belina ever believed in me.

Trusting you is the worst mistake anyone can make.

"Went that well?"

I jump at the deep voice, then look up from the ground, realizing it's Max as he steps out from a shadowed spot behind a tree. He hands me a bottle of water, and I take a big swig, swish, and spit. Then a long drink.

"Thanks," I say, my voice weak and scratchy.

Minutes pass in silence, and I appreciate that he's going to let me say what I want or maybe nothing at all. I prefer the latter because I'm in no mood to explain myself. I hardly know where to begin, to unravel why I wanted Stefano to be the killer when there were plenty of signs he wasn't.

"I really thought it was him," I say finally. "It didn't even occur to me that he was anything other than . . . not her father. I just assumed, like everyone else."

But you're not everyone else.

You did this to him.

Now you must pay.

"There's no motive," Max says. "Not for her murder."

Every fiber in my body feels pulled tight, strained from my error. I can't give up, but I can't face anything either. I start toward my car, inhale the cold wind off the ocean.

It's calling you home, girlie.

Now it's time for justice.

Chapter 35

I'm driving toward the Newport Bridge, even though it's the opposite direction of home. I hear Ester crying again, and in a panic, I glance back at the empty seat as my car swerves into the other lane, barely missing a gargantuan cement truck.

My hands tremble on the wheel. I'm losing it. Again. The lack of sleep and exhaustion and going after the wrong people in the wrong way are destroying me all over again.

You were always going to fail.

You never had what it takes.

I pull over before I reach the bridge and let it out. All of it. I cry for Belina first because I am failing her most. I cry for Ester and myself and Jack because our home is destroyed.

You have no family.

You have no one.

I cry for Stefano because it was a terrible thing to accuse him of when I had so little evidence. I cry for Ricky and my brother and my idiocy at seeing a kindred spirit where there wasn't one.

You never deserved love.

Now it's time to give it all back.

The car constricts, the air too hot, space too small. I fling open the car door, strip off my coat with my wallet inside, leave the car door open, unsure if I'll return.

I begin walking toward the bridge. My brain highlights every wrong step I've made. Each beat of my heart amplifies in my ears, repeating and building my guilt.

You failed.

You destroyed everything.

Shameful little liar.

I stand at the bridge's walking pathway for maintenance. It's locked but easy to jump. I throw a leg over, then slide down. I hurry past the **NO TRESPASSING** signs.

I need to be alone. I need to decide if I should join Belina in the water.

No one wants you here.

They'll be so much better without you.

I'm back where I started and never wanted to return: my home destroyed, as I am hearing voices and looking down at an abyss where everything can end if I let go.

This is the best for everyone.

The voice drove me here once before. Out to the abandoned mine, a hundred-foot drop to toxic water, impossible to escape. It would have all been over then too, if I had listened.

You should have jumped.

Jack would be happy now with someone better, someone worthy of him.

Belina would be alive.

On some level I know I can't blame myself completely for Belina's death. I had no idea what Alec would do to pay for Misha's lifestyle or what he'd risk to be with Belina. I wanted to protect Uncle Cal like family. That seemed to be the right thing to do. But I was wrong. And Belina was dead. Those facts are not unrelated.

Show her how sorry you really are.

Show her justice with your life.

On the Newport Bridge, the wind is at my back, shoving me along until I reach the top. My skin reverberates in the icy blasts as I lean over, only four hundred feet between me and peace.

You're ready to let go.

This is what you deserve.

I grip the railing and think of what I'd really be losing by following the voice. I close my eyes and picture Ester. I see Jack and imagine some version of happiness after all I've done.

Let go for peace.

Let go for your family.

Let go for justice.

But Jack and Ester won't get me off this bridge. Instead it is justice, my justice, what it will feel like to get a confession. To finally see someone pay for what happened to Belina.

No justice, no peace.

I hold the railing tight, turning back, sliding my hand along the cool metal surface as the wind rips at my clothes and hair. Back over the fence and to my discarded jacket, now wet with spray and dirt. I get into the car, turn the heat on blast.

About ten minutes pass, and then my phone buzzes.

"Hey, Phillip," I say, my voice sounding weak.

"You okay?" he says. "You sound rattled."

Tears burn, but I blink them back and clear my throat. "I was wrong about Stefano. Belina was his daughter."

"What?"

"He thinks Ricky had something to do with her death."

"That's why I called," Phillip says. "While I was at Miguel's house, the police showed up and searched everything. They found your copy of Belina's journal and personal papers. He's being questioned now."

I would never have pegged Miguel, CEO in training, as the kind of guy to wreck my house and my baby. "I'll be there as soon as I can," I say.

Headed for more mistakes.

More destruction.

God has turned away.

I drive through downtown Jamestown instead of Providence, creeping along the road and picturing the faces of suspects. The people I've spoken to and analyzed. Aside from Tina, they are a lot of men. I pull into the small lot by the Narragansett Café but not for a drink. There are so many men in this case that the few women involved, even tangentially, seem important.

It's after seven p.m., and a cigarette lights up from the side door. I get out of my car and head toward the glow.

"Hey, Suze," I say. "It's Devon. I was here with Ricky the other day."

She takes a long drag. "Yeah," she says. "I remember."

"You know Stefano Venantius?" I ask. When she nods, I continue. "I was just at his house."

"Good for you," she says.

I grin in the dark at the phrase. I feel like this whole day has been nothing but a *go fuck yourself.* "I accused him of murdering the local girl. Belina Cabrala."

"Oh yeah?" she says. "Ain't she his daughter?"

I suck in a breath. "How did you know that?"

"Tina and I went to high school together," she says. "She thought her ticket was punched when he knocked her up. Never really worked out for Tina or her kid."

"You knew Belina?"

"Just when she started comin' in with Ricky," Suze says.

I frown. "You think they were dating?"

"Didn't look like no kinda date to me," Suze says. "They were usually fighting. But they'd always leave together. One of those kind of relationships, I guess."

"Who else did Ricky bring with him?"

"There were a couple Mexican fellas." Suze stubs her cigarette out in the gravel. "I didn't know their names."

I pull out my phone and open a folder with photos. "Him?" I ask.

She nods at a photo of Miguel in front of his boat. "He's been in a few times. Pays cash, a good tipper. He yelled at Ricky the last time. Kinda funny."

"Was Ricky ever in with Stefano?"

She laughs, and it's gravelly and harsh. "He ain't steppin' a fancy loafer in a place like the Ganny. Not anymore."

I swipe a few over to a photo of Alec.

"I know him. They're friends." I nod, but she's still staring hard. "The one before." She taps the screen, making Max's face extralarge. "Him, who looks like police."

"You're sure Ricky was here with him?"

"Yeah," she says. "Just Ricky and that cop-lookin' guy. Only once, maybe six months ago. I hadn't seen Ricky in a while."

"Were they angry?" I ask, blinking at the photo of Max.

"No, Ricky seemed excited. He tipped me a lot that night, which is unusual for him."

Six months ago Ricky was meeting with the FBI. It would have been halfway through their investigation. But he didn't tell Stefano because the investigation continued without interruption. But maybe Ricky told someone else like Belina. Who betrayed him to tell Stefano.

"Thanks, Suze," I say.

Back in the SUV, I go too fast to where I left Max. Pulling over in front of him, I cut it a bit close to his car. I barely get the gear into park before throwing open the door. I stumble out of the car and charge toward him. "How long has Ricky been an informant?"

He takes several steps backward, hands in the air. "I'm not discussing informants."

"What's Ricky get if Stefano goes away? Immunity? Early access to the fishing licenses?"

Max crosses his muscular arms, glaring as I step closer. "Devon, he's not your suspect."

"It's hard to know without some cooperation. Where was he the night Belina was murdered?"

There's the slightest pinch between his eyebrows, a flinch really. He doesn't know where Ricky was, and I doubt he'd ever ask. That's not the justice Max is seeking.

Another one who used you.

All you're worth.

If Ricky and Belina had a relationship, even a bad one, he could have bragged about the deal with the FBI. But if she chose to tell Stefano about Ricky's plan, that would have been a problem for him. And if she decided to choose Alec, to pay off Stefano, and to start a new life that night, what would Ricky have done? Rejected, his plan up in flames because of Belina.

"What's Stefano's financial information worth? The money laundering, the offshore accounts taking in boatloads of cash?" I ask. I have a lot on Stefano, and Derek can get more. "What if there's some anonymous source who mails it all your way. Is that worth losing an informant like Ricky?"

He blinks at me, poker face not what it used be. He's intrigued.

I reach deep for confidence, grab it by the throat before I get in Max's face. "You might close this case if you sacrifice the right lamb."

Chapter 36

There's only one place to go. Only one person to see. Likely, the person who wants to see me even less than Stefano.

In the parking lot of the police station, I plug the mini–breast pump into my car. At the moment, I don't mind that pumping this way takes more time, rhythmic in and out, air and milk, until the six-ounce container is full. I screw on the yellow plastic lid and put it in a paper bag. I order my strategy in my mind and get out of the car on weak legs to find Detective Ramos.

All you know how to do is lie.

Shameful little liar.

The receptionist takes me to his cubicle, where he looks up from his small desk. He doesn't seem surprised to see me, but he's not happy either. He drops the file he was holding onto a colleague's desk and stands. "I was about to call you," he says.

"I need a refrigerator first," I say too brightly.

He frowns at the container with my milk but then gives me an aha look. "This way, and let's label it. Station is full of moochers. We don't want it to end up in anyone's coffee."

That almost makes me smile.

"We used donor milk," he says quietly. "My wife is worried we'll have to do it again." He clears his throat.

"I thought you said your son would nurse until he could ask for a beer?" I say lightly.

"Steel trap, huh?" He taps his forehead. "Anyway, need water or anything?"

I shake my head and follow him to a conference room. "Look," I begin. "I need to apologize. I screwed up on Stefano, but I can still help you close this case. If we work together, justice is possible. But we have to trust each other. Trust that my justice is the same as yours."

"Quite a speech," he says.

"I worked on it in the car," I say.

He leans on a chair, that confident cop tilt. "Your reporting with Hale blew my case to shit. If you've got some leads, I'm listening."

I sit across from where he stands at a round conference table. "First, why were you going to call me?"

"We got an anonymous tip that Miguel broke into your house and that we'd find the copy of Belina's planner there with your personal papers." He clears his throat. "That's exactly what we found."

I see on Detective Ramos's face the hesitation that I feel. "He seem the type?"

"No," he says. "He's nearly in tears in the interrogation room with his lawyer right now."

"I doubt his prints will be in my house," I say. "But you did find some DNA there that didn't belong to Jack or me, right?"

He nods. "Miguel volunteered to let us compare it."

I reach into my bag and pull out my pink-and-white Lilly Pulitzer dress. "This has Ricky Cardin's blood on it. How fast can you run it?"

He raises his thick eyebrows as if he's going to ask *how* I have his blood but takes it instead. "This isn't *SVU*, but I know a guy," he says and leaves the room.

Alone, I stand up and head to the large whiteboard on the wall. I line up the markers and begin to work. I outline the fraud triangle, detailing ways it can be applicable to Ricky or Miguel. By the time I'm done, it's clear only one had real motive to kill Belina.

But you ignored it.

You let your guilt get in the way of the truth.

Because you don't really care about truth.

Only justice as you see it.

It's been an hour since Detective Ramos left. He's likely spending time questioning Miguel while we wait for the DNA results to come back. I curl up on an old couch in the corner and close my eyes for what feels like the first time in days.

I wake up, hearing someone, and pretend to still sleep. An old survival habit from childhood. But then I remember that I'm not that girl. I open my eyes to see Detective Ramos studying my whiteboard.

"What do you think?" I ask, sitting up, rubbing my shoulder, and feeling more alert and balanced than I have in days.

He'll think you're crazy.

You'll have no one to blame but yourself.

"What's all this?" he asks, motioning toward the whiteboard.

"As you may have guessed, I saw Stefano tonight. He told me about Belina being his daughter. And that he had an alibi. Stefano and his wife believe Ricky met Belina that night. My biggest mistake, among several, was not using my expertise. This is applying the facts to a system called the fraud triangle. I know we're talking about murder, not fraud, but it could help."

"All right," he says. "Walk me through it."

That is easier than I expected. I head over to the board, starting at the top of the triangle. "First you ask, does the suspect, Ricky, have pressure to commit the crime?"

"Pressure," he says with a frown. "Another term for motive?"

"Right," I say. "But because much of this case is tied up in money, let's consider what financial pressure he had. Belina introduced Alec to Stefano. She's in charge of keeping the books for Alec. She helps them clean the dirty money. Gets it back to Stefano. So to get to the money, Ricky needs access to Belina, which he definitely had."

"Okay," Detective Ramos says. "What's next?"

"Alec needs more money, and the stakes keep getting higher. Things are going great. Stefano trusts them with a half million. It's right when Alec decides he wants a clean break to be with Belina and their baby. He spends it, thinking he can make it up with the captains. But for some reason, they don't make as much as they should."

"His fishing business mysteriously tanks?" he says with a grin.

I smirk at the lame joke and continue. "If they're underwater and on the outs with Stefano, Ricky could convince Alec to sell the licenses to Miguel. Take more control. Level up to Stefano. You need to interview some captains."

"I can do that," he says. "But was Ricky's plan to frame Alec for Belina's murder all along? Surely, with a guy like Alec, there are easier ways to get him caught."

"Murder was not the idea," I say. "That's why Ricky started informing on Stefano to the FBI. He wanted to take down Alec and Stefano for the money laundering. And shift all their lost profit to a partnership with Miguel."

Detective Ramos lets out a long breath. "If Ricky was working with the FBI and the Rossa family, he's double-crossing Stefano to get those fishing contracts. So that's a lot of pressure, if we're using your fraud triangle."

"Exactly," I say.

"Then you ask if there was opportunity to commit the crime?" he says.

"Belina herself gave us that information," I explain. "Her planner. She was meeting Ricky. The *A* with a circle was a code she used."

"According to who?"

"Stefano and his wife," I say. "It's possible Tina and Lee heard it a time or two. Tina gave me a book with the nickname she used. I can also cross-reference Belina's use of meeting with the nickname to Ricky's credit card statements."

"But going from a hustler to a murderer," he says. "That's a leap."

He thinks you're so stupid.

No one will believe you.

Shameful little liar.

I swallow my anxiety and push forward. "The last question is if there's enough in his life to rationalize doing the crime and living with it."

We're quiet while I think of what I'd have done to leave my town. I didn't have to cheat the SATs or LSAT, but I would have. I didn't sell myself for money—I got loans and a job—but I would have. Ricky doesn't see right and wrong according to the law, but his own justice matters.

"Taking down Stefano," I begin. "The boss man who ignored him." I pause because something about it doesn't seem quite right. "Ricky knew about Stefano's moonlit fishing trips with Belina. That's how he pushed me so hard in that direction. He knew everything about him. He was almost obsessed."

Detective Ramos points to a folder on the conference table. "It's my turn to use real evidence," he says. "The blood from your dress matches the DNA from the hairs found in your home. Has Ricky been there otherwise, to your knowledge?"

"Absolutely not," I say.

"Miguel says it was all Ricky's idea to break into your house to get the planner. Miguel says he was there but stayed on the porch while Ricky tossed the place. That Ricky asked him to keep what they stole."

"Okay," I say, waiting for the rest.

"Miguel is willing to talk. Ricky forced him to hide the alibi tape clearing Alec. He bragged about sleeping with Belina and said some pretty awful things about her. It won't look good in court for Ricky with Miguel's testimony. I'd like to make a deal and move forward on nailing Ricky."

I appreciate that he's pretending to ask my permission. "Whatever you need to do. Ricky is what matters."

"Good, good," he says, nodding as if relieved. "Now, I had the lab run all the DNA we'd collected for this case. It includes Stefano's, who volunteered it when we brought him in for questioning." He motions for me to open the folder.

I see the dotted bars of DNA: Belina, her unborn child, Ricky, Miguel, Alec, and Stefano. Someone has circled *100 percent match* and drawn lines from Ricky to Stefano. Then Belina to Stefano. Then from Ricky to Belina's baby.

"What the hell does this all mean?" I whisper.

Detective Ramos stands with his arms crossed. "Ricky was Stefano's son too."

I suck in air through my clenched teeth. "But . . . they were . . . together."

"For what it's worth, I don't think Ricky knew that Belina was Stefano's daughter. I don't think anyone thought she was more than a mistress." Detective Ramos clears his throat. "But it's worse than that, Devon. Belina was pregnant."

"I know," I whisper. "Alec told me . . . oh my God."

"It was Ricky's baby."

"No," I say but realize, of course, that's why she transferred money. She tried to buy her way out of this mess she'd created. First Stefano, the failed father who she was still trying to save from the FBI and make some kind of peace with over Alec's mistakes. Then Ricky, the lover she should have never had, who knew about the black market, the money laundering, all she'd done for her father, and likely, used it to control their relationship. And Alec, the man who loved her, and who despite his faults, she could see being a father to her child.

"But we don't have Ricky's DNA at the murder scene. Maybe if we book him, we get his prints, and there's a partial, but—"

This is why you're here.

There is only one way to get to justice, I realize as the anger kicks in. "I can confront Ricky. I'll wear a wire and get him to confess."

Justice at last.

"No, that's too dangerous." Detective Ramos holds up his hands, his gold wedding ring catching the light. "Ricky will know you're up to something."

You've got to try.

"He thinks we're friends," I say. "If I'm upset about Stefano, he might try to calm me down. Then I'll get him mad enough to confess."

"He might check for a wire," Detective Ramos says. "He's on edge. The break-in was sloppy. He knows we're close."

Motive is a strange legal concept. I liked uncovering motive in my corporate fraud research, building upon what I imagined a person could do to get something they wanted. Wondering when I found enough on one side of the scale to justify tipping from my theory to the truth. I see the real Ricky, not just because of Derek. We're shades drawn from the same colors. The bleeds are different, but like understands like.

You know him.

You can reach him.

"Ricky won't open up in here," I say. "But he might to me. I've gotten confessions from men like him before."

He scrubs his face. "He'll need to feel powerful. Believe he's in total control over you."

You know what to do.

Why she was given to you.

Detective Ramos can't bring himself to ask me, but it's the only answer. I hear Ester crying, even though she's not here. She's a part of all this; she wants to help. "I know how I can wear a wire with Ricky."

Chapter 37

Saturday, December 17

I told Uncle Cal I was out of the excavation business, but as I hurry down the dock toward Ricky and his boat, I'm right back in the mud and dirt and shit dumped by the hands of these men. This is my last chance to burrow out, swallow some air, and unearth justice for Belina.

I'm a good twenty yards from Ricky when he sees me, darkness wrapping us tight on this cloudy, starless night.

There must be a sacrifice for all you've done.

For the terrible mother you've become.

"Coming aboard finally," he says from the distance, but I can see the half grin. He's too eager, on edge as if he feels the reckoning, like a seagull attacking the wind, sensing the storm.

Ricky steps from the boat to the wet dock. He blows out a long breath of smoke, and his eyes go wide as his stare stops at my chest where Ester is wrapped beneath my coat. He tosses the cigarette onto the ground, not hiding his disgust. "Didn't realize there would be two of you."

"That a problem?"

There's a flinch of anger across his narrow face. "Kinda late to have a baby out."

"My only option," I say, patting her back. My hand pauses at how cold Ester is even though she's wrapped tight against me. I run my hands along her familiar shape, reassuring myself she's okay. There's just her thick fleece outfit, the wrap, and a thin wire between Ricky and us. Her hair is visible, peeking out from beneath the white cap.

You deserve whatever happens next.

I stand at the gap between the dock and the too-small boat. Claustrophobia squeezes. The sound of a belt buckle in my ears, as loud as the waves bouncing us all with a rhythmic thump, thump, thump. I close my eyes. I breathe. I let the anger come.

"I'm really glad you're here," he says. "We've got a lot to figure out."

I don't see his eagerness to create connection anymore but rather, a shark assessing where to strike to drag me under.

"Lead the way," I say.

The boat wobbles in the wind, a drunken mother's loose arms rocking us back and forth. Ricky takes my elbow, too tightly, but I don't want to risk falling, so I go along.

Both my feet on the boat, I grip the wooden rail, easing down into the main cabin room. It's small and quiet, and I can almost see my childhood twin bed. Hear the creak of a heavy body on the edge of the mattress, closer, closer, closer. The sheets I'd strip off after he was done. The comforter I eventually burned.

I hold Ester tight against my chest. My fingers tickle the edge of the microphone hidden within one of the wrap's folds. I focus on the room, how it's actually nothing like my bedroom. The wood-paneled walls, small kitchenette, and pull-out bunk in the corner. I pat Ester and adjust my messenger bag, feeling the weight of the knife at the bottom.

"What's up?" Ricky asks. "You seem spooked."

"Small spaces," I say, not hiding all the pain. "Bad memories."

You could have stopped Granddaddy.

You knew enough to know better.

"Of course," he says with a smirk. He would know exactly what I meant because he stole my papers along with the copy of Belina's planner. But it's not time for that now. "You want a drink?" he asks too quickly, and I shake my head. "Here's to the late shift," he says and takes a shot.

All along, I didn't trust Ricky, exactly, but I let myself trust his information. Assumed too many connections to my brother that weren't really there. Created a fantasy where Ricky was a survivor like me, someone who helped instead of hurt. But he'd gone the other way.

You are the same.

You deserve the same.

"Stefano really messed things up with his interview," I say, trying to focus back on what's really between us. Not the commonalities I imagined but the truth: he killed Belina.

"I saw it." He doesn't sit, but he leans against the edge of a table. "Got publicity people on payroll and journalists in his pocket. What a crock of shit."

I shrug at him but see the anger I didn't place before. The kind of hatred only a family member can bore into your heart. "I might press charges."

"You mean for defamation?"

"No, you goddamn idiot," I say, letting my tongue unleash some of my anger. "It has to be untrue to be defamation. Also, in the media, it's libel. God, Belina was right. You are stupid."

He rears back. "What? What?"

"I didn't want to *say* anything to you when we met, but she talked about you *all* the time," I lie. "Complained about you. In every single way." I pause to wiggle my pinky at him. "You know what I mean?"

"I don't . . . what?"

His stammering is a good sign. The shock will wear off, and he'll get mad. Very, very mad. "So like I was saying before your dumb-shit question. I have to decide if I want to press charges against *you*."

"What?" he whispers again, stepping toward me.

"Destroying my house to get to Belina's planner. They found hair and even a partial print. You might as well have signed your name. If you can write. I'm not sure, based on how stupid you've played all this."

The red is spreading across his sharp cheekbones. "You're mad at me because of the break-in," he says, as if he's trying to rationalize my behavior. "Miguel was freaked out. I can explain. It was just to get him to chill."

"Great defense. That'll definitely hold up in court." I take a step toward him.

But he sees weakness, my vulnerability. "Your grandfather really fucked you up good," he says with a grin. "Imagine a preacher molesting his own granddaughter. In his daughter's house. Over and over and over again. Damn, that is messed up."

You could have fought back.

But you didn't.

"He got what he deserved," I say.

"Really?" Ricky smirks. "He died of cancer. You cut him with a knife, I guess. That's what the defense said to make you seem crazy. But he got off." He laughs. "Well, obviously. But the case was dismissed. Seems like he won."

I cut my grandfather's arm when he reached for me for what would be the last time. He slapped my face, ran away screaming. Used the attack as proof I was crazy. Violent. Making everything up.

"Bad stuff happened to both of us," Ricky says, too easily. As if he'd rehearsed this connection between us in preparation for the big show.

"I feel sorry for you," I say. "You think we're the same, but we're not."

"There's a lot of money in this," Ricky says. "It's our turn to win. Not *them*."

"Them?" I throw a haughty laugh his way. "*You* are going to prison. I am going to take every last fishing contract. Miguel would *much* rather work with someone like me. He's happy to throw you over. *We* will make the money. *You* are done."

His eyes are wild, the rage and adjustment to this version of me. As I shift from friend to another bitch in the way of what he wants. "All this is Miguel's fault," he says.

"Please. Miguel is a puppy. You tried to play every side. But you're way out of your league. That blood in Alec's car was such an obvious plant."

"Fooled the cops," he hisses. "And she was such a slut that *she* brought Alec's DNA with her to the cemetery. That's destiny right there."

"But Alec is out of prison," I say. "So guess it wasn't so smart after all."

He lets out a breath as if trying to regain control of the conversation. "You're kind of sexy when you're mad. Wish you hadn't brought your fucking child here. You're a real shit mother."

He's got that right.

Tell him it's all going to end.

Tell him it's what you all deserve.

A child of yours should never have been born.

"You know a lot about shit mothers?" I say.

"Yeah, I do," Ricky says. "Mine killed herself."

The pain in his voice gets me for a second, even though I pushed the button. "And your dad? Stefano?"

"Clever, clever." Ricky winks, but there's so much disgust in his face. "Who else would I try my whole damn life to impress? Work my ass off at his dock, for years. Scrape together enough to go to those stupid charity polo matches he loves. Kiss ass long enough to get someone like Alec to work with me. Someone he actually gave a shit about. Fuck him."

"I'm sorry," I say, understanding that loneliness and longing. "Did you kill my friend?" I ask simply, with some compassion, surprised I feel it.

Ricky leans on the doorway, cocky. "You don't want to ask questions like that, Devon."

"Yes, I do."

"I can see that," he says. "But I like you—"

"Bet you liked Belina too," I say, shifting back to aggressive, where I was making real progress. "I saw her post the word *saudade*, 'a pleasure you suffer, an ailment you enjoy.' Maybe that wasn't Alec. Maybe that was you."

"You don't need to be jealous," he says with that lopsided grin that now makes my skin crawl.

"Was that part of why you decided to kill her that night? The chance to hurt someone your partner cared about? Your father?" He grunts as if I'm the dumb one. I close my eyes as the room blurs. I swallow down the *You dumb shit* scream in my throat. I can do better than that. "When was the last time you slept with Belina?"

He's quiet, measuring me.

"When was the last time?" I snap.

He shrugs. "A couple months before . . . she died. She'd come by my boat with papers or whatever excuse. Like I said, she insisted nobody find out. It's fine, though, not good to screw the boss's girl."

"You've got that right." I lean against the counter and note a block of knives about three steps from Ricky and four from me. "So Stefano never knew?"

"God no," he says. "Stefano hated me. I never told her the real reason. I didn't want her pity."

"Real reason?"

"I'm some bastard son from a one-night stand he regretted. Blamed my mom for his shitty business troubles. He even got her thrown in prison." He shakes his head, as if trying to erase the memory.

Push him.

Let justice come.

"But that's not Belina's fault."

"I was a rebellion for her. She treated me just like Stefano treated my mom." Something shifts, almost wistful. "But there was something to Belina and me. Our chemistry was rare."

You're the same.

You deserve the same.

"Incest is not that rare," I snap. "You read about my grandfather."

He blinks slowly. "What?"

Shameful little liar.

At the last words my mother ever spoke to me, I press on. "Just what I said. It's not that rare, not in this room. You must have read about it in the papers of mine you stole."

He holds up his hand, the fingers long and muscular but trembling. "What about Belina? Incest?"

"I need to explain another thing to Ricky Cardin, the genius," I say. "It was a good thing my grandfather raped me before I got my period, so no baby risk. Guess you and your half sister weren't that lucky."

His eyes focus on me, so sharp, the violence in them palpable. "What the hell did you say?"

Give him the truth.

This is what he deserves.

What you both deserve.

I step toward him. "You killed your half sister. And your unborn baby."

"I . . . didn't . . . Stefano was her . . . I thought . . . I thought . . . No, you're wrong. That was his baby. His girlfriend. You are a fucking liar."

"I'm not. For what it's worth, I thought Stefano was her boyfriend too." I reach into my bag, run my finger against the knife at the bottom, making sure it's there.

Slice his arm, and he'll slice you back.

Just like with Granddaddy.

Find justice.

I pull out the DNA report and toss it on the table with a satisfying thud.

He snatches it up, several pages dropping as he clutches the first page. I highlighted the 100 percent match in pink.

"This has to be wrong," he says, staring blankly at the report. "She was just some slut. Some woman who'd leave me. Leave her baby."

Ester begins to cry as the rage erupts in my gut, spreading through my limbs as something clicks. I bounce Ester, not apologizing for the sound, not wanting anything else ringing in his ears. "Belina told you she was pregnant."

His violent stare returns. "I yelled at her when she said she'd told Stefano about the FBI. She gave him one hundred grand to leave us all alone. As if that'd do anything. She's so fucking stupid."

"But why kill her? It was done," I yell, bouncing Ester, feeling the weight of the knife in my bag.

"I wasn't going to kill that slut," he says. "I smacked her around, and she started crying. Saying, 'Please don't do this for the sake of the baby.' She said it wasn't mine. I mean, Jesus Christ, how many people was she fucking in this town? I said, 'It's bad enough you were screwing my asshole father—'"

I watch the realization flash across Ricky's face as it twists sharp in my gut. Once he'd said those words, admitted that Stefano was his father, Belina knew what they'd unknowingly done. What they'd created.

"Then what did she do?" I ask in a whisper.

"She threatened me." He drops onto the kitchenette seat. "She wanted me to kill her and that baby."

"Don't you dare blame her, you coward," I hiss. "You wanted her dead so you could control Alec's business with him in jail for it."

He props his hands behind his head. "Alec going to prison was the only way to get those licenses. I saw it for a long time. He walked right into the murder charge."

"He walked right into you," I say.

"Fuck you, Devon." He slams his fist on the table. "Why the hell did you bring your child here? You're just like all these other fucking women."

Keep pushing.

I step closer, realizing Ester feels stiff and unnatural, her nose hard when nuzzled against my chest. I want to take her out and be sure she's okay, but she's not. Neither of us is okay and may never be okay again. "Belina was a woman who was screwed over by many men. You're just another user, stupid and dull. You killed her because she outsmarted you all the way to the end."

"You're making this so easy on me," he says, standing. "Just like she did."

Let him cut you like you cut your granddaddy.

Let justice take you.

Let justice take Ester.

My hands shake with rage, and the room narrows onto his face. My path, the only path, is clear.

"I saved Belina from being all used up and disgusting like her mother." Ricky steps closer, his lean but muscular shoulders tensing as his gaze flicks to the counter and the knives. "But I'm no altruist. This deal with Miguel is my turn at last. My ends justifying any means necessary. You get it?"

"Yeah, I do."

Some tension releases from his posture. He stares at me, desperate, cornered, searching for an out that's not the inevitable one we're careening toward. "Can you get this detective to back off?"

"I'm not doing you a favor, Ricky. Belina's life mattered. You had no right to take it."

His glare snaps back to the knives. "That's not the right answer."

"It's the only answer."

Let him stab you.

The voice is right, and I put my hand over Ester. My fingers are a warm contrast against her cool body.

Your family's better off.

You're better off.

Last chance for justice.

It's a sacrifice. But this path was always leading toward justice, no matter the cost.

"You're going to turn yourself in." I step closer to make it easy.

His eyes are wide. His stare goes from me to the top of Ester's head. As if he's calculating where to strike. "I'd rather we all die," he whispers.

I smile. "You first."

The knife is in his hand in a second. He lunges toward me, and there is not fight or flight but focus. I feel the stiffness of Ester, an unnatural hardness against my body. I realize the truth of her, of what was done to save me, of our purpose at last.

This is where it must end.

This is her purpose.

This is your purpose.

Let it all end.

I grab Ricky by the wrist, directing the jab lower so the knife tears down, through Ester, through this baby I've wanted and never deserved. I feel the knife scrape the low C-section scars and away from the wire, which is what I need.

I grab his knife because it's close, and he's surprised I'm not focused on Ester. On the sudden silence on the boat. But he doesn't understand.

"This is for Belina," I say. "For our babies who didn't deserve to die before they lived."

I drop to the ground with a scream, stabbing the knife hard into the top of his foot. My arm is on fire from the force it takes to get the tip of the blade through bone and tissue and tendons until it reaches the wooden floor.

I roll away, registering only his screams. But justice isn't done. I scramble to grab my knife as he reaches for me like a snake snapping his jaws. I lunge under his arms, stabbing the other foot, this one at a more painful angle. He drops onto his arched back like a crucified man, arms flailing, feet nailed to the cross.

Ricky's screams turn to convulsive sobs, blood from both feet pooling around us. I must have hit a vein.

I fish an empty bottle out of my bag, a small one I use for pumped milk. I take a long scoop of the thick crimson liquid now reaching my feet. Screwing the yellow cap on tight, I show him his blood, savoring his panic.

I lick my lips and whisper Belina's first words to me. "Medicine from the old country," I say but then share the truth. "Your blood will water her grave."

He is moaning and cursing, his body shaking from shock. But it's not over.

Ester is silent. The whisper in my head is silent. Pulling off the torn part of my blood-splattered wrap, I drop Ester and the wire to the ground in one terrible thud.

Ricky's mouth gapes in horror at what I've done. At what I let him do. Our gazes connect for one moment in the total silence we created.

Like recognizing like.

All the voices have stopped.

Chapter 38

The voice was wrong. I am not a terrible mother. In fact, I'm no longer a mother at all.

During that moment of focus, my instinctual reaction to Ricky's attack, Ester's crying finally stopped in my head. My mind let go of the illusion. In the weeks since I left the hospital, I have not been carrying the weight of my baby but a grief doll that's been wrapped to my chest. Cradled in my arms. Dressed and bathed and swaddled. Fed with fake bottles while I pumped real milk.

Ricky is bleeding and screaming, but I am here, past fight and flight. I have focus. I grab the wire tangled with the doll that I treated as my child for the past two months. I can't leave her, so I take the pieces—the head, legs, arms, shredded stomach with white stuffing—and shove it all into my bag.

I see the flash of the mother on Hope Street who seemed shocked at the sight of me and Ester or, I guess, me cradling a doll. Even now, only moments away from the delusion, I know I will never be ashamed. With the fullness of love, grief must be paid by the ones left behind. To carry on living after a desolation that's carved you into a new, lesser form.

Stepping outside the cabin, I am that lesser person. I hear Ricky's cries and feel some relief that he's confessed. He'll be going to jail after the hospital to treat the wounds I gave him. For weeks, months, maybe his whole life, every step will be a painful reminder of what he's done.

The boat rocks harshly in the wind, slamming against the dock. I hear another scream from inside. I think of Ricky's scars. Of mine. Somewhere in my mind I remember reading that scar tissue is not stronger than the skin that was there before the separation. But it keeps us together enough that we can go on.

All small comfort in the emptiness of my new existence without Ester.

Police officers rush the dock, and I raise my hands in the air, focusing on the red and blue lights. One officer takes me by the arm, gets me off the boat and over to Detective Ramos.

"Are you hurt?" Detective Ramos asks, and I shake my head. He frowns, unconvinced. "The ambulance is waiting."

I dig into my bag for Ester's cotton hat and press it into the slight wound.

"Ricky's feet are stuck to the floor," I say and stop walking along with him, as if demonstrating.

"Stuck?" He glances, frustrated, toward the ambulance.

"I put knives through his feet," I say. "He can't move. Doubt he'll ever walk the same again."

He blinks at me. "Okay."

"Send the medic to him so he doesn't bleed out," I explain. "I want him to spend the rest of his life in jail."

He leans toward my wound, turning on his flashlight, and quickly checks where I've held my shirt up enough so he can see. "You're still going to the hospital," he says.

"Please," I say with urgency as the two men with a stretcher near us.

"To the boat," he shouts at them. They don't slow, continuing down the dock.

I keep the pressure on the cut, and with my other hand, I dig through the cotton and plastic limbs to pull the wire out of my bag. I hand it to him, though they have the audio recorded in their van parked nearby. My cheeks heat despite the cold because I realize he knew.

"Thank you," I say, finally processing what this deception meant. Wondering who knew and who didn't. "For letting me do this with Ester being . . . not real."

He nods once and then focuses back toward the boat. I hear the radio crackle and then a voice: "He's alive but lost a lot of blood."

I smile in relief. "Can you get my knife back?" I ask. "Once it's out of his foot."

"Probably," he says.

A piece of the carrier across my chest lifts in the wind. "Where's Jack?" I ask.

Detective Ramos doesn't answer but instead takes a step back.

The weight of familiar arms comes around me. "You're okay," Jack whispers. "You're okay."

I lean into Jack's chest, inhaling his shuddering breath. I'd be crying too, if my heart didn't feel as if it were gone, left in the belly of the boat.

"She's in shock," Detective Ramos says to Jack, then faces me again. "Another ambulance will be here in four minutes. You're going to the hospital. Head that way."

At the mention of the hospital, a memory returns. The only moment I spent with Ester after she was born. The doctor tried to hand her to me. "Stillborn," I remember him explaining. Died during my C-section, as I almost did. I stared at her in the doctor's gloved hands. Her dark hair contrasted with the pale-pink blanket wrapped thickly around her small body.

But I couldn't hold her. I said no. Unable to believe it. And then everything went black. I cried for her. For days. For weeks. Until Jack said, "Do you want to hold our daughter?"

Jack's gaze goes to where Ester was across my chest and stomach. There is a flicker of hope. "I didn't know what else to do," he says in a rush. "I needed you to come back to me. I read an article about it helping someone . . . and when I handed you that doll . . . you were there for the first time since she . . . died. I hoped a few days. Then with your work. I didn't know how to reach you."

I touch his face, and he leans into my open palm. "You did the right thing," I say. "I'm here now."

He pulls me tight, a shudder in his chest as he lets out a long breath, one I imagine he's held since he put a doll in my arms and pretended it was our daughter.

We make our way toward the lights as a cold and salty blast of wind whips off the dark water. The cut barely burns, like a gentle echo of the much worse pain from my C-section incision that didn't want to heal. This cut isn't as severe, not as deep, but the same emptiness continues beyond the bloodstain. Both cuts are nothing compared to the ballast now residing in my chest at the truth.

As we near the end of the dock, I see the lights of the second ambulance approaching. I stop to untwist and remove the last pieces of the baby wrap still around my shoulders and tied at my waist. I pick up a few thin rocks stacked nearby and drop to my knees. I dig into my bag and pull out what's left of the doll.

Jack says something behind me, a question, a concern, but it doesn't matter. I wrap her one last time, gently placing the pieces onto the stretchy fabric along with the rocks, covering the perfect nose, Jack's black hair, my green eyes. I tie it all together and kiss the top of her head, something I've done a thousand times, and drop her into the water.

Epilogue

Seven months later

Cynthia rises from behind the shining marble counter at her second location, Capitol Chip, across from the statehouse. Tonight is her soft launch, and Mayor Soriano should be arriving soon.

"Detective Ramos is in the corner," Cynthia says, brushing the sleeve of her white silk shirt. "Tell me those are the olives."

I hand her the sack containing the tub of blue cheese–stuffed olives for the Uncle Cal martini she's put on the menu as a tribute. "The recipe is in there too."

"Hallelujah," she says. "Not sure the olive-stuffing business is a good fit."

"I'll keep to the pro bono," I say with a grin. I started working a few cases for Legal Aid. Mostly paperwork, but if I'm up for it, perhaps more. "Nice ribbon." I nod toward the gigantic red bow across the counter between us.

"Ah," she says, cringing, but I see how proud she is of this amazing place she's built. "I've got to find those damn big scissors."

"I'm bringing some champagne to celebrate after you close tonight," I say. "I don't care if you have a full bar. My treat to celebrate you."

She nods once and steps around to give me a tight hug. She's a hugger now. With me.

Heading over to the barista, I ask for two black coffees, mine decaf. It's still quiet. Most of the preparations have been made. The servers are gone, getting ready for opening night.

I start to sit at the two-top with Detective Ramos, but there's a padded envelope in my chair. I place my coffee down and hand him his. I slide the envelope into my messenger bag with a nod of appreciation at having my knife back.

He's already drinking his coffee in long gulps. "Thank you," he says as if I've delivered him a winning Powerball ticket. "Baby still won't sleep more than two hours."

His gaze flicks up to me. That happens now, when people who have heard the rumors mention any news about babies. I smile, almost sincerely. "It'll get better," I say. "Especially when it can't get worse."

After scrubbing a hand across his face, he takes a long sip. "Damn," he says. "Everything tastes good at these fancy places."

I wait a moment for him to take another sip. "You connected with Phillip?" I ask.

Detective Ramos grunts before answering. "Yeah, yeah, he's getting everything he needs for that damn book of his," he says. "I spend more time talking to him than my wife."

"Thank you," I say. "He got one hell of an advance, so he's feeling the pressure."

"Good for him," he mumbles.

"Stefano's sentencing is next week," I say.

"Yeah," he says. "I don't know how much his testimony against Ricky helped."

Stefano told the whole sad saga of Ricky and Belina on the stand during Ricky's trial. He seemed remorseful, but what does it matter? Ricky will go to jail for the rest of his life for the murder of Belina and illegal work for Stefano. Alec was equally tearful, but he got off with probation, thanks to his deal with Max.

Jack asked me after the trial if I felt betrayed by Belina. If she'd used my friendship to get to Alec for Stefano. It's possible, but I'd been the one to find her in Swan Point Cemetery. To have her friendship and help through my pregnancy. I wonder more if I let her down. If I'd been a better friend, if I'd asked more questions, offered more help. She didn't owe me her secrets. But I did owe her my friendship.

"Sorry to hear about your uncle," Detective Ramos says. "Seems like a lot of people were there."

It was a hell of a funeral. Uncle Cal's legacy stayed intact thanks to my basically bribing Max with Stefano's financial records to keep the Council out of court. And I still owe him a favor.

In the end, Cynthia got the grant, the last before the Council was put out to pasture. Uncle Cal pushed Jack to take it over, but he refused, preferring to pay his dues with a mayor he believes in.

Detective Ramos fiddles with his coffee cup, and I know he reached out to me for more than dropping off the knife.

"I want to apologize. We used you," he says. "Jack told me about the doll and that you weren't well. But you were still turning things up. Working the case better than us half the time."

"It got me through a tough period," I say. "I'm grateful."

He doesn't look convinced, so I change the topic.

"Are your son's days and nights confused?" I ask, trying to assure him I'm okay.

"The doc says it'll straighten out, but . . . it's hard."

I know five different techniques, but since he doesn't ask, I don't offer. "He's gaining weight now?"

Detective Ramos clears his throat, a slight flush appearing across his forehead and down his cheeks. "Yes. God. Thank you for that too."

"I was happy to do it," I say, squeezing his hand quickly. I donated my three months of breast milk to their new baby boy. Whenever the tears start, a bit fewer each day, I think of how the milk I made for my own daughter was able to be used for another life. To help another struggling family.

Detective Ramos's phone buzzes, and he sits up straight. "Another murder," he says with a rapid blink. "East Side, again, if you can believe it. I gotta head out."

"Sure," I say. He reaches for his wallet, but I shake my head. "Thank you. Really. You don't know how much—"

He clears his throat, not quite meeting my gaze. "I do know, Devon. I really do."

After taking our cups over to the sink behind the counter, I wash them and tell Cynthia I'll be back soon.

I get in my car, glancing in the rearview mirror at where Ester's car seat used to be. Where I'd watch her, and it was as real as my own face gazing back.

I leave Chip's new location near the capitol and slowly drive to my neighborhood. I pass Cole Avenue, where there's a **Sale Pending** sign in front of Alec and Misha's house. Alec hasn't returned my texts and didn't answer the door the few times I went by.

Jack didn't tell him about Ester or the lack of her. Alec never took the time to see me. To wonder at why my young child wasn't moving much, even when I thought I heard her crying.

I don't know if he told Misha about the baby with Belina, but it certainly came out in the trial. I'm not even sure if they're staying together or if they should. I miss Alec, but it's a longing for a friendship that's gone.

More than Alec, though, it's Misha who I keep hoping to see every time a blonde ponytail swishes by. I want her to still be in the right clothes with the big ring and fancy stroller, pushing a happy Emmett to story time. The wisteria still climbing, still blooming.

I park at Swan Point Cemetery and step into the cooling July evening air. I stop at the dogwood tree where I first saw Belina. I pick several blossoms, hold them to my lips, and then head to her grave.

As I walk along the pathway, I take deep, grateful breaths that the silence is broken only by the soft murmur of leaves and cicadas. The voice returned with my delusion of Ester. A voice I hadn't heard since I was a girl.

The voice has stayed silent, but I have not.

I'm back in therapy, talking about what I remember and what I don't. My therapist says I had postpartum psychosis. That my childhood trauma created in me the ability to see Ester as real. The voice telling me terrible things, the blackouts, my fixation on Belina's death, the hallucination of Ester, these were all symptoms of psychosis.

I'm able to understand my diagnosis. But I do not think of Ester as a symptom. Not when it's so easy to picture her perfect face. To close my eyes and see Jack's black hair. My green eyes. Feel the weight of her wrapped against my chest. I don't want that to disappear too.

I started taking medication. I joined a pregnancy and infant loss support group. Jack has held my hand at every meeting, and I have held his.

Arriving at Belina's grave, I sprinkle the petals on top of the large white stone. I run my fingers over the letters of her name, then the words *Beloved Daughter*. The grass is growing where there was fresh dirt through the winter, tended with both water and Ricky's blood.

I press my palm to the top of her tombstone; it's as close as I can get to looking Belina in the eyes. To let her finally see how much she meant to me. These men who used her didn't escape justice. I showed her I cared, even if it's in death, even if I'm partly to blame.

The graves are not side by side, but it's a short, pretty walk until I see the three words: *Ester Belina Burges*. Jack and I had a memorial for her a few weeks after we buried Uncle Cal. Jack read an E. E. Cummings poem. I was able only to weep.

I will cry for my daughter my whole life. She will always be mine, and as the poem Jack read said, she is carried in my heart. That's the terror and beauty of love.

Sitting in the grass, I lean against Ester's grave. I tell her about Belina. Tell her about how she was a part of bringing justice. That it wouldn't have happened without her.

There is so much pain among the four of us: two babies with lives unlived and two mothers, the life taken too soon and the life unable to be lived in its true form.

I hum one of Gillian's sea shanty songs to Ester as my fingers run over my slightly swollen stomach. Against my daughter's grave, I stare up at the thick canopy of trees. The light appears to throb through the green leaves above us, like the tiny heartbeat beneath my fingers.

Author's Note

Postpartum depression is estimated to affect one in seven families, mothers and fathers alike. Postpartum psychosis, in which a person may hear voices, self-harm, or harm others, is rarer but is a very serious medical condition. If you or someone you love is suffering from any range of issues, you can learn more at www.postpartum.net, and please contact your health-care provider. There's no reason to suffer in silence and solitude. It is not your fault, and you are not to blame.

Acknowledgments

The first thank-you is to my parents, Mike and Carla Lillie, who taught me to read, encouraged me to write, and raised me in a home that valued storytelling. Thank you to my brother, Nathan, for cheering me on. And to my husband, Zach, and our wonderful families, who have been so supportive through the years.

Thank you to my fantastic agent, Victoria Sanders, and her amazing team at Victoria Sanders and Associates (waves at Bernadette and Jessica). A lifetime of gratitude goes to my editor extraordinaire, Jessica Tribble, and everyone at Thomas & Mercer. I'm so lucky to be among your talented and well-cared-for authors.

My publishing journey took thirteen years, and fortunately, none of them was spent alone.

Thank you to Romance Writers of America, the Washington, DC, chapter in particular, where I joined my first writers group (Circle of Trust). There's also ITW/Thrillerfest, Backspace, Grubstreet, Manuscript Academy's Mid-May group, and Providence's What Cheer Writers Club—all have been instrumental in getting me over hurdles and blocks aplenty.

And then there was Pitch Wars. Thank you to the creator of this remarkable mentorship program, Brenda Drake, and to my Pitch Wars mentor, Sarah Henning, for your confidence in my voice. To my co-mentee, Kellye Garrett, you are the ultimate trifecta: great writer, great friend, and great writer-friend. My 2014 Pitch Wars alumni, you've been so generous with your enthusiasm, candor, GIFs, and many reality checks of this business.

I am so grateful to friends who have read (and reread) my writing and supported me along the way, especially Kristen Ricciardelli, Cyndi Parr, Addison McQuigg, Mayrose Wegmann, Christina Lien, John Marchant, Cat Richert, Justin and Mackenzie Oberst, and Chris and Natalie Mulligan.

Thank you to Shaterri Casteel, my dear friend and marketing support. Thank you to developmental editors who were my all-star openers and closers, Heather Lazare and Charlotte Herscher. Gratitude for the beta reader brilliance and friendship from Mary Keliikoa, Jaime Hendricks, J. R. Yates, Nina Ramos, and Meagan Blair.

The heart of this story was created during my postpartum year with my son. I made it through that time in one frazzled piece largely because of the Rhode Island New Moms Group and my magnificent mom friends: Jess, Katy, Kristen, Lauren, and Sue, we made it!

Finally, I'd like to share these lines in remembrance of Matthew Oberst from his novel: *She was standing on the moon. The same moon he wished he'd seen the night he died . . . She sang sweetly—clear and pure. The song was a lullaby. She cradled him and rocked him softly back into sleep.*

About the Author

Photo © 2018 Brittanny Taylor

Vanessa Lillie is originally from Miami, Oklahoma, where she spent a lot of her childhood investigating local ghost stories at the public library. After college, she worked in Washington, DC, until moving to Providence, Rhode Island, which she calls home with her husband and dinosaur-aficionado son. Smitten with the smallest state, she enjoys organizing book events and literary happenings around town. Sign up for her newsletter at www.vanessalillie.com.